WATCH HER DIE

An absolutely addictive crime thriller with a huge twist

(DI Temple Book 1)

DEBORAH LUCY

JOFFE BOOKS

Revised edition 2019
Joffe Books, London
www.joffebooks.com

First published as "DEATH WATCH" in Great Britain 2018

We hate typos too but sometimes they slip through.
Please send any errors you find to
corrections@joffebooks.com
We'll get them fixed ASAP. We're very grateful to eagle-eyed readers who take the time to contact us.

Please join our mailing list for free Kindle crime thriller, detective, mystery books and new releases.

ISBN: 978-1-78931-147-1

For Andrew – my chief supporter

PROLOGUE

25 June 1984

He could never quite remember how long he had tried to waken his mother before he realized she was dead. He was too young then, to register the act of murder.

When he first saw her, he thought she was sleeping. He tried to wake her, but she just lay there. He pushed at her arm, gently at first. He called to her. Pushing harder, impatiently, he called louder. Shouting, he tugged hard at her limp arms in a bid to raise her. She was playing a game.

Then, suddenly, he knew. As he studied her lifeless face with her mouth slightly ajar, his seven-year-old mind registered this wasn't normal. His young, vibrant mother was dead.

As tears filled his eyes, he felt something leave his body. He lifted his head up. A piercing shard of sunlight shone through the leafy awning outside, bleaching his sight. Looking into the sudden white light, his mind ripped through a kaleidoscope of events in a bid to try and make sense of what was happening.

He'd been out for hours that morning, under the warm summer sun of a mini heat wave. He'd virtually skipped the half-mile downhill track through a corn field to the ancient stone circle at Avebury. A source of wonder and mystery for tourists, the large megaliths were his playground twice a year.

The stones held a fascination for him. He'd run around each one of them, memorising their shape, his small fingers exploring, finding the familiar ancient dents and ridges. His eyes studied the small, sparkling lights trapped in the granite as he'd tried in vain to finger them free.

He'd tried to climb them, moving from one to another, his small feet finding natural hollows and ledges that allowed some purchase. Time and again, he fell back onto the soft grass, as if the stones themselves had shaken him off, indignant at his assault.

His mother told him they were magic. There seemed to him to be a lot of magic in his world.

At night, things moved as they didn't move during the daylight. The earth moved, literally. He'd seen it for himself as he'd wandered silently and unobserved amidst the familiar densely scented haze surrounding the smoking grown-ups as they gathered around fires and in their tents. Sometimes, the ground rippled beneath his feet and once, he almost felt he could fly. He'd learnt that if he kept quiet he could see and learn a lot. Only a couple of evenings ago around the stones, he'd seen crowds of people chanting, the beating of drums, the familiar smell of the earth and wood smoke. Amongst this, he saw the stones move, reach out to him, beckon him inside. And this morning, when he'd gone back in the light of day, to go inside, they wouldn't let him in.

Unknown to him, he'd entertained an elderly couple who watched his antics from the distance of their camping chairs. As they admired his persistence to conquer the stones, they knew his tiny frame would do no damage to the ancient solid rock of Sarsens.

Suddenly, he'd realized he was hungry and that had been the trigger for him to go back.

He'd run all the way, cutting across the fields, his feet following the thin tracks left bare from seeding. The ripening wheat came up to his waist and as he ran with outstretched arms, his hands skimmed across the tips. The heat of the midday sun enwombed him. He'd chattered happily to himself as if in the company of an invisible friend, his voice rising excitedly the nearer he drew to home and what was familiar to him. He had no cares or worries. When he reached the caravan, he leapt across the threshold of the always open door. At that point, his life changed forever.

Looking down at the lifeless body of his mother, the shock hit him. He suddenly withdrew his hand. Then, from the corner of his eye, he saw something move. Suddenly, a figure lurched forward, hand extended, reaching for his throat. Quickly, instinctively, he moved.

In seconds, the hand took a fistful of his light blue t-shirt and turning him, shoved him hard in the chest. His small body flew backwards. As his head hit hard against the side of a shelf, his jaw snapped, causing him to bite deeply into his tongue. His legs gave way and he slid to the floor against a small stove. When he looked up the figure had vanished, leaving him alone with the dead body of his mother.

Fear overwhelmed him. Blood filled his mouth. He didn't know whether to spit or drink it down. He did both.

Fright gripped him and he pressed his back against the stove, drawing his legs up away from her. He was as far as he could be from the door and he couldn't get out of the confined space. The door was open, but he couldn't move. He should run for help, but outside was his attacker.

He sat with his arms clasped tightly round his knees, shivering from the assault. It was unbearably hot inside the caravan and the body began to decompose. Gradually the place started to smell. Now and then his eyes would close. Every time he forced his eyelids open, hoping this was a dream, he saw her lying there. Still he kept his silent vigil.

Then the flies appeared. Lots of them. By then he was too rigid with fear to shoo them away. He remained like that until he was found. Two days later.

The estate manager spotted the tired old Land Rover with the long, dirty looking, lichen covered caravan towed behind. It was vaguely familiar to him, he'd seen it and the like there in previous years. They were drawn to an area on the estate, where twelve old, tall beech trees stood in a perfect circle. Up a track that was hard to find except to the initiated, the trees created a mystical atmosphere which at Summer Solstice drew people like a magnet. With this natural leafy awning as its centre, the invaders created a temporary encampment around the circle of trees by erecting a variety of odd shaped canvas and plastic sheets, using bushes for structure. Walking through it after they'd left, the estate manager thought it took on the guise of a latter day Robin Hood style hide-out.

Try as he might, he couldn't keep them off this piece of land. For all their so called 'green' credentials, these free-spirited types, 'the crusties' as they were referred to, left a bloody mess. He was left to clear up the human excrement and that of the dogs they brought with them, the remains of their spliffs and needles, tins, bottles, rags, you name it, they left it. And although they damaged the surrounding area – the trees, the crops, the flora – he knew it was much worse down south at Stonehenge.

The annual Stonehenge free festival looked like a refugee camp in a third world country. Free from the constraints of authority, thousands of festival goers pushed against the boundaries, creating their own society, determined to kick the established order hard where it hurt in the process. Thousands of them swarmed into the area in their rickety untaxed trucks, vans and cars or on foot with their tents to camp en masse in the fields surrounding the Stones. On their way there, they drove through hedges and fences, camping in farmers' fields, private gardens and roadside verges. Like locusts, they ensured they caused maximum destruction as they left their turds in the woods, on neatly edged lawns, and stole from shops. They indiscriminately cut down trees, fences and gates for their camp fires, stole washing from lines and tools from sheds, in short, ran rampant. Where they met with resistance, they pissed on shop counters, over fresh produce and in shop freezers, forcing the shopkeepers to throw out all the goods.

Over the years, London drug dealers gradually moved in and between them and the Hells Angels, supplied vast quantities of hash, LSD, heroin and everything in between, supplies and prices advertised to their customers on boards like betting odds at a race day. Into this anarchic chaos, women brought their babies and young children who were left to wander while their mothers joined the party. Some became so high on drugs that they danced in the flames of their camp fires. Those who overdosed in their squalid tents were left for dead to be found by the St John's Ambulance, a permanent presence on site. Due to the sheer numbers and incidents, the behaviour went largely unchallenged.

It was quieter at Avebury. It attracted a quarter of the numbers. About a hundred returned to this particular site on the estate year after year, despite him hiring extra security. He could see why they came back; the place did have a sense of other-worldliness to it, particularly when the haze of the smoke from their camp fires wafted through the trunks of the beech trees. But it was the vantage point from beyond the woodland that drew them back. The ground outside the beech circle was a high spot and gave a perfect view towards the Avebury Stone Circle and solstice sunrise. It was also in walking distance.

They'd all gone by now, moved off to another site, to Glastonbury Festival mostly. As an estate manager, he wasn't interested in talking to them, particularly as they were uninvited and he had to clean up after them. But the estate workers said that some of them, despite their matted hair and filthy appearance, had cut glass accents. These were the ones with public school backgrounds and were sons and daughters of barristers, stock brokers and even an Earl or two.

He saw the caravan and Land Rover just on the edge of the beech copse. On his approach he had already started to curse, thinking it had been left abandoned. He could smell the familiar whiff before he even reached the open door. He thought that the smell of death might be an animal, a dog perhaps that had been trapped inside, so he wasn't prepared for what he found when he crossed the threshold.

The moving black and white mass drew his eyes to the body. It was a woman's form, lying on a makeshift bed, her blonde hair just visible under the swarm of black noisy blue bottles and moving maggots gorging on her face. He staggered backwards, his hand instinctively covering his mouth and nostrils. Half in and half out of the door, his eyes flicked around the rest of the small space. His legs felt weak. As he was about to stagger back out, he saw something.

Another pair of eyes looked up at him. Big brown eyes, in a dirty little face.

He desperately wanted to get away from the stench, but now had to reach the little boy blinking back at him. He forced himself forward into the mass of dark flies and scooped the boy up in his arms. Easily putting him over his shoulder, he carried him the short distance out of the caravan door and into fresh air. He gulped it in and waved his free arm around at the blue bottles that had followed them out. As he set the boy down, his stomach lurched and he had just enough time to turn his head away as he vomited. The half-digested contents of that morning's full English hit the ground with such force it sprayed in all directions. The boy was forced to wipe away the glutinous splashes as it touched his legs. Still bent over, the estate manager hurriedly wiped his mouth on his sleeve. They had to get back to the office. He had to call the police.

CHAPTER 1

Present day

WITH HER WRIST tightly restrained by a knot tied underneath her palm, her limp hand dropped, like a head hung in shame. Her gut jolted. From the pit of her stomach, the leaden feeling of dread flooded through her body. She desperately tried to quell her rising panic as her heart raced, vibrating like a bass beat in her chest, the sound throbbing in her ears. Her eyes flicked to his black, leather gloved hand.

His breathing was heavy. He studied the knot, the purple veins visible under the tissue-thin skin. He was satisfied her wrist couldn't become easily dislodged from where he had tied it to the mahogany bedpost.

Her mind spun, trying to find the words that might stop him. She also knew it was important for her not to show her fear. She knew where that got her.

'It's too tight. It hurts,' she said, her mouth dry. Her free hand tried to loosen the knot.

She looked at his face, trying to appeal to him by making eye contact. Ignoring her protest and her gaze, he walked around to the other side of the bed and roughly pulled her arm. She had to act now. Or was it better just to lie there, get it over with? *It might be quicker.*

He was strong. Maybe he wouldn't hurt her if she just let him do what he wanted? Switch off, she told herself. Just switch off, like all the other times. Let him do this just once more and then never let it happen again. Ever. *This was the last time.*

Repeating the process, he took her other wrist and tightly knotted another scarf around it.

'I like inflicting a bit of pain along with the pleasure,' he said, flatly.

She knew this. She knew how much he loved to humiliate her and there was nothing like pain or the prospect of it, to control her. But he looked different this time.

Her arms now restrained, his eyes roamed over her naked body as she lay, her limbs stretched out on the bed. He suppressed his growing excitement at her helplessness and the anticipation of the gratification to come. He'd wait – but not for long.

'I could do anything I liked to you now, you're so beautiful ...' Stretching his hands in the black leather gloves, his voice was devoid of any trace of affection. Looking down on her on the bed, the sense of power he had over her intoxicated him. It always had. He hadn't had to coerce her when they first knew each other. But then he discovered she'd found someone else to give her favours to while her husband was away and that's when it started.

Unable to protect herself from his gaze and acutely aware of her vulnerability, reacting to her fear, her body started to tremble. She felt sick; the leather gloves were an indicator at what was to come.

He'd taken the greatest pleasure from the fact that he could take away everything she had.

'You're hanging by a thread, just one word from me ...' he'd say to her and she did anything he told her to do. It was this that now fostered a sense of contempt in him and had fuelled a dangerous desire to see how far he could go with her humiliation. He couldn't help himself; he couldn't resist the bait of beauty and vulnerability.

But he knew that this would be the last time he'd be able to blackmail her with the threat of discovery. He already knew she was going to lose all that she had – and she would know too, very shortly.

He blindfolded her. The dark would enhance her fear and thereby his gratification. He then looked at his watch. He needed time to think it through – think of what he could do to her, anticipation was half the pleasure. He would have her all night, all to himself.

'I'm going to leave you now. You'll have to wait until I come back.'

'What? You can't leave me like this …' she pleaded.

While it was easy for him to ignore her protests to be untied, as he looked at her, her nakedness and vulnerability stirred an almost overwhelming desire to degrade her there and then.

'I can do what the fuck I like, as you well know.' *Why wait,* he asked himself. But he'd been here before and delay always heightened the sense of release. 'See you later.'

Her senses now acute, she heard the door open. She heard him going down the stairs and the front door shut behind him.

A car engine started and wheels crunched on the gravel. He was gone.

CHAPTER 2

'Sir, got someone here reporting a woman dead. Sounds dodgy.' The experienced control room operator knew her words would catch the full attention of the inspector.

At the same time, another operator had her hand in the air, signalling for the inspector to go to her. The look of urgency on her face made him decide to see to what she wanted quickly, before attending to the report of someone already dead.

'It's Chris Rees's wife, boss. She's hysterical. She says he's just had a heart attack, the medics are with him and he's dead.'

His mind registered the words. There was nothing like the death of a serving officer to affect a workforce and this was no exception.

Inspector Bob May looked up at the Control Room clock. It was 08.09 hours. It was going to be another shit day.

May's stress levels were already high with what had come in during his 1800 to 0600 night shift, which included a vendetta kidnap and murder in Swindon. As if this wasn't enough, he'd had to stay on duty due to the sickness of the 'day' inspector and now he just wanted to find someone else he could hand the baton to and go home. Financial cutbacks ensured a skeleton staff, no overtime and demanding more for less. Everyone was at breaking point. Everyone, thought May, except those at the top.

Remaining calm, showing the operator no undue emotion, May took the call from the operator. He knew Rees, but not his wife and he set about consoling her. He spoke to a paramedic at the scene, ensuring they would stay until he could get a senior officer to them. The operator's comments had been overheard and had flown around the control room. There was a palpable sense of shock, as if a collective intake of breath had left the room without oxygen. For a few seconds there was clear disorientation. All eyes were on May and his attempts at bereavement counselling.

DCI Chris Rees had been well liked; his tell-it-like-it-is attitude to the chief officers had made him a few enemies of superintending officers, but the rank and file admired him for it. Hadn't done him any good though, thought May, as he came off the phone. Another good one gone.

He moved quickly back to his console to get the details of the suspected murder.

'What's the number?' he directed the question at the operator. The normality of his response checked the mood in the room. Suddenly it was steadied and responsive again.

'Log eighty-five, boss,' came the reply.

He looked at his computer screen as his fingers stabbed at the keyboard. He scrolled through the transcript of the log. A woman found dead, tied to her bed in the village of Ramsbury. He started to make the necessary phone calls to senior officers to give them news of both. Chief Officers first. Then the Head of Major Crime.

'Are you having a *fucking* laugh, Bob? How much more *shite* are you going to keep giving me?' the terse response to the report of another murder was spat out in the deep, gravel worn Glaswegian growl of Detective Chief Superintendent Clive Harker.

It was the third time in the previous six hours that May had contacted the Head of Major Crime for the force. The fallout from a drugs turf war with Southall and Bristol gangs using Swindon as their playground had left one local black teenager dead and his girlfriend missing, believed taken by the gang. A couple of their mates were in Great Western Hospital in Swindon with gunshot wounds from a very public shoot out and Harker was up to his neck in screaming families and community tension.

Adding to Harker's woes, Bob May had also informed him earlier that night that Harker's 35-year-old daughter, Gemma, had been picked up by a PC from a dingy stairwell in a block of flats in Penhill in Swindon. A sex worker, Gemma Harker had been left bloodied and bruised from another battering to her drug-wasted frame. May had established she'd been patched up at the Great Western and Harker took a note of the PC's name, to speak to him when he could. Harker knew better than to go to the hospital. It would serve no purpose, Gemma was lost to him. He had to do everything from a distance, for his own sake and for the job.

May was unsympathetic. His finger was in the dyke that was the control room and he felt like the tide was about to overwhelm him. He was on the last night of five, twelve-hour night shifts and that night alone he'd dealt with three serious RTCs, two sudden deaths, five misper reports and all the usual trivia that people rang in with. He had a year to go before retirement and had every intention of not dying on duty due to the stress of the job. Chris Rees's death would resonate that caution to many officers that day. It felt like every man for himself.

'I'm just the messenger. But I need an SIO to send over to Ramsbury.' May, a police federation rep, was not easily cowed by senior officers.

'Ring Chris Rees, tell him to go over there,' instructed Harker.

'That was the other bit of bad news I had. Chris's wife rang in a few minutes ago; he's had a heart attack. He's dead.'

'*What the fu…? Shit,*' he spat. Harker wasn't prepared for this and it caught him unawares.

Rees had been troublesome to Harker. He was used to keen younger colleagues snapping at his heels, but rawly ambitious, Rees had been biting his legs, causing him grief with chief officers, briefing against him, trying to undermine him. Harker had responded with counter-briefings, questioning his ability, particularly during the course of a recent important Crown Court drugs trial that Rees had lost. The situation had disintegrated into a spiteful game of brinkmanship that now it seemed Harker emerged as the victor.

Now, Harker's sense of self-preservation kicked in as his mind sped through his recent dealings with Rees. The pressure of the lost trial had obviously taken its toll. Could *he* have done more? Maybe. Had he made life difficult for Rees? Undoubtedly. There had been no love lost between them. Harker made the required but insincere noises to May because he suspected, even in death, Rees was going to be a cause of difficulty to him. But the last thing he'd wanted was to show any emotion to May.

'I've got DI Cage on call,' said May smartly.

'No, you haven't, I've got him up here with me. I've just sent him down to Bristol,' said Harker wearily, trying to hide from May his sudden preoccupation with news of Rees's death.

May looked at his screen. 'Then next on the list is DI Temple. I'll ring him,' he said.

'No,' came the immediate response from Harker, jolted out of preoccupied thoughts. 'Leave it with me. I'll see to it.' Harker cut May off the line and dialled the assistant chief constable.

May knew that Harker's choices were limited. Like all forces, budget cuts and endless reorganization had changed the landscape. Chief Officers and their accountants deployed a maverick, myopic 'now you see it, now you don't' style of operational policing that created disillusionment and was no longer sustainable. The thin blue line had become so thin that within weeks, retired officers were being sent letters asking them to return on a contract basis for half the pay they had previously received. Unsurprisingly, the take up rate was low.

May had little time for chief officers. His federation role exposed him to the wider issues. Policing on the cheap was nothing new, but chief constables making the decisions were on the same salaries as the Prime Minister and with their millionaire pensions, their next steps were typically retirement. With salaries and allowances cut for the ranks, the gulf between the chiefs and their subordinates was growing ever wider and he blamed them for the pressures his colleagues felt.

Policing was in a bad way with forty-three forces and forty-three chief constables, their expensive entourages and accountants all doing things in forty-three different ways. May often wondered how one job could illicit forty-three different responses from so called professionals at the top of policing. Why couldn't they agree on a consensus approach, amalgamate and reduce *their* numbers? It wasn't hard to do the maths; they'd done it in Scotland, merged six forces to one. Working on the same ratio you could reduce forty-three forces to just seven for England and Wales, saving an absolute fortune. No, like turkeys voting for Christmas, they would rather see staff placed under enormous pressure than give up their forty-three fiefdoms. May knew that forces ran in spite of chief officers, not because of them. No wonder, thought May, there was institutional constipation.

May knew this backdrop created a well of distrust and paranoia. Mired in internal politics, the force ran on rumours, gossip of power struggles, in-fighting, U-turns, wrong turns and back-stabbing, which ratcheted through the ranks, corridors, offices and gradually filtered down to parade rooms and canteens, where it was routinely scrutinized, embellished and lampooned. As senior officers jostled for influence, any two good decisions would be undone by five bad ones. Amongst all this had been the rumours of in-fighting regarding Harker and Rees. May also knew mentioning DI Temple would be an anathema to Harker – particularly hearing about Gemma only hours before.

The canteen had long chewed the story of the night Detective Inspector Harker had entered his lounge to discover Temple, then an off-duty probationer, reclined on his cream leather sofa with his fingers entwined in his 19-year-old daughter Gemma's hair, her head firmly buried in his groin. Temple also dodged the punch Harker had thrown at him that night, the force of which smashed into the side of Gemma's face.

It hadn't just been Gemma's jaw that shattered that evening. Her relationship with her parents was smashed to smithereens by Harker's punch. In tit-for-tat retaliation, she heaped humiliation on her father as she insisted he was arrested for serious assault. She'd fallen head over heels for Temple and Harker, in his angry possessiveness, threatened him with losing his job if he saw Gemma again. As the charge was dropped and Temple heeded Harker's words, she went missing. When she returned months later, she exiled herself from her parents for the streets of Swindon and a vortex of petty crime to feed her new heroin habit.

May knew it wasn't easy being a kid of a cop; being the only child of a man like Clive Harker must have been particularly difficult for Gemma. He knew Harker kept tabs on her through intel reports and knew that she sold herself for drugs. Something he kept from her mother. May knew that Harker now barely recognized Gemma from intel photos. In his professional life, Harker had seen many 'Gemmas' but he never reckoned on his own daughter being amongst them. He'd imagined a very different life for her. Like many of his colleagues, Harker worked hard, stayed at work late, pursuing his career through the ranks. His efforts had bought his family a good standard of living and regular holidays, which he thought made up for the demands the job and he placed on his family. But now, Harker would admit to himself that he'd always preferred to be at work, where he was most comfortable and where those around him were deferential to him, not least due to his status and rank. Gemma's situation had since brought a certain sympathy at work; God knows, he received none at home since Gemma's departure. Not once considering *he* could have handled things differently, Harker would never forgive Temple for the night that fractured his domestic relationships, culminated in his own arrest and led to the degradation and loss of his daughter.

After half an hour, May's phone rang. It was Harker.

'Contact Temple and get him over to Ramsbury, just until I can get more of the Major Crime Unit over there.' Harker rang off.

CHAPTER 3

At the sudden noise in the room, Temple's hand instinctively reached across the bed to the gun; even in his half sleep, his fingers folded themselves around the grip of the wooden handle and rested on the groove of the trigger.

In a split second of recognition, he realized where the sound came from. As if to stifle a woman's scream, his cupped hand moved from the gun to the mobile. In his urgency to stop the noise, he knocked over a wine glass on the table next to him, breaking the glass and spilling its residue.

Bob May told him he was to come on duty earlier than his scheduled evening shift.

'All hell's breaking loose here and Chris Rees died from a heart attack this morning.'

Temple was suddenly wide-eyed from the dim fog of sleep. Did he hear that right?

'What did you say?'

May repeated the message. The news of the death of his colleague punched Temple to the pit of his stomach. He had worked with Rees over the years; he was a good detective on the MCU (Major Crime Unit) and had sympathized with Temple when Harker recently blocked his move to the team.

'And you're going to be bitching for Harker, there's a murder over at Ramsbury. He wants you to deal – now,' May said.

As May read out the details of the log, Temple's thumb and forefinger manipulated his eyelids to concentrate on the information. When May finished the call, Temple slumped back into his pillow.

He thought of Chris Rees and the help and support Rees had given him over the years. He wasn't like the rest – Rees didn't fawn and lick up to senior officers and yet he was able to engage with them, making him more genuine. The mention of Harker forced Temple to remember that before he died, Rees had advised Temple to transfer to another force. The early run-in with Harker over Gemma had cast a long shadow over Temple's career. The only reason Temple had reached the rank of inspector was due to Harker being on secondment for three years and since then, Harker had practically held him in a head lock. Transferring was a good idea, but Temple had another reason for staying. It had become a physical need. It was the reason he joined the job in the first place and what drove him on.

The sharp cool rays of the May morning sun cut through the cheap material of the curtains at the window, obscuring the pattern to give a half-light to the room. Temple's clothes were scattered on the bare boarded floor where he'd stepped out of them. The air smelt stale and his eyes were drawn to the broken wine glass and spilt contents on the bedside table. A thin red line had dribbled its way across the cream thick cream-coloured paper of a solicitor's letter. He stood the glass upright and with the back of his hand, pushed a broken shard across the paper. A red smear now appeared across the large black printed heading of his wife's name.

He could do without a murder investigation. His domestic problems needed a plan that meant full on commitment for the next week but the phone call had now rendered that impossible.

He took the letter in his hand. It had lain on the doormat when he came home last night. He read the words through a red circle stamped by the base of the glass. The same dark wine stain was on his lips and as he moistened them, wincing at the dog shit smell of his own breath, he read again of his wife's intentions to divorce him for adultery.

Not for the first time he drew parallels with mistakes he'd made in the past and those he continued to make. It was as if a fault line had embedded itself into his life, causing him to screw up at regular intervals. He felt as if he was in a constant battle to subdue the unrelenting destructive power the past seemed to have on his life. "Moving on", they called it now; he needed to move on. But he couldn't. If he could just discover the truth, he could bring himself peace.

As he read the letter, he knew he couldn't give up on his wife Leigh. It was in his nature to screw up but it wasn't in his nature to give up. He figured a psychologist would make sense of this and the reasons he took unnecessary risks.

In a bid to understand him, Leigh had suggested that his behaviour was all wrapped up in 'survivor syndrome'. That his infidelities were perhaps a subconscious Oedipus complex, not an idea Temple was especially keen on, but he'd complimented her on her attempt at reverse psychology on him.

He loved Leigh; she understood him and he needed her for that alone. She was his best friend, lover, or at least, had been. And they had their daughter, Daisy. But she'd run out of patience following his denials regarding a female who rang asking for him in a series of phone calls to the house. He had no idea who the woman was, but seven months ago, Leigh threw him out. OK, he was no saint and it wasn't the first time, or the second she'd had reason to throw him out. But a divorce was the last thing he wanted, especially for something as far as he was concerned, he hadn't done. She'd upped the ante this time, though and gone further; moved a boyfriend in. Into the house they had shared, the house he still paid the mortgage on. Into the house where he should be, their home.

Temple took hold of the gun and momentarily felt its weight in his hand. It was a French Chamelot-Delvigne double action officer's revolver from 1874. As a child, Temple had listened avidly to his grandfather as he told the story of how he had been given the gun by a brave female resistance worker in WWII following the liberation of Ghent in 1944. He opened the drawer in the table and put the gun inside next to a packet of sleeping pills. Before closing the drawer, he hesitated; should he take the gun with him after all? Temple had trouble of another kind and right now he'd kill if he had to. He shut the drawer.

CHAPTER 4

RAMSBURY SITS ON the east side of Wiltshire, situated alongside the River Kennet. In what estate agents termed 'desirable commuter land', residents travelled to work in London and Reading on the Great Western line from nearby Great Bedwyn or Pewsey, or dashed along the M4. Typical of fodder for Sunday supplements, it was the prime example of country life; a self-contained village community, where people rubbed both their monied and benefit-receiving shoulders in its two pubs and the village shop. A school and ancient church completed the perfect pastoral package.

Temple drove on through the High Street. He hadn't been to Ramsbury for years, but he could see it had changed little. At the sight of The Yew Tree public house, his mind recalled the two or three visits here with his archaeologist uncle, Richard, as a boy. His uncle had taken him to the restoration of a Roman mosaic at nearby Littlecote Manor. One of the finest in the country, Temple now remembered how his uncle explained the meaning of the pattern to him and the tale of Orpheus. They were as good as strangers then, but due to Richard's persistence, they became friends. So much so, Richard took him everywhere with him, on archaeological digs and surveys around the county. Surprised at his remembrance of these events, his thoughts were suddenly broken as a horse and rider appeared from his right, forcing him to brake sharply.

Temple continued and bore left at The Phoenix into Oxford Street and through to the Whittonditch Road, looking for Wedwellow House. As he followed on through the village, Temple observed a smattering of social housing amongst the rest of the newly built semis and large detached houses of the wealthy and older terraced cottages. He continued to drive on, slower now, so that he could see the names of the houses.

Usually, circumstances dictated a sizeable circus of police vans and cars at the scene of a murder, but as Temple drew alongside a high brick wall where the house name was carved in stone, he could see only two police vehicles, one a large marked CSI van and a white Honda. Turning his car through a pair of open wooden gates, Temple was approached by a young uniformed officer. Temple didn't recognize him and took out his warrant card to identify himself to the officer who had leant down to register Temple's face. Waved on, he drove slowly, the wheels of his car crunching across a neat pea gravel drive.

He parked beside the police cars and recognized one of the two white paper suited CSIs coming out of the house as Jackie Newly. He looked at the house; E-shaped and detached, it was a substantial pile of Victorian red brick with a new and expensive looking wing extending to the right of a heavy oak door.

Standing in the open doorway, his white forensic suit straining to contain his bulk, Temple recognized DS Simon Sloper.

'For fuck's sake,' said Temple under his breath, instantly on the defensive. Temple knew Sloper was a friend of Harker's from way back. His well-honed paranoia told him that Sloper would be reporting back to Harker every decision he made.

Sloper was well known for gaining the largest overtime record in the force and for relying heavily on his friendship with DC/Superintendent Harker. Rumour had it that Harker's friendship had sorted many a situation that would ordinarily have resulted in Sloper receiving disciplinary action.

'At last, the cavalry,' Sloper quietly quipped, unimpressed by Temple's arrival. Harker had confided enough times for Sloper to know Temple was an anathema to Harker.

Sloper cultivated and milked the relationship with Harker for all it was worth. A pre-PACE cop, the short time he'd spent as an RMP before that gave him a swagger he had never lost, something that was useful moving in the circles he did. With nothing to retire for, at fifty-eight, he knew he was viewed by the younger cops as a relic, but he could still teach them a thing or two.

Sloper knew Harker was grateful to him for keeping tabs on his daughter Gemma and Sloper had been quick to exploit this pretext. He was well known to the movers and shakers around drugs and prostitution, and particularly liked to mix with the sex workers in the county. With Harker as top cover, Sloper moved effortlessly amongst them. He loved their seedy underworld and as he observed those who ran it, he was like a fox guarding a hen coop. He told himself – and any local response team who might register his presence around Swindon's red light district – that he was gaining much needed intelligence and information. The reality was, he'd been sucked in.

Sloper had been at the scene in Ramsbury for nearly two hours and although an old hand at murder scenes, he wanted to hand over the burden of covering some 'golden hour' basic actions. If Harker wanted him to chaperone Temple he was happy to oblige, but he wasn't being paid for being the SIO.

Knowing Temple was a close colleague of Chris Rees and that Rees had been a source of aggravation to Harker, Sloper decided to leave him in no doubt where his loyalty lay.

'Poor old Reesy, eh? Apparently his missus found him slumped in the shower this morning, bare arse naked. Dead.

Nothing they could do for him. Fuck all. Poor cow. Must have let the last job really get to him, poor bastard.'

Temple was still unable to believe Chris Rees was dead.

'He was a good bloke, he'll be missed,' was all he could say. Temple wondered why it was that a man like Sloper survived in the job, when Chris Rees sacrificed his life for it.

'I never really took to the man,' said Sloper, pointedly. 'He was a prick.'

Temple shot him a look of disdain.

'Let's get on with what we're here for, shall we? What's the score?' asked Temple, wishing he hadn't drunk so much the previous night. He'd need to be sharper to counter Sloper. Truth was, seeing Sloper had put him on the back foot.

Sloper briefed Temple as he changed into a forensic suit handed to him by the CSI.

'The body's upstairs on the bed. The doc's pronounced life extinct and left and I've called up the path, we're just waiting for him to get here. Coroner's got us a slot at the mortuary at 15.30. The deceased is a Mrs Greta Ashton-Jones, thirty-four years old, very fit, well, at least, she was. She lived here with her husband, Maxwell Ashton-Jones. He's a pilot for British Airways, older than her by some nineteen years, currently away on a long haul flight to Sydney. There's a son, James, seventeen years old, from Mr Ashton-Jones's first marriage – he was a widower before his second marriage. The son's at boarding school.'

'Who found the body?' Temple asked.

'Their cleaner, Irene Cresswell, she rung it in just after 8 a.m. She turned up as normal at 0700 this morning, and let herself in with her key. All seemed to be in order, there were no signs of forced entry. She'd finished her cleaning downstairs, gone upstairs to do the bathrooms and found the body when she went to go into the ensuite.'

'So she was here cleaning any clues away for an hour. Great start,' said Temple, flatly.

'She's next door at the moment. They've given us a police staff investigator, Kelly Farmer, who's taking her statement.'

'So let me get this straight; there's us two, this Kelly Farmer and two CSI, *is that it?*'

Temple started to feel uneasy. He knew the chief constable had to shave about £25 million off the budget and everyone had to do more with less, but this was ridiculous. With police staff investigators costing half than a detective constable, employing more of those was the way forward and an obvious bone of contention amongst detective officers.

'Who gave Harker the initial assessment?'

'I did,' Sloper replied, archly. 'As I said to Clive, it's probably a straightforward domestic. She's in her own bed, how hard can it be? We either nick the husband, or she was over the side and we nick the bloke she was shagging.'

In the majority of murders, Temple knew the perpetrators were close to home, but he also knew it was important to keep an open mind, particularly in the early stages. He didn't want to clash with Sloper, but it had taken just five minutes and he was already beginning to feel seriously pissed off with him.

Temple, Sloper and the two CSI went inside the house. An oak wooden staircase led off a flag-stoned hallway. Temple's paper covered feet sunk into a strip of snowy white deep piled carpet as he put his foot on the first stair. Looking up the flight of stairs, he hesitated slightly.

'You all right?' asked Sloper sarcastically, as he almost knocked into Temple.

'Fine. This all feels quite new to me, like the builders haven't long been gone,' said Temple, looking around. 'There have been people working here, see what they have to say about Greta and Maxwell Ashton-Jones. Write an action down to find out who was here and go and see them.'

All four went into a large bedroom. On a mahogany-framed bed in the middle of the room lay a naked blonde woman, lying on her back with arms stretched out and her wrists tied to the bedposts, her hands hanging like wilted flower heads. Her legs were together and crooked to the side. The rest of her naked form displayed a slim, lightly tanned and very attractive figure. Temple scanned her face; her head was slightly to the side, her eyes were shut, her mouth was half open and her blonde hair was splayed across pillows behind the head. She looked as if she was sleeping, a sleeping beauty, thought Temple, even in death. There were no obvious signs of violence, no signs of robbery; she was still wearing expensive looking diamond rings on her fingers. Looking around the room, the windows were closed.

Standing next to him, Temple became aware of Sloper's laboured breathing. Turning to look at him, he saw Sloper's eyes busily scanning the naked body tied to the bed. He had an urge to cover her from Sloper's view but knew he couldn't. In an attempt to distract him, Temple spoke his thoughts out loud, turning away from the bed.

'So the cleaner has come in this morning; after cleaning downstairs, she's come up here, opened the door and found Mrs Ashton-Jones like this and phoned us.'

Sloper continued his study of the body.

'Did the doc say how long she'd been here?' Temple asked, directing the question at Sloper who finally broke his gaze from the body to the CSI.

'He thinks twenty-four to thirty-six hours,' said Jackie Newly. 'The hypostasis has settled in the shoulders, back and on the legs. We've taken photos of the room, the body, close shots of the hands, wrists, face and we'll get the video up here next and run it round.'

'Good,' said Temple, as he walked around the room, taking in the scene. He could feel Sloper's eyes following him and wished he could be in the room alone.

It was sparsely but tastefully furnished. The heavy, king-sized wooden bed dominated the room; discrete built-in wardrobes and two free-standing chests of drawers made hardly a dent in the space of the room and there was an elaborate painted chandelier. He went into a large modern ensuite. Looking around, he noted various products in expensive looking bottles. Above a 'his and hers' double marble basin, was a glass shelf under a large gilt mirror.

Amongst paracetamol and ibuprofen, he saw a small bottle of medication with Greta's name on it, which he wrote down. Walking back into the bedroom, he went over to a set of closed French doors. These led to a small balcony that looked over a swimming pool in the rear garden and into fields and the River Kennet beyond. There was a garage and stable complex to the left. It was an idyllic setting.

Back in the room, his eyes were drawn to a large framed charcoal drawing of a naked woman hanging on the wall – it was clearly a portrait of Greta Ashton-Jones. On a chest of drawers were framed photographs of Greta. They had a professional style to them. As he looked at them, Temple was struck by her eyes. Their almost feline shape and grey colour gave her a very attractive, exotic look and her tumbling blonde mane of hair and dusting of freckles across her nose, made her look younger, vulnerable even. She had clearly been at ease with both the camera and the taker – there were other photos of her with a man, older than her. She looked effortlessly sophisticated – the photo showed her in a wide brimmed hat, smiling broadly, her generous lips revealing perfect teeth. Temple lingered on the image before he turned and looked back at the bed.

'She was a bit of all right, wasn't she? Good body.' Sloper had joined Temple looking at the photos.

'Who's the guy, do we know yet? And what about this one, who is he?' Temple pointed to another frame with a picture of a different man.

'Yes, we ID-ed them earlier with the cleaner; that's her husband, Maxwell, and that one is her father.' Sloper walked back to the bed. 'He goes off to work, she gets her bit on the side in, we've just got to find out who it is – after all, she can't tie her own wrists.'

Irritated by Sloper's comments, Temple gave him a list of instructions. A mobile sounded; Sloper drew two out of his pocket, turned and walked away, putting one to his ear, the other back in his pocket. Temple watched him. The call was short and their conversation resumed. Temple wondered if it was Harker. He continued to list the initial actions.

'As a matter of priority, I want to know what time Maxwell Ashton-Jones left for work, what time his plane left and where he is now. Have we covered the phones? I want the last number called and the last number received. Seize any mobile phones and laptops and get them back to HQ for examination. Search her handbag and purse. Ring the Financial Investigation team at HQ, I want a full financial profile of husband and wife. I'll leave you to run the video camera all over the place while I go and see the cleaner.'

Temple divested himself of his forensic suit and walked to a neighbouring house. He knocked on the door. It was answered by a woman wearing a grave expression who showed Temple into the kitchen. Sitting at a pine table was Kelly Farmer. She looked up at him. Recognition hit him as soon as he saw her. A tall, striking brunette, with a sharp cut bob hairstyle, he had last seen her in the police bar at a recent leaving do. Temple had watched from afar as friend and colleague, Paul Wright, attempted to chat her up, only for her female partner to turn up and promptly plant a full kiss on her lips.

Kelly Farmer had finished taking the statement and Irene Cresswell was reading it whilst sniffing into a paper hanky. Temple drew Kelly to one side and spoke to her in a low voice.

'Kelly, we haven't met before, I'm DI Temple, I'm the senior investigating officer. What's she saying?'

Kelly referred to a hard back notebook as she started to recount the information given to her. Temple sensed her inexperience.

'Slow down, Kelly, slow down. Where do you usually work?'

'I'm normally on burglaries and ABHs in Swindon.'

'You won't have been involved in a murder inquiry before then?'

'No, boss, I haven't, but I'm up for it,' she replied confidently.

'That's just as well because there's not many of us at the moment, which is even more of a reason to ensure we cover all the bases. So, how long have you got in?'

'I've been investigating for nearly a year now, done my courses, started on tier 2 interview course last month.'

Kelly knew this was a chance to prove herself. She didn't want to fuck this up. If she could prove herself in this investigation, she might get on the MCU where her pay would increase. She and her partner were struggling to pay a chunky mortgage on a townhouse on a new executive estate in Swindon. While investigating was a far cry from her previous work in a car insurance call centre, the situation demanded further ambition and Kelly already had her sights set elsewhere. If she could acquire enough interview skills and experience, she could work in more lucrative areas, such as fraud and money laundering investigation in London.

'OK. So, tell me everything she's told you, *slowly*.'

Kelly took a breath and began.

'Right, Irene Cresswell is the cleaner for the Ashton-Jones. Maxwell and Greta live here, their son James, who's seventeen, is a full-time boarder at Stilcombe Public School – that's near Newbury – but comes home at weekends and holidays.'

'Where is he now, do we know, did he come home this weekend?'

'She says that he came home on Friday, but that he didn't stay the whole weekend as he was going to stay at a friend's from school.'

'And what's Irene's routine?'

'She turned up this morning at 7 a.m. as she does on every Monday and Friday. She cleans on Fridays *for* the weekend and then on Mondays *from* the weekend to take them to the next Friday. She last saw Greta Ashton-Jones alive last Friday morning. Greta told her that Maxwell had left for Sydney the evening before, on Thursday. Maxwell is a pilot for British Airways and he does long haul trips. Greta told Irene that Maxwell would be away for nine days – this is normal apparently. Irene says there's a twelve hour flight to Singapore, then a forty-eight hour stopover. She knows this because Greta used to be an air hostess, that's how Greta and

Maxwell met. If her timings are right, by my reckoning, he's now in the air going to Sydney or thereabouts.'

'Good work. Have you asked her what she actually did this morning?'

'Yes, she thought Greta was out this morning as she usually sees her car on the driveway, it's a red Porsche. She didn't know the registration. Maxwell drives a black Range Rover Sport. Her car was not on the drive so Irene let herself in and came straight in here to the kitchen to tidy up. She said she thought she might have driven over to some nearby stables to have an early morning horse ride as she did this sometimes; her own horse died two years ago apparently. She washed up and gathered up some rubbish, washed the floor, opened the French doors to let the floor dry, went into the lounge, tidied and hoovered.'

'Was the house secured when she arrived?' asked Temple, impressed by the level of detail that Kelly was providing.

'She says so.'

'When did she discover the body?'

'She'd finished in the lounge and went upstairs to collect any washing and start tidying the bedrooms, that's when she went into Greta's room and discovered her lying on top of the bed, dead.'

Sloper rang. 'Temple, the path's here, just dressing up.'

'I'm coming back. Is there a red Porsche or black Range Rover Sport in the garage?'

'I'll have a look.' Sloper rang off.

'OK, finish it off, Kelly. I want to find out about Greta and Maxwell, everything she knows about them, anything. I also want to know what she cleaned up – what was there to tidy? We'll get together later for a debrief.'

Temple walked back to the scene to see Sloper in the driveway.

'There are no cars in the garage.'

'Right,' said Temple, 'get the reg number for the Porsche and ring into PNC, get them to run Greta as the registered keeper and put a marker on it to stop it if seen and ring me immediately. We need to find that car.'

Temple and Sloper met the pathologist and after introductions, went back upstairs. In his early fifties, Tim Yardley was a big, avuncular man with a distinctively deep voice. He had just joined the regional consortium and had travelled up from Exeter following the call. Yardley, Sloper, Temple and Jackie Newly stood around the bed, looking at the body.

'What do we think then, guys?' said Yardley, as he reached into an open briefcase to retrieve a pair of latex gloves and a thermometer.

'Death by auto-erotic asphyxiation, sex game gone wrong is my bet,' Sloper ventured. He'd worked on something similar in the past.

'That's what it could be.' Yardley examined the face, gently raising the eyelids with his thumbs to look at the eyes. 'There are slight signs of petechiae, a characteristic of death by strangulation. Of course, I'll only be able to give you what you want once I've done a full examination back at the mortuary.'

Sloper watched as Yardley continued to conduct a quick check of the body with his latexed hands and finished with a temperature check.

'No obvious signs of a struggle, finger nails are in place, no bruising to legs or arms although there will be once we remove the ties on the wrists. There's some bruising coming through around the ankles so looks as though the legs were restrained at some point.'

'Estimated time of death?' asked Temple.

'Notice the weather this weekend? Clear skies at night and particularly harsh frosts for late May. This would have kept the temperatures down and help to slow decomposition. I'd say she's been dead for twenty-four to thirty-six hours, late Saturday, early hours of Sunday morning.'

'Thanks, Doc, I'll see you later at the mortuary in Salisbury.'

As Temple assimilated the information, he watched Jackie put a bag over the head and untie the hands and feet of the body to ensure any forensic evidence that might have been left were not lost in transition.

He knew, with Greta Ashton-Jones's husband apparently out of the country at the time of her murder, this was not the cut and dry 'domestic' that Sloper had assessed. Conscious of Sloper's direct line into Harker, Temple's experience of similar inquiries was enough to tell him that he would need more resources if he was to make ground in the next couple of days. The local press would soon pick up on the story and the public would know there was a killer on the loose. He gave Sloper a further list of fast-track actions.

'Kelly said the Ashton-Joneses' son, James, stays over from boarding school at weekends. He was here on Friday apparently, find out where he was this weekend. Once we get confirmation of the route to Australia, we'll need to get word to Ashton-Jones that his wife's dead. I want a family liaison officer to meet him when he gets back at Heathrow. Are her parents alive? We'll need to get formal ID of the body.'

'Yes, Greta's mother, Dianna Forrester lives at Harnham, Salisbury, and her father Brett Forrester lives at Marlborough, Hyde Lane. I've got both addresses, we can do one each if you like?' Sloper suggested. He'd use the time to give Harker his first update.

'Yes, I'll see Brett Forrester and ask him to ID the body,' said Temple. He knew Sloper was weighing his every decision; watching as he assimilated and evaluated every piece of information. He felt him breathing right down his neck.

CHAPTER 5

TEMPLE PASSED THE town hall as he drove into Marlborough's wide High Street. It was heaving with barely moving traffic as drivers slowed to double-park, or try to snatch a free parking space along the kerb side, rather than pay. He stopped to wave across a group of teenage schoolgirls standing in the road. A dominant presence in the town, female students of Marlborough College were marked out by their distinctive uniform. Temple watched as they strode in front of his car. Clutching their books, they looked like heroines from Victorian novels, as the hems of their voluminous long black skirts skimmed the tarmac. He drove on through to the end of the High Street and turned right to Hyde Lane.

As he drove down the winding lane, passing bespoke, detached houses, he stopped to check the number Sloper gave him. There were cars parked either side of the lane, leaving a narrow channel through which to drive and Temple had to negotiate some bad parking in order to drive on through. As the lane carried on, Temple stopped the car and checked the number again.

'Shit,' he said, as he realized he had the right address.

Temple had arrived at The Sidings, Brett Forrester's address and it looked as though he was entertaining. The cars he had passed were those of the many guests Temple could now hear in the garden that ran to the left of the property. He could see the tops of expensive garden parasols over a manicured laurel hedge and through his wound-down window, he heard music, laughter and the sound of a party in full swing. He drove on and found a space to park and got out. The afternoon sun had a touch of warmth and the breezeless air held the music above the chatter.

Temple walked through a wooden gate and onto a brick path, which took him towards an open front door. At the door he could see down the hallway, through to the end of the house to the garden. The rich, sonorous sound of jazz music drifted through the house from an outside sound system and its relaxed vibe permeated through into the high spirited, joyous mood of the party goers. Momentarily, Temple wished he could disappear; come back when the party was over, when there weren't so many happy people around. To the rising lilt of an alto saxophone, Temple went inside, unable to escape the task he was there for. He walked down the hall and stopped at the open doorway of the kitchen to the left. Temple interrupted a small group of chattering people.

'I'm looking for Brett Forrester?' he said awkwardly, feeling the burden of the message he had to deliver.

A slim woman in a shocking pink dress at the sink turned her head.

'He's in the garden, darling,' she said, smiling, wondering why she didn't know him.

Temple approached her and standing next to her, looked out of the window onto a large lawn. There had to be more than fifty people out there.

'Can you point him out to me, please?' he said quietly. He didn't want to draw attention from the other people in the room if he could help it. The cadence of the saxophone created a warm sense of joy and wellbeing about the place and he was conscious that he was about to change that.

The woman looked at him quizzically.

'Yes,' she replied and looking out of the window, pointed to a man, 'That's him, in the striped blue shirt and cream panama hat.'

Temple looked through the window and saw Brett Forrester, a tall, well-built man, in his early sixties. Standing in a small gathering of other men, he was holding a half empty glass of champagne in one hand, while his other arm rested over the shoulders of a male companion. Clearly at ease in each other's company, they were laughing noisily into each other's faces.

Feeling like the Grim Reaper, he went into the garden, weaving his way around people who were chatting and laughing, dancing and chinking their glasses, until he reached Forrester. He stood close enough to his left shoulder to make him turn around.

'Mr Brett Forrester?' he said quietly.

'Yes?' Forrester, interrupted by Temple's formality, turned from his companions. Making eye contact, Temple continued to speak in a low voice.

'Sir, I wonder if I could have a word with you. I'm Detective Inspector Temple—' he said, showing his warrant card. Before he could finish, Forrester interrupted him.

'Look, if it's about the parking …' he said, dismissively, half turning back to the group.

'No, sir, it's not about the parking. Could we go inside, I really need a word with you in private.'

Forrester turned from his companions and, for a few seconds, studied Temple's face. Something in Temple's expression and the sound of his voice told him he should do as he was being asked. He turned back to his friends.

'Hang on, guys, let me deal with whatever this is and I'll be back.' He put his glass into the hands of one of his friends and strode purposefully back to the house.

Temple could see he would be in no mood for a preamble and used the walk to the house to decide he'd be straightforward in delivering the death message. Irritated by the intrusion, Forrester led Temple into his study at the front of the house, took off his hat and shut the door behind them, muffling the sound of the music. Temple quickly studied Forrester's face and spoke.

'I'm afraid I have some bad news, sir. This morning I was called to Wedwellow House, in Ramsbury, where the body of your daughter, Greta Ashton-Jones, had been discovered. She has been murdered. I'm sorry.' Temple knew that with those few words, he had just shattered Forrester's world.

Brett Forrester looked back at him in disbelief and took a small stagger backwards. Temple reached out and took his elbow to steady him.

'Are you *sure*?' Brett Forrester looked questioningly back at Temple, barely able to say the words and desperately wanting it to be a mistake. His mouth went dry.

'I'm afraid so, sir, she was found by her cleaner this morning.'

Tanned, with thick dark hair, slightly greying at the sides, Forrester was well spoken and held himself very straight, straighter since Temple imparted the news. He closed his eyes and tilted his head back slightly. After taking a deep breath, he seemed to recover himself. He turned his back and walked towards the corner of the room to a drinks tray.

Temple took this opportunity to look around the room. An old kneehole desk was situated in a large bay window, with a well-worn leather settee and chair either side of an open fireplace. In one of the chairs was a khaki canvas bag, brimming with expensive looking cameras and lenses. On the floor were small exotic rugs. The room contained various indigenous objects, the kind of trophies acquired from a life spent travelling in faraway places. On the walls were two artistically arranged patchworks of different sized framed photographs.

'Would you like a drink, Inspector?' Forrester was standing near a table containing various decanters. Temple saw Forrester's hands shake as he negotiated the liquid into a glass. He declined.

'I wonder if you could tell me when you last saw your daughter.' Temple watched Forrester intently as he answered.

'I last saw Greta on Saturday,' said Forrester, his deep voice momentarily weak with emotion. He cleared his throat before continuing. 'We had lunch together, here,' he said, finally letting out a deep sigh as he held a half filled, cut glass whisky tumbler up to his lips.

His body had taken on a feeling of other worldliness. He knew this was real because no one would play such a bad trick, but his mind was still having trouble actually processing the words. The man said Greta was dead. All at once he felt as though the top of his head had been sliced open and his guts ripped out. He felt laid bare. Raw. Weak. However, instinct told him he should still try not to betray his feelings and to hold himself together.

'According to the pathologist, she died on Saturday evening, or the early hours of Sunday morning,' Temple informed him. 'You could well have been one of the last people to see her alive.'

The words caught Forrester unawares. He looked back at Temple, startled.

'What, you think that *I killed her*?' His tone was incredulous.

'No, sir, I mean apart from the person who killed her, you could have been the last, or one of the last people to see her alive. Can you tell me about your daughter, sir, how did she seem when she left you?'

Forrester closed his eyes as if to shut Temple out of a private memory he was reliving.

'She was beautiful, full of life, vital.' Forrester's voice trailed off as finally, he seemed to succumb to the shock of the news and, as his legs gave way, his body sank heavily into the settee. 'Look up there,' he said, gesturing with his head, his voice obviously weaker. 'That's how she was on Saturday, how you see her there.'

Temple's gaze went from Forrester to the photographs on the wall. There were black and white images of a younger looking Greta at a party, talking animatedly, a scene similar to what Temple had witnessed in the garden. She was striking;

another photograph showed a full head shot, looking full on into the camera, blowing a kiss. There were others too, but it was the way they were taken as much as the subject, natural, yet professionally executed, as if a photoshoot. Temple could see there was not one bad take.

'How did she die?' asked Forrester, his voice at a whisper, barely able to form the words.

Temple turned back to him.

'We're waiting on the result of the PM, sir, post mortem …'

'I know what a PM is, Inspector. Who would want to kill Greta?' Forrester's voice tailed off.

'That's what I'm hoping to find out, sir.'

'Only hoping, Inspector? I'm going to want you to do more than hope. I shan't rest until I know who murdered my daughter.' Forrester's voice faltered at the word 'murdered' as if he couldn't believe he had to say it.

'It was a clumsy use of words, sir. I will find out who murdered your daughter. I have all the force resources at my disposal and will use them to get to the truth.'

Temple said the words knowing that he lied. Forrester didn't need to know his immediate lack of resources and that every inquiry was largely determined by the force accountant, scrutinizing every penny spent. Temple knew that justice had a cost now, a finite budget, with a financial cut off point which any SIO knew he could not go beyond without being called to meetings to justify further inquiries. Not only did Temple have to find the murderer, he knew he also had to outwit the anonymous bean counters. They would ultimately call time on his inquiry when their spreadsheets calculated the tipping point and question his ability not to have drawn things to a close beforehand.

'I will need to ask you some questions to build up a picture of Greta's background, her life.'

As he watched Forrester, Temple was sure he saw Forrester's face cloud a little when he had mentioned questioning him. Temple felt his mobile vibrate in his pocket.

'I just need to take this call, sir, it may be important to the inquiry.' Temple was grateful for the chance to leave the room and stood in the hallway. It was Sloper; Dianna Forrester insisted on going to the mortuary to identify the body so Temple instructed him to take her to Salisbury hospital and he would meet them there. He returned to Brett Forrester.

'I'd like some time, Inspector, to be on my own, to let this sink in properly.' Forrester was ashen. He had visibly shrunk from the man Temple had seen in the garden.

'Of course. Are you going to be all right, sir?'

'Yes, I'll be all right.' Forrester tried to rally himself. 'I'm used to seeing death and destruction, murder and savagery …'

'Sir?' Temple suddenly wondered what Forrester was going to say.

'I was a photographic journalist, Inspector, travelled all around the world witnessing atrocities and various genocides … it makes you hard when you've seen so much. I didn't think anything else could really touch me …' His voice had shrunk to a whisper.

Temple watched as Forrester shook his head in disbelief.

'Can we make an appointment tomorrow, sir, I can come here?' asked Temple.

'Yes, come back tomorrow, about eleven.'

Temple saw himself out. As he closed the front door, he suddenly heard a loud roar from inside. Forrester was screaming, crying out at the top of his voice. As Temple reached the gate at the end of the path, the music stopped. He hated giving death messages, seeing what it did to people, he'd done it enough times following accidents. But telling people their loved one had been murdered – that someone had deliberately ended their life – that took things to a different, darker, more destructive level, where your life would never be the same again. Temple knew all about that. He headed off to the mortuary.

CHAPTER 6

RUNNING LATE, BY the time Temple arrived at Odstock Hospital, the identification was over. Sloper and Dianna Forrester were stood in a corridor. Temple extended his hand to introduce himself.

She was small and slim, with tidy grey hair pulled back behind her head and a tight mouth. Her face was hardened although it was evident that she had once been an attractive woman. She showed little in the way of emotion, despite just seeing her daughter's dead body. She wore a light beige mac, with flat shoes. Plain and restrained. Already, he couldn't imagine her as a wife to the larger-than-life Brett Forrester.

She acknowledged his words but seemed to have no desire to ask questions. Temple knew that she was probably in shock. As Sloper went to take Dianna Forrester back home, Temple watched as Sloper put a gentle arm to her shoulders as if to guide her. The sympathetic gesture was unexpected; he had a heart after all, thought Temple; deep down, buried under all that sarcastic, nasty bulk. He arranged to meet him later to debrief.

Temple went into the mortuary. Greta Ashton-Jones's body was already on the cold white porcelain table with Yardley standing over it. The post mortem began. The impersonal environment always reminded Temple of a public toilet; the walls of the room were covered with square white tiles and the floor was grey concrete, all of which was easy to wash down. The sickly sweet smell of a pungent air freshener pervaded the room, ready to mask the smell of deteriorating flesh. Temple got dressed in theatre greens and stood opposite Yardley.

'It's not that often I get to do the honours on such an attractive woman,' remarked Yardley.

Temple looked down on his victim. Yardley was right; she was lovely, so who would want to destroy that?

'Right, let's get down to business. This is our able assistant for the day; hello, Kim.' Yardley turned to acknowledge a woman entering the room, with what looked to Temple to be a vacuum cleaner. Temple was slightly taken aback by her prettiness which seemed totally at odds with the surroundings. Temple welcomed the temporary distraction from what he knew was to follow. She put on protective glasses.

'Feel free to leave the room at any time. If you want to, you can use the viewing gallery,' she said confidently to Temple as she turned to a tray to select a knife.

'No problem, I've done a few PMs so I know what's coming, but thanks,' Temple said, trying to match her confidence and settle his stomach for what was to come. He watched as Yardley took the offered knife and made a deep Y incision starting at the shoulders, meeting in the middle of the chest and going on down past the navel.

As the knife cut into the dead flesh, it released the fetid stink of rotting meat so forcefully that it seemed to instantly cling to everything in the room. Temple's immediate reaction was to obstruct the smell fighting to invade his body by holding his breath, but it was useless. It worked its way into his throat like a vile poisonous gas, all the time threatening to make him gag. Despite the stench and repulsion that he felt as his gut knotted from the rush of evil odour, Temple managed to recover himself. The smell seemed not to register with Kim and Yardley.

Temple watched as Kim deftly used rib shears to release the heart and lungs from their bony cage. Both then become engrossed in the removal, weighing and recording of organs. Eventually, Yardley broke the silence of studious dissection.

'I'm taking tissue samples for toxicology purposes. There is some petechiae on the eyes – as I said before – and the hyoid bone just above the larynx is broken, with some soft tissue damage on the neck. I can also now tell you that our young lady had engaged in sexual activity prior to death, semen is present in the vagina and I'll get you the samples for DNA retrieval. She was also approximately nine weeks pregnant.'

'Pregnant?' repeated Temple, surprised.

He looked at Greta's face. Kim had her knife poised to slice into the hairline.

'Yes, which might give you a further dimension to your inquiry. You can make an inquiry with her GP. I'll send off the DNA to the lab of course,' offered Yardley helpfully.

Temple watched with a morbid fascination as Greta's face was skilfully sliced and rolled apart from its bony structure as if a mask.

'Thanks.' Temple's attention was taken by the sound of an oscillating saw.

'Right, we're just going to open the skull now.'

He knew he'd seen enough.

'Well, if you both won't mind I've got some phone calls to make. I'll catch up with you outside, Doc.'

Temple went outside into an office area to write up his notes and make calls. Yardley joined him an hour later.

'So Inspector, I can confirm cause of death as strangulation. It appears that her windpipe was compressed, which would have prevented her from drawing in any air and although there is some local bruising, I've seen a lot worse. This isn't a throttling. This was quite a controlled act; consciousness would have been lost as quickly as ten to twenty or so seconds.'

'Could this have occurred during sex?' Temple asked.

'Well, we know she had sex prior to death, she was tied when found and there is nothing under her fingernails to suggest any sign of a struggle prior to them being tied. However, there is significant bruising where the ties held her arms to the bed – and the ankles I might add, suggesting they were tied too at some point and also suggesting some resistance to the ties – but there are no other significant bruises on her body, all of which may suggest some compliance with the act. This could very well be a case of auto-erotic asphyxiation. I'm inclined to bet she was strangled by someone who knew what they were doing. What I mean is, knew where to put their hands – their thumbs have found the windpipe and closed it off spectacularly. Your victim would not have had much of a chance of a struggle and death would have occurred quite quickly, I'm talking seconds not minutes.'

'Could it have been an accident?'

'Well, it depends. It's a possibility that during the throes of passion they got carried away and forgot the release … that's one for you. But if she hadn't been restrained and she wasn't compliant, we would have been looking at a significantly different scene. As I said, there is an amount of bruising from the ties that bound her so that would have restricted her movements somewhat.'

'Sex after death?' asked Temple.

'Not sure about that. It floats some people's boat I know.'

'Thanks, Doc.'

It was early evening when Temple left the mortuary and drove back to Marlborough Police Station to meet Sloper and Kelly for a debrief. During the drive, he turned the post mortem over in his mind. Bruising from being tied to the bed. *Who had been with her?* Not her husband by all accounts. Strangled during sex. He'd get a DNA profile at least. Pregnant, Yardley had said. He'd also get a DNA profile on the foetus. He touched the radio button. The sound of Andy Williams came out. '*Oh pretty baby, now that I've found you stay, and let me love you, baby, let me love you …*'

Temple pulled his car into the nick. He found Sloper and Kelly in the main office where Sloper was writing Greta's details on a whiteboard. Temple informed them of the results of the post mortem and Sloper recounted details of the initial statement he had taken from Dianna Forrester.

'I felt sorry for her. There's no love lost between her and Brett Forrester, or it seems, between her and Greta. She says she hasn't seen Forrester for many years and she refused to go to Greta and Maxwell's wedding. Brett Forrester walked out on her when Greta was two years old. She was young and inexperienced when they married. He was a journalist and went away for long stretches at a time, trying to carve his career. She says he went away one day and basically never came back. Her relationship with Greta was difficult; Dianna Forrester is quite a religious woman, a practising Catholic and Greta was convent educated.

'She describes Greta as quite a wilful and wayward child and admits that she brought her up quite strictly. After Brett walked out, Dianna and Greta lived with Dianna's father, a retired Army Major. Yes, Forrester sent money to her, but he never came back. It appears that Greta rebelled against the constraints of the convent and home life. The usual stuff; truancy, wearing make-up, then boyfriends – Dianna says that she was strict with her because she was obviously pretty and became more so in her early teens. But she says she also found her difficult to control, that she was moody, which she put down to her being a stroppy teenager. At some point, Greta ran away from home and turned up at her father's home in London. He was a photographer and journalist. Dianna Forrester described him as selfish and self-absorbed.' Sloper continued to read from his notes. 'Seems then, from about aged fifteen, Greta moved in with her father. Having tracked him down, after all those years, he welcomes her with open arms. Greta practically shut her mother out after that. I've run him through PNC, no show.' Sloper finished and turned his attention again to the whiteboard, before finishing. 'She's right uptight and despite her quiet demeanour, I bet she could be a bitch when the situation demanded.'

'She's just lost her daughter ...' stated Kelly, wide eyed, expecting more respect for the victim's mother.

'I'm telling you what I think. Giving you the benefit of my experience, take it or leave it, *love* ...' Sloper answered, turning back to the whiteboard.

Ignoring the pair, Temple remembered how Brett Forrester looked when he told him he would need to question him about Greta. He logged onto a computer and put Forrester's name into Google. Described as a gifted and award winning photographer, Temple discovered he had freelanced for all the major press outlets: Reuters, Associated Press, *The Times*, the Press Association and *National Geographic*.

He found numerous entries of examples of Forrester's work from around the world, including Northern Ireland in 1981 when, for *The Times*, Forrester had photographed the inside of an IRA stronghold, complete with hooded men standing with their weapons drawn facing the camera. He had also been to Sudan, Israel, Palestine, Mexico and Columbia, covering internal conflicts and all manner of drug barons, as well as being in a party of journalists who travelled from Bangkok to the Thai border at the end of the Khmer Rouge in Cambodia. Temple found a photo of him dated 1979, taken in Palestine; the suntanned and bearded Forrester was pictured on a dust track, in front of a car shot through with bullets, wearing a black and white shemagh around his neck, with a cigarette hanging out of his mouth, his camera slung over his shoulder. Forrester was right. He had seen it all, he was fearless. He would be, after seeing all that. Then by contrast, from 2000, his photographic work began to feature women and be exhibited in art galleries.

'Well, we'll get Brett Forrester's side of the story tomorrow. In the meantime, capture all this about him.'

'Irene Creswell gave me some interesting stuff, boss,' Kelly followed on, looking at the screen over Temple's shoulder.

Sloper turned to watch her. She was irritating him and he couldn't quite nail why. She was slim and well dressed in her aubergine coloured trouser suit, he'd give her that. A lot of the women at work, especially policewomen, dressed like maiden aunts in his experience. But there was something that irked him. As he watched her, he knew what it was. Ambition. That was it. There was nothing worse, a pretty dyke with ambition. He'd seen it before. They'd stab you in the back to get a pencil, rather than ask you for it, he thought.

'Greta and Maxwell had been married for twelve years; his son James is from his first marriage to his wife, Olivia. She was an air hostess and drowned in a swimming pool in Saudi Arabia when their son was three years old.'

Temple and Sloper exchanged knowing looks. Sloper wrote in his notebook, just as a mobile went off in his pocket. He ignored it, leaving it to ring as Kelly spoke.

'Greta and Maxwell married within a year of meeting; she was also an air hostess. James goes to boarding school, coming home most weekends, Irene says that Greta told her he would not be home this weekend as he was staying with one of his friends instead. She's been cleaning for them for six years, starting when Greta was still flying; she stayed on when Greta gave up work four years ago.'

'Did she say why she gave up work?' asked Temple.

'No, and I didn't ask, sorry, boss,' replied Kelly, annoyed at herself. Sloper snorted and muttered under his breath, taking his two mobiles out to check for the caller.

'That's all right, we'll find out,' Temple reassured her, watching Sloper.

Kelly carried on. 'She felt there had been a change in the relationship between Maxwell and Greta in the last eighteen months, with Maxwell spending more time away, leaving Greta on her own. She also said, pointing to her head, that Greta was a bit troubled. She wouldn't say any more than that on the matter. A regular visitor to the house when Maxwell is away is his friend, Jonathan Silvester. He's a retired pilot and dabbles in investments, she thinks he managed some of Maxwell's money for him. Greta has a girlfriend, Caroline Black, another hostess, who she says she saw intermittently; they travelled the world together when Greta was working. With time on her hands, Irene says that Greta 'got about a bit' with other men, one being the local builder. Despite all this though, Irene says she liked her. Greta treated her well, gave her stuff, bits of jewellery, handbags. She said she loved working for her because it gave her a window to a different world.'

'Thanks, Kelly, that's great. We'll need to follow up the friend and the builder. We also need to find out what happened in Saudi Arabia – Ashton-Jones has got two dead wives now – that gives us an obvious insurance motive and puts him at the top of the list as a suspect. Anything on the other actions?'

Sloper nodded. 'I've pulled a favour with the Financial Crime Unit and they've come up with some initial inquiries into bank accounts. Maxwell has a joint bank account with Greta and also a separate one, using the middle name of Thomas to distinguish the two. There's also a savings account in this name too. They're not short of a bob or two, either; there's about £25k in the joint bank account and £200k in the single bank account, with £96k in the single savings account. There's signs of investments in an offshore account which we probably won't be able to access, so who knows how much that's holding.'

'Nice work. We need to find out how much the insurance paid out for the first Mrs Ashton-Jones and what Greta is insured for. Let's find out how he's getting all this money. How the other half live,' said Temple, drily. 'What about Maxwell's movements, Si?'

'Well, BA have provided me with an itinerary. Maxwell would have been away for nine days but that'll be cut short. He left Gatwick on Thursday evening at 21.45, arriving at Singapore at 10.30 on Friday for a forty-eight hour stopover. He left for Sydney at 12.05 on Sunday afternoon, arriving at

Sydney at 19.50. He's actually in Sydney now on a further forty-eight hour stopover. I explained the situation to the head of their HR. They are going to break the news to him and ring me when he's on the plane back. We can then make arrangements for him to be met this end. I reckon we'll be seeing him in twenty-four hours.'

'OK, when they ring you back I want to know how he took the news. So at the time of Greta's death, he would have been in Singapore?' Temple asked.

'By my reckoning, yes,' said Sloper, 'on a forty-eight hour stopover before going on. It actually takes twelve hours give or take, from here to Singapore. I'll see what I can find out about Saudi – I'll start with the coroner's office.'

'We need to make sure we capture all this stuff.' Temple reached inside his pocket to answer his mobile. It was PC Gregory on scene guard duty.

'Sir, I've got a guy here called Marcus Hussain, he's turned up in the red Porsche. I thought I'd better let you know.'

CHAPTER 7

The Porsche was parked opposite the gates of Wedwellow House when Temple arrived. In the dark he could see there was a man standing next to PC Gregory. Temple approached the pair, as Kelly and Sloper drew up behind and joined him. Marcus Hussain, dressed in a sharp suit, was handcuffed and clearly agitated by the situation he found himself in.

'Marcus Hussain, sir,' said Gregory, addressing Temple. 'I have detained this man under Section 1 of the Theft Act.'

'I want to make a complaint,' spat Hussain.

'You can take the handcuffs off, Gregory,' instructed Temple. 'We're dealing with a major incident at this address, sir, a murder, in fact.'

'Murder?' Hussain repeated, his eyes widening.

'Yes, Mr Hussain,' replied Temple, satisfied that he had said enough to distract Hussain from pursuing any grievance with Gregory.

In his late twenties, Hussain was neatly groomed with close cropped hair and a sharply tailored electric blue suit. There was a gold ring on his little finger and a gold chain visible at his expensive, open neck, black striped shirt. Temple immediately sensed his self-assured, cocky attitude.

'This car, does it belong to Greta Ashton-Jones?'

Hussain made a show of rubbing his wrists before he answered.

'Yes, I'm bringing it back for her, it's been at the garage. I'm the assistant manager at the Green Range Porsche garage at Great Western Way in Swindon.' He drew himself up to his full height as he spoke.

'It's quarter to ten in the evening – do you usually work this late?' asked Temple.

'Greta's an important client. It was actually before nine when I got here but this monkey wouldn't let me through the gates,' replied Hussain, staring at PC Gregory.

'When did you last see Mrs Ashton-Jones?'

'Saturday evening,' replied Hussain. 'Look, who's dead, who's been murdered?'

'At what time?' Temple asked, ignoring the question.

'I don't know, man,' replied Hussain.

'I think you do,' said Temple.

'I don't.' Hussain's voice was rising.

'That's quite an expensive watch you've got there on your wrist, are you trying to tell me that you don't use it?' Temple asked.

'Look, I don't know what time I saw her, all right.'

'Mr Hussain, you probably have important information in relation to my inquiry and you've turned up in the victim's car. You're obstructing my inquiries. You're coming with us to the station.'

'Hey, hang on, hang on, man,' Hussain protested, as Sloper and Kelly moved in to take hold of Hussain. 'What victim? D'you mean Greta? Get off me. Are you talking about Greta?' Hussain was working himself up.

'Greta Ashton-Jones has been found murdered at this address. You had her car and you've come back to the scene and are not cooperating. You're being arrested on suspicion of theft.'

Hussain was left speechless as Sloper and Kelly put him into their car and drove off to Gable Cross Police Station on the outskirts of Swindon. Temple joined Sloper and Kelly in the custody suite.

'He's been processed, boss, and he's in the interview room,' said Kelly. 'We've got his clothes, DNA and a photograph.'

'Right, I'll go in and interview him, you and Sloper go and carry out a Section 18 search at his house.'

Temple entered the interview room and sat down. He unwrapped the cellophane from a pair of discs.

'Do you want legal representation, Marcus?' asked Temple.

'I don't need it, man, because you're going to let me go,' he said quietly.

'It'll speed up your release from custody if we can commence this interview now. Just so that you know, I've instructed my officers to conduct a search of your home address …'

'Oh fucking hell, man.' Hussain rose in his seat. 'You've got no right, you need a warrant. I haven't done anything.'

'You watch too much telly, mate. Now, sit down and tell me about Greta Ashton-Jones.'

'Look, I'm no murderer, why would I kill Greta? I thought she was great, she was beautiful …' Hussain's voice trailed off.

'Did you have a sexual relationship with her?'

'No, it was a strictly professional relationship.'

'I don't believe you,' replied Temple.

'Look, man, I want a brief now, we're having no more parley until I get one.'

'OK by me, we'll take you to a cell and you can wait for one to turn up.'

While waiting for the solicitor, Kelly returned to the station from Hussain's address in Swindon.

'Sloper sent me back with this, boss, thought you might want it for your interview.' She handed Temple a sealed bag with an A4 brown envelope and some latex gloves for him to take out the contents. Temple pulled out a series of A4 photographs.

'Just what I needed. The lying bastard.'

'We've also found a small amount of cocaine, enough for personal use.'

With a solicitor representing him, within the hour, Marcus Hussain was brought back to the interview room. Hussain was keen to get the interview over and be released. In company with Sloper and with a series of sealed bags resting on the table in front of him, Temple began his questioning again.

'Marcus, the last time we sat here an hour and a half ago, I asked you if you'd had sexual relations with Greta Ashton-Jones. You told me you had a strictly professional relationship with her. Is that a true representation of what you said?'

'Yes.'

'Do you want to change that response?'

'No,' replied Hussain, locking eyes with Temple.

'Officers have searched your home and during the course of their search, they have found this envelope. Do you know what's in here?' Temple pushed a sealed evidence bag containing the envelope across the table.

Hussain looked at the ceiling.

'Yes, I know what's in there.'

'Perhaps you can tell us what the contents are?'

'You fucking know what the contents are, man, you've been looking through all my personal stuff.'

'Can you tell me what was in the envelope, Marcus?' Temple's tone was calm in contrast to Hussain, who was becoming more and more agitated.

'You know what's in the fucking envelope, man. Photographs. Of me and Greta. Having a fuck in Savernake Forest.'

Temple slowly placed a sealed bag containing each photograph onto the table in front of Hussain.

'So, you lied to me. And do you know what I'm thinking now, Marcus? If you lied to me about that, you could be lying to me about the last time you saw Greta.'

'Look, man, I did see Greta on Saturday, about 7 p.m. and I left her at the house. I didn't tell you about us because for one, she's married and two, my boss has warned me not to get involved with clients or I'll be fired.'

'I need to know everything, Marcus. I need to know everything you know about Greta and everything about your relationship. How did you come by these photographs?'

'I don't know. I mean, I come home from work one day and there they are, on my doormat. No address, no stamp, just pushed through the door.'

'So you didn't commission them?'

'What?'

'You didn't get someone to take them for you, of you and Greta together?'

'No, man, what do you think I am? The envelope was on my doormat. I picked it up and looked inside ...'

'Did you show them to Greta?' asked Temple.

'Yeah, of course, man.'

'What did she think?'

'She was shocked, man, and worried that Maxwell might see them. I said to her, "You're worried!" I was worried her husband was going to turn up at the garage and cause a scene. Nothing happened that day, the next day I gets a text message. Said £500 in cash or husband gets the photos. Then she got one too, same message, different amount. She got stung for two grand,' said Hussain.

'Greta also got a text asking for money?' Temple asked.

'Yeah, man.'

'Any photos?'

'No photos, just the text message,' replied Hussain.

'What did you do?'

'Text back, telling them to fuck off.'

'Then what?'

'Well, then I gets another text back telling me to leave both amounts in a Tesco's carrier bag, at a picnic spot in Savernake or my boss will get the photos as well as the husband. Says drop the bag and drive off.'

'And did you?' asked Temple.

'Yeah, man, I did. I mean, I couldn't risk it. I wasn't fucking happy, though,' said Hussain.

'And when was this? Have you still got the text message on your phone?'

'This all happened about two, three months ago. I changed the phone not long after that for a new iPhone, so no, I haven't. I chucked it.'

'Why did you keep the photos?'

'I fucking paid for them, man, didn't I?' said Hussain, indignantly.

'Were you keeping them to blackmail Greta as well, Marcus? To get your money back?' asked Temple.

'What? No, man. We were both in it together. She didn't tell me to get rid of them so I didn't. She didn't ask for them back. She was sorry for the trouble caused. She gave me a couple of hundred quid back.'

'I've only got your word for that because she's dead. So, what were your feelings for her exactly, Marcus?'

'Look, man, her husband was away. A lot. She was like one of those bored housewives. Loads of money and loads of time on her hands and fucking gorgeous into the bargain. I mean, she was a real head turner. I first met her when she came into the showroom with Maxwell and bought her Porsche. Then she would turn up at the garage with real or imaginary problems with her car and it was obvious it was a come-on, so I obliged. Last Saturday she came in saying the brakes felt spongy. I told her we'd have to look at it and I took her back to her house,' explained Hussain.

'What time was this?'

'She came in about 5.30, just before maybe, we close at 6 p.m. in the showroom but the garage room guys go home at 4 o'clock on a Saturday. She had to leave the car with us for them to look at today, I mean yesterday now,' remarked Hussain as he looked at the clock showing 1.30 a.m. 'I drove her home and drove the Porsche back here ready for Monday, as we'd arranged.'

'And what time do you say you left her?' asked Temple.

'I reckon 6.45, 7.'

'And how did you leave her?'

'I admit, I almost expected her to ask me in but she said she was busy and that we'd catch up on Monday night, as Maxwell would still be away,' said Hussain.

'What sort of busy, Marcus?'

'She didn't say … oh yes she did, she said she was "entertaining".'

'So you turn up at 9.45 p.m. expecting to see her yesterday?'

'Yeah, only it was about 9 p.m., man. The plan was to stay a few hours, you know, then get off home.'

'Did she know you'd have her car all day?'

'I rang her mobile and left a message. Told her we'd done some work on the brakes. I had to deliver another car as well yesterday so I told her I'd be late and to ring me back if it was a problem, which she didn't …'

'So, you expect me to believe that you left her, alive and well, driving off in her car. How do I know that you didn't go in on Saturday night and things got out of hand and you killed her?' asked Temple.

'No way, man. I'm not a murderer.'

Temple observed a bead of sweat slowly travelling down the side of Hussain's face. Hussain was obviously starting to feel the heat of the four bodies in the small room. He kept up the pressure on him.

'Am I going to find your DNA in the house, Marcus?'

'Well, yeah, I suppose so, I mean, I have been inside.' Hussain shifted in his seat.

'Am I going to find it in the bedroom, Marcus?'

'Don't know what you mean, man.'

'I think you do – have you been in Greta's bedroom? Am I going to find your fingerprints, Marcus, traces of you?' asked Temple.

A previous visit to Greta flashed into Hussain's mind; in her bedroom, in her bed, his hands gripping the wooden headboard as she writhed beneath him.

'You don't have to answer these questions,' the solicitor put in.

'Oh, you've taken your time,' quipped Hussain. 'Yeah, of course I've been in the bedroom.' Hussain hung his head in realization of his situation.

'This isn't looking good for you, Marcus. You say you last saw her at 6.45 p.m. or thereabouts and you've been in her bedroom—'

'Look, man, I ain't got no reason to kill anyone, let alone Greta, no way.'

'What kind of sex did you have, Marcus? We know you take it outside the bedroom, what other activities did you indulge in?' Temple kept up the questioning, sensing Hussain's guard had dropped.

'What's that supposed to mean?'

'Did you play games, did things get out of hand?' asked Temple.

'Fuck off, man.'

'Well, having sex in the open is different, isn't it – what else did you do that was different?'

'Nothing man, just the normal.'

'Your normal and mine are likely to be totally different. Did you ever play games? Did you hurt each other, did you ever, let's say, tie her hands?'

'I never tied her up, man, no way, I've never done that.'

'Never tied her hands?' Temple persisted.

'No, never.' Hussain looked from Temple back to his solicitor.

Temple and Sloper briefly exchanged glances and Sloper took over the questioning.

'I'm going to want to know exactly where you went, Marcus, from the time you left Greta at 6.45 p.m. until the time you turned up there yesterday. So, let's go through it again.'

Hussain retraced his steps and then Sloper asked him to go over things yet again, going through all his movements for the whole evening. When Hussain started to yawn, his solicitor insisted his client be given a break until morning.

Temple took Simon and Kelly into an office.

'What do you think?' Sloper asked Temple.

'I don't know,' said Temple.

'I do. He's got to be favourite. We just need his old phone number to try and trace the text message for the £500,' said Sloper.

'It would be easier and quicker to get the details of his bank account to trace the withdrawal of the £500. Also check with Greta's account for £2,000. Send the photos and envelope to forensics for fingerprinting. We'll need to seize some CCTV and ANPR of the routes he says he drove on Saturday night to corroborate his story. He says he left Greta at about 6.45 or 7 p.m. and went back to the garage where he left her car. He drove his own car home and went out in Swindon, clubbing at The Palace until 2.30 a.m. before going home. The CCTV at the club will confirm his movements. Si, can you pick it up in the morning and brief someone from Neighbourhood Policing to look through it?'

'Sure,' he replied. 'It's him all right,' added Sloper, convinced of Hussain's guilt. 'His recall of where he was at any particular time is too neat, it's too good. Almost as if he's rehearsed it and let's face it, he's had enough time for that. He won't have accounted for CCTV – I bet it's not as tight as he says.'

'We'll have to see what the DNA results are, and they won't be for another twenty-four hours so there's lots of ground we can gain until then. I want the information around the flights from Singapore back to Gatwick. I'll leave you with Hussain in the morning while I go to see Brett Forrester to get his account of the last time he saw Greta on Saturday. We need to find out who was taking the pictures of Hussain and Greta in Savernake Forest. Who's the peeper, the blackmailer? I want to know who that was,' said Temple.

CHAPTER 8

TEMPLE STOOD THE team down at 3 a.m. and made his way home. Once off the main A roads, the journey was largely along unlit winding country roads. At that time in the morning with no moon, it was pitch black. Adrenalin from the day's events had kept tiredness at bay. His mind continued to run through tasks that would need attention later that day, as he drove down the decline from Stanton St Bernard towards All Cannings. Turning left into the village, in the distance he could see blue flashing lights signalling out in the landscape. As he approached The Green, he was waved down by a uniformed officer in a reflective jacket.

'You can't go any further, sir, there's been a fire. Where do you want to go?'

'I live just past the next house, number fourteen …' Temple wanted to get to the house.

'That's where the fire is, are you the only inhabitant, sir?'

'What … yes, what's happened?' Temple asked.

'Neighbours put in a 999 call when they saw flames at the door of the property. They also reported a light on in the front bedroom. We're glad you've turned up as the neighbours said there was usually one occupant.'

'I rent it. How bad is it?' All he wanted was to get through the cordon. His eyes darted around, seeing who was standing about.

'It looks like some kind of accelerant was put through the letter box and ignited, probably petrol from the smell of it. Luckily, one of the neighbours was late home and saw the flames before the fire took a real hold.'

Temple half listened to him; his preoccupation was trying to see if he recognized anyone hanging around in the darkness. As he went to question the officer further, they were both interrupted by the shouts of a blonde woman in a black leather biker's jacket and blue jeans, striding towards them in high heeled boots.

'Christ, thank God you're all right,' she said, on seeing Temple.

'I've been working late. Jane, what are you doing here?'

'The neighbours called me, the fire brigade wanted the homeowner. Thank God it hadn't got a chance to really take hold. Derek saw it on his way home and called 999. The fire officer says it's too bad to go into now though, you won't be able to move back in until I've had the work done. Why would anyone want to do anything like that?'

'I don't know, we'll have to see what they come up with. Look, Jane ...' Temple needed time to think. He'd been expecting a visit.

'Have you got anywhere you can stay tonight?' she asked.

'No, if I can't go in, I'll just sleep in the car. I only need a couple of hours ...' Temple knew he had to get back in the house and he couldn't leave the scene until he had. He'd sit there all night if he had to.

'Then come back to mine, follow me back. I've got a spare room, I'll get us a brandy. Come on.'

Jane's instant reaction to the situation was to provide shelter for her tenant and try to work out who would want to burn down her house. With these thoughts occupying her, she didn't register Temple's reluctance. Temple didn't want her to think he wasn't appreciative of her offer but knew he had to get inside.

'Just give me a few minutes. I'll see you there.'

With the brigade getting ready to drive off, he seized his opportunity. He parked a little way from the house, away from the small collection of neighbours who had gathered on The Green. He slipped down a sideway to the rear of the house. The back door was open; a pane of glass near the handle had been broken. He went inside. The floor of the small kitchen was wet from the water hoses. He saw the empty wine bottle and the broken glass that he'd left on the draining board. Stepping through the kitchen, he looked down the hallway. Even in the darkness, he could see the charred black area by the front door where the fire had taken hold and had begun to eat into the ceiling.

Temple walked down the hallway, his shoes squelching in the soaked carpet. The smell of smoke was strong and clung to the air he breathed, making him cough to rid it from his throat. With the stairway untouched by the fire, Temple leapt up the stairs, taking two steps at a time, up to the bedroom. The room was as he had left it, with no apparent fire damage. He'd come for one thing only – the gun.

He opened the bedside drawer and put his hand inside. It was gone. The solicitor's letter was also missing.

He looked across the room to a corner where there was a box of papers, files and a laptop – all as he'd left it. He thrust his hand inside the drawer all the way to the back; only the packet of sleeping pills was there. He put them in his jacket pocket. In his desperation to find the gun, he looked under the cabinet and the bed. Logic told him it couldn't just disappear, but it wasn't there.

He suppressed a rising sense of panic. He looked around the room; he considered the firemen having searched the room and taken it but since when did they start going through drawers after a fire?

He looked around. Someone had found and taken a loaded gun. As he walked around the room, desperately hoping against hope that the gun would miraculously appear, he berated himself. 'Fuck, you silly fuck.' In his desperation to find it, he pulled all the bedclothes from the bed, but still there was no trace of it. He looked again in the drawer and in frustration and anger at his own stupidity for leaving it, threw it across the room. He continued to search, looking under the bed, despite knowing exactly where he'd left it. Eventually, he scooped up the box of papers and made his way out of the house. The fire. The gun. It had to be King. Paul *fucking* King.

As he approached his car, the police officer stopped him.

'I thought I recognized you, you're job, aren't you? Do you know why someone would have done this or who they are?'

Temple fingered a growing pain of tension in his neck.

'I've no idea, mate,' he lied. 'It's late and I'm tired. Perhaps when it's light, I'll be able to think clearer and help you.' He could think of nothing but the gun. His heart had begun a sickening dull thud against his chest.

Temple found himself back at Jane's, on her leather button backed sofa, a half filled brandy glass in his hand. He took a deep gulp from the glass. The alcohol hit his head and hollow stomach at the same time. He sank back into the sofa. He needed to think.

Jane sat forward in an adjacent armchair, elbows resting on her knees, cradling a brandy glass in both hands. Her expensively dyed blonde hair fell to her shoulders and her long shellac nails tapped the glass she was holding. In her mid-forties, her divorce from her estate agent husband had given her six rental properties in various villages which gave her a good income. She vetted her tenants personally, liked to install professionals and banned pets. Temple was on a twelve month let; Jane thought he was a safe bet, being one of her better employed and paid tenants. He'd told her he had just separated from his wife and the little-boy-lost look about him at the time appealed to her, so much so, that she waived the deposit in the hope that the gesture might help develop a relationship between them. Looking across at him now, she considered that perhaps there was a silver lining to every setback in life; she now had Temple staying with her.

'God, I'm shaking! I'm just trying to think if I've upset anyone,' she said, holding her hand out in front of her.

Temple felt as guilty as if he'd started the fire himself.

'Don't think about it now.' He wasn't really interested in the conversation. 'You are insured?'

'Yes, of course I am, but what will you do?'

'Don't worry about me,' he said, wishing he could be alone to think.

'How bad was the damage?' she asked.

'I don't think it had taken hold too much, the ceilings were scorched but intact and there will be a lot of smoke damage.'

'Your clothes will be ruined,' she replied.

His clothes were the last thing on his mind. All he wanted was to be able to think, think of King, where he'd go, what he'd do next. Temple knew he was in the shit and there were limits to what he could do now before he would have to report what happened.

'Did you take out contents insurance like I told you?' Jane asked.

'No, I didn't anticipate this.' Temple downed the rest of the brandy.

'Do you want another?'

'No. I really must get some shut eye,' Temple rubbed his forehead. 'I'm a bit busy at the moment. Got a lot on.' He stood up.

'The room's at the top of the stairs, help yourself to everything in the bathroom. Look, you can stay here if you like, until I get things sorted,' Jane offered, hopefully.

'I might take you up on that, thanks, Jane.'

Temple found the room. Without undressing, he lay on top of the bed and stared at the ceiling. Had it been a random attack? Had Jane upset someone? Or had what he'd been waiting for come to pass?

Paul King had threatened revenge from the dock at Bristol Crown Court four years ago when he was convicted for seven years' imprisonment for aggravated burglary. 'I'll kill you, Temple, and your fucking family. I'll burn your fucking house down,' King proclaimed calmly, as he was led away to the cells. Although threats like that were commonplace from criminals, Temple's instinct told him he meant it. King was evil.

Paul King came from the travelling fraternity and made a lucrative living out of stealing what didn't belong to him until Temple stopped him. He'd put the fear of God into his elderly victims, whom he preyed on for money, persuading them they needed tiles replacing, trees cut down, or their drives tarmacked. Just one case had netted him £80,000 in cash, after he repeatedly targeted the same old couple, taking them to the bank until he'd emptied their account. If he met any resistance, he'd fire up a blowtorch and threatened to burn them. On one occasion, he'd started a fire and left an elderly woman screaming and alone. She died terrified, curled up in the corner of her own kitchen. Forensics couldn't prove it, but Temple knew it was him. During hours spent sitting across a table in an interview room with King, Temple had had to listen to him telling him explicitly what he would do to him and his family in answer to every question Temple put to him. This added threats to kill to his charge sheet and a few more months onto his sentence.

Temple had registered his concerns at work as soon as he had been told of King's imminent release. He knew King was dangerous but with no recent intelligence other than the threats King made four years ago, there was little to suggest that King would target him and as such, resources weren't committed to it. But he was the one who had sat facing King in the interview room. He felt his evil and the strength of his intent.

King had come out of prison a month ago. He was out on licence and Temple knew that he only had to name him for the fire to put him back inside. But had he done it? Had he taken the gun? Perhaps the fire brigade had taken it after all, perhaps they'd done a search and found it, perhaps they were in the process of handing it in. Temple knew even if that was the case, it would spark an inquiry by the Professional Standards Department (PSD) and he was looking down the barrel of dismissal and prosecution. Whilst the gun was antique, which ordinarily required no firearms licence, the fact that it was loaded made it a prohibited firearm.

If it was King and he was arrested with the gun in his possession, he was bound to say where it came from and how he found it.

What made him feel sick was the thought that the gun would be in circulation within the criminal fraternity. He knew how it worked. It was clean, uncirculated, untraceable. It would be rented or sold up and down the country, used by teenagers to kill other young teenagers, used by drug gangs for vendettas, kidnaps, in gang and drug turf wars. It was highly valuable in monetary terms. And deadly. He knew he had to call it in. It would be the end of his career and likely prosecution, but he couldn't live with the thought that his firearm would cause untold misery.

He had started sleeping with the gun since King's release. Had he really intended to shoot King if he'd been confronted by him in the night? Yes, even now, as he asked himself the question he knew he would have, because King had threatened not only him, but Leigh and Daisy. He would have stopped King in his tracks even if it meant shooting him. As to the consequences, he'd let a jury decide. He was still too affected by the past to let anyone get away with harming his family again. But what now?

He tried to recall the detail in the solicitor's letter. There was no address; he was sure there was nothing in it to take King to Leigh. They'd moved since King had been imprisoned. Eventually, the brandy kicked in and dulled his senses enough for him to sleep and stop thinking how he could protect his family when they no longer lived under the same roof and somehow get himself out of a mess that would see him lose his job and potentially release a loaded weapon onto the streets. He decided to give himself twelve hours to resolve things before handing himself into PSD. At least it would give him an excuse to contact Leigh.

CHAPTER 9

Sitting outside in his car, Temple put in an early call to update Harker on the inquiry. He'd managed to get two hours' sleep but didn't seem to feel any better for it.

'We'll get Hussain's account checked out and go from there,' Temple explained.

'Simon seems to think you've got your man. Young woman, older husband. Over the side as soon as he's out of the country. Don't fuck about with it, Temple, don't string it out. Make sure you fast-track fingerprints and DNA, we could do with a quick resolution on this one. The Swindon job is still ongoing and burning more resources and money by the minute. I need the Ramsbury job closed off as soon as possible.' Harker ended the call with one of his signature grunts.

The call confirmed what Temple suspected – Sloper was giving Harker every detail of the inquiry. Perhaps Sloper was right, perhaps Temple had his man, but Hussain just didn't feel right. His mobile showed a missed call. It was Jackie Newly. Temple called her back.

'Just to keep you updated, knowing that you want this urgently, I put in an early call. Things will be a little delayed with the DNA profile.'

'What timeframe are we working to, Jackie?'

'Well, things are a little more complicated given that there seems to be a mixed profile.'

'Hang on, what exactly are you saying?'

'On first examination, there appears to be two distinctive DNA profiles coming from the semen.'

'Let me get this right, are you saying our victim had sex with two different guys prior to death?' Temple asked, his whole concentration now on what was being said to him.

'That's what they seem to be saying, but they'll need more time to be sure.'

'Once this is established, check it against the foetus,' instructed Temple.

'OK, so we could end up with three different profiles. In order to make sure this is right and to distinguish these, the lab will need twenty-four hours, maybe sooner.'

'OK, Jackie, look, make sure they get another DNA sample over for comparison. Contact the custody suite at Swindon to get the sample of Marcus Hussain. I'd be grateful if they could check against this profile in the first instance. And keep on their case, will you, keep the pressure on?'

'Sure, will do, I'm just sorry for the delay, boss.' Jackie Newly was a good sort and Temple trusted her to do her best for him.

Temple met Simon and Kelly at Marlborough Police Station and updated them on the situation.

'We should have the DNA profile in twenty-four hours, a slight delay but nothing we can do much about.' Temple withheld the fact that there was a mixed profile, specifically to keep Sloper in the dark. He would impart this information to Harker himself to show him that Sloper wasn't in possession of all the facts of the case.

'Fucking scientists,' said Sloper, 'How hard can it be? It's not like that they're not doing this every day. Still, they'll have Hussain's to compare with now and that'll be game over. I can go up to Swindon. It's him, I just know it's him. He looks like a slimy, shiny little shit, with his poncey suit and gold round his neck.'

Kelly flashed him a look.

'And what would *you* know?' he said.

Sloper was finding it increasingly difficult to temper his frustration at having to work on a routine domestic, with what was going on at Swindon. He needed to know first-hand what was happening up there with the drug gangs and he was having to work harder than he wanted to. He was more comfortable dealing with the crackheads and heroin addicts of Swindon than dancing around the refined likes of Dianna Forrester.

Sloper prided himself with the fact that street dealers and pimps couldn't so much as take a shit without him knowing about it, as he kept across their scummy lives. He spoke their language and walked their walk and he needed to. He had his own interests to protect. Normally, he had free movement, but at Harker's behest, he had to stay put, stay with Temple. Get a quick resolution, he said. In the meantime, his phone was ringing its tits off with dealers and pimps wanting to know what was going on with all the cops swarming all over Swindon, asking questions, making arrests, pulling the place apart. That's what they paid him for, to keep the heat off.

Through tracking Gemma, the deeper she sank, Sloper had gone a step further. The world was changing; the eastern Europeans had moved in and from his position, Sloper was ready. As a Romanian head case moved in to pimp Gemma, Sloper had his number. They'd eventually come to an agreement. Sloper had learnt a lot and come a long way since he'd first dragged Gemma out of a punter's car in Manchester Road. It was a whole different ball game. But, in order to protect his investment, he had to find out who the local scum was who'd beaten and left Gemma in a stairwell as she made her way back to her flat. Meanwhile, cops were crawling all over the place in Swindon and Sloper was firefighting from a distance. The sooner he got a result here the better, but he felt he was having to work with fucking amateurs, leaving him to do most of the work.

For his part, Temple knew Sloper wouldn't do him any favours whilst he was still with his investigation, but with no one else on the horizon, he had to get as much out of him as he could. Feeling the tension between Sloper and Kelly, he knew all he could do was try to protect her from the worst of Sloper's extremes.

Kelly stood up and walked over to a window to put some space between them. She was already sick of working with Sloper; she saw what he thought of her; he viewed her with contempt. She was uncomfortable. Temple sensed how she felt and knew he had to keep what team there was together as much as he could. He could do without their bickering. It was all he could do to concentrate in light of the missing gun. He had a plan, but it was desperate and depended on another's help.

'In the meantime, there's plenty for us to be getting on with around Hussain and Mr Ashton-Jones. When's he due in by the way?' asked Temple.

'The airline rang me back earlier,' said Sloper, 'Maxwell left Heathrow at 21.45, on Thursday evening, arrived in Singapore at 10.30 on Friday and arrived in Sydney at 19.50 yesterday GMT. British Airways's HR department broke the news to him last night. They said they would have him back on a flight out of Sydney later today to Singapore, in time for another flight out with Singapore Airlines back to Gatwick. He'll be with us tomorrow.'

'OK, so there's nothing we can do but wait,' said Temple. 'You continue some inquiries with Dianna Forrester, Si, and I'll make an appointment with Greta's GP and go back and see Brett Forrester. I'll ask him if he has a contact number for Greta's friend, Caroline Black, and I'll ring you with it, Kelly, for you to make contact. Right, we'll meet here tonight for a debrief, let me know any developments.'

Glad to get away from the office, Temple drove off to meet Brett Forrester. On his arrival, the door was opened by a pretty young girl with an elfin-like face and close cropped dark hair. She looked back at him through doe-like, heavily kholed eyes. She wore a black, short silk slip dress that emphasized her waif-like thinness, as it skimmed the contours of her bra-less body, while on her legs, cream coloured socks ended mid thigh, leaving creamy white flesh exposed. She gained height from high platform shoes. As she walked away from Temple to show him into the study, she reminded him of a foal trying to walk for the first time.

'And you are?' Temple asked, following his own introduction.

'I'm Alice.' Temple was disarmed by her well-spoken voice and wanted to delay her departure to find out more. As she spoke, Temple studied her face. Her heavily made-up eyes looked enormous and her full, soft, pink painted lips looked babyish.

'Do you live here?' he asked.

'I sometimes stay over,' she replied, 'with Brett.' She could have been talking about a teenage boy.

She could be no more than twenty, he thought, perhaps younger.

'If you go in here, he'll be with you in a minute.'

She opened the study door. Temple went inside and she closed it behind him. Old bastard, thought Temple. He finds out his daughter's been murdered and calls in Alice for some comfort. There had to be forty years between them.

He looked around the room where they had met before. He was looking for the canvas bag of cameras and equipment but it wasn't there today. Within seconds, Brett Forrester joined him; he seemed subdued but in possession of his emotions.

'Sorry to keep you, Inspector. I didn't sleep too well last night but then dropped off in the early hours.'

I bet you did, thought Temple, thinking of a way he could question him about his choice of companion.

'I can get you a family liaison officer, sir, to help you through the investigative process,' offered Temple. If he could get an FLO in here, he could find out what was going on.

'I don't wish to be ungrateful, Inspector, but I was a journalist. My friends are journalists, two are crime reporters and so I know how this works. You appoint me a family liaison officer, I tell them all I know and they feed that back to you for your investigation. Let's cut out the middleman, shall we? I'll deal with you, if that's all right. Just ask me what you want to know.'

Temple agreed.

'You last saw Greta on Saturday afternoon, you said, was that a regular visit?'

'We would meet up, now and then, for lunch, to spend the afternoon together, just to catch up. We were close. She wasn't close to her mother and Maxwell was away a lot. She took an interest in my work, she helped me in it. We connected, if you see what I mean.'

'Was there a specific purpose to her visit on Saturday, was it just social?' asked Temple.

'We had lunch, didn't you hear what I said? She came here at about 1 o'clock, 1.15 p.m., we ate, had a catch up, you know how it goes, Inspector.'

'What time did she leave?'

'About 4 p.m.'

Temple scanned the pictures of Greta on the wall.

'She was beautiful,' said Forrester, wistfully.

As Temple surveyed a number of photographs, his eye was drawn to a series of black and white photos which, on closer inspection, he realized showed close up images of a naked woman's body.

'These are striking,' offered Temple. 'It's not apparent at first what they are, I mean, they almost look as if they're of a landscape. Is it your work, Mr Forrester?' asked Temple.

'Yes,' replied Forrester, quietly.

The light and shadow-play of the black and white photographs attempted a clever conceal of the hollow of an armpit, the rise of a woman's abdomen, the cleft of a woman's buttocks, both of which could only have been taken from an interesting angle from between the legs.

'It's not immediately obvious what they show, but when you realize what you are looking at, they are really quite intimate. And very clever. Was it the same model in all of them?' asked Temple.

'Yes.'

'She must have been very trusting,' said Temple, thinking of Alice, the young girl who had opened the door to him.

'She was. They were part of an exhibition I had in London. Caused a little bit of a stir at the time.'

Brett Forrester attempted to distract Temple from looking at the pictures by asking him if he wanted a cup of coffee. Temple said yes in the hope that it would bring Alice into the room where he could see the interaction between her and Forrester. Forrester left the room instead and returned alone with the coffee. Temple continued to look at the detail in the photographs.

'Could you describe your relationship with Greta, Mr Forrester?'

'As I said, we were close, we connected. I wasn't there much for her when she was growing up, her mother and I went our separate ways when Greta was only two years old. I had a job to do, I spent a lot of time away, abroad. I suppose her mother and I were basically incompatible. I looked after them financially but I kept my distance. We had no contact. One day, I came home to find Greta sitting on the doorstep of my London flat, she was fifteen. I didn't recognize her. I didn't *know* her. She'd had a row with her mother and had run away. Due to my work, she had tracked me down and just turned up, decided she would come and live with me.'

'That must have come as a bit of a shock, I mean, kids aren't easy, let alone a teenager and a daughter you've not seen for such a long time,' said Temple.

'She was actually fine, very like myself, either fortunately or unfortunately. It seems we both discovered how difficult it was to live with her mother.'

'Did she return home?' Temple asked.

'No, she stayed with me. We lived together until she met Maxwell.'

'Was she a difficult teenager—'

Brett Forrester cut Temple off.

'What has this got to do with the fact that Greta has been found murdered?'

'I just need to try and establish a picture, the background of Greta's life. It helps us to try and understand her, understand the things she did, her thought processes, character, likes and dislikes. As you said, you know how this works. Victimology. It may bring us closer to her killer if we know more about her, what she did. You'd be surprised at how helpful to inquiries the past can be sometimes.'

'She was beautiful, she wouldn't harm a fly,' said Forrester, becoming increasingly irritated with the direction the questions were taking. 'She wasn't a difficult teenager, she was bright. Happy.'

'What was her relationship like with her husband, Maxwell, were they happy?' asked Temple.

'He gave her everything she wanted and she loved him. They met at work and he adored her. Who wouldn't? She came home one day and said a pilot had told her he'd fallen in love with her, within months they were married. So far as I know, their relationship was good. If you're asking me if I think he killed her, for a start he was out of the country and as far as I'm aware, he loved her. They were good together.'

'Was that based on things that you observed, or …'

'Look, Inspector, it was based on what she told me and what I saw. The only thing that I would say is that she shouldn't have given up work as this left her on her own too much when Maxwell was away. She didn't like being on her own, she liked being with people.'

'Why did she give up work, do you know?' Temple asked.

Forrester looked vague and his eyes left Temple's face to focus on a white fleck on his trousers, which his finger lightly picked at as he spoke.

'She, she was fine all the time she was living with me, I didn't notice any such behaviour. But when she married, she seemed to become increasingly highly strung; this is the only way I can describe it. Maxwell said she didn't like him having to go away so often, being separated for days at a time. It made her moody. Got worse when she gave up work. He said she'd have mood swings, becoming depressed when they were apart but conversely, very happy as soon as they were together again.'

'And this made her give up work?' asked Temple.

'Yes, Maxwell told me that eventually she found it hard to function at work. He actually got her professional help and she took anti-depressants as a result. She had to give it up in the end. She didn't seem to change that much to me, she was still her normal self.'

'I'll check with her GP, thank you for that. Did you know her routine, the things she did during the day?' asked Temple.

'She shopped, she went riding, went to the local pub. When Maxwell wasn't there, she did all this on her own and she was on her own more often than not. But we would meet on a regular basis.'

'What about friends, acquaintances?' Temple asked.

'Well, she had Caroline, Caroline Black but then Caroline also continued working – she's also a hostess – so they saw each other when they could. That's why I think she may have been a little lonely with Maxwell still at work.'

'Do you know if she was bothered by anyone, Mr Forrester?' asked Temple.

'What do you mean by "bothered"? Say what you mean, Inspector.'

'Well, did she ever express any concerns to you about anyone – or did she confide any extra marital relationships to you?'

'No, she didn't. Why do you ask?' said Forrester.

'Well, if you think Maxwell was not responsible for her death, it means someone else was and I need to find that person.'

'She certainly confided no such thing to me.'

'Just one more thing; have you ever photographed Greta in Savernake Forest?' Temple watched Forrester intently.

'No, I haven't, it's not somewhere we've been together,' he replied.

'That's enough for me at the moment, Mr Forrester,' said Temple. 'Do you have a contact number for Caroline Black? My officers will need to speak to her.'

'Yes, I have her mobile number. I'll ring her and break the news.' Brett Forrester provided Temple with the number.

'I'll send my investigator to go and see her. James Ashton-Jones attends a boarding school, I understand. We will need to speak to him as well.'

'I'll contact the school. I think Maxwell's friend, Jonathan Silvester, will need to be contacted too; between us we'll make some arrangements to see that James is picked up,' Forrester replied.

Temple could resist no longer.

'And Alice, sir, was she a friend of Greta's?' he asked.

'No, Inspector. Of course, I've explained what's happened, but they didn't know one another. Alice is a friend of mine.' Forrester put an emphasis on the word 'friend'; Temple pondered the forty-year age gap. He wanted to know how they met, how it worked but he knew he couldn't ask without alienating Forrester, who, he felt, was already irritated by his questions regarding Greta.

'Thank you, sir. I'll call back in a day or so. If you have no questions for me, I'll get back to the station.'

Temple drove back to Marlborough Police Station. What was it Forrester had said about the model? She had been very trusting. His thoughts were interrupted by his phone bleeping with a text message from Sloper, telling him he had finished with Dianna Forrester. Temple pulled over and rang him.

'How did it go, Si?'

'Got some good background stuff. She's a strange woman, Dianna Forrester. She doesn't seem to have a lot of sympathy for Greta, almost like this was her just deserts. Needless to say, they didn't get on. Greta was convent educated at a day school near where they lived with Dianna's father, after they were abandoned by Brett Forrester. That's how she puts it, that he abandoned them and then they divorced. Dianna was a committed Catholic and between her and her father, the retired Major, they attempted to instil discipline into Greta's life. Dianna Forrester thought this was necessary because it was obvious to her that Greta was very pretty but also very wilful. She says that she was trying to protect her as any mother would against the attentions of boys. She describes Greta as becoming increasingly rebellious as a teenager, make up, boys and so on, and they basically entered what she described as a battle of wills.

'This came to a head when Greta told her she had had sex with a local boy; she says she had just turned fifteen. Dianna said that their relationship deteriorated as she tried to exert more control over Greta. Greta also told her mother that a priest at the convent had made a pass at her. Mrs Forrester says that this is when they had a huge row and Greta left to live with her father. She didn't believe Greta about the priest. Thought she just said it as an attack against her religion. She was fierce when it came to talking about Brett Forrester. Said he was a bohemian type character, had no regard for the rules of society. In fact, near the end, she worked herself up into a right state, saying they were both pretty much damned by the devil.'

'What prompted that response?' Temple asked.

'I asked her if she visited Greta when she lived with her father.'

'Had she?'

'Yes, once. The visit was not long after Greta first moved in. It was a flat in London by the way. She hadn't registered with a school and was being left pretty much to her own devices. By the time of her visit, she said she sensed that Greta had changed to the point that she said their mother and daughter relationship was basically over. In fact, her exact words were – I've written it down – "evil had found evil."'

CHAPTER 10

Sitting in his car, Temple made a call.

'Hello, Tara. It's DI Temple.'

'Hang on.' He listened to stiletto heels clipping across a wooden floor almost in tandem with the beat of 'Voulez-Vouz' playing loudly in the background. Then he heard the sound of a door opening and shutting and a metal bolt being put across it.

'What do you want?' she hissed.

'I need your help.' He paused. 'King's out.'

'I know,' she said quickly. 'He turned up here at the pub, looking for somewhere to stay.'

Temple had been banking on King sticking to old habits.

'Where are you now?' asked Temple.

'I'm in The White Bear, at Trowbridge, I work here now,' she said in a low voice.

'I need to know what King's up to, Tara.'

'I'm not doing it again. I was fucking bricking it for months. Fuck off, I ain't doing it.' Tara grew increasingly nervous with the conversation. By talking to Temple, she was putting herself in danger, but at the same time, having King around was equally dangerous. She knew King saw her boyfriend, Zac Finch, as an easy touch and that Zac was intimidated by him. She knew all about King and the dregs he associated with and hated the way he exerted control.

Zac had inherited a nice little garage from his father and was himself a good mechanic. It had steady regular custom, which allowed it to tick over. She was proud of him. It was clean and legit, and then King had come along. Before Temple put him inside, King used the garage as a base which acted like a magnet for all his associates. When Temple pleaded for her help to put King away, she was ready to oblige. She knew far more than she let on, but it was enough to help convict King. Then, when he was let out, King made the garage his first port of call.

'It's too late. My house was set alight last night. I know it was him, Tara. You know what he's like. This isn't a game. He threatened my family and you of all people know he doesn't forget. Where is he now? Where is he?'

Tara sensed the desperation in Temple's voice. She tried to hold out.

'I don't know,' she lied. She shouldn't even be talking to him. It was too dangerous.

'Yes, you do, where is he, Tara?' insisted Temple.

There was silence.

'He's with us. He's fucking with us, in Finch's flat, which is why I can't do this.'

She was scared. Scared of King. He was premiership nasty and she didn't want to be anywhere near him. But if he ever found out that she'd helped Temple put him away, she knew he would kill her.

Temple heard the rising panic in Tara's voice. He needed her help and was desperate for her not to end the call.

'All right, all right. Can you just do a favour for me? Can you just ring me and let me know what he's up to? I need time to sort my family out, to get them out of the way. That's all I ask. Get back to me later today.'

'OK, but don't ring me again,' she said.

Temple ended the call, relieved that he had at least located King. He just had to wait and hope for Tara to keep her word. But he knew he couldn't wait too long.

He drove towards the Medical Centre in George Lane at Marlborough, where Greta was registered. After explaining the purpose of his visit, he was shown into a waiting room and after a short wait, Greta's GP collected him.

He introduced himself to Temple. 'I'm Dr Williamson. We'll go into the surgery. All the patient notes will be on my computer.'

'I just wanted some background information on Greta, if you can give it.'

'Of course, I'll cooperate as far as I can.'

'The post-mortem showed that Greta was nine weeks pregnant. Had she been to see you in the run up to her death?'

'Yes. That would have been the last time I saw her. Three weeks ago, I gave her a pregnancy test here in the surgery.'

'Don't patients usually do that for themselves?' asked Temple.

'They do, but we need to be sure so we do another. Especially in Greta's case.'

'Meaning?'

'Meaning, she came in to tell me her news and I wanted to check that she hadn't misread her own pregnancy test. I'd have to book her in for a scan quickly if it was positive, which it was, of course. It was important for me to see the test for myself as she was on medication and we had to talk about that.'

'What was the medication? Her father told me that she was on anti-depressants,' Temple said. He looked back in his notes to the name of the medication he had found in the bathroom at Wedwellow House; the doctor confirmed them to be the same as prescribed.

'Yes, she was. As I understand it, she had a mild form of cyclothymia.'

'Which is what exactly? How does that manifest itself?' asked Temple.

'Her husband expressed particular concern saying that she was becoming increasingly depressed when they were apart. From memory, he's a pilot. She displayed other behaviour too, such as excessive spending and paranoia. I referred her to a psychiatrist who diagnosed her as suffering from a mild form of cyclothymia which is often a precursor to bipolar disorder. It sometimes has a hereditary aspect. An 'attack' or 'episode' is usually triggered by an event, or experience, usually a sad or traumatic event.'

'So would this be her general behaviour?' asked Temple.

'No, not by any means. This was how she might behave when going through an episode but this was treatable, manageable and in between these times, she was able to function perfectly normally. I mean, if you'd met her you might not even think there was anything wrong. Her husband was particularly concerned about the excessive spending, I remember. The key was recognizing the symptoms of an 'attack' if you like, before it took hold. She was determined to manage it, I mean, she understood what was happening. You might want to speak to the psychiatrist for more background.'

'Yes, I would. This is really helpful. And the pregnancy, was she happy about that?'

'She did appear to be, yes. We discussed ongoing support throughout the pregnancy and made a series of appointments.'

'I take it there was no issue around who the father was?'

'I assumed it was Mr Ashton-Jones.'

Temple left the surgery and went back to the police station to make contact with the psychiatrist. He found Sloper in the incident room and interrupted him looking at the photographs of the scene taken by the CSI.

'Anything I've missed?' asked Temple, suppressing his paranoia of Sloper constantly checking on him.

'Just having another look-see,' replied Sloper, as he thumbed through the photographs contained in a number of blue A5 sized books.

'Have you got the photographs of the body there?'

'Oh, you want a look at them too, do you?' Sloper smiled as he handed the book he was looking at to Temple.

'I want to check something,' said Temple, as he took the photographs from his hands.

Sloper put on his jacket to leave. Temple leafed through the album of the photos taken by Jackie Newly. Yes, it was as he'd thought. The photo confirmed a birthmark on the inside of Greta's right thigh. Temple had seen the same mark in one of the photos on Brett Forrester's wall. Temple wondered at the circumstances in which Brett Forrester could come to take such intimate photographs of his own daughter.

CHAPTER 11

LATER, AT SWINDON Police Station, Sloper looked over the shoulder of a female PCSO as they viewed CCTV from The Palace night club in search of Marcus Hussain.

'That's him, that's him leaving there. He's alone,' exclaimed Sloper, looking at the black and white, grainy image of Hussain. 'It's 1.15 a.m., he said he left The Palace at 2.15 or 2.30, that's an hour spare. There's still time for him to have gone to Ramsbury.' They continued to watch the image.

'He's walking round the back to the car park, no sign of him being drunk. He's getting in a car – that's a Porsche. I bet it was Greta's, the cheeky bastard. He told us he'd left it at the garage.'

Sloper's inquiries with ANPR confirmed that Hussain had driven out of Swindon in the general direction of Ramsbury in Greta's car. Sloper rang Temple.

'He's lied to us, so we need to interview him again. The super's signed a twelve hour extension for us, so he's not going anywhere,' explained Sloper.

'OK, set it up, get the brief in. Make sure his DNA has been sent up to the lab.'

'It has, I've checked, Jackie Newly sorted that. We should have a result very shortly,' replied Sloper.

'Good. I'll chase Jackie up again later if necessary. If it's Hussain's DNA, he's lied about not being with her that night. It doesn't necessarily make him her killer,' said Temple.

'He's our man, I'm sure of it,' replied Sloper, eager to put Hussain under pressure to explain his lies.

'I've just had a call from the Financial Investigators so I'm going to HQ to see them. I'll see you at Swindon in a couple of hours.'

Temple drove to the Headquarters complex. A financial profile of Maxwell and Greta Ashton-Jones was handed to him by DC Graham Mellor.

'As I told Simon Sloper, they were pretty well off, so on the face of it, there were no apparent money worries. He has his British Airways income and other payments coming in. Maxwell Ashton-Jones had a large financial payout of life insurance about fourteen years ago, when his first wife, Olivia, died; £350,000 from Prudential Insurance. We're going through the bank accounts. It's taking a little time as there is a fair bit of activity and we're looking for anything unusual amongst the usual utility bills and so on.'

'Look for a cash withdrawal for £2,000 in the last three months ...'

'Will do. There are a number of ISAs and offshore companies registered in Panama and Lichtenstein. There will be accounts behind these but we won't be able to penetrate the financial jurisdiction in these countries.'

'Thanks, Graham. How much was Greta Ashton-Jones insured for, do we know yet?'

'Yes, there's a policy for £350,000 with Zurich Insurance. Two dead wives is pretty unlucky,' said Mellor, sarcastically.

'And financially lucrative. So he'll have netted £700 grand from the deaths of two wives. I'll go and speak to the Interpol liaison officer about getting me the case file on the death in Saudi. How long before you complete, Graham?'

'Another twenty-four hours. There are a range of investments, the usual sort of thing. Looks like he could be your man, though.'

'Give me a call soon as you know,' replied Temple.

Impatient for news on the progress of the DNA, Temple rang Jackie Newly.

'Anything for me yet, Jackie?' he asked.

'Not yet, boss, you must have read my mind. I've literally just come off the phone to the lab guys. They assure me it won't be long now.'

'I could do with it in the next few hours, keep on to them.'

With an appointment booked at Salisbury Hospital to see Greta's psychiatrist, Temple also took the opportunity to see Dianna Forrester. Her comment to Sloper that 'evil had found evil' had kept him wondering and he needed to question her to compare what Brett Forrester had said about Greta. He drove to Harnham and found himself at a modest terraced house. Dianna Forrester answered the door to him and he went inside.

Facing Temple, as he entered the hall, was a large wooden crucifix that hung on the wall, with rosary beads strung through. Temple wondered if it was supposed to act as some sort of Catholic feng shui. The house was tastefully furnished and so tidy it was almost holy; Temple offered to remove his shoes.

'There's really no need, Inspector, come into the kitchen,' Dianna Forrester instructed.

He followed her and they both sat down at a pine table. Her face was showing the strain of someone who was stoic and desperately trying to bear the pain of her tragic loss. Her swollen eyes were testament to the fact that she'd cried long hours in private when she was overwhelmed by rushes of grief. But now she sat across from him composed.

'I wonder if you could shed more light on Greta's teenage years,' said Temple.

'I have already given a statement to your other officer, I'm not sure what more I can tell you, really,' she said in a quiet voice, her hands resting on the table.

'I understand that she left home and went to live with her father, Brett. How old would she have been?' asked Temple.

Dianna looked at him suspiciously. 'Have you spoken to *him*?'

'Brett Forrester, you mean? Yes, I have. He says she just turned up one day on his doorstep and didn't return home to you.'

'Yes, that's fair. We had a row and she left. Eventually, I went to see her there, at his flat ...' Her voice trailed off as she remembered. 'She opened the door to me and I knew I had lost her forever. She was different. Completely different.'

'How long was it before you went to see her and when she left you?' asked Temple.

'It was about three months, I suppose. She rang me to tell me where she was straightaway, so I wasn't overly concerned for her. I was angry with her; she had been difficult so it was a bit of a relief to get some respite from her, which sounds bad, I know. But when I turned up, to take her home ...'

'Yes?'

'I knew. I just knew.' Silence fell on them.

'What did you know, Mrs Forrester?' ventured Temple, gently.

'It's actually hard for me to say this, Inspector, but I just knew ...' her voice had dropped to a whisper.

'What did you know?' pressed Temple.

'She answered the door in one of his shirts. That was all she had on. It was the middle of the afternoon. She thought I was him at the door, although why would he have knocked? She wasn't pleased to see me, her face was crestfallen, no, embarrassed. Embarrassed to see me, being dressed like that. I walked past her, into his flat. I went from room to room, looking around, looking at his things. It was all very contemporary, bohemian. And then I realized. There was only one bed, one double bed. The sheets were crumpled where she'd just got out of it. I remember looking at her and she looked back at me, at first shame-faced at being caught, but then with almost a mocking look. I've never forgotten it. He loves me, she said. He loves me and I love him. It was depraved. Evil. I ran out. There's no doubt what she meant.

They were lovers.' All the time she spoke, she'd looked down at the table.

'Is there any way you could have been mistaken?' asked Temple, his mind going back to Alice. She immediately looked up at him.

'No.'

CHAPTER 12

Kelly had established contact with Caroline Black who had wanted to see her at once to find out what happened. An hour and a half later, Kelly sat in the bar area, watching the steady stream of passengers filter in and out of the Heathrow Hilton Hotel reception. At the reception desk stood a tall blonde with a mane of highlighted and flicked back hair. Looking in her direction, Kelly stood up and identified herself by waving her hand in the air. Perfectly groomed and smart in her British Airways uniform, Caroline Black gracefully sashayed towards her and introduced herself. Standing and firmly shaking her offered hand, Kelly introduced herself. She noticed that Caroline Black's eyes were red and swollen from crying.

'I'm sorry to have to meet you in such circumstances, Caroline. I understand you were on your way to New York when Brett Forrester gave you the news, are you sure you are all right to talk so soon?'

Caroline Black looked expensive; she was gorgeous, with her perfectly made up face, manicured pink painted nails and gently waved shoulder length blonde hair. They both sat down.

'Yes, of course, I just can't believe it. I just *cannot* believe that anyone would want to kill Greta. Did you say you were a detective?' Her voice was soft, yet commanded attention through perfect diction. Kelly felt that it would be easy for her to feel intimidated by Caroline Black but instead, she felt compelled to study her closely, for anything she could pick up and take away for her own benefit. She didn't meet the likes of Caroline Black in Swindon.

'I'm not a police officer, I'm a civilian investigator. We have some of the same training as detective officers and basically do the same job. That's why I've been sent here to speak to you about Greta. What can you tell me about her?' Kelly knew she needed to get Caroline on side if she was going to find out all she could.

Caroline leaned forward, shaking her head. 'I can't believe she's dead, I just can't. We were like sisters. How did it happen?' Her eyes brimmed with tears.

'I'm sorry for the shock this has caused you. Greta was found yesterday, by her cleaner, in her bedroom. A pathologist has determined that she was murdered,' explained Kelly, being careful to follow Temple's instruction not to reveal the exact nature of Greta's death.

'I can't believe it. She was such a lovely person.'

'Well, that's where you can help our inquiry,' said Kelly gently. 'We need to find out as much as we can about Greta and her life in order to catch her killer. If you can tell me what you know about her, it will be a great help. When was the last time you saw or spoke to Greta?'

'About three weeks ago. We didn't have to speak on the phone every day. Any time we spoke to one another, we just picked up where we'd left off, the time in between didn't matter. We had busy lives but we caught up with each other when we could – if not by phone, we used FaceTime. I suppose the last time I saw her would have been three weeks ago, I can't really remember exactly when right now, just what we did.'

'Which was?'

'We had lunch in the pub, The Phoenix, at Ramsbury.'

'Do you remember what you spoke about, how Greta was that day?'

'She was fine. It was a lovely day, she told me she'd been riding early that morning and I drove up from my home in Newbury to meet her at the pub. We had lunch, we went back to the house, had coffee and sat outside, around the pool.'

'What can you tell me about Greta, her lifestyle, her relationship with her husband, Maxwell?'

'She was lovely, my best friend. We met one another when we were training as air hostesses, we had such a laugh. Sometimes we were able to work together and we travelled around the world. We would borrow each other's clothes, although she was slightly lighter than me, we shared rooms, went out on the town, had too much to drink … all the things mates do.'

'Did she confide in you?' asked Kelly.

'Of course.'

'What was her relationship like with Maxwell?'

'Maxwell is a great flirt, as was Greta. She had men in the palm of her hand, I mean, look at her, this was us in New York,' Caroline reached into a red leather bag and produced her phone and a photo of the two together. 'Those cat's eyes. She was feline, so striking. She was vibrant, full of life. When we were together, we were mad.'

Kelly looked at the photo. It was taken in a busy bar, both smiling, facing the camera with their arms around each other's necks and glasses raised, their faces tanned, surrounded by people. A happy moment caught in time.

'We need to find out who killed her, Caroline, and to do that, we need to know what was going on in her life at that time and find out how she came to be murdered in her own home. Nothing you've told me so far indicates that there were any problems, was her life really so perfect?' Kelly enquired.

Caroline Black stiffened a little in her chair.

'We all have some problems, even Greta,' she replied.

'I need to know what they were – did she have problems with Maxwell, with money? You said she was a flirt, was she having a relationship with anyone other than Maxwell?'

'The thing is – I'm sorry, what did you say your name was?' asked Caroline.

'Kelly.'

'The thing is, Kelly, I'm not sure that I'm happy talking about her like that. I've always felt a bit protective towards her. Will what I say get back to Maxwell?'

'Possibly, it depends what it is. Look, if it makes it easier for you, shall I ask you some direct questions? Remember, we need to find out who killed her.'

'I know, I know, but Greta never wanted anyone to get hurt. She's dead and I just want people to remember that she was a good person.'

'Was there someone else she was seeing?' asked Kelly.

'There was more than one. Look, she was insecure in her relationship with Maxwell. He is a good looking guy, a pilot. She didn't just think he was faithful to her, in fact, she thought there was someone else in his life. She knew something was going on. As beautiful as she was, she suspected that he had another woman. She said he was behaving differently, she sensed it. The usual thing at first, a bit distant when he came home, distracted, and then she said things started to go missing. Some of his clothes, his belongings, like cufflinks. Then he said they should get rid of some things as they'd had them for some time. He sold an old MG he had, then he sold his favourite painting which she thought odd. She told me that – asked me what she thought it all meant.'

'What was it like, the painting?' asked Kelly.

'It was a picture of a white beach, with palm trees and blue sea and sky, painted in the Seychelles, it reminded him of an island he'd once visited.'

'And what *did* you think?'

'I don't know. There's all kinds of things you could read into it, some sort of midlife crisis, wanting to get rid of familiar things, get in new things, I don't know.'

Kelly wrote it all down as Caroline continued to speak.

'She regretted giving up work, she missed the lifestyle, the travelling—'

'Why did she give up work?' Kelly interrupted.

'Personally, I think she found it difficult being married to Maxwell. He's a good looking guy and because of the lifestyle, she knew that Maxwell would stray. She met him through work, on a long haul flight. They fell in love, got married but they didn't work together often. He worked long haul flights, there were stopovers in luxury hotels with gorgeous young hostesses. She knew how it went. I think she discovered he was unfaithful pretty early on and I think she found that a real strain. It affected her, I know she was on anti-depressants.'

'So you think she compensated herself with affairs?'

'Sort of. An outsider might describe her as a little needy when it came to men but I blame Maxwell. Yes, I blame Maxwell for that. If he'd given her the attention she deserved there wouldn't have been other men. They fell at her feet, but I think she only really wanted him. So when he went away, she would just turn her attention to someone else. She was full on and men were flattered of course. But it did get her into some tricky situations.'

'What do you mean?'

'Well, for one, Jonathan Silvester, a friend of Maxwell's. He was a former BA pilot, they used to work together. Jonathan left BA and went into finance. Greta said that Maxwell used him as a financial advisor, put a lot of business his way in terms of stock buying, investments and such like. When Greta gave up work, Jonathan started to visit the house when Maxwell was away.

'I don't like the guy. He's arrogant and I didn't like the way he treated Greta. He hit on her one day when Maxwell was away and at first, Greta said she enjoyed their time together. But when she tried to call it off, he wasn't at all happy with that. She told me that he threatened to tell Maxwell about her sleeping with him and that he said he would decide when they were over. When he delivered that message, he also forced himself on her.

'She told me he continued to visit her, infrequently dropping by when he knew Maxwell was away and they'd have sex. She said he was forceful if she attempted to stop him. And she let him get away with it. It really annoyed me the way she let him use her like that. It was as if she just resigned herself to the situation.'

'So you're saying that Jonathan Silvester visited her for sex when Maxwell was away and Greta continued to let this happen? Did she actually tell you it was against her will?'

'That's what made it difficult for me to understand. She let him do that to her. She didn't seem to want to try too hard to deter him. When I said to her to not let it happen, she said, it's only sex, she just didn't want Maxwell to know about it. He even had a key to the house, he'd let himself in and she'd suddenly find him sitting in the lounge or even standing by the side of her bed. The bloke's a complete shit.'

'Was there more than one man?'

'Yes. This was why she wanted to call it off with Jonathan Silvester. She fell for the builder who they hired to build their extension. He was fit, walking around with his shirt off all last summer – even I was tempted. She really liked him, though. She actually talked about leaving Maxwell and she said he talked about leaving his wife and kids. They were both in deep – it was serious. Trouble was, he lived in the village, at Ramsbury, and when the job was finished, he struggled to find the time to see Greta. When it ended, she took it really hard.'

'We'll have to see him, what's his name?' asked Kelly.

'Mike Cooper.'

CHAPTER 13

Temple sat opposite Dr Brigitte Jacques, senior psychiatrist at Salisbury Hospital. He hoped she might go against the usual stereotype when the police wanted information from the medical profession and lend herself towards a shared understanding between two professionals which would result in the disclosure of the contents of Greta's file. However, as Temple outlined the circumstances of the case and the request for information, the doctor stared back at him seemingly, he felt, unimpressed with him both as an individual and his profession.

She was shocked, of course, at the murder of her patient but death, she told him, did not signal open access to what were essentially highly sensitive and confidential patient files. She didn't care how forthcoming Greta's GP had been, she was not a GP and this was not a surgery.

Experience told him that getting doctors and nurses in A&E departments, their so-called health care 'partners', to disclose anything about patients, was usually uncooperative bordering on obstructive. Temple knew they guarded their information more effectively than anything MI5 could achieve. 'Patient confidentiality' may as well be a euphemism for 'state secret', he thought as he tried again to negotiate disclosure of what was contained in Greta's notes.

'Look, I found anti-depressants at the house,' said Temple, 'and Greta's GP confirmed that she had been prescribed them for a mild psychiatric disorder. All I want to find out is, did she give you any indications as to the history behind her condition?'

The doctor remained silent and looked back at him expectantly. He realized the pressing nature of his inquiries were not going to make any impression on her. She had what he needed and Temple acutely felt the inequality of his situation. He pressed on.

'My inquiries indicate that she may have had an incestuous relationship with her father. In fact, I think her relationships with men were complicated in general and it would be useful to know anything that can help me with my investigation,' Temple explained.

As he outlined the case, Temple felt as though he was on the couch himself, being assessed. She continued to look at him in silence as he spoke, as if weighing his every word. She made no movement, not a nod of the head, not a gesture, except keeping direct eye contact. He felt as though she was looking right through him, into him, into his mind. As much as he wanted the information she could tell him, he started to feel as though he wanted to get out from under her gaze more. For some reason, she unnerved him. He wanted out of the room but knew he had to put up a better argument for the facts he wanted and knew she had. He shifted in his chair.

'I strongly suspect that her killer may well be in her inner family circle, certainly, it's an avenue I have to explore thoroughly and any information that you can give me that enables me to arrive at a conclusion sooner rather than later, will be an obvious advantage,' said Temple, trying but failing to match the doctor's coolness. He started to sound desperate. At last, she spoke again.

'You can't have any access to my notes or the file itself. But, hearing what you say,' she said, slowly, 'I am willing to relay to you a little of what I know. She did say that she had a very loving and intense relationship with her father. She adored him.

One day, she came home to find him with another woman, her own age she said, in bed. By this time she was about nineteen. In hindsight, she could see that he had deliberately wanted her to find him thus, and that this coincided with him encouraging her to get a job and see the world.

'She then became an air hostess. This was the trigger, in my opinion, for her separation anxiety; such had been the intensity of their relationship, the shock of seeing him with someone else and him rejecting her, as she saw it. There were also underlying issues with her mother and an early sexual experience with a priest that was non-penetrative. The separation anxiety manifested itself again later, when separated for short durations from her husband who was a pilot. She strongly suspected that he wasn't faithful and again, felt feelings of rejection. This, coupled with the other issues I've mentioned, escalated into cyclothymia – a mild form of bipolar.'

'What did she say regarding the relationship with her father – how did their relationship develop?' asked Temple.

'That's all I'm prepared to say – which, I think, is more than adequate.'

'Her husband – what did she say about him – his treatment of her?' Temple persisted.

'As I say, I will not divulge any more information. The things that were disclosed to me were done so in the knowledge that there was complete confidentiality – but under the exceptional circumstances, I have complied with your wish,' replied Dr Jacques.

'So these things are actually contained in your file?'

'Yes, they are.'

'Did she say anything about a man called Jonathan Silvester?' asked Temple. After a short silence in which she had thought through her reply, the doctor answered.

'She did say that a relationship had developed between them. The nature of it was complex. We spoke about it at length and she did concede that this relationship confused her.'

'In what way?'

'Difficult to say in brief. She described it as both repelling her and compelling her. That's really all I'm prepared to say.'

She stone-walled him to any further questions on the subject.

'What was the regularity of your meetings – when was the last time you saw Greta?' asked Temple.

'We met as and when directed by her GP, or more often, if her condition warranted it. I guess I met Mrs Ashton-Jones once or twice a year. The last time would have been five months ago,' Dr Jacques said.

'And, as to Mrs Ashton-Jones's condition, what would it be like?'

'It's important to remember, Inspector, that in my opinion, this was a condition that was still very mild and treatable, hence we were still at an anti-depressant stage, which, in the rounds are not the norm. This is a much undiagnosed condition generally. Some leaders, high-flyers, academics may well exhibit traits. Medication naturally changes to suit the prevailing symptoms. In Mrs Ashton-Jones's situation, it was mild but both she and her doctor decided that she would benefit from my sessions and medication. She would exhibit classic symptoms – risky behaviour, such as spending large amounts of money, she would confess to an increased sex drive and a desire to make new sexual relationships, a need for love and acceptance; this is typical behaviour as she sought security and physical closeness. There was also a lack of need for sleep. She would feel excessively happy and in this state, would have appeared as interesting and good company. Of course, this is only a bare outline, as I say. There are quite startling figures as to how many people actually have the condition and function without ever being diagnosed.'

Temple thought he fitted some of those traits himself. Maybe that was his problem; Leigh went so far to say he was damaged.

That was all she was prepared to divulge. Temple persisted, but happy that she had complied with her duty, Dr

Jacques sat back in her chair and said nothing more. Temple thanked her for her time and left.

Back in his car, Temple's mobile rang.

'It's me,' Tara whispered. 'Something you should know.'

'OK,' said Temple.

There was a long silence at the end of the phone.

'I overheard King saying he's got a gun,' she whispered.

CHAPTER 14

Temple's gut knotted. He knew he'd been right. King had had every intention of carrying out the threat he made in court to burn his house down. King had burnt an old lady alive and Temple suspected King had had much the same fate in mind for him the night of the fire. Instead of finding Temple at the house, he had found and taken the gun. Tara was his only chance of staying a step ahead. His mind raced.

'Did he say where he'd got it?' Temple held his breath. If she said she knew it was his, he was finished.

'No, just that he had one.'

'OK, thanks, Tara. Where are you now?'

'I'm at home, in the flat,' she said. 'I'm going back to the pub later.'

'Where's Finch?' he asked.

'He's still at the garage, he had a lot on today. He's meeting King in the pub later. I fucking hate this. I don't want King here, he scares me. *This* scares me.' She sounded desperate.

'I know, I know. Tara, look, if you help me, I'll get him locked up again. Do you know where he might keep the gun?'

'He's got a big bag, a holdall, in the spare room, but I'm not looking through his stuff. He'll know it was me,' she said.

'I just want you to tell me if it's in the bag. I don't want you to touch it or move it, can you do that – please?' Temple pleaded.

'I don't know,' she replied. She was alone in the flat but King could return at any moment.

'Please, Tara. Come on. Just go and look,' he coaxed. '*Please*.'

'Hang on,' she said.

Temple listened on the phone as Tara went into the spare room. He heard the holdall being unzipped.

'My hands are fucking shaking,' she said. 'He'll know it was me, he'll know.'

'He won't know, Tara. Just look inside,' Temple continued to talk gently.

'It's here. It's in the bag. It's just sitting on top, he hasn't even hidden it.'

'Describe it to me, Tara, what does it look like?' he asked.

'It's a gun, with a barrel.'

'Describe the grip to me.'

'It's wooden, with like crosses across it …'

'OK, don't touch it. Is there a letter in there with it, a solicitor's letter?'

'The gun's resting on top of a folded piece of cream paper,' she replied.

'OK, that's good. Just don't touch it. Zip the bag up and leave it as you found it,' Temple instructed.

'I want him out of here, Temple. He's a fucking psycho.' Tara's voice faltered with fear.

'Leave it with me, Tara, I'll sort it. Listen to me now. Leave your door key on the top of the door ledge outside the flat. Go with Finch to meet him at the pub tonight and text me when you are all together. Ring me straightaway if King leaves the pub or the holdall leaves the flat.'

Relief flooded through him. At least he knew where the gun was. His urge to go round to the flat there and then and seize it was overwhelming, but he knew he had to fight that and think it through. The last thing he wanted was a confrontation with King. He had to get the gun back, he just needed to work out quickly how he could do that and ensure Tara was protected. He knew he owed her for this.

Temple made his way back to Swindon Police Station to meet Sloper and Kelly, hopeful of recovering the gun, but he needed to think quickly. He had to concentrate on the inquiry for the next few hours. He had to get everyone up to speed with the information from the Financial Unit, Caroline Black, Dianna Forrester and Dr Jacques and direct the next set of inquiries. He found Kelly in the general CID office.

'How are we getting on with locating Jonathan Silvester and Michael Cooper? I want Jonathan Silvester – have you got him yet? In the absence of Maxwell, he will be very useful.'

'I've located both. I've got Silvester coming in tomorrow,' Kelly replied.

'I'll go and see how Simon's doing.'

Temple went off to join Sloper interviewing Marcus Hussain. Knowing that Maxwell Ashton-Jones would profit from another hefty insurance payout made him a prime suspect. Temple suspected that Hussain was just in the wrong place at the wrong time.

Sloper had made a start. Marcus was sitting across from him in the interview room with his solicitor when Temple joined them. Looking at him, Temple saw that Hussain had lost some of his earlier bravado. A night in the cells sometimes did that, he thought. He observed while Sloper continued his questioning.

'CCTV shows us that you left The Palace and drove off in a car, a Porsche – or someone's Porsche – was it Greta's?' asked Sloper.

'Yeah, it was Greta's car, man.'

'Where did you go?'

'Just drove around before going home,' replied Hussain.

'You're lying. How do I know you're lying, Marcus?'

'I don't know.'

'Because ANPR caught you going out of Swindon, in the direction of Ramsbury.'

'So you know I was in Greta's Porsche,' said Hussain.

'Of course, I know everything, Marcus. Just testing you. Now, are you going to tell me the truth?'

'Look, man, OK, I did. I did drive out that way, but it wasn't to Greta's. I didn't drink in the club because I was going out to get some coke, the stuff you found at the house. I was meeting a dealer on the road at Cadley.'

'What road?' asked Sloper.

'The A346.'

'And where did you stop? It's a long road, Marcus, where did you agree to meet?'

'In a layby, there's a road sign and I pulled up, just past there.'

'I think this is a cock and bull story, Marcus. You've had long enough to think about it,' Sloper challenged.

'Look, man, you found it, you found what I bought that night when you searched my house.'

'Are you telling me you couldn't have got that in The Palace? The place is heaving with the stuff,' Sloper said.

'I've got my own dealer, had him for years. I use the same guy, that way I don't get any shit.'

'So why didn't you tell us this before?' asked Sloper.

'Because I was going to buy drugs, man.'

'You know what I'm going to say next, don't you, Marcus?'

'Precisely, man. That's exactly the reason why I didn't tell you.' Hussain threw up his arms in exasperation.

'I'll ask anyway. Who is it, who's your supplier?' asked Sloper.

'I'm not saying, man.' His eyes looking down onto the table, Hussain sat and shook his head.

'Let me concentrate your mind for you. I'll think you'll find you're still in the shit here, Marcus,' said Sloper.

'I did not kill Greta, I've done nothing wrong,' Hussain insisted.

'That's where you're wrong. You've constantly lied to us, Marcus. We've given you every chance here to tell the truth. I suggest you think carefully about not revealing your alibi. You can't account for your time. It's not looking good for you, Marcus. You had a good job there, at the Porsche garage ...' Sloper was enjoying himself.

'All right, all right. I got my gear from Shaun Wheeler. I arranged it on my mobile. You can check my call list.'

'We will, Marcus, you can be sure of that. Shaun Wheeler – Wheeler the Dealer. I know Shaun Wheeler. But I tell you something, Marcus, if I was you, I wouldn't want to rely on him.'

The interview was suspended while Sloper tracked down Shaun Wheeler.

While Temple tried to concentrate on reviewing the growing amount of information they were gathering, his mind tried to work through the logistics of having King arrested at the pub and him being able to retrieve the gun from Tara and Finch's flat. For his plan to work, he needed to be in Trowbridge when Tara texted him – *if* she texted him. His mobile rang.

'Boss, it's Jackie, I've got some news for you.'

'Is it the DNA results?'

'Yes. Two profiles with one a match to the foetus. I'm sorry, boss, but it looks like there's no match to your man in custody for either of the profiles.'

'Don't be sorry, if it's not him, it's not him. Thanks, Jackie.'

Temple rang the custody unit and instructed Hussain be released on bail.

CHAPTER 15

TEMPLE DIALLED HIS wife's mobile number.

'Hello?'

'Leigh, it's me.'

'What do you want?' she replied flatly. As soon as she heard his voice she remembered the hurt he'd caused her. She couldn't help it, but her voice changed automatically. She couldn't hate him and that annoyed her more than anything. Every time she heard him, like now, she just felt an overwhelming sadness.

'Can you talk for a minute? I just need to sort of explain something. How are you? How's Daisy?' he asked, trying to read her mood through her voice.

'Fine. Just say what you have to say.'

She hated the way he dropped into her life with his calls, interrupting the flow. She was torn between screening his calls, not talking to him at all and still having a chance to hear his voice. That's what the sound of him did to her. Momentarily wish things back the way they used to be. The sound of him confused her, made her turn against herself for the thought of taking him back.

Temple persevered. 'Do you remember the Paul King case, aggravated burglary and he threatened to kill me, us, when he got out?'

'Not really, no.' Temple could hear the tension in her voice as she spoke to him.

'Well, he did. He's out now and he tried to set fire to the house last night. I just want you to be careful until I can get him arrested.'

'How careful do I need to be?' she asked. 'Don't think that you're going to see Daisy while this is going on, I'm not having you put her in danger,' she said, the words tumbling out, her voice much edgier than she thought she was capable of and with more force than she had meant.

It proved to her just what the sound of him did to her. How had they got here, she wondered. She was all right all the time she didn't hear from him but in one phone call, there it was again and she hated herself for it. She missed him and she hated admitting it. Even now, eight months on, with Roger in her bed, it wasn't the same. She could tell this to her secret self – perhaps everyone felt like this when they split up, perhaps she just had to persevere, try not to miss him, adjust. She was all right until he rang and his voice was soft.

'Of course I won't put her in danger, I don't want either of you in danger which is why I'm ringing. Perhaps I could drop by and explain, see Daisy – later on today?' If he could just meet with her today, they could talk, properly.

'No, I'm taking her to the doctors. She's not eating properly.'

'You said she was fine!' he almost shouted, regretting it instantly. The hard edge to his voice snapped her out of her thoughts and she was angry again.

'No, I said *I* was fine. I expect it's all this bloody upset you've caused. I'll talk to Roger when he comes home, you don't need to come round. I can't talk anymore now.' She wanted to end the conversation and knew any mention of Roger would do it.

'I'll ring later on then, to see how you got on at the doctors.'

'Whatever.' Leigh ended the call. Temple sensed the hurt he'd caused her in every word she forced herself to speak. Every time they spoke they seemed to end on a row. If he could just get to see her, speak to her, he knew they could start to sort things out.

CHAPTER 16

SLOPER HAD TRACKED down Shaun Wheeler to his home in Liden, Swindon, a new housing estate, full of three storey townhouses in cream coloured Cotswold stone. Sloper looked into the window of the BMW parked on the small tarmacked drive before ringing the bell. Wheeler answered the door.

'All right, Shaun?' said Sloper sarcastically. 'Remember me? DS Sloper, CID. Can I come in?'

'And you're here because?' Wheeler stood his ground. Standing in front of the door, he barred Sloper's entrance.

Sloper drew himself up to full height, pushing out his large stomach, in contrast to Wheeler's skinny physique.

'Well, we can do this here, on the doorstep – and, *we will* – or you can invite me in. What's the matter, caught you on the hop, have I? Weighing out the gear?' asked Sloper.

He eyed Wheeler. He'd watched the little shit dealing drugs for years, since he was fourteen, but his intel record showed that he hadn't been caught for some time. It was shits like Wheeler that gave Sloper the run around, the ones that took most effort. They didn't know the 'rules' and made out like there weren't any. Well, Wheeler was about to find out there was.

Wheeler stood aside and gestured Sloper to go in. Sloper took a quick scan of the room, looking for evidence of dealing. The living room was fashionably off-white, with a new cream leather settee and a fifty-five inch flat screen television mounted on the wall. Sloper noticed the place was clean and tidy, not the usual drug den he was used to seeing. This was a dealer on the up.

'You live here on your own, do you, or are you still living with your mum and dad?' he asked.

'On my own. This is my place,' Wheeler replied.

'Is it now? And where did you get the money for this, as if I didn't know? Who'd give you a mortgage – one of Jake Shaw's dodgy mortgages, is it? One of Jake's loans?'

'What have you come here for?' Wheeler asked, looking bored by Sloper's questions and annoyed at the way he was looking at his things.

'Don't get cocky, Wheeler. I need to ask some questions and I need you to think very carefully before you answer me. Marcus Hussain – do you know him?'

'No.'

'Well, he knows you and he's telling me that you and him met up in the early hours of Sunday morning, out at Cadley – what do you say about that?'

'Don't know what you're talking about.'

'He says that you're his dealer. Says he's always used you, in which case, you'd know all about him. So, I'll ask you again, do you know him?'

'No.' Wheeler hunched forward and thrust his hands into the long pockets of his cargo pants.

'That's a shame for him and good news for me. He says that you met him at Cadley and you sold him a wrap of coke. We found the wrap in his house when we searched it. Now, I'm going to cut you some slack. I'm not interested in the coke. All I'm interested in is if he's telling me the truth because I need to know where he was that night. Now, do you know him and did you sell him some coke?' Sloper asked.

'I don't know the guy and if he says I do, then he's a fucking liar,' replied Wheeler.

'You see, Shaun, he's in a bit of a tight spot. I suspect he murdered someone that night, but he denies it. He says he drove out to Cadley to meet you and buy some coke. Now, it doesn't mean that he couldn't have done all that and still carried out the murder, but I still need to know what he did that night.'

Wheeler was wide eyed. Hussain was a good customer but he never had him down as a murderer. Shit, if he was violent, a murderer, who knows what he'd do the next time he wanted his drugs.

'I know Marcus,' he said, slowly.

'That's better. And?'

'I'm not admitting to supplying any drugs. I don't know who he gets his drugs from but it wasn't me. I did see him out at Cadley, though, as he says, in fact, I raced him in his Porsche back to Swindon. What sort of murder's he committed then?'

'Never mind that. What route did you take coming back?'

'Up the A346 and then A419, then onto the motorway.'

'I can check that with CCTV and if you're lying to me, I'll be back to get you. Are you sure it was the early hours of Sunday morning?'

'Yeah, course I'm sure.'

Sloper started to wander around, going into the kitchen.

'While I'm here, what do you know about Gemma Harker taking a beating? And don't say you don't know who she is, all you scum know who she is. You feed her the shit she takes.'

'I'll ask about.'

'You'll do better than that, you piece of fucking shit. You'll find out and then let me know or, see all this, it'll be gone. Seized. Proceeds of Crime Act. I can make it happen. It's up to you.'

It wouldn't do any harm to have Shaun Wheeler under his control – in his experience, you could never have enough dealers. He made his way back to Swindon Police Station.

CHAPTER 17

Temple's mobile bleeped. It was Tara texting to say that they were all in the pub together. This was his chance.

Temple drove through the village of Hilperton, on into Trowbridge, the county's administerial hub. The once prosperous and significant wool and mill town had none of the obvious beauty or charm of Salisbury, or other Wiltshire towns. Its past affluence hadn't translated into striking architecture; it was a mixture of utilitarian buildings and served little use than as a thoroughfare through the county for all HGVs and cement lorries. The buildings that did exist in Bath stone were darkened by the black grime from weather and diesel emissions.

Temple remembered that it had once featured on an internet website as one of the worst places to live. To him, it was a shithole. He'd done a short stint in CID in Trowbridge as a DC and remembered it for its depressing number of rapes, domestic violence incidents and GBHs. The dark clouded early evening sky mirrored his feelings about the place.

He drove into a cul-de-sac and parked outside some purpose built brick flats. Sitting in his car, he dialled into the local station and spoke to the duty sergeant. He gave instructions for King to be arrested at the pub on suspicion of the arson and for the flat to be searched.

Knowing that this would take time to arrange, he let himself into the foyer of the flats and took the stairs. At Tara's flat, he quickly felt around the top of the door frame until his gloved fingers found the key. He opened the door, replaced the key and went inside.

Tara was no domestic goddess. The air was stale and smelt of cooking and sweat. Treading across thin stained carpets, he made his way to the bedrooms and went into the smaller of the two. By the side of the bed was the blue holdall she had described. He unzipped it. The gun was there. He quickly put it into his suit pocket and covered the protruding grip with the pocket flap. Folded underneath the gun was the solicitor's letter with Leigh's name on it. He left it in the bag, zipped it up and left the flat.

As Temple put the gun in the glove compartment of his car, his phone rang. It was Sloper.

'Temple, where are you? Hussain's brief says he's getting bail. What the fuck's going on?'

'I'm on my way back, I'll be there in about forty minutes. Did you find Wheeler?'

'Yes, he confirms that he met Hussain that night. I still don't know what's going on. Why is Hussain being released?'

'Hussain's DNA didn't match the profile they had. We've got nothing new on him, we have to let him go.'

Without replying, Sloper ended the call and rang Harker.

Back at Swindon Police Station, Temple listened as Harker summoned him by tannoy to the management suite. Attempting to avoid him and going down to the parade room, Temple walked straight into him on the main stairs.

'In here,' grunted Harker and gesturing with his head to a small room. He shut the door.

Temple looked at him. Whilst he could match him in height, Harker was a broad and heavy man and his six foot frame was as big as his reputation for being a belligerent bastard. His wiry short cut greying hair exposed ears that were gnarled and deformed from past rugby battle, where he'd ground his boot studs into many an opponent's flesh as a way of neutralising frustrations at work. His thin lipped mouth was now permanently set in a snarl. Temple noticed that his eye bags had eye bags and his large eyes bulged out of a face that was flushed red. Harker's blood pressure was through the roof and it hadn't been helped by Sloper telling him the prime suspect in the Ramsbury murder had been released on bail on Temple's say so.

'I'm up to my fucking eyes in ACPO alligators so this better be good. Why are you letting this Hussain bloke go?' His deep voice had sunk to a growl. Feeling the oppressive heat of the room, Harker hooked his finger at his collar to undo the button at his neck and loosen his tie. He turned his back on Temple, walking over to a window, leaving a desk between them. Being in such close proximity to Temple still made Harker feel as though he wanted to reach out and pound his fist into Temple's face as he had meant to do all those years ago. The compulsion to do so hadn't gone away after all this time.

'His DNA isn't on the victim. She was pregnant and indications are that there is a mixed profile of DNA found inside her, giving us two DNA profiles for identification. One of the profiles already matches the foetus and Hussain's wasn't one of them. We've got his account, but there's no motive. I don't think he was the one who was with her when she died,' replied Temple. The room was small and he wanted to get out. He was speaking to Harker's back and he could see his shoulders twitching.

'I thought we found her with her hands tied to a fucking bed and she was strangled – sex game gone wrong. There wouldn't be any fucking motive,' said Harker, his voice remaining low. A quick outcome with Hussain would have suited him; it would wrap the job up and it would be largely due to Sloper's inquiries that they'd have such a quick result.

It would also start to take the pressure off him a bit, letting him throw it at the chief officers who kept appearing in Swindon, wanting to grab him by the balls to make sure he had a grip on what was going on with the Swindon murder and kidnap.

'It's not Hussain,' Temple repeated, knowing it wasn't what Harker wanted to hear. 'I've spent time with him and it's not him. He doesn't deny seeing her, or that they had sex on occasions, but it wasn't him she was with that evening. Hussain dropped her off, as she was expecting a visitor. He was one of the last people to see her alive, but he didn't kill her.' Harker turned around but remained at the window.

'So, who was it then?' Harker asked, his bulging eyes staring back at Temple. He was losing his patience but Temple stood his ground.

'I don't know yet. But no one that's been spoken to so far has mentioned that she was pregnant so I'm guessing she hadn't made it public. Someone took photographs of Hussain and Greta Ashton-Jones together a few months ago having sex in Savernake Forest and blackmailed them. She was in a sexual relationship with her husband's best friend, Jonathan Silvester. She was also having a relationship with a local builder, both men we've yet to see. Maxwell Ashton-Jones flies in tomorrow morning at 6.30 a.m. We've got a reception party waiting for him at Gatwick to bring him here. He's due a large insurance payment for Greta's death. I don't know if he knew about the other men, or if she was pregnant. I need his DNA and the other men that I've mentioned to go through a process of elimination,' Temple explained.

'You need to get this moving, Temple. The Chief's had a phone call from the Police and Crime Commissioner, who's also a friend of Ashton-Jones and lives in Ramsbury. He wants to know what progress we've made, says he wants to see the SIO to make sure we're putting in enough effort. He says there's a killer on the loose in his local village and he's not convinced that we're doing enough. Then he says he's coming up here to see me.'

'I didn't know the Crime Commissioner lived at Ramsbury,' replied Temple.

Anthony de la Hay was a retired Brigadier and had made himself an active presence in the force since his election. He'd quickly assimilated the talent of the Chief Officer team; as hirer and firer of the Chief Constable post, both the deputy and assistant chief constable were deciding on just how much they needed to court de la Hay as the Chief was due to retire in a year. De la Hay was carefully managing the relationships as the politics played out between them. With a murder on his doorstep and with many of the local community having elected him, they now looked to him to get involved, much to the annoyance of the Chief.

'Get hold of the press officer from HQ and sort your holding statement. Keep this contained, Temple, don't let the press or de la Hay start doing their own fucking inquiry.' Harker knew that press intrusion into the Swindon inquiry was one of the drivers for the Chief Officer's concern; the press could whip up community tension in just one headline.

'One thing de la Hay is right to pick up on is that I need more resources. I need a few more statement takers and a Holmes inputter.' Temple returned Harker's gaze. Harker struggled to contain his contempt for Temple and felt his face grow redder.

'Yeah well, de la Hay will need to understand about priorities. A dead boy and an abducted girl are where the resources are focussed, just keep on top of it, Temple. I'll give you one Holmes inputter—'

They were interrupted by a knock on the door. Graham Mellor came into the room, with a paper in his hand. He had gone to Swindon to enlist the help of his colleagues.

'Thought you might like this.' He handed Temple a list. 'We've been going through the bank accounts of the Ashton-Joneses. I've highlighted those unusual transactions. In the joint one, there's the usual activity of direct debits coming out and salary going in, shopping and so on. There are four cash withdrawals of £500 over four days in February. But in the last six months, every month, there is a withdrawal of £2,400. Four withdrawals are in cash but there are two cheques for the same amount, last one last month. When I made inquiries with the bank, they said the cheques were made payable to Curtis Coleman Ltd.'

'Who or what are Curtis Coleman?' asked Temple.

'It's a London based security agency. I looked them up on the internet and they supply security services, body guards and anti-hostage trained chauffeurs.'

CHAPTER 18

TEMPLE HAD TAKEN Jane up on her offer to stay with her until the fire damage was sorted. His initial thought was that he could sleep in his car, but even he could see the sense in accepting the offer of comfort with everything that was going on. On the way back to Jane's, Temple called in the custody suite where Paul King was being held. King had finished being interviewed and was in his cell, awaiting recall to prison when Temple arrived. He spoke to the custody sergeant.

'We're just waiting for the prison van to come and get him. He's got an alibi for the time of the fire, but can't account for having a letter of yours in his possession. So he's going back on receiving stolen goods.'

'Who's his alibi?'

'Zac Finch.'

'*Finch*?' As Temple said his name, Finch appeared through the security doors with a detective constable, showing him the way out. Short and lean, Finch was no match for the likes of Paul King.

'Mr Finch, could I have a word?' Temple gestured to a small anti-room. Zac Finch went inside and Temple closed the door, just about keeping his anger under control.

'What's this about you giving King an alibi for setting fire to my house?'

'He didn't do it. He was with me and Tara in the flat that night. It wasn't him. Tara's making a statement now. I'm just waiting for her.'

'Are you fucking mad?' Temple asked.

'Honest, Mr Temple …'

'Don't make me laugh, Finch.' Temple could see he was lying.

'He was with us, with us both, watching the telly. I bought some porn films. He's not long been out, so we were on the sofa watching telly and Tara was doing the ironing behind us. He took one phone call all evening, went to the door of a caller at one point, but he didn't leave the flat.'

'You fucking liar, Finch. You tell me what's going on. Now,' Temple demanded.

'He didn't do it. He didn't torch your house. He didn't go out that night.'

'Who called at the door then?' asked Temple.

'I don't know. Didn't see them.'

'You're a liar. You didn't see them because nobody called. This is serious, Finch, so I suggest you think about what you've just done. Your business would soon go downhill if it was known that you like giving information to the police and that would be the least of your worries.'

Finch lost his temper.

'What could I do? He's a fucking psycho and I can't rely on your lot keeping him under lock and key. What if they release him again and he comes back to me?'

'You shouldn't associate with scum like him. Since you do, I want to know if he comes to you again. When he gets out again, I'll expect a phone call and for you to tell me everything he does.'

Watching Finch leave the room, Temple was faintly pleased with the fact that although both Finch and Tara lived together, neither had any idea that the other gave him information. There was heavy procedure and legislation around Covert Human Intelligence Sources (CHIS) with information given to police being strictly controlled between only a handful of specialist officers. But both Tara and Finch refused to speak with anyone but Temple.

He knew he could rely on Tara. Tara hated King because he put the fear of God into her. She hated to feel afraid of anyone, so she would always go to Temple with any information that would keep him locked up. She also hated to see how he manipulated Finch. Temple didn't mind her making a statement with Finch, all the better, she had to look after herself; she'd done him a service and he wouldn't forget it. Finch, it seemed, was a different matter and he needed to make it quite clear to him where his loyalties should lie.

With King heading back to a cell at Horfield, Temple drove back to Jane's.

Back at Marlborough Police Station first thing in the morning, Temple was called to say that the eagerly awaited arrival of Maxwell Ashton-Jones would be delayed until later that afternoon due to delays in departure at Singapore. He was being brought straight from the airport to the station by PC Carrie Smith, a family liaison officer that Harker had released to the team.

Armed with some further detail around the death of Olivia Ashton-Jones, Temple hoped that the meeting with Maxwell would move the inquiry forward. Olivia Ashton-Jones's death certificate cited 'accidental death by drowning' and a coroner's report provided the detail.

During a stop-over in Riyadh, Olivia, Maxwell and Jonathan Silvester were on the same British Airways flight, Maxwell and Jonathan co-piloting and Olivia one of the hostesses. On landing at King Khalid International Airport, they checked into the Hilton Hotel. They met up with other employees and a discreet party ensued, involving some illicit drinking of duty frees bought from Gatwick. The party continued around the hotel pool. Later that evening, Olivia Ashton-Jones was found floating face down in the pool. The party goers had described leaving the pool at various stages, going back to their rooms, leaving dwindling numbers at the poolside.

Maxwell Ashton-Jones had confessed to sleeping with a fellow hostess in her room at the time of his wife's death – corroborated by the hostess. Jonathan Silvester had also been indulging himself elsewhere, although witnesses did say that they had seen Olivia and Jonathan together in the pool, talking by themselves. Olivia was found by hotel staff who tried unsuccessfully to revive her. She was taken by ambulance to the Green Crescent Hospital in Riyadh where she was pronounced dead. The initial examination at the hospital showed there were traces of alcohol in her bloodstream. It was decided that she had simply had too much to drink and had either become tired in the pool whilst swimming and had drowned due to the effects of alcohol, or had simply fallen into an alcoholic sleep.

The body was embalmed and repatriated. However, back in England, a subsequent post mortem revealed a trauma to the back of her head, consistent with it hitting a hard surface. The coroner gathered statements from those present and recorded that in all probability death was caused by accidental drowning. He concluded the amount of alcohol in the bloodstream may well have caused the deceased to have slipped or caused herself some injury prior to death, but he did not believe it to have been sufficient to have played a part in her death, hence the verdict.

As Temple read the file, Temple wondered how the case had not prompted further investigation. Now, Maxwell Ashton-Jones had two dead wives; one had been murdered, the other an accidental death. Maybe he'd got away with the first one and decided to have another go? But how could he have done it when he wasn't even in the country? The other common denominator was Jonathan Silvester – were these two working in tandem? Or was it simply a case that Maxwell had been tragically unlucky?

Temple would ask Kelly to make further inquiries with the coroner and authorities in the Foreign Office and in

Riyadh. Saudi Arabia had strict anti-drinking laws and the case must have involved the British Consulate's diplomatic skills during the repatriation of Olivia Ashton-Jones.

Kelly watched Jonathan Silvester standing in the foyer of Gable Cross Police Station. She observed him through the door without him knowing, as he waited for her to collect him. She was intrigued after her meeting with Caroline Black as to what he would look like, so she took a few moments before she made herself known to him to weigh him up.

He was tall and broad shouldered and had a thick head of blond hair which made him look younger than his fifty-nine years. He had disarmingly vivid blue eyes and a sickeningly white and broad smile. She also noticed that he was casually, but expensively dressed, from his tweed jacket with fashionable leather elbow patches, down to his brown leather brogue shoes. To her, he was the archetypal slime ball, but as she stood and watched him turn on the charm to two female police officers entering the foyer, she could easily see how he would attract women.

'Like flies around shit,' she mumbled under her breath as the officers stopped to chat to him, remarking on his tan. She interrupted their conversation to make herself known to him and held the security door open for him to pass through.

She showed him into an interview room and sat at a desk opposite him. Armed with her notes from Caroline Black, despite another long day, she was up for the prospect of taking a statement from Jonathan Silvester. Given what Caroline Black had told her, she masked her distaste for the man sitting opposite her. She managed to smile at him, giving him no clue as to how she really felt about him.

Jonathan Silvester hadn't seen the inside of a police station before and he had every intention of leaving it as soon as he could. Just how did these things go, he wondered. He eyed Kelly, weighing her up; she was a smart looking woman, who wasn't even a police officer. He wasn't sure what he could read into that, but he had contacted a solicitor after her call, who said he would come out immediately if required. He put his mobile phone on the table between them.

'Mr Silvester, how long have you known Maxwell and Greta Ashton-Jones?'

He confirmed that he and Maxwell had worked together for years and were very good friends.

'I left piloting for a more lucrative role in finance and investments. I have a few clients, Maxwell is one of them.'

'Did you know Olivia Ashton-Jones, Maxwell's first wife?' Kelly watched him intently.

'Yes, of course, we were all good friends. I was actually with Maxwell when Olivia drowned in the pool in Riyadh. It was a terrible time. A terrible time both for him and his son, James. And then he met Greta.'

'How would you describe their relationship?' Kelly asked.

'Very loving. She was a very pretty woman and she loved James as if he was her own son. He's known her since he was five years old. They were a very loving family. Maxwell is shattered by this.' Jonathan Silvester shook his head.

'How do you know how he feels, have you spoken to him?'

'Of course I have. He rang me from Sydney, he broke the news to me. He'll be back in the country later today,' he replied.

'And what do you think, Mr Silvester, of Greta's death?'

'Well, it's terrible, why would anyone want to kill Greta? We're all shaken by it, really shaken.'

Kelly felt that this was the first sincere thing that Jonathan Silvester had said.

'When was the last time you saw Greta, Mr Silvester?'

'Oh, well, let me see, perhaps a week or so ago, perhaps longer. My girlfriend wanted Maxwell to bring back some orchids for her from Singapore. I visited them both to put in my order.'

'Orchids?' questioned Kelly.

'Yes, you can order them from the plane in Singapore, they are very cheap and come in a box of twenty cut stems, very pretty. She shares them amongst her friends and family. The ladies love them,' he replied.

Kelly could see that he didn't seem the least bit fazed about being in a police station.

'I spoke to Greta's friend, Caroline Black, yesterday, Mr Silvester.'

She paused, deliberately, watching him to see if the mention of her name prompted a reaction. Nothing.

'She told me that Greta told her you would visit Greta at home when you knew Maxwell was away. She said that you and Greta had a sexual relationship, would you tell me about that, please?' Think about that, you cocky bastard, she thought.

'We did have a relationship, a sexual relationship as you say, some years ago, but it was over. I can't account for what Greta might have said to Caroline.'

'Did Maxwell know about this?'

'Yes, he did actually. He was away a lot but not always flying. I mean, he told Greta he was flying, but he wasn't.'

'Wait a minute. A moment ago, you told me that they were in a very loving relationship – how does that fit in with you and Greta having a sexual relationship?'

'Maxwell still remained very fond of Greta. He loved her, she just wasn't enough for him.'

'He was having an affair?'

'Yes, he would go and stay away for a weekend, or a few days with whoever took his fancy at the time. We didn't exactly have a conversation about it, but I knew he wanted me to distract Greta while he was away, call it an 'arrangement,'' replied Silvester, matter-of-factly.

'How did you know if you say no conversation took place?'

'He would ring me and ask if it was all right to return at a particular time, ask if we would be together.'

'Did Greta know this?'

'God, no. Not about our arrangement, but I think she knew about Maxwell.'

'Did you ever threaten Greta by saying you would tell her husband of your relationship, and thereby prolong it when she lost interest? Caroline Black says that Greta told her you did.' Kelly watched him as he answered.

'The answer to your question is no,' he replied. He was masking a rising annoyance at Caroline Black, but only just. She was obviously fuelling the inquiries and no doubt was the reason he was there. *Fucking bitch.* He'd never liked her. 'As I said, Maxwell was well aware. I was … helping him out, if you like. I can't account for what Greta had told Caroline. Caroline Black doesn't like me so I wouldn't put too much emphasis on what she tells you,' he said, doing his best at being dismissive.

Kelly continued, trying her best to ignore Silvester's apparent arrogance.

'So, Maxwell had more than one affair?' she asked.

'Yes. I think it's fair to say Maxwell likes variety.'

'What do you mean by that?'

'Well, he's surrounded by pretty women at work. He's a handsome guy, especially in a pilot's uniform. They fall at his feet, even now, at his age. What's he supposed to do, turn it down? It was no secret.'

'Caroline says that Greta suspected that he had another woman – was there any *one* woman, Mr Silvester?'

'Look, Maxwell will be back later, perhaps you can ask him that.'

'But do you know if he had someone in particular?'

'As I said, you can ask him that question yourself soon.'

'Caroline Black says that Greta told her that things started to disappear from the house – some of his clothes, he sold a car, a painting – do you know anything about that?'

'It seems to me, Ms Farmer, that Caroline seems to have an awful lot to say. Look, I'm not going to speculate on what Maxwell has or hasn't done,' he said, casually shrugging his shoulders.

'So if we go back to you, you said that your sexual relationship with Greta ended – when exactly?'

'Oh, perhaps we haven't been together for a year or so.'

'How long was your relationship, would you say?'

'It went on for a few years. As I said, it seemed to suit all of us.'

'How do you know it suited Greta?'

'Look, I did. She was a very willing participant in our relationship if you get my meaning. I paid her attention, I know what women want, know how to treat them. She and I were a good match in many ways.' Looking directly at Kelly, he said, 'We had a very healthy and active sexual relationship. As much driven by Greta, as me. Without wishing to be arrogant and crass, she couldn't get enough of me, she was very demanding. She was a lovely woman, but could also be quite child-like in some respects.'

'Meaning?'

'Well, she believed in love and all that stuff. Thought that love and marriage was forever.'

Kelly sat forward in her seat.

'And you think that's childish, do you – commitment?' she challenged.

'I think I said child-like. What I meant was, it was an innocent take on the world for her to have. When you set your expectations so high … I think she was pretty disappointed when Max started to stray.'

Kelly stared back at him, expressionless.

'Do you know if she was seeing anyone else?'

'I suspect she was. Greta seemed to need a lot of attention. That's not a bad thing.'

'And what about you, Mr Silvester, you said you had a girlfriend?'

'Yes, I have.'

'Were you with her on Saturday night?'

'No, I wasn't. She was at her home and I was at mine.'

'Were you in all night?'

'Yes, I was.'

'Mr Silvester, did you see Greta on Saturday night?' asked Kelly. Again, she stopped looking at her notes and watched him as he answered.

'No, I didn't. I stayed at home.'

'What did you do?'

'Probably caught up on some paperwork, had a drink, listened to some music.'

'It was only Saturday, four days ago. Don't you know?'

'Yes, as I said, caught up on some paperwork and listened to some music,' Silvester replied, slowly, giving her a half smile back.

'On your own?'

'Yes.'

'Do you have keys to Greta's home?'

'I expect so … somewhere,' he replied, vaguely.

'I'd like us to write a statement now, going through the points we've covered, if that's OK with you?'

'Yes, fine. I'm only too glad to help, just wish I could be more helpful.'

Kelly and Jonathan Silvester locked eyes as he spoke. She thought of Greta and what Caroline had told her. Now, Silvester seemed to be saying that her husband was complicit in their relationship. Two dead wives and two men. Jonathan Silvester read Kelly's thoughts through her eyes. He'd need to speak to Maxwell. Seeing Silvester off the premises, Kelly rang Temple's mobile.

Sitting in the main office at Marlborough waiting for Maxwell's arrival, Temple was contacted by a PC at the front desk.

'Sir, the Police and Crime Commissioner's here to see you in the front office. I know the office is closed but he was banging on the glass doors to get attention. Says he wants to see you.'

'I'll come down.'

Temple introduced himself to former Brigadier Anthony de la Hay. Dark suited, de la Hay's handshake was like a vice.

'You're a busy man, so I'll get straight to the point.' Temple appreciated his directness. 'I have concerns about the inquiry you are conducting into the death of

Mrs Ashton-Jones at Ramsbury. I live there and I know Maxwell Ashton-Jones, who, as you know, is currently out of the country. The community is shocked by events and want to know what is being done to catch the killer. I'd like to know what progress you're making and whether or not we need to issue crime prevention advice.'

'I can assure you that we are doing all we can to bring Mrs Ashton-Jones's killer to justice and the inquiry is progressing well. I am, in fact, waiting to receive Mr Ashton-Jones here at any moment, sir.'

De la Hay leaned in closer; Temple could smell his aftershave.

'Spare me the usual well practised bullshit. I'm not a journalist and don't tell me the crap that's fed to parish councils and community groups. When do you expect to make a further arrest? I see you've already released one man from custody – with what's going on at Swindon, we don't want the public to lose confidence in the force or the Chief Constable, do we? I need to know how this is going.'

'The man you refer to was arrested for theft, as Mrs Ashton-Jones's car was missing, and released on bail until I am satisfied that he did not steal her car. I can understand that there will be concern in the community, but at this stage, I think I'm looking closer at Mrs Ashton-Jones's close associates for my inquiries.'

'Do you have sufficient resources at your disposal? This has affected the local community—' Before he could carry on, Temple interrupted him.

'Sir, I understand your anxiety, as you live in Ramsbury, and the concerns of the community. I appreciate your input, but inquiries are at an interesting stage at the moment and I can give you my reassurances that resourcing is adequate for the time being.' Temple toed the party line, as instructed by Harker, but it was his first direct contact with Anthony de la Hay and he wanted to keep him on side.

'I have made a press release via my press officer—' Again, Temple interrupted.

'The press will be dealt with by me and the Force Press Department, sir, so if you can direct any inquiries to me or to them, I'd be grateful.'

'If you don't mind, Inspector, I have my own press department and I'll issue what I see fit.' De la Hay was in no mood to be told what to do. Temple quietly persisted.

'I'll also be issuing a press release outlining the case so far. If I can take your contact details, perhaps I could keep in touch with you in the days ahead to update you on progress?' Temple was under no obligation to do so, in fact, de la Hay was overstepping his authority, but Temple knew that by offering to keep him in loop, he might just keep in line.

'Yes, please, that would be helpful,' de la Hay replied.

As de la Hay wrote his mobile number, Maxwell Ashton-Jones arrived at the station. They both greeted one another with a long handshake.

'I can't tell you how good it is to see a friendly face,' Ashton-Jones said as he smiled at de la Hay. 'The journey back was hellish, not knowing what's going on.'

'It's a bad business, Maxwell, terrible. If there's anything further I can do for you, just call, you know that. I've spoken to the Chief Constable and the inspector here and they assure me that the case is progressing well.'

'Thanks, Anthony. You know what it's like, when you're out of the country and you don't know what's going on the ground, you need someone you trust to find out what's going on,' replied Maxwell.

'Any time. Call by at the house afterwards. If you need somewhere to stay, you and James are most welcome.'

Temple got Ashton-Jones seen into an interview room and put his hand on de la Hay's elbow, as he was about to depart.

'Am I right in thinking that you've already been in contact with Mr Ashton-Jones?' Temple asked in a low voice.

'Yes, I made contact with him. We're neighbours, we meet socially and I was concerned for him.'

'He's now a person of interest in my inquiry, so I would appreciate it if you wouldn't make further contact from herein. Given your position, you might be compromised.' De la Hay gave a small nod and left the station.

Before going into the interview room, Temple spoke to the FLO, Carrie Smith.

'What's he been like, Carrie?'

'No outward emotion in terms of tears or anything like that all the time I've been with him. A couple of deep sighs now and then. He stared out of the window for most of our journey. I've told him that the house is still a crime scene and that he and his son will have to find alternative accommodation. You wanted to know how he responded to being told of his wife's death; the BA guy who gave him the news said that he was really shaken.'

I bet he was, thought Temple.

He went into the room. He'd been waiting to see Maxwell Ashton-Jones for two days and now had the opportunity to eye him up. Maxwell was tall, slim and somewhere along his journey, he had changed out of his pilot's uniform into an expensive looking suit. He looked like a mannequin. Perfect hair, cleanly shaved and completely self-possessed in his conversation with de la Hay. Assuming he was actually grieving, he was paying great attention to his appearance. Temple knew this first contact was an ideal opportunity to get as much as he could out of Ashton-Jones.

'Can I first of all offer my sincere condolences,' Temple said, before outlining the circumstances around finding Greta's body.

'You say my wife was found tied to the bed?' Ashton-Jones looked genuinely taken aback, as he took in what Temple told him. He wasn't expecting that, thought Temple.

'Yes.'

'Do you know yet what happened?' asked Maxwell, regaining composure.

'No, but I'm beginning to trace her last known movements. We've already conducted a number of inquiries with Greta's friends and of course, her parents, to try to build up a picture of her lifestyle. If you could add to that picture, that would be most helpful. How would you describe your relationship?'

'We had a good relationship. You know how it is, we've been married for about twelve years now and I was away a fair bit.' He looked down onto the desk in front of him. 'I'll cut to the chase with you, Inspector; if you're asking was I a faithful husband, then no, I wasn't. That's rather difficult, given the nature of the job I do. Was Greta faithful to me, I happen to know she wasn't. Did I love her, yes, of course. I think we understood each other.'

'Thank you for being so candid,' said Temple, realizing that Maxwell had obviously spoken to Silvester and was forewarned as to the potential line of questioning Temple would take.

'We've spoken to Jonathan Silvester and Greta's friend, Caroline Black. Caroline gave us a picture of her relationship with Jonathan Silvester that he says you knew about and pretty much gave your consent to, would that be right?' asked Temple.

'As I said, I am away a lot. A long while ago, I noticed an attraction between Jonathan and Greta and as I have my own "distractions", I er, encouraged their relationship. I certainly didn't object to it, no. That might seem strange to outsiders, but these were two people I loved; Jonathan's like an older brother to me and Greta was just adorable.'

'Was there anyone else you encouraged Greta to have a relationship with? I just want to get a picture of what was going on here,' said Temple.

'No, Inspector.' Ashton-Jones eyed Temple. 'Like I say, Jonathan is like a brother to me and so I knew he would treat her well. I realize this might sound unconventional to you, but there it is.'

'And how did you feel about the relationship between Greta and Jonathan?'

'As I say, I sort of encouraged it. Look, we were all very close. If your angle is did I feel jealous – no, I didn't. I've no idea why someone would want to kill Greta.'

'I agree with you that your arrangement is not something that I've come across before and I'm not here to judge, just to try and get to the facts. I'm aware that Greta had a medical condition. Could you tell me about that?'

'Ah, who told you about that?'

'Her GP,' replied Temple.

'Greta's medical condition, as you put it, did cast a bit of a shadow on her life, our lives. She was beautiful but not always easy to live with, at least, not from my perspective. All the time she worked, she was fine, but when she gave up work and we parted company, sometimes for weeks at a time, she found that challenging. My fault; I guess I made her feel insecure. It started not long after we married. She would miss her shifts and turn up to meet me at the airport when I got back. The purpose of this was to see who the other crew members had been, the women of course. But when she gave up work, her behaviour became increasingly erratic every time I went away. Frankly, it quickly became tiresome.

'She started to spend her way through our bank account. She'd go on spending sprees, spending huge amounts on clothes, shoes, bags, jewellery, things – anything. I'm talking thousands, in one hit sometimes. Tens of thousands all told. I had to move money out of the current account in order to limit the damage she could do. I had to get help for her to see what was wrong with her and to see what could be done.'

'So, what did you do?' asked Temple.

'Went to the GP who put us onto a psychiatrist. He diagnosed her and she'd been on anti-depressants since,' replied Maxwell matter-of-factly.

'Did she have any other conditions that you know of?'

'None that I know of.'

He's got no idea of the pregnancy, thought Temple. He wanted to keep it that way for the time being.

'DNA evidence has been left at the scene, so I'm currently trying to find a match for that. Can I please have a sample from you after we've spoken so that I can compare with that found at the scene?' Temple withheld the fact that there was a mixed profile.

'By all means, I'll give you a sample, but I wasn't even in the country at the time of Greta's death.'

'I'll still need a sample. It will be a process of elimination. I understand that increased sexual activity can be a symptom of the medical condition your wife had – were you aware of this?' Temple asked, watching for Maxwell's reaction.

'Yes, I am aware that can be that case,' he replied.

'To your knowledge, was Jonathan due to visit Greta the night she died?'

'No.'

'How can you be so certain?'

'Jonathan told me that the relationship had run its course,' replied Maxwell.

'But he could have?' asked Temple.

'No, I don't think so. The relationship was over.'

'You're sure about that?'

'Yes.'

'Someone gained entry to your home and killed your wife,' said Temple.

Maxwell nodded.

'Had the house been burgled? Was there any sign of forced entry?' asked Maxwell.

'Apparently not. Your cleaner, Irene Cresswell, is clear that things were normal in the house when she turned up that day,' Temple replied.

'What are your thoughts, Inspector?'

'That Greta knew her killer. That it was someone she trusted, someone she let into the house. It is, of course, entirely possible that death occurred following an initial consensual act which went wrong. As you see, I need to continue this line of the investigation.'

'Of course, I see.'

'Your son, sir, will he be joining you at some point? We will need to speak to him,' said Temple.

'James? OK. Jonathan is looking after him at the moment. Why would you want to speak to James?'

'He was due to stay at home that weekend, I understand, but went to a friend's instead. In any case, again, as I've explained, we need to build up a picture of Greta's relationship with him and she was his stepmother.'

'Of course. Of course. We shall both be staying with Jonathan, so by all means, make contact.'

'That's all I want for now, I'm conscious of the long journey you've had, but if I could direct you downstairs to take the DNA sample, I'd be grateful. The FLO will take you to where you want to go.'

Temple had never seen someone so intent on holding their composure as Maxwell had. Perhaps he was already making space in his bank account for the insurance payout. There was no display of anger, rage or tears of despair; no plea to find her killer. Temple was convinced the answer to this was close to home.

The DNA sample acquired, Temple instructed that it be fast-tracked to the Forensic Lab.

CHAPTER 19

Sloper pulled up into a builder's yard at Ramsbury. His arrival was noted by a man talking to two others on the far left side who were loading a flatbed van. As Sloper parked, the man approached him.

'Michael Cooper?' Sloper asked.

'Yes?'

'I'm Detective Sergeant Simon Sloper, I'm conducting an investigation into the death of Greta Ashton-Jones and I wonder if you could help me with my inquiries?'

Michael Cooper looked around him.

'Why don't you speak a bit louder, I'm sure the blokes over there didn't hear you,' he said sarcastically, referring to the two men he had been speaking to, who had stopped what they were doing and were now interested in what was taking place.

'Well, it was either come here or go to your home address. Now, which would you have preferred?' said Sloper, not lowering his voice.

'All right, all right. Come in the office.' He'd been expecting a visit since hearing of Greta's death.

The office was a beaten up portacabin, with two desks and filing cabinets. As Michael Cooper extinguished music blaring out of a radio, Sloper looked around. Heavily stained tea cups sat on a tray on one of the desks, along with a white hard hat.

'I'm not sure we can talk here,' ventured Sloper, 'won't the men be in and out?'

'I'll shut the door. They won't come in,' said Cooper, not wishing to give the men outside the spectacle of seeing him leaving with a police officer.

Michael Cooper was a big, muscular man. Dressed in denim jeans and a short-sleeved torn t-shirt, his broad shoulders, biceps and pectoral muscles bulged through the cloth. Why did builders seem to wear clothes that were too small, mused Sloper. He could see why Greta would have been attracted to the man, especially stripped to the waist on hot days. He had a mass of untidy blond hair, bleached by the sun and a deep, outdoor suntan.

'Did you know Greta Ashton-Jones, Michael?' asked Sloper, perching his weight on the corner of a metal desk.

'Yeah, we did some work on their house, so of course I did. From May last year till the end of January.' Michael Cooper leant his back against a steel filing cabinet and faced Sloper, arms crossed.

'How would you describe your relationship with her?' asked Sloper, as he cast his eye around the portacabin.

'Oh look, shall we stop wasting each other's time? I know what you're getting at. They've been talking down at The Phoenix. Look mate, they've put two and two together and come up with six.' As he spoke, he walked across to an adjacent desk, clearly uncomfortable in the confined space.

'Michael, I don't know who "they" are. We haven't got our information from The Phoenix but thanks, I shall be going there next. Now, you and Greta, what went on?'

'Look, mate, I just did a job, a good job and they was happy with it.'

'Were you and Greta shagging – because a little bird tells me you were?' asked Sloper.

'Hey, hang on a minute. Are you supposed to talk to me like that?' said Cooper, rising to Sloper's bait.

'Well, I can piss about going round the houses if you want and we can do this down the station. I just thought, you being a busy man, that you might thank me for getting straight to the point.'

Cooper acquiesced. 'Yeah, all right, all right. Look, I fancied her, she fancied me, her old man wasn't about much, she was lonely ...'

'What were *you*, Michael? Were you lonely? Oh no, you've got a wife and kids, I understand ...'

'All right, steady on. Look, we fell for each other, you know. And I admit, for a second I did think about leaving the missus, but after the job finished, having to sneak round to her place, it all got a bit much. It just ended.'

'Is that what you do, Michael? Is that your MO, your *modus operandi*, wherever you go, you shag the missus of the bloke that's paying you?' Sloper was goading him, pushing Cooper to lose his cool.

'No, it isn't. She, she was lovely, never met anyone like her. It was like, she knew what made men tick, well, me anyway. She was good company, not like a lot of women who keep on for things. She'd tell me about the places she'd been to, the things she'd seen. We'd talk about travelling together, where she'd take me – she seemed to know all the best places and she'd describe them to me.'

'Fascinating,' said Sloper sarcastically.

'It was to me, yeah,' said Cooper.

'You sound like you've never been out.'

'We go on beach holidays, to Menorca with the kids, but that's pretty much all we do.'

'Very nice. So when did this relationship end?'

'About four months ago.'

'You're sure of that, are you?' asked Sloper.

'Yes, not long after the job finished.'

'How come it ended then?' Sloper asked. 'Did the wife find out?'

'No. She never suspected. I got spooked,' Cooper said, looking down momentarily.

'What do you mean?'

'What I said. Not long after the job there finished, one night, I said to the missus that I was going down The Phoenix. I was also going to see Greta. I would go in the pub. I'd have a pint and then leave and walk round to Greta's. I wouldn't go by the road, I'd go by the field at the rear of her house, there's a footpath – if you're local, you know it's there. This night, there was a man sitting in a van up the footpath, like he was hiding, sitting in his van, reading a paper.'

'Did you see what he looked like, get a registration number at all?'

'No, it was dark. I just didn't like the feel of it so I didn't go to see her and I rang her mobile, told her he was out there. This is an out of the way footpath, with a bloke sat in a van, not a local, pretending to read a newspaper in the dark, in the cold – it was all wrong. And there I am, sneaking around going into someone's house. I thought he might be waiting for me.'

'Big bloke like you, you could have anyone,' Sloper observed.

'I didn't know who or what he had in his van, did I? And my wife and kids are a couple of streets away. Anyway, as I said, I just got a bad vibe. Suppose I got a wake-up call. Stopped seeing her, ended it.'

'How did Greta take it?'

'She was upset. I was upset – but it was like, that night, well, I saw it for what it was.' Cooper shrugged.

'So how long would you say you saw each other?'

'Probably the best part of nine, months, I suppose. All the time I had the job and a few weeks after.'

'What – and she let it go just like that?'

'After a few calls to my mobile and she turned up here once, but I told her it was best for both of us. There was no animosity, she wasn't threatening me, threatening to tell the missus or anything. She just backed off.'

'Did you know she was on anti-depressants?'

'Yeah, so what? Mate, most the women at the school gate are on anti-depressants, my missus takes them now and then,' replied Cooper. 'Look, I wasn't horrible to her, I didn't have to be, didn't want to be. As I say, after a few phone calls and coming here on one occasion, she didn't bother me again.'

'And you say your missus didn't know?'

'No.'

'How can you be so sure?'

'Because I am. She'd soon let me know if she thought anything was going on,' replied Cooper.

'Did you not recognize or remember anything about the guy in the van?'

'No, only that it was a dark blue transit. I didn't know if he had a van load of blokes in it or hammers or whatever. And he definitely didn't want me to see who he was because he was just looking into his paper, using it to cover his face. Sitting there in the bloody dark.'

'If you're telling me a load of old shit, I'll come back for you, you know that, don't you?' said Sloper. 'While I'm here, I'll have a DNA test off you.' Sloper went back to his car and returned with a buccal swab kit.

'You're barking up the wrong tree here, mate,' said Cooper as Sloper bagged up the sample. 'You want to get on and find out who did it, so don't waste your time on me. She didn't deserve that.'

Sloper left. His next call was at The Phoenix, one of the local pubs. Situated in the centre of the village, its modern interior provided nooks and crannies in which to either sit in sofas, or at tables around a central bar area. Planting his bulk on a bar stool, Sloper leant on the bar and looked at the menu which contained offerings such as sea bass and puddings sprinkled with bee pollen. Pretentious shit, he thought. He held an outstretched hand containing a five pound note to get the barman's attention. Lunchtime trade was brisk.

'And what would you like, sir?' a barman enquired.

'Half a 6X, please,' Sloper replied.

'What are you,' said the barman as he poured the drink, 'a hack?'

'No mate, police. Had the hacks in, have you?' asked Sloper.

'Yeah, yesterday. It's all anyone here can talk about. We're not normally this busy at lunch times but the murder seems to have brought in a load of rubber necks.'

'Come in here, did she, Greta?'

The barman gave him a look.

'Yeah, her and Maxwell were good customers.'

'How did you find them, then?' ventured Sloper, glad to have stumbled upon an unexpected source of information.

'Easy going. They spent loads, they'd come in regularly when they were about together. The three of them would come in for an evening meal on a Friday – Maxwell, Greta and young James. Just Greta and James when there was no Maxwell. You could tell she loved the kid, even though he wasn't hers, more near his age group, I suppose. Loved their champagne they did. We started serving it by the glass because of them.'

'When was the last time they were in?' Sloper asked.

'Friday last week.'

'You sure?'

'Yep, Greta and James, the boy. Sat over there.' The barman pointed to a table in the bay window. 'He had lasagne and she had a Caesar salad. They came in most Friday evenings.'

'What time was this?'

''Bout 7 p.m. They left after about an hour or so.'

'They seem all right?'

'Yeah, perfectly all right.'

'And Greta, what was she like in general?' Sloper asked, looking out over the top of his glass, taking a long sip of beer.

'She was all right, nice bit of stuff mind, not that she'd look at the likes of me, but she was nice enough, not snotty either, considering they must have loads of money. They drove around here in their flash cars but she was pretty down to earth. Liked the men. Liked the attention. Not too popular with the women, though, the wives.'

'Why do you say that?'

'Well, bit of class, wasn't she? You could see that. She could wear a bin bag and still look like she'd come off a catwalk. Not that she ever wore a bin bag – expensive stuff, it always struck me.'

'Seen a lot of catwalks, have you?' asked Sloper sarcastically.

'No, mate, I haven't,' replied the barman, rising to Sloper's sarcasm, 'but you know what I mean. Anyway, when are you going to get anyone for it? Got suspects, have you?'

'Working on it, mate, working on it. Let us know if there's anything you can help with,' said Sloper.

'Yeah, I will.'

Sloper turned and surveyed the customers, making short work of his drink. He wondered what they would read in the local paper.

Graham Mellor had been looking into Curtis Coleman Ltd., and rang Temple with an update.

'We've done the usual checks, Companies House and all that. As I said, they're a security firm with an office based in London, in South Kensington, one in Melbourne and another in Kuwait. Their CEO is a guy called Adrian Coleman. He's ex-military, the website quotes that he retired as a Major in the Grenadier Guards.'

'Who's the Curtis in the partnership?'

'Well, that's what's interesting. Charlie Curtis is a pilot, ex-BA. Curtis Coleman also provides a private plane chartering facility, offering a world-wide service. Perhaps Maxwell Ashton-Jones was moonlighting on the quiet.'

CHAPTER 20

Temple made an early afternoon appointment to see James Ashton-Jones and travelled just outside Newbury to where he and Maxwell were staying with Jonathan Silvester. It was a large, new executive-type house, one of four in an exclusive cul-de-sac. Temple was greeted at the door by a woman in her mid-forties, dark hair piled up with a clip, clad in white jeans and teetering on red heels.

'Hello, Inspector, I am Rachel Hurst, Jonathan's girlfriend.'

'Hello, Rachel, how's everyone doing?'

'Oh, you know, bearing up. James is taking things very hard. He and Greta were close.'

'Did you know Greta?' Temple asked.

'Yes.'

'I will need to speak to you as well, while I'm here, if you don't mind.'

Rachel took Temple through the house to the garden. They walked through a large open plan kitchen/living space, where they stepped out onto a large paved area that framed a rectangular shaped pool. The late May sun was high in the sky and with no clouds to act as a filter, the sun had an intense heat. Temple saw Maxwell, James and Jonathan stood around the far corner of the pool, their heads together, talking quietly amongst themselves. You had to hand it to them, thought Temple – another pool – a seemingly innocent mechanism by which to look at practically naked women. He was curious to meet Jonathan Silvester; Kelly had told him about her meeting. What was it she had said – she'd never met a more arrogant bastard and believed Caroline Black's version of events.

Rachel alerted them to Temple's arrival and went into the kitchen to make coffee. The men moved to a parasoled table and the four sat down. Temple introduced himself to James Ashton-Jones.

James was tall, broad shouldered and muscular and looked older than his seventeen years. He quickly looked up at Temple from downcast eyes, red rimmed from crying. His eyes were partially hidden under a long thick fringe of hair that he had to keep sweeping to one side with his hand every time he looked up. Then each time, his hand returned and tucked securely back under his thighs.

'Do you play a lot of sport, James?' Temple ventured, in an attempt to put James at ease.

'Yes, rugby. Prop forward. A bit of cricket too.' His quiet voice was deep and respectful.

'No doubt your father and Jonathan have already explained some of the circumstances of your stepmother's death. I'm here to see you and for you to give me a statement, basically outlining your relationship with her and the last time you saw her. Does that make sense?' Temple spoke gently.

'Yes, of course,' he said, quickly looking across to his father.

'When did you last see Greta, James?' Temple asked.

'When I came home on Friday.' His downcast eyes focused on a spot on the table.

'You came home on Friday? It's just that the information I had from the cleaner, Irene Cresswell, was that you stayed with a friend last weekend.'

'No, well, yes I did, but I came home first. I was going to stay with him on the Friday night, but his parents weren't ready for me until Saturday, so I stayed at home on Friday and then went off.' He quickly looked up at Maxwell and Jonathan as if for affirmation.

'So can you talk me through, please, from when you arrived home on Friday?'

'Yes, sure,' he said shyly, still avoiding eye contact with Temple. 'I arrived home from school about half five. I'd caught the train to Bedwyn Station and got a taxi from there, home. Greta was by the pool when I got home so I showered and joined her for a quick swim before we walked up to The Phoenix for dinner.' James was quietly spoken as he gave his account.

'When you say she was by the pool, where exactly was she?' asked Temple.

'She was on a recliner, sunbathing,' he replied.

'What was she wearing, James?'

'Well, her bikini,' he said, reddening and looking across to his father and Jonathan Silvester.

'It's OK,' said Temple, 'You're doing great. So, you have a swim and then you go off, down the pub for dinner. How long do you think you were there for?'

''Bout an hour or so,' he replied, quietly.

'And then what?' Temple asked.

'We had dinner and then walked back to the house.'

'And then?'

'We watched some telly and then I went to bed.' Again, James looked up at Maxwell and Jonathan as if he was looking for approval, for confirming his story.

Rachel Hurst came out with a tray of coffee in cups and saucers. When she offered James his cup, he was forced to take his hands from under his thighs and as he took hold, the cup rattled in the saucer as his hands shook uncontrollably.

Jonathan took hold of it, with barely detectable annoyance.

‘Ray, do you think James could have a mug, please, I’m sure he’s more used to that than a cup and saucer.’ He tried to brush the matter off.

Temple scrutinized James intently; James had closed his eyes, whilst his father moved to put his arm around his shoulder.

‘I’m sorry, this must be so upsetting for you. If you like, we can stop?’ offered Temple.

‘Not too much longer, Mr Temple,’ said Maxwell, with a glare in his direction.

‘I won’t be, sir. If you can just tell me what time you left the house in the morning, James, and where you went, please?’

‘Yes. I, I think we left about 10-ish, I suppose. Greta gave me a lift to the station and I caught the train back to school where I was being picked up by the parents of my friend, Felix, Felix Harmon-Fford,’ he replied, trying a fleeting attempt at making eye contact with Temple.

‘And was this in the Porsche?’ asked Temple.

‘Yes.’

‘And do you know what Greta intended to do with the rest of her day?’

‘Yes, she said she was going to visit her father, Brett.’

‘And you? What did you do?’ Temple asked.

‘I just hung around with Felix.’

‘Did you return home at all?’

‘No, I went from Felix’s back to school,’ James replied, looking up into the middle distance.

‘And how would you describe the relationship you had with your stepmother, James—’ Temple asked.

‘Look, Inspector, I think he’s had enough now,’ interrupted Maxwell.

‘It’s all right, Dad.’ Staring down and fixing his eyes on the wooden feet of the table, James continued. ‘She was really fun, really sweet and she was really good to me.’ With that, he put his forefinger and thumb to his eyes.

‘That’s enough now, Inspector,’ said Jonathan.

'Yes, that will do. Thank you, James. I would like to see you for a few minutes, Maxwell, if that's OK?' Temple said. 'Perhaps we could go inside?'

They left the poolside for the kitchen area, as Silvester put a reassuring arm around the boy.

'You told me when we last spoke that you saw other women. Is there anyone in particular?' asked Temple.

'I am seeing a woman, yes,' said Maxwell, slowly.

'Did Greta know?'

'No, not to my knowledge. Our relationship might seem rather unconventional to you, Inspector, but I was nevertheless discreet,' Maxwell replied.

'I am going to need to know who she is, can you tell me her name and whereabouts, please?'

Maxwell sighed. 'Yes, Inspector. Antonia Peronelli, she lives near Windsor.'

'Sounds Italian to me,' said Temple.

'Yes, she's Italian. She's actually a countess of some small former province or township in La Marche,' explained Maxwell. 'Which makes her sound a lot grander than she actually is. But she's nothing to do with this, nothing at all.'

'I will have to go and see her. How long has your relationship been going on?'

'A year or more.'

'And were you planning on taking it further?' Temple asked.

'Yes. You may as well know, I was going to file for divorce. I love Antonia and she wants us to be together.'

'Can you see what I'm thinking, Maxwell?' Temple asked.

'I can see how all this might look, yes,' he conceded.

'That, suddenly, things are all rather convenient for you. They've turned out just a bit neatly for you, haven't they?' asked Temple.

'I didn't kill my wife, Inspector. I may not have been in love with her but it's easy for me to remember what attracted me to her. I'm just not good at being faithful. I guess I'm always looking for something better. And, of course, Antonia is easy to be with.'

'Meaning?'

'Meaning, I suppose, that I don't have to put up with any histrionics like I had to with Greta. I haven't got to wonder what I'm walking into every time I arrive home, wonder whether she's on an even keel. If she was down, she might be already half cut, if she was up, it was as if she was wired. Now I have love and consistency,' replied Maxwell.

'Does Antonia know that you are married?'

'Of course, I'm totally honest with her. Antonia and I spoke of my divorcing Greta. She knew that was my intention. There was no jealousy there, Inspector. Antonia has nothing to be jealous about. I was with Antonia more than I was with Greta in the last year. I wasn't always where I'd say I was and this allowed me to spend a lot of time with Antonia while Greta thought I was flying.'

Temple finished with Maxwell and went back out to the poolside. Jonathan was sitting on his own.

'I'd like to see Rachel now,' said Temple.

'What do you need to see Ray for?' asked Jonathan.

'She says she knew Greta,' said Temple, looking across to James, 'so I will need to speak to her.'

'Ray, Ray,' Jonathan called out. 'Can you come out here, please, the inspector wants to see *you* now.'

'That's OK, Mr Silvester, I'll go and see Rachel in the kitchen,' said Temple.

'Well, you can see her out here, with me.'

'No, that won't be necessary. As James is classed as a minor, it is only proper that you are with him when we talk. I can see Rachel on my own, thanks.'

Temple walked off to the kitchen where he found Rachel. She didn't quite seem his type, thought Temple, looking at her. She was attractive enough, but not in the same polished way as Greta.

'You said you knew Greta?' he asked.

'Well, when I say 'know' I mean, know socially. We used to meet up now and then of course, I met Greta and Maxwell through Jonathan,' Rachel explained.

'How long have you been having a relationship with Jonathan?' Temple asked.

'About a year now, perhaps a little more,' she said.

'And Jonathan, he works in finance; I believe he takes care of some of Maxwell's investments, would you know?' asked Temple.

'Yes, he does. Keeps a close eye on them for him, although I don't ask too much detail around that. All I know is, he says some of it is quite complex and often needs Maxwell's signature so he would often go over and leave paperwork at the house with Greta if Maxwell was away,' said Rachel.

I'm sure he did, thought Temple. And you didn't suspect a thing.

'And where were you last Saturday evening?' he asked.

'I was out with some girlfriends. Jonathan wanted to stay in and catch up with some paperwork so we agreed to meet up on Sunday.'

'Thanks, Rachel, that's all I need for now,' said Temple.

After explaining that he may need to speak to them all again at some point as the inquiry progressed, Temple left. His mobile rang, it was Sloper.

'I've just been over to the local pub. Greta and James were there on Friday,' he said.

'I know,' said Temple, 'I've just finished there, just seen James and he said the same. Interesting, though, he was a very nervous and upset young man. Only he and Brett Forrester have shown any emotion about Greta's death. I want some house-to-house done, Si, just two houses either side of the scene, as they're quite spaced out, do you think you and Kelly could manage that?'

'Sure.'

'I want to know what the neighbours thought about the comings and goings at Wedwellow House, what they saw. Go in the garden, Si, see if the pool was overlooked at all.'

'If she was my neighbour, I'd want to have a look,' said Sloper.

CHAPTER 21

Temple pulled over in a lay-by. He had been trying to gauge when best to put a call to Leigh to find out how Daisy had got on at the doctors but realized that as far as talking to him was concerned, there would be no good time for Leigh.

'Leigh, it's me. What happened at the doctor's?'

Expecting his call about Daisy, this time, her voice was hard edged.

'It was all right. She tried to get to the bottom of why she wasn't eating properly. She examined her, looked down her throat, examined her stomach.'

'Did they find anything?' Temple asked.

'No. She suggests that she goes to a child psychiatrist and we're waiting for a date,' Leigh replied, her voice hard and accusatory.

'A psychiatrist? Oh fuck.'

There was silence between them. Temple felt the guilt wash over him. This was his fault. He'd caused this situation. Even though he had no idea who the female was who had kept phoning their home, he'd done enough in the past to deserve Leigh throwing him out. And Daisy, caught between the two of them, had now it seemed been really affected by it.

For her part, Leigh was frightened and angry with herself, as well as with Temple and felt helpless. Their little girl was being damaged by them; perhaps she should have kept her family together, not been so hasty to have thrown Temple out. Perhaps she should have forgiven him. And there she was again, blaming herself. She felt her anger suddenly rise up.

'Is that it? That's your answer to everything, isn't it? I'm going off my head here with worry. This is what you get, these are the consequences of your actions, you selfish bastard.' She ended the call.

A familiar pain shot up inside Temple's neck as it jarred with tension. He couldn't just leave things like that. He tried to continue the conversation using a quick round of texting which ended with him having to turn down an offer of a few hours with Daisy due to the commitments of the investigation, giving Leigh the opportunity to end the text exchange with more abuse. At least he'd been able to text her that King was no longer a threat. The pain in his neck began to creep up into his head as he stared at the phone cradled in his hand. He had barely time to digest the news about Daisy when his mobile rang. It was Finch.

'I've got some news for you, Mr Temple.'

'Go on, Finch, make my day,' replied Temple, drily.

'I got a visit last night. Someone came asking if Paul King had left anything behind in the flat. Said they were after a gun,' said Finch.

'Who was it, Finch?'

'Georgie Munt. The Fortunes sent him round. Paul King got in touch with them from prison. Took a mobile in with him. Your boys obviously didn't fancy an intimate search,' Finch replied.

'Get on with it, Finch. What did you tell him?'

'Well, I searched his room, didn't I? Couldn't find anything. King says that it came from your house and that I must have it because the pigs didn't find it when they nicked him.'

'You've got a problem then, Finch,' said Temple.

'I haven't got his fucking gun – *your* fucking gun,' said Finch, his voice rising.

'Then you'd better tell them there was no gun.'

'But there was. He told me about it.'

'Did you see it?'

'No,' admitted Finch.

'Then there was no gun. If the cops didn't find it when they searched his stuff and you haven't got it, it didn't exist in the first place. He's just told you some moody old story about finding a gun at my place to fit me up. Despite what you say, Finch, he was at my place because he set it on fire and then stole a letter of mine with my wife's name on it. They found this at your flat, in his bag. He was going to go after her next. So for all your trouble in giving him an alibi that night, you can now deal with the Fortunes and King on your own. That's what you get for being a lying bastard. Perhaps it'll teach you where your loyalties lie.' Temple was in no mood for Finch.

'Thanks a fucking bunch, Temple. Perhaps you'll get called out to investigate my fucking body in a ditch next. You won't have to look far, it'll be the Fortunes,' spat Finch.

'Oh piss off, Finch.' Temple ended the call.

He thought getting King back into prison would be an end to it. Now the Fortunes were looking for the gun – he didn't need this aggravation.

Finch was right to be bothered though, thought Temple. From the time he'd worked in Trowbridge, he knew Munt had a reputation as a nasty bastard. The Fortunes were a domiciled gypsy family, led by brothers, Caleb and Elijah. They had an unofficial four acre set up, referred to by the local police as 'South Fork' on former waste land. They had created an impenetrable gated community for themselves and their extended family, unchallenged by authority. The Fortunes, Munt and King were cousins, brought up alongside each other and as teenagers, had formed a strong bond. Hierarchy was calculated by how much money they brought in. This motivated the younger ones who wanted to emulate their elders but knew they needed to earn their right to swagger.

Like a pair of modern day Fagins, Caleb and Elijah unleashed their offspring on the unsuspecting community and surrounding counties. Using their extensive and collective cunning, they preyed on the frail and elderly to confuse and bewilder them into parting with life savings for gardening and repair work, or, disguised variously as gas, water, electric or other officials, they blatantly burgled. And while the kids went out to play, Caleb and Elijah were part of a thriving network processing high end stolen goods, mainly gold and gems. A spot of metal theft and harbouring also kept the wolf from the door.

But King, always the wildest of the bunch, had gone too far. His violence and imprisonment had put the spotlight on them. Raids by the law were to be avoided at all costs and King had made himself a liability. When he came out, the Fortunes told King to leave Temple alone, that it would be like stirring a hornet's nest, but he wouldn't listen to them. But then King came back with a gun. Currency. Then suddenly the gun disappeared. Now back inside, Munt took King's instructions for dealing with Temple and retrieving the gun.

Temple knew Tara would be bothered by Munt. The last thing he needed was her panicked phone calls to him about the Fortunes. They might give Finch a good slap; as Temple saw it, he deserved that for lying for King. With the Fortunes and Munt after the gun, he knew he had to get rid of it. More than that, he was breaking the law and with King back in prison, he had no excuse for this. He took the ammunition, three bullets, out of the gun and put them in his pocket. He'd throw them in the Kennet and Avon canal at his first opportunity.

Temple searched for some painkillers in his pockets. He found the sleeping pills. Unbroken sleep was something which eluded Temple at the best of times. The constant stream of information about the case, about King, Tara and Finch, reduced his ability to sleep further still. When the case was over he promised himself a sleeping pill, until then he'd have to bear the consequence of lack of sleep. He looked in the glove compartment; under the gun was a packet containing the last two Anadin. Needing them quickly in his system and with no water to hand, he chewed them as he drove back to Marlborough Station.

It had been a long day and in company with Kelly, Temple read through the recent statements they had obtained.

'The new one, boss, from Michael Cooper is interesting. It mentions a van down beside the lane next to Wedwellow House,' said Kelly.

'What kind of van?' asked Temple.

'A blue transit. The house-to-house might pick something up. He might have been just passing and sitting up to take a break in his journey, but Cooper suggests he was a bit too far down the lane for that.'

'We need to trace it,' said Temple. 'We still need to find who took the photos in Savernake Forest and it could be this guy.'

'The Hi Tech guys have also finished with the iPads from the house too,' said Kelly.

'What took them so bloody long?' said Temple.

'We were at the back of the queue, the Swindon job took priority. It seems that Greta had a Facebook page but wasn't too regular a user. Neither did she have a Twitter account. She used her iPad mainly to email and FaceTime Caroline Black and Maxwell. There was nothing untoward found on it. The computer found in the study had accounts on it, which have been passed to the Financial Team. Again, nothing of note, no porn or anything extreme,' reported Kelly.

'OK, put these statements into the Holmes inputter.'

'When you read all the statements, boss, the picture of Greta's life is emerging ...' ventured Kelly.

'When you read the statements, Kelly, it tells you that people are lying. The information from Dianna Forrester and

Caroline Black suggest that Greta was being manipulated by the men in her life. Ashton-Jones now has two dead wives which stinks. Caroline is our star witness at the moment and I don't think she's telling us all she knows. Everyone's holding back. They're all withholding information.'

The peace in the room shattered as the office door banged loudly against the wall and Sloper entered.

'I see you've made the local papers,' said Sloper throwing the *Wiltshire Daily Record* onto a table.

'I haven't spoken to a rag,' said Temple.

'You've been verballed then. We'll be lucky to keep this out of the nationals. "Sex Murder Riddle", they're calling it,' said Sloper. 'And believe me, you don't want them breathing down your neck.'

Temple picked up the paper to see the banner headlines on the front page. He was quoted and misquoted.

'That's fucking de la Hay. Everything I said to him and things I didn't. That would be Rob Carroll's input,' said Temple, referring to the editor, who wasn't known for his pro-police stance or respect for the truth. Locals had expressed their 'shock' and 'horror' at the murder, amongst the comments about Greta and Maxwell described as being 'a lovely couple.' Carroll stoked public concern by continuing with a two-page spread, containing a timeline of events.

'Who gave him all this information?' asked Temple, as he looked at the coverage.

Sloper pulled a face and shrugged.

With hacks on the trail, Temple knew he now had to step up the pace of the inquiry. He had to keep ahead of the press in terms of information. He had to make a further arrest soon, or the hacks would publicly crucify him in the absence of a suspect and the desire to show their investigative superiority over the police. And enjoy doing it in the process. He had to get the DNA results and make some real progress soon.

Temple suspected it was also only a matter of time before he was expelled from the inquiry by Harker, courtesy of Sloper's reporting back on the lack of progress. Yet so far, Harker had left him there. His eyes went to Greta's picture on the whiteboard again. Piecing together her life and last moments of it was now all consuming. He wanted to bring her killer to justice. And he had to do it before the press used him like a punch bag and offered him up to Harker on a plate.

'How did you get on with the house-to-house?' Temple asked Sloper.

'Greta was my kind of woman, I wish I'd met her.'

'Like she'd have given you a second look,' said Kelly under her breath.

'I heard that. Like you wouldn't have had a go too, given half the chance,' Sloper shot back.

Kelly looked at him with loathing; she hated it when people thought they had a right to comment on her love life. He was getting on her nerves, just his presence was starting to annoy her. There were times when he stood way too close to her and she didn't like it.

'Fuck off,' she spat.

'Now, now,' taunted Sloper, 'you can't tell me you wouldn't have fancied her?'

Kelly rose to the bait. 'You don't know anything about me.' She stood up to confront him.

'I wouldn't be too sure about that,' said Sloper, 'you and your little girlfriend who works up at the bank. I can just imagine what you get up to … in fact, I *do* imagine.'

'You're like something out of the fucking Dark Ages, I bet imagine is all *you* do these days—'

Before Sloper could retaliate, Temple cut in. 'All right you two, enough.' Kelly sat down.

'So, who would like to hear what I have found on house-to-house?' said Sloper, as if their spat hadn't happened.

'Come on, Si, don't fuck about,' said Temple.

'Well, I went back to the scene. I went outside, into the garden, by the pool. And looking up, you can just about see the top bedroom window of the nearest house next door to the left. That's right in direct line with the poolside. So I went to the house on the left and spoke to a nice couple who let me in. I went upstairs to their back bedroom and lo and behold, there was a pair of bins on the window shelf. They'd been watching all the activity going on in the inquiry. On speaking to the husband though, on his own, he told me that on sunny days, he'd catch a peek at Greta laid out by the pool. The incentive for him was that she would often sunbathe topless.'

'I don't suppose he was out twitching last Friday, was he?' asked Temple.

'Oh yes. He's retired, and knowing Greta's habits, he knew that twenty-two degrees would fetch her out to the pool and sunbathing. He actually said that about the temperature. Brings a whole new reason for listening to the weather forecast in the morning. Twenty-two degrees and he knew he was on for a peek,' chuckled Sloper.

'Anyway, more to the point, he's seen Greta and James having more than a step-motherly peck on the cheek. According to him, they were more likely to have their tongues down each other's throats and hands all over each other. And more besides, I wouldn't mind betting. Seems they were more like boyfriend and girlfriend. A real wicked stepmother.'

CHAPTER 22

Right then Temple's mobile rang.

'Hi, boss, its Jackie. Just thought you'd like to know we had a negative DNA result for Michael Cooper and a result for Maxwell Ashton-Jones.'

'And?' he asked, hanging on her every word.

'Negative.'

'Negative on all counts?'

'Yes, no familial, including the foetus,' she replied.

That should also put James Ashton-Jones out of the picture in terms of DNA, thought Temple. So, Greta was carrying another man's child, or would have been, if she'd lived.

'OK, thanks, Jackie.'

Temple updated Kelly and Sloper. He looked at his watch and rang the Telecommunications office to request mobile phone data.

'I need some inquiries done around four names in my case – Brett Forrester, Jonathan Silvester, Maxwell Ashton-Jones and James Ashton-Jones. I'm interested in activity between them a week prior to the murder and since and where Maxwell Ashton-Jones is concerned, a list of calls he made two months prior to the murder.'

'OK, we'll identify the service providers for each, put a priority one on them and request the information.'

'How long do you think it'll take?' Temple asked.

'Well, once we get the superintendent's sign off, depending on who the providers are, could be twenty-four hours or two to three days.'

Temple knew he had no choice but to wait while his colleagues conducted the inquiries he had requested of them. He knew that the lack of DNA evidence meant he would need to cast the net wider, but he remained convinced that the murderer would have been known to Greta.

'Doesn't the fact that we couldn't match Maxwell's DNA rule him out?' said Kelly.

'All that tells us is that Maxwell wasn't one of the two men who last had sex with Greta, neither was he the father of her child. The fact that she was carrying another man's child gives him a motive,' said Temple.

'He was still abroad when she was murdered so how can he have done it?'

'For all we know Greta could have told him she was pregnant when she found out. Maybe he worked out that he couldn't be the father. We have to be absolutely sure that he could not have come back from his stopover in Singapore. Si, can you make inquiries with BA? I want to know if it's possible for someone, a member of staff, to get aboard a plane without appearing on any inventory or booking system. Whether it's just possible to slip back into the country under the radar.'

'It's a bit far-fetched. He'd still have to get through passport control and get back to Singapore to carry on the next leg of his journey,' said Sloper, thinking that Temple was becoming increasingly desperate. He'd look forward to his next conversation with Harker; he felt sure he'd pull Temple off the inquiry once he told him of his latest thought processes.

'I know, I know, but maybe that's what Maxwell wants it to look like. I just think we need to make the inquiries before we can discount it and until it becomes an absolute impossibility, it's still a possibility. I want someone to tell me it's impossible.'

Sloper shrugged.

'If he knew about the pregnancy, he could also have put someone else up to it, commissioned it, while he was out of the country,' said Temple.

'But I thought you said he didn't seem to know she was pregnant,' said Kelly.

'That's how it seemed to me but maybe I'm wrong,' said Temple. 'We're going to need DNA samples from Jonathan Silvester. I'll need to question Brett Forrester again and we'll need to find out exactly what Maxwell's involvement was with Curtis Coleman. We'll also need a DNA sample from Brett Forrester.'

'What, her own father?' questioned Sloper, thinking he'd have to ring Harker sooner than he anticipated.

'Yes, they were close, according to Greta's mother, too close. She suspected them of having a sexual relationship although her psychiatrist didn't confirm it. Perhaps they were and that relationship was still ongoing,' replied Temple.

The more he thought about it, the more he was convinced that the answer lay with the men closest to her. They were all covering something up.

*

In the morning, Temple instructed Kelly to go and see Antonia Peronelli at Windsor. He also knew he needed to try and break into the close relationships of Ashton-Jones and Silvester.

'Si, can you ring Maxwell and make an appointment to see him and James this afternoon? We need to time this right. I'm going to see Forrester this morning and I want you to see them at 12.30, no later. Can you see if you can arrange that and ring and let me know?'

Temple had received a text message from the force press office. The media interest in the case was ramping up and the local news station wanted to do a piece to camera. Temple met the crew outside the Headquarters building and finished in one take, before driving off to see Brett Forrester.

Sloper rang him en route.

'The meeting is set up for 12.30 as you asked. What are you up to?' asked Sloper.

'None of them are being as forthcoming as they should, they're all hiding their own bits of information about Greta. And they're very tight. I want to shake things up a bit. None of them have said they know about Greta's pregnancy. I'm going to tell Brett Forrester when I get there. I suspect that he'll be straight on the phone to Maxwell when I've gone. Now you've made your appointment, you'll see the effect the news has on them when you turn up. Tell them you also want a DNA sample from Jonathan Silvester and James Ashton-Jones.'

'But any familial DNA would have shown from Maxwell's DNA sample,' Sloper pointed out, thinking that now Temple really was going all over the place.

'Just get it, please, Si,' Temple instructed.

'I'll report back,' said Sloper. He'd been watching Temple closely and now he was sure he'd lost the plot. Still, he was happy to follow his orders – it would help him inform Harker, give him more reason to drag Temple off the inquiry.

It was 11.30 in the morning and Forrester met him at the door with a tumbler half full of Jack Daniels.

'How are you, Mr Forrester?' Temple knew he wouldn't take kindly to any advice from him about staying away from the bottle. He needed him to be fairly sober if what he had in mind had any chance of working.

Shown into his study again, Temple's eyes went immediately to find the pictures on the wall that he'd seen previously. The wall was bare.

'Coping, Inspector, just coping. Is there a break-through, are you here to tell me you've made an arrest?'

‘I’m actually after some more information to help us and to give you some information. As you know, we’re trying to build this picture of Greta, of her lifestyle, to help find her killer. Seems she led a more complicated life than one might expect. She was having a relationship with Jonathan Silvester that her husband knew about. Were you aware of this?’

‘Yes,’ he replied.

‘You didn’t say previously,’ said Temple, surprised.

‘You didn’t ask,’ Forrester retorted. It was clear the glass of whisky wasn’t his first or his second that morning.

‘I think I asked you if you knew if she had any extra marital relationships and you said no.’

‘I don’t think I was actually thinking, Inspector. Yes, I knew about Jonathan, she confided in me.’ He ran his fingers through his hair and drank deeply from the glass.

‘What did she say about that relationship?’ asked Temple.

‘I don’t remember, Inspector,’ Forrester replied, clearly agitated with Temple’s questioning.

‘Did she say whether she was happy with the way he treated her, for example?’ Temple persisted.

‘What do you mean?’ Forrester walked away for a refill.

‘Meaning that Caroline Black has suggested Greta was under some duress to continue the relationship with Silvester. She suggests that he told Greta unless their relationship continued, he would tell Maxwell, when in fact, Maxwell knew all about their relationship.’

‘I, I didn’t know that. She never said that she was unhappy in her relationship with Jonathan,’ Forrester replied, walking slowly towards the door.

‘Did she say if it had ended?’

‘She said she didn’t see him so much anymore. Look, perhaps Caroline got the wrong end of the stick. She can be a bit highly strung.’ Forrester turned his back on Temple as he refilled his glass. At the rate he was going, Temple knew he had to speed things up.

'The pictures that you had on the wall there, they've gone,' said Temple, wanting his eye contact again. Forrester turned round.

'Yes. I couldn't bear it, I couldn't bear to see her … so alive.' Forrester looked at the empty wall, his voice now broken with emotion. 'I had to take them down.'

'I saw James Ashton-Jones yesterday, sir. James confirmed he had visited home on the Friday but was with friends on Saturday and the rest of the weekend,' offered Temple.

'I see.'

'We have also had the results of DNA tests from Maxwell; they were negative.'

'Well, I would have been surprised if they hadn't been, since Maxwell was out of the country.'

Temple tapped his pocket.

'Excuse me, sir, my phone is vibrating. I'll just take this call.' Temple went out of the room and down the hallway. He feigned a quick conversation before going back.

'I have to make my way back to the station, sir. Further developments. You said you would have been surprised to find Maxwell's DNA at the scene? I also came here to tell you that Greta was nine weeks pregnant at the time of her death.'

Forrester's eyes widened. 'She was pregnant?' He wasn't expecting this.

'Yes, sir. As I say, I have to go back to the station.'

Forrester was sufficiently distracted by the new information as Temple hoped he would be.

The prospect of also losing a grandchild – Greta's child – had suddenly completely overwhelmed his thoughts.

Temple left and drove back to Marlborough Police Station where he met Sloper.

'I think it worked,' said Sloper. 'What time did you leave Forrester?'

'Quarter past twelve. Told him I had to come back here and left him having just told him about Greta being pregnant.

He must have been straight on the phone to Maxwell as soon as I left.'

'I arrived at 12.30 on the dot and the door was opened by some Rachel bird,' replied Sloper. 'I said I wanted to see James as arranged and she said she didn't think that would be possible as he was upstairs with Maxwell. He was being sick.'

CHAPTER 23

'They know something,' said Temple. 'They all know something and they're all covering up. Did you see James at all?'

'No. Maxwell came down to see me in the hallway. He said that James had been violently ill, must have been something he ate.'

'Where was Jonathan?' Temple asked.

'Apparently with James, in the bathroom. Maxwell looked grey. I asked him if he was all right and he said yes, but he thinks they all must have suddenly got a bug as he didn't feel so good.'

'They're lying,' said Temple.

'I said I'd go back later, about five. I'll take a buccal swab kit with me and get James's DNA,' said Sloper.

'James must be involved for them to have told the kid and it's turned his stomach.'

'If he was your weakest link though, you'd have thought they would have withheld it from him,' observed Sloper.

'You would, unless he's involved in some way. Something's going on and we need to find out what it is. There's not enough to nick any one of them yet and I don't want any of them running to Anthony de la Hay crying foul play with us. We need to get them out and get some intrusive surveillance in there.'

'You'll have to get it past Harker first,' remarked Sloper.

Temple returned to Brett Forrester. There was no answer from the house. Temple peered into the windows of the study. There was no sign of Forrester. He walked around the back, peering into the windows of the kitchen; still no sign. Looking through another window, Temple looked into the lounge and although Forrester was not there, the French doors had been left open onto the garden. Temple walked round to them. Looking down the garden, he could see a summer house. He walked across the lawn towards it. Sitting inside, Brett Forrester was slumped in a chair, looking at the floor, a whisky glass cradled in his hands. He looked up as Temple approached.

'Twice in one day,' quipped Forrester, as he drew himself up straight in the chair.

'I knocked on the door, sir, no answer,' replied Temple.

'That would have been an indication to some that I didn't want to see them,' said Forrester, unimpressed with the intrusion.

'Is now not a good time, sir?' asked Temple, with no intention of leaving without speaking to him.

'There's probably never going to be another good time, Inspector. Let's go back into the house, into the study.' Forrester led the way, heading straight for the drinks tray to top up his glass. He hadn't intended for Temple to see him like this again and thought he'd seen the last of him for the day.

'Mr Forrester, on a previous visit, you had a series of photographs on the wall depicting a naked woman, but almost in the form of landscapes. Do you still have them?' Temple asked.

'Yes.'

'Could I have a look at them, please?'

'I put them somewhere, I'm not sure where,' said Forrester.

'Why did you take them down?' asked Temple.

'They were on the wall with the pictures of Greta. The wall looked bare once I took the pictures of Greta down, so I took them all down,' Forrester explained.

'I'd really like to take a look at them. If you remember, I remarked on them. They were extraordinary, once you realized that what you were looking at was a woman's body and not a landscape at all,' said Temple.

Forrester became evasive.

'I'll look them out for you at some point, Inspector,' he replied.

'Who was the model in the photos, Mr Forrester?'

'I ... I'm not sure where I've put them but perhaps the next time you come ...' said Forrester in an attempt to deflect the question.

'The model, who was she?' Temple persisted.

'Look, I'm not sure what the relevance of this is,' said Forrester, sighing.

'I'd like to see them again, do you remember who the model was?'

'Yes, I remember, of course I do.'

'Mr Forrester,' said Temple slowly, 'I was at Greta's post mortem.'

Understanding of what Temple was saying suddenly hit Forrester. It would be no use trying to lie. Forrester realized Temple knew. He looked back at him.

'It was Greta,' he said, 'but then, it seems, you know that.'

'Well, there was a birthmark that looked familiar. With the model's face not being revealed, it would be difficult to tell unless of course you knew the model intimately. From memory, Mr Forrester, those were very intimate photos. Very cleverly shot, but all the same, very personal.'

Forrester's face hardened. Temple could almost see his brain working away, working out through the whisky what he would disclose, what he thought he could get away with not saying.

'How long ago were they taken, Mr Forrester?' Temple asked.

'I'm not sure now ... a few years ago ...'

'You said they were part of an exhibition if I remember rightly?'

'Correction, they *were* the exhibition, Mr Temple.'

'Where was that?'

'A gallery in Chelsea, a friend of mine had it and let me exhibit there,' Forrester explained.

'You lived in London, didn't you, Mr Forrester, when Greta came to stay with you?'

'Yes, I did. You know that, Mr Temple.'

'How old was Greta when you took the photographs, Mr Forrester?'

'I actually don't remember.'

'How old was she? Was she in her teens?' asked Temple, ignoring Forrester's attempt at an apparent selective memory lapse.

'Maybe. I can't remember.'

'Was she over the age of consent?' Temple persisted.

Forrester flashed a look at Temple.

'You see, Mr Forrester, I have a problem with those photographs. They're strangely erotic but erotic nonetheless. And they are of your daughter. How does that happen?'

'What do you want me to say then, Inspector?' said Forrester, clearly annoyed. 'Eh? What is it you want?'

'The truth, Mr Forrester. Dianna Forrester made a comment to my officer that "evil had found evil" when she visited Greta when she was living with you.'

Forrester snorted at the mention of Dianna Forrester's name.

'You won't find a good word about me from that woman, or for Greta come to that. Look, me and Greta, we had something, something unique. I had lived as I wanted, did as I pleased, answered to no one and lived my life completely as I wished. And then Greta turns up.'

'And then what?'

'And then she had to fit in with it. Which she did. I was busy at that time. I'd settled in London from travelling around the world, experiencing many cultures, places, people, conflicts, war. My work was in demand, *National Geographic*, *The Times*, *Times* magazine. I had quite a portfolio to unleash and I also wrote about my experiences. I was a free agent and I settled in London and basically just carried on. In my own way.'

'Did you have girlfriends?' asked Temple.

'Many. Mostly models. Once they find out you're a photographer, they latch onto you and can't wait to take their clothes off. Is that what you wanted to hear?'

'Only if it's the truth. And what about now?'

'I've no shortage of women, Inspector. You've seen Alice, another model, no doubt she thinks I can help her career in some way. So our arrangement suits us both. There are others besides.'

'And can you help Alice's career?' asked Temple, thinking she had the rough end of their bargain.

'Maybe. I don't force her to come here; she's a willing participant – very eager to please.'

Forrester met Temple's gaze. Arrogant bastard, thought Temple.

'And how old is Alice?'

Forrester snorted. 'Alice is nineteen.'

'And so, back to the photographs. They're of Greta,' stated Temple.

Forrester remained silent.

'Mr Forrester?'

'She too was a willing participant, Inspector. You can't make someone lie for hours while you get the light right and their position in a certain way. A lot of work goes into that kind of photography. It's not point and shoot,' he said, disdainfully.

'You're quite a charismatic man, Mr Forrester. I suspect you can get people, women, to do pretty much what you want them to,' said Temple, thinking of Alice and the age gap between her and Forrester.

'I can't answer that.'

'What did Dianna mean, Mr Forrester?' asked Temple.

'As I've told you, you can't set any store by anything that woman says. She's very bitter and has always been jealous of Greta.'

'Why would she be jealous of her own daughter? What do you mean by that?' asked Temple.

Forrester stayed silent, drinking deep from his glass.

'Mrs Forrester also said that when she visited her daughter at your flat, that there was only one bed,' Temple continued, slowly, looking at Forrester intently. 'She says that Greta had made it quite clear to her that you were in fact sleeping together.'

Forrester looked back him, his face hard.

'Listen to what my ex-wife says at your peril, Inspector. She's a very bitter woman. It won't lead you to Greta's killer,' Forrester said, dismissively.

Temple persisted. 'Someone took some photographs of Greta, a few months ago, while she was having sex with a man called Marcus Hussain. Did she say anything to you about this, Mr Forrester?'

'No, she didn't,' Forrester answered, with a shrug.

'Did you take the photographs of them?'

'No, Inspector.'

Temple watched Forrester intently, but he gave nothing away. Even with the best part of a bottle of whisky on board, Forrester's guard was up. Temple knew he had to be careful not to alienate him, despite his suspicions regarding the relationship with his own daughter. He backed off. He believed him about the photos.

'You understand why I had to ask, Mr Forrester, given your background and the photographs you have taken of Greta.'

'I understand, Inspector, but this won't find Greta's killer. I adored her, Maxwell adored her, and what worries me is that you're not casting your net wider. I would have thought the person who took the photographs might be a main line of your inquiry,' replied Forrester.

'They are, sir, hence my questioning. The majority of murders are carried out by someone known to the victim. Talking of Maxwell, were you aware that his first wife, Olivia, died by drowning in Riyadh?'

'Yes, I am aware. It was tragic.' Forrester busied himself emptying the whisky bottle.

'Yeah, tragic is one way of putting it,' said Temple, insincerely.

Temple watched Forrester's face; watched as he took in the intonation of Temple's words. A barely perceptible look appeared in Forrester's eyes and he looked back at him. Temple reckoned he'd planted a tiny seed of suspicion and now he had to water it.

'Did Maxwell tell you about it?' asked Temple.

'Yes, briefly.'

'And now he's lost his second wife ...' As he spoke, Temple could see Forrester was thinking. Temple waited, hoping that Forrester was considering the prospect of a man losing two young wives. 'I have to go, Mr Forrester, back to the station. If you don't mind, I'll come back later, perhaps tomorrow.'

'If you have to.' Forrester was relieved.

'Yes, if you don't mind, I'd like a DNA sample. I'll bring my kit tomorrow.'

Temple went back to the incident room to look through statements again to make sure he hadn't missed anything. Although he was alone, he had to try hard to concentrate on what he was reading. He felt as if he was trying to take on more information than his brain would allow. His stomach was empty and yet it didn't crave food. He had hardly slept or eaten and yet adrenalin pumped through his body like an injection of speed. He looked at the photo of Greta stuck on the whiteboard.

Here, in the quiet of the room, Temple studied her image again, remembering all that had been said about her. On the outside, it must have appeared she had it all; beauty, adoring husband, designer clothes, money, fast cars – the perfect lifestyle. When she's murdered, along comes the inquiry team who strip all that away and lay it bare for all to see, examine every crevice of her life and pull it apart. It was, in fact, as far away from perfect as you could get, thought Temple. The press would have a field day when they got hold of it.

He was jolted out of his thoughts as Kelly came in, back from her visit to Antonia Peronelli. She was eager to impart her information. Much to her annoyance, Sloper came crashing in before she started. He took up his position leaning back in a chair with his feet up on the desk.

'She was quite a nice woman, actually,' said Kelly.

Sloper eyed her from across the room.

'Oh yeah?' he said, suggestively. Kelly looked back at him, not disguising her dislike for him.

'In that she was really respectful towards Greta—' she said.

Sloper cut across her. 'What, considering that she was screwing her husband—'

'In terms of Greta being dead. She said it was an enormous shock, she had held Greta no malice and was in fact now quite remorseful of her affair with Maxwell. She said she loved Maxwell and would shortly be coming here to be with him, now their circumstances had changed.'

'Fucking waste of time you going there, wasn't it?' said Sloper. 'If that's all you've come back with. You could have spoken to her over the phone.' He'd rung Clive Harker earlier and told him that the inquiry was heading for disaster.

Kelly ignored him and continued.

'She did, though, have an MG on the drive and a rather nice painting on the wall, very much the same as described by Caroline Black.'

'So not sold, as Greta told Caroline,' said Temple, 'but moved to the new love nest.'

CHAPTER 24

AT 5 P.M., Sloper drove back to Jonathan Silvester's house to speak to James Ashton-Jones. His reception was rather cool, with Silvester showing Sloper into the open plan kitchen where both Maxwell and James were sitting together on a sofa.

'Evening, gents,' said Sloper. 'Look, I won't keep you long. We're continuing our inquiries, as you would expect and part of those inquiries are forensics. We need to cover all bases and that includes fingerprinting and swabbing at the crime scene. Since the crime scene was your home, I'd like to take fingerprints and buccal swabs for DNA. This will help us to identify any DNA that is not from one of you. So I'll need a swab from both yourself, James and you too, Jonathan.'

James looked at his father next to him and then to Jonathan Silvester, who was still standing next to Sloper. He watched them. Despite their best efforts, Sloper could see there was obvious tension between the three of them.

'Anything wrong?' asked Sloper.

'No. No, Sergeant, you do what needs to be done,' said Jonathan.

Sloper pitched his briefcase onto a marble work surface. He took out two buccal swab kits, an ink pad and blank fingerprint forms. He invited James to the table. As Sloper grasped James's hand, he felt it shake as he pressed his fingers into the ink pad and onto the blank squares of the fingerprint forms laid out on the table in front of them.

'You all right, James?' said Sloper, attempting to sound genuinely concerned.

'Yes,' he whispered, feigning confidence.

'Them sudden stomach bugs are vicious,' said Sloper. 'Right, next hand,' and he continued the task.

The silence ratcheted the tension in the room.

Sloper continued to watch James's face as he proceeded to ink his fingers and press them onto the sheet, filling the blank spaces. James was clearly in turmoil. The rims of his eyes brimmed with tears so precariously that Sloper expected at any second they would cascade down his cheeks. Sloper continued to observe as, miraculously, somehow, James's ever-swelling lower lids acted as perfect dams to ensure no breach occurred and, in a blink, his tears remained swimming in his eyes.

'Right, now for the buccal swab. If you just rub this stick on the inside of your cheek for me, give it a good wipe round,' Sloper instructed, as James took the swab. Sloper was willing James to break down but somehow he managed to blink away his tears and recover himself.

Sloper repeated the process for a none too pleased Jonathan Silvester. Once the tests were taken, Sloper packed away the kits.

'DI Temple also wanted me to update you further on tests from the pathologist. It appears that Greta, Mrs Ashton-Jones, was nine weeks pregnant.' Sloper looked at all three; James immediately hung his head and looked at the floor as Maxwell and Jonathan both went to speak at once.

'That's shocking news,' said Maxwell. 'I mean, I, I didn't know that.'

Jonathan put his hand on his friend's shoulder. James remained silent. Sloper knew that Temple was right; they had already digested this information by their controlled reaction.

'As spoken about already, be on your guard concerning the press. They may try to phone you or turn up on the doorstep. I suggest you check anyone who asks you questions before making your answer. If they say they're police, ask to see their warrant card. It will look like this.' Sloper showed his warrant card.

'That's me done for now, gents, unless, of course, you have any questions yourselves?' said Sloper.

'No, Sergeant, thank you. We'll see you again soon, no doubt.' Jonathan Silvester showed Sloper out.

Back at Marlborough, Sloper gave himself a fanfare as he walked through the door.

'I have the DNA,' he said, as he put his haul onto a desk.

'Thanks, Si. Make sure you get it over to forensics and fast track it. I want a twenty-four hour turnaround,' said Temple, intently looking at a computer. 'So, how did it go – how was James?' he added, looking up from the screen.

'He's one very nervous young man. He's going to crumble. Talk about the weakest link. He's it,' said Sloper.

Kelly came in from an adjoining office.

'I'm making progress with Olivia Ashton-Jones, boss.'

'Enlighten us, Kel,' said Temple, taking another look through a file containing Maxwell's financial records.

'I've found the link to Curtis Coleman,' she said, coolly.

Temple looked up.

'The Saudi police were all over Olivia's death when it was discovered she had alcohol in her bloodstream. They forbid drinking but expats are known to obtain it illegally either by smuggling it in or by making their own. Even now, expats usually stick together, living in their own communities, often in gated compounds and because they're not out amongst the locals drinking, turning a blind eye is tolerated, so long as no one is caught of course. Hotels don't serve alcohol either so back then, when crews flew in, they generally had some stashed on them.

'The coroner's file contains witness statements. All involved denied drinking that evening, except one hostess, Ann Powell, who provides the only account of the party. Even she waited until she was back in the UK before she gave her statement. She says that as was the norm, they started having a room party where they broke out the booze. The room was booked by Jonathan Silvester. Other English hostesses and pilots were invited. During the course of the evening, someone suggested swimming in the pool and they traipsed between the room and pool at various times, via the hotel lift.

'Powell says that the party quickly got out of hand as drunken men and women flirted with each other in the pool and in the lifts, using the opportunity of going between both to go off to each other's rooms. Olivia had been seen talking with Jonathan Silvester in the pool that evening and was pissed off with Maxwell flirting with other women. He disappeared at one point and Jonathan and Olivia were together in the pool. Ann Powell said they started to argue when Jonathan also continued to flirt with women. Powell says that two different hostesses told her that Maxwell was having sex with another hostess at the time Olivia was found in the pool. Silvester was left to find him and tell him. Anyway, as soon as it becomes known about Olivia, the partygoers clear the room of all traces of alcohol, the cups and bottles and go back to their rooms, they pack up and get ready to leave on the next plane out of Saudi. Maxwell and Jonathan are left behind to go to the Green Crescent Hospital; when the authorities find out about the alcohol in Olivia's bloodstream, Maxwell and Jonathan deny any knowledge or involvement. Once they realized their predicament, they took steps to get out of Saudi using a private carrier, Curtis Coleman. The coroner asked other witnesses to corroborate Powell's account but they wouldn't.'

'We'll have to speak to Ann Powell,' said Temple.

'I'm already on it, boss. I've tracked her down. Going to see her tomorrow.'

Looking at the computer, Temple was concentrating on the train times from Pewsey to Paddington. DC Mellor's inquiries with Curtis Coleman had come to a halt; Adrian Coleman and Charlie Curtis were quite elusive characters. Only an hour away by train, Temple decided to visit them himself.

CHAPTER 25

The office of Curtis Coleman was off Gloucester Road. A tiny doorway was wedged amongst a charity shop and obscurely named boutiques; having checked the street numbers, Temple nearly missed it. He looked down a dozen named security buzzers before he found Curtis and Coleman. He pressed the buzzer and waited.

'Hello, how can I help you?' asked a female voice.

'Hello, my name is Detective Inspector Temple. I've an appointment to see Adrian Coleman.'

'Push the door. We're on the second floor, first on the left.'

Temple went inside, up a narrow and steep flight of stairs. A small landing and another flight of stairs took him to a further landing with three doors, one signed Curtis Coleman. Temple pushed the door which didn't open. There was another security buzzer to negotiate before Temple was invited across the threshold. Once through the door, Temple was struck by the decor and atmosphere; it had the air of an exclusive club.

Subtle lighting came from picture lights which shone on gilt framed paintings of race horses and on one wall, lights were directed at a full floor-to-ceiling bookcase. He walked across a plush Wilton carpet. At a reception desk stood a tall, exotic looking, immaculately suited receptionist, her long dark hair falling to one side across her shoulder. Looking up, Temple observed a security camera in the corners of the ceiling. He saw that a monitor on the desk had charted his progress up the stairs. The fact that Curtis Coleman were obviously so alive to security Temple felt he might be able to use to his advantage.

'Hello, Mr Temple,' said the receptionist, in a slightly accented middle-eastern lilt, as she greeted him with a wide white smile. With a confident authority that belied her years and slight frame, she said, 'Mr Coleman will see you in just a moment, he's just finishing a phone call to our Kuwait office. If you would like to take a seat,' and gestured over to a seating area.

Temple sank into a deep seated, green leather wing chair in an alcove to the side of the reception desk. He continued to look around him. A glass table had a well arranged array of magazines and a vase of huge lilies. Another vase of the same lilies was on the reception desk. They scented the room. Before he had time to observe more, the receptionist spoke.

'Mr Coleman has finished his call, you can go in now.' She waved her arm towards a door.

Temple went in, to be greeted by the outstretched hand of Adrian Coleman. Coleman was tall, straight and expensively though casually dressed; he looked freshly out of the barbers and with a slightly plumy voice and athletic build, Coleman looked as if he'd just broken from a pose in a magazine shoot. Still in a suit he'd worn for days, Temple felt like a tramp in comparison.

'Sorry to keep you waiting, Inspector, I'm Adrian Coleman, co-founder and CEO of Curtis and Coleman.'

They shook hands. Very soft, Temple registered.

'I understand you think we may be able to help you with your inquiries?' said Coleman. He sat back in his chair, confident and in total command of the situation.

'Yes. I'm currently conducting a murder investigation in Wiltshire. During the course of financial inquiries, Curtis Coleman Ltd came up. Two payments were made by cheque for £2,400 from Maxwell Ashton-Jones and I'd like to know what those payments were for.'

'I appreciate your directness but this is where we may run into difficulties, Inspector. I'm not sure I can help you.'

Temple tried a different tack.

'In what capacity do you know Maxwell?' asked Temple.

'He is a friend, a former employee and a client. His status as a client means that I cannot divulge any information about him.' He paused. 'Sorry.' Coleman looked back at Temple with a wry smile.

'Can you at least tell me how you met?' Temple asked.

'I met him through Charlie Curtis, my partner. Charlie is a former pilot and he and Maxwell worked together at British Airways. Charlie left BA to work privately, mainly piloting small jets for the rich and famous. Charlie and I met in a nightclub here in London, became acquainted and thought, with our combined contacts, that we could do some business together when I came out of the army. We set up Curtis Coleman Ltd.'

'What exactly does Curtis Coleman do, Mr Coleman?' asked Temple.

Adrian Coleman leaned forward.

'We're in the security business. When we started, there were very few firms like ours around but now, we've got some healthy competition. We provide a bespoke security service, anything from live-in and live-out close protection, anti-hostage trained chauffeurs, pilots, sea captains, to private investigators and computer encryption specialists. Our clients are mainly foreign diplomats, rich and titled people, some celebs – or at least, those who think they are – who want to move around this country and the world quietly, quickly and safely. We provide them with the means to do that.' Adrian Coleman sat back into his chair.

'And Maxwell, where does he fit in?' asked Temple.

'As I said, I met Maxwell through Charlie. Maxwell's piloted for us in the past and he's become a friend.'

'You said he was also a client, what did you mean by that?' Temple asked.

'I also said that I couldn't divulge any information about Maxwell as he was a client. Why don't you ask him yourself?' Coleman enquired.

'I intend to,' said Temple.

'What's he got to do with your murder investigation anyway, Inspector?' Coleman asked.

'His wife, Greta, was found murdered last weekend and I have to conduct inquiries into her and the people close to her.'

'My God, is that so? Poor man,' said Coleman.

Temple had the distinct impression that Coleman knew about Greta's murder. He hadn't been making a call to their Kuwait office, he'd been speaking to Maxwell.

'Did you know Greta?' asked Temple.

'Yes, well, no, not really. I met her once, so didn't really know her. But I do remember that she was a very attractive woman, very attractive …' Coleman's voice trailed off.

'Are you still not prepared to tell me in what capacity Maxwell was a client? Was he frightened of someone, did you provide him with security?'

'Client confidentiality means that I cannot disclose any further information to you, Inspector,' said Coleman.

'As an employee, did Maxwell work for you whilst still working for BA?'

'Look, I don't mean to be evasive, Inspector, but you should really ask him yourself.'

'The private jets, airplanes – do you own a fleet or …?'

'We own a few and we lease the rest.'

'And where are they kept?'

'We keep them at various locations around the country and the world, ready for whoever needs them. As you might expect, we need to be able to respond quickly, as the need arises.'

Temple could see that Coleman wasn't going to betray Maxwell's confidence.

'And Charlie Curtis – where is he?' asked Temple, thinking he might try him instead.

'Ah. Charlie's in Mauritius at the moment, been there for a month and I don't expect to see him for a few weeks yet. He's got a bar and tends to spend a lot of time there now. More of a silent partner, as a consequence.'

Temple could see that he was wasting his time; on his own turf, Coleman was impenetrable.

'Thanks for your time, Mr Coleman, I'll see myself out.'

Temple left and went to catch the Circle line to Paddington. He thought about Maxwell's connections with Curtis Coleman as he stood on the crowded tube train. He was obviously piloting for Curtis Coleman whilst still working for BA but it was his client status that intrigued Temple. Two cheques for £2,400 to Curtis Coleman and then four more cheques for the same amount, un-attributable. What did £2,400 buy from Curtis Coleman, wondered Temple. Was it enough to get him back to England from Singapore and back again using one of their aircraft? His mobile rang.

'Boss, it's Kelly.'

Temple could barely hear her and tried to speak above the noise of the tube train as it screeched to a halt along the metal tracks to stop at High Street Kensington.

'Kel, I can't hear you properly, the signal keeps cutting out, I'm on the underground.'

'Boss, you need to know … urgent …' The line broke again.

'Boss … hospital …' The signal dropped out completely.

He'd have to wait for the train to stop at the next tube station. His phone rang again.

'Hello?' he shouted.

'Boss, we've just had a call. It's …'

The phone signal dropped out again. Temple rang Kelly back as the train halted at Notting Hill Gate but after two rings, the signal disappeared as soon as the train started again.

The phone signal continued to drop in and out. Frustrated, Temple looked up at the tube map above the doors. The next stop was Bayswater, then Paddington, five minutes, tops. The train suddenly slowed to a stop. Temple looked at his watch. It was eight minutes to three and his train left for Pewsey at 3.05. He had to get it as the next was an hour and a half later.

The train started again, stopping at Bayswater and onto Paddington. With three minutes to spare, he ran along to the terminal and up the stairs where his train was boarding at platform three. Temple ran across the concourse and just managed to jump on the first class carriage at the end of the train. Temple sank down into the leather seat while he caught his breath. He decided he'd stay put until the ticket collector came along. Searching his pocket for his ticket reminded him it hadn't been a completely wasted journey. On his arrival at the station before catching the tube, he'd managed to nip outside to the Grand Union Canal that ran alongside and drop the three bullets into the water. That was at least now something he could forget about. As the train moved off, he returned his call to Kelly. She was desperately awaiting his call.

'Boss, I was trying to tell you about James Ashton-Jones. He's in the Great Western. He's taken an overdose. He tried to commit suicide.'

CHAPTER 26

The words stung him. *Fuck it.* He hadn't anticipated James taking such action. He stared out of the window through his reflection. He had plenty of time to think. There was nothing he could do until his journey ended.

Temple met Sloper at Great Western Hospital in Swindon.

'How is he?' asked Temple.

'Silly little bastard took a load of paracetamols,' said Sloper. 'Maxwell found him and called an ambulance. First we heard of it was from Jonathan Silvester.'

'And how is he?' Temple asked again.

'Touch and go. He took a lot, must have been during the night or early this morning. When he didn't stir, they just thought he was lying in. They didn't find him until nearly midday.'

'Shit,' said Temple, annoyed with himself that he hadn't seen it coming.

'He's obviously involved in what's happened, either that or he knows who is. The burden of his knowing has obviously tipped him over the edge,' offered Sloper.

'I better tell Harker,' said Temple, knowing that the prospect of telling him of the near demise of a potential suspect was not a conversation that was going to go well.

'I, er, already have,' confessed Sloper.

'Oh thanks, Si,' said Temple sarcastically. 'Of course, you would.' Temple could imagine how Sloper had put it across – 'the wanker's really fucked up, boss.'

Sloper defended himself.

'Well, you weren't here. You were on your way back from London. A lad attempts suicide after police contact. I had to tell him. He'll have to inform the Independent Police Complaints Commission.' Sloper enjoyed delivering that news.

'And that's all I fucking need.' Temple couldn't help but think that Harker would capitalize on having him investigated by the IPCC.

'Right, let me see if I can find a doctor.' Temple needed a prognosis for James before he spoke to Harker.

He went to a nearby office and found the doctor who had tended to James.

'He's being closely monitored at the moment. We are doing various tests, liver damage, brain function etc. I'd say he was found just in time. Just a few minutes longer and he would have been in a very bad way indeed, possibly fatal,' the doctor told him.

'What's generally the process of recovery in these cases?' Temple asked.

'Well, it depends on the results of the tests. Paracetamol is very harmful but we are hopeful that there will be no long lasting damage. The road to recovery will, however, be a slow one, even in the event of minimal damage. Our tests will show us quite quickly what further support we need to provide and if minimal, he'll be sitting up in a couple of days. But he is far from out of the woods yet. He will, of course, need psychiatric help. Given the heavy dosage taken, it was obvious he intended to end his own life and we will need to know why.'

'I'm as interested as you are in that question. I'm investigating a murder in which James is a very important witness. I'll need to speak to him at the earliest opportunity, Doc. When will I be able to speak to him?' Temple asked.

'His recovery takes priority and only when he is ready will that happen.'

'Of course.'

Temple rang Harker.

'I've informed the IPCC, Temple. The only saving grace here was that he wasn't in police custody, but as he had come into contact with the police, I had to let them know.'

'What are the chances of them investigating?' asked Temple.

'Depends. If they haven't got a lot on, who knows, they might take it on. Simon says the lad was under pressure,' Harker snarled.

'I think he was, but not directly from us,' said Temple.

'He says you told the family about the victim being nine weeks pregnant.'

'I told her father that and I believe he told her husband and son,' Temple explained.

'What was that all about then? They're victims, aren't they? Have you even got a proper grip on this, Temple?' asked Harker, his voice rising, but feeling a sense of satisfaction that his judgement on Temple had proved to be right. He wasn't up to this and he'd take great pleasure in informing chief officers at the earliest opportunity. Harker needed them to rely on his judgement and this would do very nicely.

Temple was fuming, listening to Harker questioning him. Sloper had done a good job on him. He continued.

'They're actually potential suspects, as Sloper knows, sir. At the very least, there's more they could be saying to help us with our inquiries.'

'Simon said the lad was ill when you instructed him to go and see him,' Harker persisted.

'He wasn't ill. He was clearly nervous, I saw that for myself but I suspect what made him sick was the news of his stepmother's pregnancy. From information given by a witness, I think there's a chance the child could be his, given his reaction and the course of action he took today.'

'Well, I hope you can prove that, Temple. I'm coming down to do a seven day review in two days' time. Depending on progress, you can come off the inquiry,' said Harker.

'I'm also after some technical, sir,' said Temple, doing his best to ignore the last remark and seizing his chance.

'What? Where?' asked Harker, surprised at the request.

'At Jonathan Silvester's house. Maxwell is living there at the moment. Given the turn of events in the last six hours, this might yield a quick result.'

'And who do you think is going to monitor that for you?' said Harker, dismissively. Feeling the pressure of the lack of progress of his own inquiry, Harker's gravel voice took on a menacing tone. 'My investigation takes priority, Temple. I've got more fucking plates spinning at the moment than Paul fucking Daniels and I can do without—'

Temple cut in. 'Well, if you're refusing, I'll have to put it in the policy book—'

'Don't get fucking smart with me, Temple. If you can find someone to monitor it, come back to me,' growled Harker and terminated the call.

Temple went back to Sloper. He was just going to launch into him when, over Sloper's shoulder, he saw Maxwell coming towards them. Temple walked towards him.

'Maxwell, I'm sorry to hear about James. Have you managed to speak to him?' asked Temple.

Maxwell was tight-lipped. His confident, easy going manner was clearly dented by events. He was tense and strained.

'No, I haven't. How long will my house remain a crime scene, Inspector? I'd like to take my son home as soon as he has recovered.'

'It'll be out of bounds for some weeks yet, depending on the progress of the inquiry; I'm sorry. Will that cause you a particular problem?' Temple asked.

'No, no, Inspector, I was just wondering.' Maxwell stopped himself speaking any further. It was as if James's suicide attempt had made him momentarily drop his guard. Temple could see he was taking the event hard – much harder than the death of his wife. Their game-playing hadn't bargained for this, thought Temple. They'd lost control of the situation and it was written all over Maxwell's face.

'I'm going to head back to Marlborough, now, Maxwell. If you have any questions, please give me a call. We will be keeping in touch with James's progress,' said Temple. He wanted to put some distance between him and Sloper. 'Jonathan not with you?'

'No, he was earlier, but he's gone home,' said Maxwell.

Temple wondered if the cracks had begun to appear in the relationship. Suddenly, a woman spoke from behind him.

'I'm from the *Wiltshire Daily Record*. We're following the story at Ramsbury, can you talk to us, Inspector?'

Before he turned round, hearing she was from the *Daily Record*, Temple's instant reaction was to tell her to fuck off. He was still trying to digest his situation with Harker and the IPCC and he wanted to continue his conversation with Maxwell.

'No, not now. If you want to talk to me about the inquiry, make an appointment at Marlborough Police Station and I'll talk to you there,' said Temple.

'I just want a quote,' she persisted. 'The young boy, the one who took the overdose, is he a suspect in your inquiry?' She had attitude. Temple concluded this was exactly what he didn't need, a lippy journo.

'How did you know he'd taken an overdose?' asked Maxwell.

'I've been here, sitting over there …' she gestured.

'But how did you know to come here?' asked Maxwell, his voice rising.

Temple looked over at Sloper who shrugged. He had tipped off the hack, to put more pressure on Temple.

'What's your name?' asked Temple.

'Sophie Twiner,' she replied, holding out her hand. Temple ignored the gesture.

'Right, Sophie, make an appointment at the station and I'll give you want you want. In return, I'd ask you not to hassle this man now.' Temple turned to Maxwell.

'OK, I'll come and see you tomorrow,' she said.

'I'm promising nothing. If I'm free, I'll see you, if not, I won't,' said Temple.

Finishing his conversation with Maxwell, Temple left for Marlborough, leaving Sloper at the hospital. He couldn't trust himself around him any longer. The urge to put him up against the wall and punch him was becoming overwhelming.

Kelly arrived back at Marlborough at the same time as Temple. She had been to see Ann Powell.

'She was reluctant to talk. I tried to engage her with the coroner's report and her witness statement but she said it was all too long ago now and she couldn't remember,' she explained.

Temple was distracted by James.

'Just as well she made a statement at the time then,' said Temple. 'Go back and see Caroline Black, see if she was aware of any gossip about Maxwell and Olivia from when they were married, they all worked for the same organization after all.' He was only half listening to her.

'Hang on a minute,' said Kelly. 'All I said was that she was reluctant. I didn't say she didn't speak to me. After a while, she spoke. She said that she remembered Olivia and Jonathan Silvester talking together, at a table. She said there were people getting in and out of the swimming pool but they sat apart from them. She said she thought they were having an intense conversation and that she didn't seem particularly happy that evening. She said she probably wouldn't have remembered this but for the fact that Olivia died soon afterwards and she often wondered what it was that she and Jonathan were talking about.'

'Did she say what she thought happened that night, how Olivia died?' asked Temple.

'I asked her that. She said that the way Maxwell and Jonathan disappeared quickly gave rise to a lot of speculation within BA. She said what she thought was odd was that she saw Jonathan holding Olivia's arm as he guided her into the pool and that she was obviously reluctant to go in. Jonathan got in with her but she said they continued to carry on talking in much the same way as she'd seen them at the table. That was the last time she saw Olivia alive.'

'Well done, Kel, she seems to have remembered more than in her original statement to the coroner. Caroline Black may be able to add to this, see if she knew what the rumour mill was saying about it.'

'Will do, I'll ring her tomorrow.'

Temple picked up the phone and dialled an internal number. He knew it was even more urgent now for him to try and move the inquiry forward; he had to stay focused. He had to follow up on his meeting with Adrian Coleman.

'Is that Callum Naylor?' asked Temple.

'Temple, you old bugger. How you doing?' DS Callum Naylor answered.

'Fine, fine,' Temple lied. 'How's Special Branch these days?'

'Busy as ever, you know how it is. How can we help you?'

'I need some information about aircraft landing strips and airfields. I know there's an airfield at Old Sarum near Salisbury and one at Kemble in Gloucestershire, but how many more are there?' Temple asked.

'There's quite a few, mate. You'd be surprised, so much so that we have ports officers who keep tabs of them and who's coming and going – well, at least, that's the theory.'

'You got time to go through them now?'

'Yes, come up to the office at HQ.'

Temple went to Naylor's office. There, Naylor showed Temple a detailed map of all Wiltshire landing strips and airfields.

'What's your interest?' asked Naylor.

'The murder inquiry at Ramsbury. The husband is a pilot for BA and I think he's been moonlighting for a security firm. I want to check out local landing strips before I speak to him again.'

'Well, there's one near Ramsbury, at Clench Common. Ramsbury has an old World War II airfield, closed in 1946. The 101st Airborne Division – you know, the "Band of Brothers" from the TV series – was based there. That's now part of a farm, but Clench Common Airfield has two grass airstrips in the shape of a cross, with an aviation club set up over there.'

'Any others?' asked Temple.

'Take your pick,' said Naylor, nodding at the map, as Temple looked at the spread of various landing strips and airfields.

'I didn't realize there were so many,' said Temple.

'People don't. There's bloody loads, mate. Some are disused or dummy WWII airfields, like the one at Ramsbury. Some are new, set up by enthusiasts, micro-lighters and gliders. And then there's the private ones.'

'Private ones?' asked Temple.

'These are marked out in designated fields. In the main, it's the great and the good, the monied, your landed gentry, a few farms. They keep them for their helicopters, light aircraft and small jets.'

'Are those on this map too?'

'Some are, but not necessarily all, but we'd like to think we know who and where they are,' replied Naylor.

'So, how are these monitored, who knows who's coming and going?' asked Temple.

'Well, the CAA, Civil Aviation Authority, are supposed to know and local clubs such as Clench Common will keep a log of who comes and goes. There's designated flying times. But we ask about for people to give us sightings, particularly when an aircraft is heard at night,' Naylor explained.

'So chances are, if there is any activity, you will know about it either through official channels or through information received?'

'By and large, yes.'

Temple continued to study the map.

'Can I get a copy of this?' he asked.

'Yes, no problem, I'll get a copy and send it over.'

'Could you also do me one more favour? Can you check with Singapore Airlines and any others that run flights from Singapore to Gatwick to see if a Maxwell Ashton-Jones was on a flight from Friday to Sunday last?'

'Will do. We'll let you know.'

Temple drove back to Marlborough. He rang the HR department.

'I want you to find me a DC on light duties,' he said. After some toing and froing, they came back with DC Craig Toff.

'He's got a broken ankle,' said the girl on the end of the phone. Toff had broken it playing hockey.

'He'll do,' said Temple, 'get him to report to me at HQ tomorrow morning and tell him to bring a sleeping bag and an alarm clock.'

Looking down at his mobile, he saw he had a missed call from Jackie Newly.

'Hi, Jackie, you rang?'

'Yes, boss, got some news for you, on the DNA.'

'I'm listening.'

'I have a negative on Jonathan Silvester for the mixed profile,' she said.

Temple held his breath.

'But it's come back as a positive match for James Ashton-Jones, both for one of the mixed profiles and for the foetus.'

Temple closed his eyes and the calmness of his voice belied the relief he felt at the breakthrough. 'That's good news, Jackie, thanks for that. But hang on a minute, if Maxwell's profile was negative, – surely James's wouldn't be a positive match?' asked Temple, suddenly wondering if he'd understood what Jackie was saying.

'Well, that's precisely why. There was none. When there was a match with James, a check was run again for familial

DNA to Maxwell. No match. However, there is familial DNA between James and Jonathan Silvester.'

'Them two?'

'Yes, it became clear when checking the mixed profile and the DNA of the foetus. It means they're father and son. That's why Maxwell's sample showed no familial because he's not James's father. Jonathan Silvester is.'

CHAPTER 27

Temple's phone rang. It was Sloper.

'Things have taken a turn for the worst here. They've just put James on a ventilator and are doing more tests. They say that he's suddenly deteriorated.'

'Oh *shit*.' Temple had been hoping that his recovery would begin to progress. He needed him to stay alive, not just to find out what he knew. 'Stay there and let me know if there's any further change,' instructed Temple, glad to keep Sloper out of his way for now.

Temple knew he still had to identify the outstanding DNA profile, particularly should James's condition deteriorate further. Whilst it further added to Maxwell having a motive, especially if he knew that James wasn't his son, Maxwell was still out of the country at the material time.

Temple wondered if he knew that Jonathan Silvester had an affair with his first wife and that James wasn't his son. Maxwell knew about and encouraged an affair with his second wife, perhaps it was the same for Olivia. But if Maxwell didn't kill Greta, then who did? Jonathan Silvester said he was alone at the time. Temple knew that despite the welcome breakthrough, he was still no nearer to finding Greta's killer.

Temple informed Kelly of the new developments.

'I want you to go and see James's friend, the one he says he stayed with on Saturday night, Felix somebody or other ...'

Kelly flicked back through her notebook.

'Felix Harmond-Fford, boss.'

'Go and see him now and get a statement. If he hasn't heard about James taking an overdose, don't tell him and obviously don't disclose the DNA evidence. He's probably back at school, but I want that statement, Kel.'

'Will do, I'll find out where he is and go and make arrangements to see him.'

Temple's phone rang again.

'Sir, PC Gregory here, at the scene at Wedwellow House.'

'Christ, I'd forgotten about you. You haven't been standing there since I last saw you, have you?' asked Temple.

'No. sir, I've been relieved by a colleague. Between the two of us, we're covering the scene on a twelve hour shift. I rang to say that a witness approached me today. I've taken all her details. She says she can remember a van in the area in the weeks preceding Greta's death. She doesn't know if it's significant, but it was a blue transit. She saw it once down the lane by the side of the crime scene and again, parked up, away from the premises but on the same road.'

'Don't suppose she got a registration number?' Temple asked.

'Well, because it was suspicious and because she's in the Neighbourhood Watch, she did write it down. I haven't run it through PNC, I thought I'd pass it on to you first, sir.'

'Good work, Gregory.'

Temple took the registration number and rang PNC. He took the details of the woman ready for Kelly to go and get a statement. The PNC inquiry came back negative. Either it had been written down wrongly or the plates were false.

Kelly came back into the office.

'I'm just off now, boss, off to Stilcombe School to see Felix. While you were on the phone, the Financial

Investigation guys rang. They've located a safety deposit box, in Knightsbridge, near South Kensington. It's Maxwell's.'

Temple rang the Financial Investigation office.

'How did you find this?' asked Temple.

'Just trawling through all the bank statements, boss. It's paid for once a year, £500, to Knightsbridge Safe Deposit Boxes.'

'Interesting, thanks, guys, do you have an address?' Temple asked.

'Yes, they're a kosher firm, all above board, albeit, why do people have safety deposit boxes? Still, that's one for you, boss.'

The address was close to Gloucester Road and Curtis and Coleman.

CHAPTER 28

It was late and dark outside. Felix Harmon-Fford stood waiting for Kelly in the headmaster's office. As he looked out of the window into the blackness of the night, his own reflection looked back at him. Using the window pane as a mirror, he stared at his image, eyeballing himself. He was nervous – this was serious shit. He'd found out Greta was dead from the house Dame when she'd told him why James was absent. He would keep quiet, he decided. No comment, like he'd seen on TV.

Kelly had never been to a place like Stilcombe. Fucking Hogwarts, she thought, as she drew up to the floodlit sandstone castellated facade in one of the force's Ford Corsas. She walked up to the main door. Without stepping over the threshold, she felt the atmosphere thick with high achievement and potential; it was almost palpable. She felt just being there tonight, some of it might rub off on her.

Expected, she was shown into the headmaster's room by a harried-looking school Dame who thought the room was fitting for a visit from the police. She closed the door behind them all and sat on a straight backed chair, by the door. Kelly introduced herself to Felix Harmond-Fford and pulled two chairs together and sat opposite the boy. She sensed Felix's nervousness and did her best to put him at ease. He sat down awkwardly in front of her. She spoke to him gently.

'All right, Felix? Cool name you have there. As you probably know, Greta Ashton-Jones was found murdered on Monday and James may have been one of the last people to see her alive. I'm here to take a statement from you so that we can verify what James has said, do you understand?'

'Yes,' said Felix, crumbling, all ideas of going 'no comment' dissolving as soon as he saw Kelly and she began to speak.

She was younger than he had expected her to be and prettier. He judged her to be fit. Her gentle tone disarmed him, he had been expecting more of an interrogation when they'd told him the police were coming to talk to him.

Kelly weighed him up; he shared the same height and muscular build as James, making him look older than his seventeen years.

'James says that he stayed with you last weekend, from Saturday afternoon, would that be right?' Kelly asked.

'Yes. He arrived by train from Bedwyn and we picked him up from the station at Newbury,' Felix explained.

'Who's we?' asked Kelly.

'Me and my mother, she was driving.'

'And then what did you do, Felix?'

'Then we went home, hung around the pool, listened to music ...'

'How was James when you picked him up from the station?'

Felix shrugged. 'Normal, I guess.'

'Was he happy, or sad, or was he agitated at all?' asked Kelly. She could see Felix was finding it a struggle to maintain eye contact with her.

'No, he was perfectly happy, buzzing I'd say, good spirits.'

'Did he say anything to you about his morning, or Greta?'

At this question, Felix succumbed to Kelly's gaze.

'Um, no, I don't think so,' he said, as he looked away, colouring red as he tried to think of what to say.

'It's really important, Felix, that you tell us what you know. So, did he say anything to you about his morning or Greta?' Kelly asked, as he continued to avoid her gaze by staring at a breakfront bookcase that was behind her.

'Um, only that he'd had a good morning.'

'Did he say anything about Greta, Felix?' She said his name in an attempt to regain his eye contact. It failed.

'Um, Greta, um, I don't think so.'

'Did you know Greta, Felix?' she tried again. It worked. He looked at her.

'Yes.'

'Did you visit James at his home, like he visited you at yours? Did you stay over?'

'Yes,' he replied, his eyes downcast.

'What did you think of Greta? Was she a good mum?' asked Kelly.

'Yes, Greta was great, she was a laugh.' Felix's face lit up momentarily, as if from an instant memory of happy times.

'In what way?' Kelly asked, softly.

'Well, she'd sit with us around the pool, she'd join in on our conversations, liked listening to our music. She wasn't like my mother. She was fun to be with, understood us. She was just really cool, I mean, seriously cool.'

'Let you have a few beers, did she?'

'Yeah.'

'Do you know how James felt about her, did he think she was a good mum?' Kelly asked.

Again, the eye contact dropped.

'James thought she was fun too,' he said, slowly.

'Did James ever confide in you about Greta? She was a very attractive woman, wasn't she? Did you think so, Felix?'

'She was really fit, yeah.' He coloured again.

'Did James confide in you, did he tell you things about Greta, about him and Greta?'

Shifting in his chair, Felix was clearly uncomfortable from the line of questioning and Kelly sensed, from his body language, he knew more than he was letting on. She was on the right course.

'It's OK, Felix, you can tell me. You won't be in any trouble. This is a police investigation, it's serious. You'll help us and help James in the process,' she coaxed.

'I don't, I don't know what it is you want,' he mumbled.

'Just for you to tell me what James told you of his morning with Greta.'

Again, Felix shifted uneasily in his chair. He looked around him. The Dame moved forward. Kelly caught her movement out of the corner of her eye and for a moment, she thought she was about to call time on their session.

'Look, I …'

'Just tell me, Felix, all I want is the truth,' pleaded Kelly gently.

He felt cornered. He let out a sigh and blurted it out.

'He loved her. He wouldn't hurt her. He really loved her.' His face reddened and he looked into his lap as he spoke.

'How do you know that, Felix?' asked Kelly, softly.

'He told me. He told me he loved her, loved being with her. She was so cool.'

'And yet he spent the day with you?'

'That was because she told him to. James didn't mind me coming over and staying the weekend at his, but he didn't like being away from Greta if he could help it. She told him she was going out on Saturday and said for him to go and have some fun and stay with me. So he did.'

'Despite him not wanting to?'

'He was OK about it. As I said, he was really happy.'

'What made him so happy that day if he was doing something he didn't really want to do?' Kelly asked.

Felix again dropped his gaze and looked down at the floor.

'What had made him happy, Felix?' Kelly insisted.

'He told me that she had made him happy.'

'How? In what way? How had she made him happy?' she pressed, cognisant of the Dame moving again and about to leap to her feet.

Felix shook his head.

'You know,' he mumbled.

'No, I don't know,' said Kelly gently. 'I wasn't there so I need you to tell me. What did he say, Felix, what happened?' She had one eye on the Dame.

'That they had sex and that made him happy,' he said quietly.

Kelly momentarily let silence hang between them before she continued.

'Was this a regular thing or something that happened for the first time that day?' she coaxed.

Felix rubbed his face with his hands and looked round the room, as if searching for an escape route.

'It's what they did. Just what they did. He was in love with her and she loved him.'

'So, this wasn't the first time?' asked Kelly.

'No,' Felix mumbled.

'So you knew about this. How long to your knowledge had this been going on?'

'I don't know.'

'When you stayed over at the house, do you know if they had sex?' Kelly asked.

'I guess so, sometimes,' he said, quietly.

'Did they know you knew?'

'No, I mean, she didn't know that I knew, but James told me. He swore me to secrecy. She's not his real mother, see …' Felix hung his head, ashamed at the betrayal of his friend.

'OK, Felix, you've done really great, I'll write out a statement now for you to sign. Just tell me, what happened last weekend? Did James go back to school with you on Sunday evening?'

Felix's relief at Kelly telling him they had finished was obvious. He visibly relaxed as the tension left his body.

'No. He left. He was going to stay over, but he went back home late on Saturday evening, back on the last train to Bedwyn, to see Greta. I haven't seen him since. He didn't come back, he didn't come into school on Monday.'

CHAPTER 29

Temple received Kelly's brief over the phone. 'Nice work, Kelly, really well done.'

'He's just reading through the statement now.'

'Get it signed and get back here with it and get it onto Holmes. In the morning, sort out capturing the CCTV at Bedwyn railway station and checking with cabs that might have taken James back to Wedwellow.'

With James Ashton-Jones at the scene of the murder at the right time, Temple was now frustrated by his medical condition. He rang Sloper for an update and told him Kelly's information.

'I've just been speaking to the doc,' said Sloper. 'They will be doing a blood transfusion very shortly. Maxwell's just doing a blood test now as he wants to help out.'

Temple realized the doctors may be about to tell Maxwell some unwelcome news.

'We've got the results of the DNA test for James. They've come back positive on the mixed profile and for the foetus,' explained Temple.

'Thanks for telling me,' said Sloper sarcastically. 'Dirty little bugger, no wonder he was so nervous and in the state he's in; he was shagging his stepmother.'

'Keep a watch on Maxwell and let me know any change in demeanour, it's important. And let me know of any change in James's condition, of course.'

'What's going on?' asked Sloper.

'I'll tell you later,' said Temple.

Temple set off early the next morning to see Brett Forrester, who reluctantly provided a DNA sample.

'I suppose you've heard about James, Mr Forrester?' asked Temple.

'Yes, Maxwell rang me from the hospital. I can't imagine what the lad must have been thinking. I suppose he's taken Greta's death harder than we realized. It seems as though it's one thing after another.'

'It would seem so. You can't think of any other reason why James might take an overdose?' asked Temple.

'No, I can't. He's a fit, healthy, intelligent young lad, I can't think of any reason except that Greta was a mother to him and that he must have been thinking about her murder.' For once, Temple felt that Forrester was telling the truth.

Temple left and went to Headquarters to the Telecommunications team. They had mapped out a timeline for the call traffic between the mobile phones. Of significance was a phone call at 23.58 on the Saturday evening in the vicinity of Ramsbury from James Ashton-Jones to Jonathan Silvester. This would tally with Felix's assertion that James got the last train to Bedwyn and would have been after James would have arrived home from Bedwyn station. This was further evidence that had him squarely near the scene of the murder at the time Doctor Yardley had given for the time of Greta's death. Temple studied and checked the detail – this made James his prime suspect.

Following this was a call from Jonathan Silvester to Maxwell's phone at 05.17 on the Sunday morning. There was also a call from Brett Forrester to the home of Jonathan Silvester, coinciding with Temple's visit to Forrester when Temple had given him the news about Greta's pregnancy.

It confirmed for Temple the conspiratorial nature of the relationship between them all.

But the more he thought about it, Temple couldn't believe the lad had killed Greta. He couldn't believe that he wouldn't have totally broken down when he had first seen him. Yes, he had been distressed, and the results of the DNA tests had shown why that was, but he didn't look or feel like a killer. Temple needed to know why he called Jonathan Silvester at 23.58 on the evening of Greta's death and what prompted Jonathan Silvester to call Maxwell in Sydney. He had to speak to James, while he was on his own in hospital.

Temple also knew he had to get some technical equipment into Jonathan Silvester's house; he needed to know what was said between Jonathan and Maxwell. He needed to know what they knew, particularly around James's paternity. If the doctor disclosed to Maxwell the fact that there was no blood match to James, he would know that James was not his son. Temple wanted to fracture their relationships, and cause doubt and suspicion amongst them.

Temple rang Maxwell Ashton-Jones. He was at the hospital.

'I'd like to speak to you, sir, when convenient. When would be a good time?'

'They've managed to stabilize James's condition, things are better here now, so yes, perhaps I could meet you at Marlborough, on my way home, Inspector?'

'Will Jonathan Silvester be with you?' asked Temple, sensing an opportunity.

'No, I can leave him here with James, just in case he comes round.'

'We'll meet at Marlborough station if that's all right, in an hour maybe, twelve noon?' he suggested.

The meeting was set. Temple seized his chance. He rang the control room and the duty inspector put him in touch with the on call superintendent. Temple explained the urgent nature of his inquiry and requested authority to insert technical equipment into Jonathan Silvester's house. After twenty minutes on the phone, the paperwork was set in motion and an appointment was made with the chief constable who would ultimately give sanction. Temple was told he would receive a phone call when the paperwork was signed.

Impressed with the speed of the bureaucratic trail for once, he rang the Technical Support Unit.

'I need some listening equipment put in a house near Newbury as a matter of urgency. Can you get a crew over there? The occupants will be away for a couple of hours.'

'We could do it, where do you want it?' came the response.

'In the kitchen,' directed Temple.

'We'll need an Authority.'

'I'll get you Authority.'

'Give us the address.'

Before he left Headquarters for Marlborough to meet Maxwell, Temple met DC Craig Toff. His stocky frame hobbled towards him on crutches, his toes poking out of a heavily plastered foot and ankle. Temple opened the door to a tiny office. With no windows, it looked like a cleaning cupboard. Inside, there was only enough space for a desk on which was a listening device and headphones and a chair; the rest of the floor space would be needed for Toff's sleeping bag.

'I want you to go in there, Toff, make yourself comfortable and then put the headphones on and listen. Record any conversation you hear and only go to sleep when the people you're listening to go to sleep and only for a few hours. I don't want you to miss anything and ring me with anything that you think I'm going to be interested in. Do not, under any circumstances, leave this room unmanned. And don't ring your CID mates and tell them what you're doing. This is strictly covert.'

'I'm hardly likely to go far, am I?' said Toff, balancing on his crutches. 'I've brought my sleeping bag and clock as you said. I'll even piss in a bottle if it makes you happy.'

'It does, Toff, I like your initiative.' For the first time, Temple felt as though he was on the front foot with his inquiry.

CHAPTER 30

TEMPLE WATCHED AS Maxwell drew up at the station in his car. He alighted carrying a briefcase. Temple watched him as he walked to the foyer, looking for any signs of stress. Maxwell certainly looked less composed. With them all out of the house, it would give the technical crew a chance to rig a listening device in the kitchen. Temple showed Maxwell into a small interview room.

'I just need to clarify some points,' said Temple. 'You told me about Antonia Peronelli. I'm curious,' he said, 'why not just end it with Greta before now?'

'There's a lot to sort out, Inspector. I had to prepare my finances. I know it sounds mean now and perhaps even distasteful, given the current circumstances, but I had to prepare for divorce. Financially, it wasn't something I could just do without causing myself a lot of financial damage. I was in the process of trying to mitigate my financial losses in that kind of scenario.'

Temple watched him.

'Go on. What do you mean by "mitigate"?'

'I was speaking to Jonathan regularly, who is my financial advisor. We were liquidizing certain assets, ISAs, some art, paintings and such like, stocks and shares, that sort of thing. A flat was sold.'

'You were basically trying to hide money from Greta then. That's pretty calculating of you, if you don't mind me saying so,' said Temple.

'I know, I can see how it looks, particularly as I said, under these circumstances. I was only doing what many men in my position would do.' Maxwell looked back at Temple, impassively.

'And what position is that exactly?'

'Well, finding someone that they want to be with when they are married to someone else. You start to think of your new life and start preparing for it.'

'Is money very important to you then, Maxwell?' Temple suspected he already knew the answer.

'Look, I've worked hard and I realized that if I divorced, I'd lose half of it. I was trying to make that as minimal as possible.'

'Did all your money come as a result of your hard work, Maxwell?'

'Most of it, yes.'

'Sure of that? We've been through your finances and we're talking of some pretty big numbers, aren't we? You had a payment of £350,000 when your first wife, Olivia, died, didn't you? And now you find yourself a widower once again and with another insurance payout due, so the financial side of things and domestic side of things have resolved themselves rather neatly for you, haven't they?'

'I can appreciate how it looks.'

'I've also been looking at the coroner's report into Olivia's death. Death by accidental drowning. In Riyadh.' Temple watched him.

'Olivia's death was an awful, tragic accident.'

'And did you have the same arrangement with Jonathan Silvester and Olivia as you did with him and Greta? Did you agree to an affair between them? Was it your intention to divorce Olivia at some point?'

'No, Jonathan didn't have an affair with Olivia.'

'Were you a faithful husband to Olivia?' Temple asked.

'Not that it's got anything to do with your inquiry – no.'

'Was she faithful?'

'No, Jonathan told me that she was having an affair with a steward.'

'What did you think about that?'

'We'd reached the stage by then whereby I was looking at other women. Things change once you have a child. I wasn't very good at turning down opportunities when they presented themselves. Good looking women, easy access to hotels, sunny and exotic climates, I don't need to draw a picture ...'

Temple knew that he himself had a few difficulties when the opportunity arose, but this guy, he was in a different league.

'You still haven't answered my question – how did you feel about your wife having an affair?'

'If you're asking me if I flew into a jealous rage, no, I didn't. I'm not like that. How did it make me feel – disappointed, I suppose.'

'And what about Curtis Coleman, Maxwell, what can you tell me about your involvement with them? Adrian Coleman told me that you were a friend, employee and a client – what did he mean by a client, Maxwell?'

Temple stared back at him; the awkward look on Maxwell's face told him that at last, he'd hit on something. He hadn't been expecting that.

'This isn't a formal interview is it, Inspector? I don't think I am obliged to tell you all my business.'

'No, it's not a formal interview as you know, but I do want to know what he meant by you being a client and if you don't tell me, then I might think that you are obstructing my inquiries. If you don't tell me, I'll apply for a Production Order to gain access to Curtis Coleman's records. I don't suppose they'd be overly pleased with that, do you? The police sifting through all their records, looking at their client list, what they get up to ... Might not be a good advert for their claims to operate a fully confidential service.'

'OK, OK, Inspector. I used to pilot for them, in between periods of leave at BA. It was lucrative work, every other job was cash in hand, one went through the books, one didn't. There were other perks too, like tips from wealthy clients—'

'That makes you an employee, not a client,' Temple interrupted.

'I'd charter an aircraft every so often. When I was seeing Antonia and on occasions with other women before that, I sometimes used a plane belonging to Curtis Coleman to get from one end of the country to another. Antonia used to live in Cheshire until she moved and when our relationship developed, I could get to her quickly and easily by plane. Clench Common airfield is nearby at Ramsbury, which is partly the reason I chose to live in the area.'

'What sort of plane are we talking about? Not the jets you fly around the world?' asked Temple.

'No, the jets are a small, personal but expensive way of flying; internal flights can be undertaken by good semi-light and light aircraft.'

'Did you always stay in England?'

'By and large, although I flew to France and the Channel Islands too.'

'And what was your first introduction to their services? How did you get yourself out of Riyadh?'

'If you know already, Inspector, why don't you say?' Maxwell asked.

'Because I want to find out if what I know correlates with what you tell me, Maxwell. Why and how did you get out of Riyadh?'

'Olivia was dead. Drowned in the pool. We'd been drinking, as was the norm when we stopped over there. A whole group of us, we'd get together, break out smuggled duty free booze in the room, leave the drinks in the room while we went downstairs to the pool. When they took Olivia off to hospital, they found she had alcohol in her bloodstream. As you know, alcohol is prohibited there and so, as her husband, they wanted to know how this had occurred. I told them that she had drunk on the plane on the way and that I thought she had sobered up by the time she went swimming.'

'Was this the same story you gave to your employers?' Temple asked.

'Yes, it was the only way to avoid being arrested, losing my job and being incarcerated in a Saudi jail, maybe everyone else being arrested and locked up too. Security was tight at Riyadh. Our bags were searched for booze so we had to smuggle it in shampoo bottles. I remember once having the inside of a wine box under my cap. Others would fill their socks with miniatures; bottles would be strapped under the arms. They made a thorough search of bags but never of the person.'

'So, what did you do?'

'The next BA flight out of the region was a twelve hour wait; Jonathan knew Charlie Curtis had just set up this firm, flying wealthy Arabs and businessmen around the region on private Learjets so he contacted him and he picked us up at the airport and got us out of there. I'll always be eternally grateful to Charlie Curtis for getting us out so quickly. There was nothing more to be done for Olivia. It was a terrible tragedy, but if I hadn't got out of there, James would have been left without both of his parents. I've maintained my association with Curtis Coleman ever since.'

'How did Olivia come to have a head injury?'

'I've no idea. I'm told she was in the pool, with others. Next thing, she's found dead.'

'A witness tells me that she was in the pool with Jonathan.'

'Yes, Jonathan was there, in the pool, as were a few other people.'

'And so when Adrian Coleman refers to you being a client, it is this capacity that he means, you chartering his aircraft to see Antonia?'

'Yes, exactly,' replied Maxwell.

'Tell me about the payments for £2,400 that has been coming out of your account to Curtis Coleman for the last six months.'

Maxwell shifted in his seat and Temple could tell that he was quickly trying to work out whether or not speak. Whether or not to tell the truth, thought Temple. Temple didn't say anything, choosing to keep the silence between them. Eventually, he saw Maxwell's shoulders visibly drop, as if a weight was coming off them.

'I, I did something that I'm not overly proud of…' said Maxwell hesitantly. 'It was actually Jonathan's suggestion. We were working out my finances, putting a figure on my wealth for the divorce. We both knew Greta, both knew of her excesses – she would go on spending sprees. I had to limit the amount kept in our joint account, siphon the rest off into savings accounts because she could whip through it in an afternoon, especially online.

'If you've looked inside her wardrobe, you'll see any number of designer handbags – Chanel, Burberry, Givenchy, Chloé – they're all in there, at two to five thousand pounds a throw. Pairs and pairs of Jimmy Choo's, racks of designer clothes, a lot of it not even worn. Then she'd buy more. She'd have a clear out and give it to the cleaner, the girls down the stables and suddenly, I'm buying designer bags and clothes for half the village. It wasn't just clothes either, jewellery, cars – she had five cars at one point and then she started buying animals. I came home one day to find ten carp in the pool. She once bought a horse off the internet. This was what she could be like, during an episode.' He was eager to justify his actions and was almost shouting.

It was the first time Temple had seen Maxwell actually lose his cool. He could see why Maxwell had got Greta professional help, although not for any concern for her, but out of concern for his bank account.

'So Jonathan suggested that we should continue to try and negotiate as low a sum as possible by citing her adultery, but I'd need proof of it. Whilst we both knew he had slept with Greta, he also suspected her of having other relationships with a local builder, a guy called Mike Cooper, who I employed to build an extension nearly a year ago and a guy from the Porsche garage where we bought Greta's car. He said I should employ the services of a private investigator. So, I used Curtis Coleman.'

'How long ago was this?'

'Six months ago,' replied Maxwell, looking up at the ceiling. 'Look, this didn't sit comfortably with me. I'm no saint, that's for sure, but I was never comfortable with Jonathan's suggestion. I knew she wasn't faithful – neither was I – but he felt we needed to go in strong.'

'And what did you discover?'

'The investigator discovered exactly what Jonathan suspected. He took photographs of Greta together with Mike Cooper and the guy from the Porsche garage. So, it vindicated my actions, but it wasn't something I was happy with. She could easily have done the same to me over the years and would have had the same result,' he said.

'Who is he, this investigator?'

'I don't know, I never actually met him. There was no need. Once I told Adrian Coleman I wanted a PI and what for, he saw to it and then set up a safety deposit box where the photographs were left for me to collect and I left the money to pay him. We intended to use what was discovered as a lever during divorce negotiations. As I say, I'm not proud of what I did. There seemed to me to be something particularly seedy about employing someone to spy on one's wife, even if it did produce the desired outcome.'

'What kind of photographs did he show you?'

'Photographs of Mike Cooper coming and going from my house and the timings. Greta in her Porsche with the guy from the garage, Hussain, I think his name is. They showed her kissing him, her arms around him. Another showed him going to and leaving the house. Nothing more, but enough, as neither Cooper or Hussain had any business being there, except to be with Greta. His notes with the photographs said that he found it a challenge to get the photographs I needed. That he'd had to wait some time. That's why he stayed with it for nearly six months.'

'So nothing more explicit than kissing and hugging?' asked Temple.

'No, but hey, I'm sure that's not just what took place inside my house,' said Maxwell.

'What did you do with the photographs you were given?'

'They're here.' Maxwell put his brief case on the table and opened it. 'I brought them to you as I wanted you to know that Greta had relationships with these men and this is the proof. It was also weighing on my conscience about the private investigator. I should have told you before. It might have been pertinent to your investigation. These men might be able to help you.'

As he spoke, Maxwell put a brown envelope onto the table. Temple saw that it was the same as that found at Marcus Hussain's house. Maxwell took the photographs out and passed them to Temple. Although similar to those he had viewed, these were tame by comparison.

'You're right, you should have told me this before. And these are the only photos he has sent you? It's important that I know if there are any more.'

'This is what he sent me, this is all I have.'

'Given the fact that you were going to great lengths to keep your money, don't you think that you've paid over the odds for what amounts to a couple of dozen photographs, Maxwell?'

'In his report, he said that he had had to wait some time to take these. I first received those with Michael Cooper in January, then these in April with the guy at the Porsche garage. These things take time, I guess.' Maxwell looked back at Temple. 'You're judging me, Inspector,' he replied in answer to the way Temple looked at him.

'I have to form an opinion. You've kept information that you should have told me from the outset. You see, it seems to me you're sitting pretty – your wife's murdered, there's no expensive divorce and you've got yourself another big insurance payout. What else are you holding back and not telling me?'

'Nothing more. You know everything.'

'I'll need to find this private investigator, urgently. I want you to tell Adrian Coleman to give me full access to your client file.'

Temple ended the meeting, knowing he now had the listening device installed.

CHAPTER 31

KELLY HAD FINISHED making inquiries at Bedwyn Station. CCTV was non-existent; they had cameras but they had broken down a few weeks before and had yet to be repaired, much to the annoyance of the Bedwyn Trains Passenger Group, the local driving force for improvements to the station. More helpfully, only one cab firm was used at Bedwyn. She went to the cab office. Those who were on duty were unable to help so she had the manager contact each of the others at home to ask them if they had picked James up on Saturday evening. The last man he contacted confirmed that he had taken a young guy, fitting James's description from Bedwyn Station to Wedwellow House at around 11 p.m. when the last train came in, on Saturday night.

'James has clearly lied about not returning home, it also fits with what Felix has told us,' said Kelly, as she updated Temple back in the incident room. As she spoke, she wrote the information on the whiteboard. 'The train got in at 11 p.m., he gets a taxi home – what's that, twenty minutes? The pathologist timed her death late Saturday to early hours of Sunday morning and his DNA clearly shows they've had sex. Then we've got a call going into Jonathan Silvester at 23.58.

Given that he's also taken an overdose, isn't this tending to suggest we've actually got our man, or rather, boy?'

'Well, he's built like a man, but I'm not convinced he's got it in him to kill Greta.'

'He's tried to kill himself, boss,' said Kelly quietly, her hair swinging across her face as she turned from him to the whiteboard.

'I've got to speak to him again. I'm going to go back up to Great Western Hospital to see if he's recovered enough by now,' Temple replied, looking at the timeline Kelly had written on the whiteboard against James's name.

The phone rang in the office, Kelly picked it up.

'Boss, phone call for you, Social Services.'

'Social Services? I'm not here.' Temple put his jacket on; Leigh's visit to the doctors and Daisy seeing a psychiatrist must have triggered the nosy bastards wanting to get in contact, thought Temple.

Another phone rang in the office. On his way out, Temple answered it. It was the front desk telling him that Sophie Twiner, the reporter, was in the foyer.

'I don't remember making an appointment with her but keep her there, I'll be down.' Temple saw an opportunity. He needed to trace the private investigator fast and Sophie Twiner could help.

Sophie Twiner was waiting in the front foyer of the station. Temple buzzed her through and took her to a small room off a short corridor.

'What brings you here, Sophie?' She looked younger today, he thought, the paper must be the first she'd worked for.

'I thought we made an appointment,' she said.

'I'm sure we didn't. Anyway, you're here. I haven't seen you before, how long have you been with the *Wiltshire Daily Record* then, Sophie?'

'A little while,' she said vaguely, not wishing to indicate her inexperience.

Temple guessed this would be her first major inquiry. She was as green as grass. The *Wiltshire Daily Record* were obviously covering Harker's job with their most experienced journalists. He didn't like dealing with fresh faces; they were particularly dangerous when trying to make a name for themselves. The established ones didn't fuck you about, pull stunts or turn up unannounced. At least she'd be easy to control, thought Temple.

'I think you can help me. I think we can help each other,' he said, which he knew was exactly what she wanted to hear.

'Rob said much the same thing to me; you know Rob Carroll, the editor?'

Temple watched as she brushed her fingers through her shoulder length blonde hair, sweeping it to the side. A move obviously for his benefit, he thought, as she stroked it into place.

'I know Rob,' said Temple. 'Although from my experience, he's more like Lewis Carroll from some of the stuff he prints. Doesn't let facts get in the way of a good story, old Rob. Why have annoying little things like facts when you can just make it up.'

Sophie withstood Temple's short rant against her employer. Carroll had had a call from a crime reporter from the *Daily Mail*; they'd exchanged notes about the Ramsbury murder and Temple as the SIO. Carroll had looked into the news archives and sent Twiner on a mission. Carroll could smell a good angle for a story a mile off.

'We just need to have a couple of ground rules, Sophie. No tape recorders and if you print anything I haven't said, we won't speak again. If you piss me off, I'll tell all my colleagues to avoid you like the plague. For instance, I don't want anything appearing in the paper about the boy in hospital,' said Temple.

'OK, it's cool. I understand what you're saying. It's all a matter of trust. But in return, will you stop patronizing me?'

Undaunted by him, Sophie Twiner was already eager to add Temple to her growing list of police contacts, not least of which because she had found herself attracted to him when she saw him at the hospital. Most people dismissed her as just another blonde and underestimated her sense of determination and ability to get her story. She was keen to build this particular relationship and change his attitude towards her. She'd let him get away with talking to her like a schoolgirl this time, for the sake of what she had in mind. She liked the look of him and had already begun to speculate what he might be like in bed and had every intention of finding out.

'There's something you can do for me,' said Temple. 'I need to find a man with a blue transit van who was seen in Ramsbury. You can print me an appeal for sightings and keep your ear to the ground in The Phoenix.'

'Leave it to me,' she said.

Following a text from Kelly, Temple returned upstairs to the incident room.

'Boss, just to let you know, Jackie Newly rang. She's says that the DNA profile of Brett Forrester is negative.'

'OK. So, we've got an unidentified DNA profile, outside Greta's immediate circle, which means I'm missing something and someone. I've got to know what happened that night with James, I've got to find out why he's taken an overdose. I'm going to go up to the hospital to see if I can get in to see him.'

He had just driven onto the short motorway stretch to the Great Western Hospital when his mobile rang. It was Sloper.

'You still at the hospital?' asked Temple.

'Yes.'

'I'm on my way, we need to get to James and speak to him,' said Temple.

'That's what I was ringing to tell you, you can slow down. He's dead.'

CHAPTER 32

TEMPLE ARRIVED ON the ward and stood outside the room where James's body lay. Sloper's words left him feeling as if he'd been punched in the stomach and the fist had left its imprint in his gut.

James had been in a room on his own which was now closed to the outside world. Temple positioned himself so that he could just see into the room through a gap between the shutters at the window. Inside, Maxwell and Jonathan stood around the bed, looking down disbelievingly on the lifeless muscular body of the boy they both loved. As nurses worked quietly to remove the drip and the numerous wires from a heart monitor, a doctor explained in hushed tones the reason for James's sudden demise. As Temple watched, Sloper nudged his elbow, holding a cup of coffee.

'Do you know what happened? I thought he was making progress,' asked Temple, fingering his neck.

'So did they. I managed to speak to the doctor briefly. He said it was heart failure, the pressure on his other organs was too great apparently and his heart just gave up.'

'Kelly found the taxi driver who picked him up at the railway station. He was going back to see Greta the night she was killed. Looks like he was there at some point, which is why I was coming up to see him,' said Temple, not quite able to believe James was dead.

'Kelly told me. I suppose that's it then. Circumstantial evidence to show that he was probably the last person to see her alive and most likely killed her, hence the overdose,' said Sloper quietly.

'He didn't kill her, Si,' said Temple, disagreeing with his theory.

'Then how come he's lying in there, dead? There had to be a reason for his overdose and that was his conscience. He couldn't live with what he'd done,' replied Sloper. 'You saw for yourself, how he was.'

'If I thought he'd killed her, I'd have nicked him. He wouldn't be lying in there; he'd be in custody, being watched round the clock. We'd have his account of what happened and we'd be talking to the CPS. He didn't kill her. What weighed on his conscience was sleeping with his father's wife, his own stepmother, is my guess – who he then found out was pregnant and doing the sums, he worked out it could be his. He was scared shitless as to how he was going to explain it.'

They looked back at each other.

'Suppose I better let Harker know,' said Temple, feeling the weight of the situation and not relishing the conversation.

'I already have. I've outlined the circumstances to him, about James lying about his whereabouts on the Saturday night and the DNA results. He's asked me to start at Swindon tomorrow on his job. Says for you to ring him.' Sloper slurped his coffee. He couldn't wait to get up there, he needed to smooth a few ruffled feathers and see what state Gemma Harker was in.

Temple wondered how Harker had taken the news. He had heard that the Swindon case was getting messy. They were no nearer finding the girl who had been abducted and the community and family of the murdered boy were becoming increasingly hysterical at the lack of arrests. As Wiltshire surveillance officers drove through the unfamiliar streets of south London and needed the support of already stretched Met resources, Harker had had to negotiate with a number of different local Met commanders who were up to their necks with their own issues, never mind his.

Temple needed to put some space between him and Sloper. He didn't want him to hear his conversation so he went outside and contacted Harker from his car.

'The way I see it, Temple, and the way Simon sees it, is that James Ashton-Jones murdered his stepmother, hence his overdose,' said Harker, in no mood to listen to Temple.

He'd given Temple a straightforward domestic to investigate and he was trying to string it out.

As far as Harker was concerned, the last few days had proved to him that he had been right to intervene in Temple's recent application to join the Major Crime Investigation team. He was incompetent, thought Harker, congratulating himself at his foresight in the face of pressure to have deployed Sloper to watch Temple.

'James lied about his whereabouts, he was at the scene at the material time and his attempt at suicide has succeeded. It was him,' said Harker, impatient to end the call.

'I don't think it was him,' countered Temple. 'He had no motive I can think of ...'

'She was pregnant, Temple,' said Harker, his voice starting to rise. 'His own stepmother was carrying his *child.* That's good enough a motive for me. He was seventeen years old. They were at it, having a bit of kinky sex and she decided to tell him she was pregnant and he lost it. Tell me that couldn't have happened?'

'It wasn't him,' Temple persisted. 'I saw him, sat with him, talked to him, and yes, he was distressed but it wasn't him. I don't think he even knew she was pregnant and it was finding that out, I think, once she was dead, that sent him over the edge. Apparently he loved her. It was the burden of hiding his illicit affair with her and finding out that she was pregnant that pushed him over the edge, but he's no killer. I've got an outstanding DNA profile at the moment—'

Harker cut in. He had had enough.

'The outstanding profile merely tells you that she had sex with someone else that day. She had form for it. There was no sign of forced entry into the house, the boy would have been the last person to see her alive and he had access to the house. He lied, Temple. People do that. Murderers do that when they're trying to cover their tracks. Men who say they love women, murder them. I want you to write up your policy book to this effect and close the inquiry. Go and see the husband and her father, tell them all we've found out and close it down. I'll cancel the scene guard. I'll give you a day to finalize things and then come and see me with your policy book and I'll sign it off,' instructed Harker.

Temple managed a curt, 'Sir,' in acknowledgement. Staring back at his phone in his hand, he had no intention of following his orders. He couldn't. Harker wasn't right.

Temple threw the phone onto the seat beside him in frustration. He needed to think.

He returned to the incident room at Marlborough and informed Kelly about Harker's instruction to close down the inquiry. He told her of Maxwell's disclosure of employing a private investigator.

'Sloper starts in Swindon tomorrow. I don't want to get you into any trouble so you'd better go back to your normal duties. I'm going to pursue the private investigator before I write anything further in the policy book. Above all, I don't believe James Ashton-Jones was Greta's killer. I can't walk away until I've found out who the outstanding DNA profile belongs to,' said Temple. As he spoke, his eyes looked at the photo of Greta on the whiteboard.

From all that Temple heard, Greta had been badly used by most of the men in her life. She was heavily insured with a husband who wanted a divorce. James Ashton-Jones being Greta's murderer was a hypothesis, of course, but it just didn't feel right. And if it wasn't James, a murderer remained at large and he seemed to be the only one who cared about that. The least she was owed was to find out exactly who killed her.

Kelly's inexperience left her undecided as to who was right, Temple or Harker. The statement she had taken from Felix Harmond-Fford and from the taxi driver saying that he had taken James home on the evening in question had made her feel as though her skills as an investigator had uncovered lies told by James to cover up the crime. But she could see that Temple was unconvinced and that the outstanding DNA profile was something he wasn't going to leave. She was in no hurry to move off the inquiry; statement taking for burglaries and ABHs were waiting for her back at the office where she worked. There was no way she would rush back to that from a murder inquiry. Besides, she liked working with Temple, she was learning from him and gaining confidence in her own abilities. He didn't seem to differentiate between her and detective colleagues, unlike those she normally worked alongside. And she'd heard that Sloper was off up to Swindon.

'I'll give you another couple of days, boss. It'll take me all that time to tidy up here and start putting the file together for the CPS. If anyone asks, that's what I'll tell them I'm doing. Besides which, I'm still trying to work out Maxwell's journey times. I've also booked another appointment with Caroline Black for tomorrow and Antonia Peronelli the day after.'

She showed Temple a list of dates and times.

'Sloper told me that he spoke to BA and asked them if it was possible for a pilot to land at Singapore and take a flight back to the UK without showing on a manifest. According to them, it's not possible for anyone to come into the country with them without it being known.'

'I asked Special Branch to check other flights from Singapore for me, have they given that information back yet?' asked Temple.

'No, I'll chase them for you.' Kelly picked up the phone.

Deflated by his conversation with Harker, Temple left.

Driving through Harnham, Temple pulled up outside Dianna Forrester's house. Kelly had been updating her on progress by phone but Temple knew it was time for him to pay a personal visit to inform her of developments. When she opened the door to him, the strain she was under was clearly etched in her face. She had obviously been doing much soul searching since they last spoke so Temple knew he would have to tread carefully in what he chose to disclose. However, although she looked fragile, she was steely in her questioning of him. Temple knew he couldn't withhold information from her, so he sensitively outlined the facts so far, including what the psychiatrist had told him, Greta's infidelities and the pregnancy.

'It all just makes me feel so very sad,' she said, tearfully. 'But I should have done more, Inspector. At the time, I should have done more, listened more and done something about things.'

'Teenagers can be very difficult, Mrs Forrester. In hindsight, we could all perhaps do things differently,' said Temple, knowing that Greta's death and the circumstances around it would stay with Dianna Forrester forever. He knew that she would spend the rest of her life replaying the events of Greta's life in her mind, wondering if she had done this or said that, Greta's life would have taken a different course. Finding that one thing that could have been done or said, at the right time, that would have made all the difference, something that would have caused a different outcome than the one she had. He looked back at her from across the table where they sat.

'What I would like, Inspector, is to see some action taken against my former husband. I know there are things that I am to blame for, but I also know what I saw that day in his flat and, to my great regret now, I should have taken things further. I shouldn't have been content to be rid of Greta as a teenage problem, I should have done more. I should have taken her away from that situation. I didn't. If I had, who knows – she might not be dead now. No, I know she wouldn't be dead now. She certainly wouldn't have been so promiscuous. She was wilful and impressionable. Brett and

I were like chalk and cheese and so were Greta and I. Why did I ever marry him in the first place?' she asked of herself.

'Do you know the answer to that, Mrs Forrester?' asked Temple. He'd asked the question himself as he and Leigh were obviously so different.

'I was in a similar situation to Greta, very strict parents and then when this handsome and, to my mind, sophisticated man came along, he being a little older, I fell for him. Even back then he was charismatic and I was very easily seduced. To my shame, we had to get married,' she whispered.

'When you say you want action taken against him, what do you mean exactly?' asked Temple.

'What I want, Inspector, is to see him pay for what he did to Greta. I want him arrested. I want him imprisoned,' she replied.

CHAPTER 33

In the morning, Temple contacted Adrian Coleman's office. He was in a meeting but would ring back. After an hour passed, Temple's impatience got the better of him. He rang again.

'Mr Coleman is still in his meeting,' said the receptionist.

'I want you to interrupt him,' said Temple. 'This is an urgent matter and I need to speak to him. I'll hold on while you get him to the phone.'

After a minute's wait, Temple heard Adrian Coleman's voice.

'Mr Coleman, I've spoken again to Maxwell Ashton-Jones and he has disclosed to me that he engaged the services of a private investigator through your company. As a matter of some urgency, I need to know who the investigator was.'

'I don't actually know who it was. We outsource that sort of work,' Coleman replied.

'Well, I'll need you to tell me who your contacts are, who you outsourced that out to,' Temple told him.

'I'll look on the file and get back to you,' offered Coleman, determined not to give any information to Temple on demand.

'I can't stress enough how urgent this is,' said Temple, getting the feeling that Adrian Coleman was fucking him about, but he could do nothing else but wait for Coleman to return the call.

As he contemplated the action he would take if Coleman didn't call him back within the next two hours, the phone rang. It was Coleman.

'Looks like we engaged a firm called Dobson and Byrne.'

'When you say "we", what do you mean? Was it you personally?' asked Temple.

'Well, no, a member of our team. Maxwell would have given me the brief and I would have passed that on to a member of our team. We have a number of PI firms to choose from that we use on a fairly ad hoc basis. It saves us employing someone direct and keeping them on our books. The brief is then passed onto them and they get on with the job.'

'And where are Dobson and Byrne?' asked Temple.

'In London,' said Coleman brightly. He passed him back to the receptionist who gave him the contact details.

Temple rang the number provided.

'Hello?' a female voice answered.

'Is that Dobson and Byrne?' Temple asked.

'We're not in business anymore. Sorry,' came the reply.

'Wait,' said Temple, sensing the phone was just about to be put down. 'I need some information and you're the only one who can give it to me.'

'We've stopped trading, mate. The firm's gone tits up,' said the girl.

'But you're still answering the phone,' said Temple.

'I'm just here clearing out the office. There's a lot of paperwork to get rid of,' she said.

'I just need to ask a couple of questions, do you think you could help me, please? It's really important. Did you take on work from a company called Curtis Coleman?' Temple asked.

'Yeah,' came the reply.

'I understand that you provided them with the services of a private investigator.'

'Yeah. Who are you, anyway?'

Temple had to think fast.

'I work for the accounts department at Curtis Coleman and you may have some outstanding payments due.'

'Oh, yeah?' the woman said. Temple sensed that he now had her interest.

'I'm particularly interested in a job started in November last year. It ran for six months but we'll need the name of the investigator if we're to release the payment. Can you tell me who it was, please?'

'Um, I dunno.' Temple could hear the rustle of papers. 'I might have just shredded the papers I'd need in order to tell you that.' Temple heard more rustling of papers. 'I can't find it. Can I ring you back?'

Temple gave the girl his mobile number and then slumped forward on the desk in frustration.

He looked at his watch – it was 12.30. He'd had a text from Daisy earlier, using her mother's mobile. More often than not he ignored them, not wanting to encourage her, knowing he'd be bombarded if he replied but this time he texted back and agreed to take her out for an hour. He needed a break, needed some normality. Perhaps it would help her to be with him, too, he thought.

Half an hour later, Temple drew up outside the home he once shared with his family at Beckhampton. They'd chosen it because of its quiet location and setting, being largely hidden from view from the main road. It offered the peace and privacy Temple craved after a day at work. Looking at the house now, Temple knew he had to return there. Leigh was angry with him and he deserved it. But she also knew him. Knew him better than he knew himself. All that he wanted was in that house, he thought.

Seeing his car draw up from the window, Daisy ran out to meet him. Waving at Leigh in the doorway, she got into the car and strapped herself into the front seat. As Temple drove down the road, it was obvious she relished his company; as they chatted, he looked at her animation and it felt like old times. Temple felt instantly relaxed. As he experienced their closeness and realized how much he missed her, a sudden wall of tiredness hit him. At the temporary absence of having to constantly make decisions, the adrenalin of the last week faded away. It was replaced by happy elation as he looked at her by his side.

'Daddy, no!' Daisy shrieked suddenly.

Temple saw the rabbit in front of him and because Daisy was with him, he swerved the car to miss it, rather than drive straight on and hit it. The rabbit moved in the same direction, causing a rumble, as it fought the crush under the wheels. Daisy knew exactly what had happened and in a reflex action, she spun round in the front seat to see the vivid red carnage the wheels had left splattered across the road behind. She screamed hysterically.

'Dais, he just ran out,' shouted Temple, startled by the pitch of her cry, as he drove on. 'It's a wild rabbit, not like the one you've got, there's thousands out here,' he said, trying to reason.

'It might not be dead! Stop, stop!' she started to scream.

As he continued to try to placate her, to stop the high pitch of her screaming going through his head, he heard his mobile go off in his pocket.

'I can't stop. We're not stopping, Dais, it just ran out,' he shouted above her screams and the sound of his mobile.

Tears fell down Daisy's cheeks as she cried loudly. Temple pulled over, his brief moment of tranquillity shattered. He put his arms around her; she was strangely inconsolable as she clung to him, her little body wracked with great tearful sobs. This was a Daisy he didn't recognize and it shook him. He'd never seen her like this before. No matter what he said to try to console her, he failed. He knew this wasn't about a dead rabbit, it was about the last eight months. He should be able to take her home now, go inside and be with her but he couldn't. He'd broken that happiness and she'd been damaged in the process. He U-turned and stopped back outside the house.

'You'll have to go back in, Dais, go and see Mummy. We can't go out with you being so upset,' he said.

Daisy clung to him again, her arms locked round his neck. Refusing to let go, he had to prise her arms away. Tears streamed down her face.

'Why can't you live with us?' Daisy sobbed.

'Look, I'd love to live with you and Mummy again. You know that. But Mummy's got someone else now,' said Temple, trying to calm her down.

'I don't like Roger,' she said, simply, her mouth now wet with her own tears.

Temple hated him. He hated everything about him. Couldn't even bring himself to say his name. Hated the smug grin Roger Hunt gave to him when he turned up to see Daisy, as if he was superior, the way he started to possessively put his arm around Leigh and his hand on Daisy, which she shrugged off. He hated the way Roger turned away from him when he was talking, deliberately, as if Temple bored him. His haircut, his shoes, his fucking black Chrysler 300 car parked on his drive. In Temple's eyes, he was so fucking *square*. He knew Leigh and knew that he'd hurt her badly and that Roger was her revenge. She was using him to hurt him – and it worked. Living in his house, lying in his bed with Leigh – the house he still paid the mortgage on. Every time he saw him, he wanted to punch him.

Through gritted teeth, Temple asked Daisy, 'He's all right, isn't he?'

'I don't like him, Daddy,' she replied, quietly.

'But why don't you? He's nice to you, isn't he? Dais?' Her red, wet eyes were cast down, glued to the foot well. She refused to look at him. He pressed her further. 'Daisy?'

Temple's mobile ringing again broke the silence between them. As he looked at it to determine the caller, Daisy took the opportunity to get out of the car. She ran to the front door which was opened for her by Leigh. On looking at her tearstained face as she pushed past her, Leigh looked out at Temple in the car, her face hard and angry. She went back inside.

As there was nothing more he could do, Temple drove back to the incident room.

Back in the office, Temple interrogated his phone; the only missed call had been from London, the woman at Dobson & Byrne had left a message saying she would call back. While he waited for the call Temple and Kelly went over the timings for James Ashton-Jones arriving at Bedwyn station and getting a taxi to Ramsbury again.

'Thing is, boss,' said Kelly, 'if James did get to Wedwellow House that night, where did he go afterwards?'

Temple looked at the mobile data. There had been a call from James's mobile to Jonathan at 23.58.

Temple's mobile rang. It was Leigh. It had been two hours since he'd left Daisy.

'Leigh, I'm a bit busy right now and I'm waiting for a call to come in, so if it's not urgent can I call you back?'

'You told me to ring you if anything strange happened.' Her voice was raised and tense. 'I-I've just been into the kitchen and there was a man standing outside, looking at me through the kitchen window. He was holding a lighted match in his hand, just standing staring back at me.' Leigh was obviously shaken.

'All right, all right. What did he look like?' Temple asked.

'He was a big bloke, dark stubbly hair, number two I suppose, tattoo on his neck. Grubby looking. He frightened the life out of me,' she said.

From Leigh's description, Temple recognized Georgie Munt.

'Then what did he do?'

'He just stood there, then blew the match out while he was staring at me and then walked off. Didn't run, just walked off out of the garden.'

Temple realized that he must have been followed by Munt when he'd gone to get Daisy. He must have been watching him and he'd taken him straight to the front door.

'Make sure you lock everywhere and stay there until I get there. Is Roger with you?' asked Temple.

There was silence at the end of the phone.

'Leigh?'

'I've chucked him out. I rang him at work. I've gathered all his things up and he's gone ... Daisy's told me that he's been hitting her. After you dropped her off, I asked her what the matter was. She was so upset that it just tumbled out of her. That's why she stopped eating. He's been hitting her.' Leigh started to cry.

Temple's sudden rise of anger brought him to his feet, sending the chair he had been sitting on flying behind him.

'What? And you hadn't noticed?' he said angrily, his focus changing from Munt threatening her with a burning match to Roger. 'For fuck's sake, Leigh. He's been hitting her? Where were *you*?'

Leigh continued to cry. Conscious that Kelly was still in the office, he resisted the urge to continue the argument.

'Look, I've got to free this phone up. I'm coming over now.'

Kelly looked over at him.

'I've just got to sort out some domestics.' Temple left the office and went out to his car.

Seething with anger at the two fold assault on his family, Temple drove out of Marlborough Police Station down a congested George Lane, putting his response driver training to use as he forced his way through traffic in his unmarked car. He continued down the A4 and onto the Beckhampton Road at 120mph, one hand on the steering wheel, his other fingering the base of his neck. What sort of bloke hits a nine-year-old girl, he thought. His mobile rang, forcing him to slow down as he wrenched the phone from his pocket.

'Hello? Is that the accounts department?' the female from Dobson and Byrne asked.

Temple quickly overcame his confusion at the question. 'Yes, yes, it is. Do you have something for me?'

'Yes, I managed to find what you need. How much are we talking about?' she asked.

'Um, about three grand,' said Temple, just desperate for her to tell him what he needed to know so that he could drive on.

'Well, the person that inquiry was given to at that time was a man by the name of Ian Turner.'

'Was it definitely him?'

'Yes, that's what it says here, in front of me,' she replied.

'How can you be so sure?' asked Temple.

'Because that was the only matrimonial case we took on from Curtis Coleman. He specialized in it, or at least that's what he liked to deal in. He told us, just matrimonial, nothing else.'

CHAPTER 34

TEMPLE TOOK ANOTHER call from Kelly straight afterwards.

'Boss, Special Branch got back to us. Thought they'd passed on the information already. They've checked the passenger manifests for BA and the other airlines coming out of Singapore that day and Maxwell's not shown on any of them. Looks like he did spend his stopover in Singapore. They've found him booked into The Stamford Hotel. Check in and check out times correspond with the flight he came in on and his outward journey to Sydney.'

Temple continued his journey to Beckhampton. The new information forced him to calm down and think more rationally. He needed to get back to the office to start inquiries on Ian Turner but before he could do that, he had to get Leigh and Daisy out of the house, somewhere safe. Just until he'd finished this case. Then he'd take care of them himself; with Roger off the scene it would be easier. At the thought of Roger, his anger surged again.

He pulled up outside the house and knocked on the door. There was no answer. He opened the letter box and shouted through it. There was no one in. With a rising sense of panic, he rang Leigh's mobile. She answered.

'Leigh, where the fuck are you?' he asked, relieved to hear her voice.

'I'm over at the pub.'

'I told you to stay put.'

Temple drove round to The Flying Bull. He found Leigh sitting inside at a table, near the open doors to the garden.

'What are you doing round here?' he said quietly, trying desperately to keep his temper under control.

'Giving Daisy her tea as a treat, trying to be normal.' Leigh nodded outside to where Daisy was sat on a swing.

'I told you to stay indoors until I came round.'

'I didn't want to be indoors. We're safe here. There's people about.' Her eyes were red and her voice shaky. Temple's rage found him standing by the table, unable to sit down.

'And where's he gone?' Temple asked, referring to Roger, his jaw tightly suppressing his instinct to shout the words. As he spoke, he looked out at Daisy in the garden.

'He's gone.'

'No, where is he, I said? I want him nicked.'

'I don't know where he's gone. I don't care. I don't want to see him again, he makes me feel sick. When I phoned him and told him what Daisy had said, he didn't even argue the toss, the bastard.'

'If I see him, Leigh, I'll kill him. So, what's been going on? What did Daisy say?' demanded Temple, trying to keep his voice low.

'She said that he'd slapped the back of her head a couple of times and on her legs. She said that he hurt her and she'd cried. Thing is, I'd seen some marks on her legs and asked her what she'd done.' Leigh could no longer meet Temple's gaze. Looking out at Daisy, she knew she'd let her down badly. 'I didn't for a minute think that he would touch her and she wouldn't say what had happened. Why couldn't she tell me?'

'She did tell you. Eventually. Just makes me sick she was so worried that she stopped eating. She stopped eating,

Leigh. They were going to send her to a shrink, for fuck's sake.' He looked back at Daisy who was still on a swing. His guts knotted as he suppressed other thoughts. 'Are you sure that's all he's done to her?' asked Temple, barely able to say the words.

'You can't think…?' Leigh looked up at him.

'I don't know what to think, who knows what's been happening. You were fucking clueless …' He stopped speaking as he looked at her. He wanted to shake her, ask her what was she thinking letting Roger move in. But he knew the answer to that – she had wanted to hurt him as he had hurt her.

She looked back at him, tears brimming in her eyes. 'I feel sick. I'm sorry, I'm so sorry …' Her voice trailed off.

Temple tried to curb his anger towards Leigh. They shouldn't be in the pub, they should be at home where he could shout and vent his pent up anger like anyone else would. The surroundings felt as though they were closing in around him. He was feeling attacked from all sides, as his heart pounded, sending adrenalin coursing through his body. He knew he had to calm down, he had to think.

'Look, where are you going to stay tonight? You can't go back home, I can't leave you there now.'

'We'll be all right.' Leigh sniffed into a tissue, feeling the weight of guilt and her own self-loathing at having brought Daisy into contact with Roger. The situation removed the sense of righteous indignation she had felt towards Temple since she was sure he had slept with another woman. Her guilt told her she had failed to keep Daisy safe through her wish to hurt him. She'd just wanted him to know how it felt. She suddenly knew she hadn't loved Roger and had played a silly game and hurt Daisy and herself in the process. The revelation about Roger made her suddenly question everything about herself.

'Look, here's my credit card,' said Temple, putting it on the table in front of them. 'Book into The Bell Hotel tonight, for a couple of nights. Tell Daisy it's some kind of adventure.

I'm committed on a job at the moment and I need to know you're both safe.'

'I'll just call 999 if I get any trouble,' said Leigh.

'I can't trust *them* to look after you,' he said as he looked back at her, unable to hide his feelings as anger rose up in him again. Temple knew how thin resources were in the more rural parts of the county and he didn't want to leave his family at the mercy of how fast a response car could get to them should Munt put a match to the house. 'I'm not asking, Leigh. I need to look after you both.'

He pushed his credit card towards her. She looked back at him and the tears spilled from her eyes. She gave in. She could see his anger towards her in his eyes, he'd never looked at her like that before.

'Come on,' he coaxed, 'let's go home and get some stuff together and I'll take you down there, book you both in.'

After collecting some things and putting them in a case, Temple drove them down to Devizes and into the car park of The Bell Hotel. Dating back to the sixteenth century, The Bell as it was locally known, dominated the Market Place. Although there was parking outside, they went in through the rear entrance to the reception where Temple booked them a double room. Temple's anger continued to bubble and was tempered only by Daisy's presence.

He felt an overwhelming urge to shake Leigh and ask her how she could have let Roger near her. His gut knotted at the thought of Daisy being so frightened of Roger, but he also knew that he wasn't blameless. If they hadn't separated, it wouldn't have happened. He knew he'd really hurt her and tit-for-tat, she'd hurt him back. On top of that, he had also put them all in danger; doing his job had now also left them vulnerable to Munt.

Before he left, Leigh moved forward to kiss him on the cheek by way of seeking some sign of forgiveness. She leant against him, wanting him to draw her into him. He'd have given anything in the last few months to be this close to her and wrap his arms around her again but right then, he found it hard to have her near him. He pushed her gently back to arm's length. He looked into her tearful eyes.

'I'll try and get back to see you later,' he said quietly, 'and find out if all he did was hit her.'

CHAPTER 35

TEMPLE USED THE drive back to Marlborough Station to calm down. He rang the PNC bureau and asked them to run the details of Ian Turner through the computer.

'Got a breaking and entering thirty years ago and an indecency twenty-eight years ago, against a female. There's an alias too, Ian John Taylor. I can also confirm there is no DNA for him on the national database.'

Temple questioned the operator again until he was happy that this was the Ian Turner to pursue. He also asked for an 'of interest' marker to be put against him. There was an address in Croydon, a flat. Temple wrote the information up on the whiteboard and left the office. In doing so, he bumped into Sophie Twiner.

'Just the man I was looking for,' said Sophie as she saw Temple coming through the door in the front office foyer.

'Sorry, Sophie, I can't stop, I'm off to Croydon.'

'Oh. Well, can I come with you?' she asked.

'No, this is business,' Temple replied.

She looked at her watch; it was 6 p.m. She followed him out to his car.

'Perhaps we'll catch up when I come back,' he offered. She took her opportunity when he pressed his key fob. Opening the passenger door, she got inside.

'I tell you what. I'll take a few hours off and come with you. I could get an insight into an inquiry, perhaps do a piece for you?' she said.

'I don't think so. I really do need to move, if you don't mind. I'm not in the mood for this.' Expecting her to get out of the car, she instead pulled the seat belt round her.

'I'm not taking no for an answer,' she said and pushed the seat belt firmly into the catch and looked at him. 'Get a move on then.'

'Sophie, get out,' instructed Temple, programming his sat nav with a post code.

'No, I won't.' She sat, facing forward.

Annoyed, he pulled his car out of the parking space and down onto George Lane. With a clear run, he put his foot on the accelerator and stopped hard at the junction. If he meant to scare her, he failed; his reaction only excited her.

'Please get out,' he said forcefully.

'I'm not going anywhere except with you,' she said, fixing his gaze.

He drove on, irritated at her insistence and knowing that he could hardly physically manhandle her out of the car without the possibility of her lodging a complaint against him. The journey continued in silence, Temple not quite sure what he was going to do with her.

He intended to make the two-hour journey without stopping and Sophie grew restless as a result. Turning the heater on, she shifted in her seat. From her position, she could observe Temple comfortably, in profile. His quietness and distant stance towards her only made her more determined to make him warm towards her. Her boredom at his lack of attention drew her to touch the glove compartment. Temple's silence finally gave way.

'Don't ...' he said. The tone of his voice made her stop. She sat back in her seat.

'What do you keep in there, then?' she asked.

'Just police stuff. Not for public consumption,' he replied.

He glanced sideways at her, irritated. He should have thrown her out in George Lane, she was a fucking nuisance.

She shifted in her seat. Temple watched her from the corner of his eye. She looked back at him and his eyes returned to the road.

'What can you tell me about 'the Fyfield Down murder' case? Operation Acre, isn't it?' she said slowly, looking at Temple.

He looked at her. She knew she had his interest.

'I've been doing my research.' She was pleased with herself. 'You found her body, didn't you? She was dead, naked on her bed, surrounded by pills, wasn't she? By the time they found you, her face had been eaten by maggots.' She looked at him, knowing her words were provocative.

Temple remained silent.

'The pills turned out to be contaminated, didn't they? The PM was able to establish that she had them jammed into her mouth and down her throat before being strangled. Have you never been tempted to get to the bottom of it?'

Had he been tempted to get to the bottom of it? She continued.

'Didn't you have contact with the suspect or something like that? They've never convicted anyone, have they?' She looked at him, waiting for him to answer.

The trouble with crap journalists is that they were depleted of human sensitivity and emotional intelligence. Temple knew the drill; say or do something that would provoke a response, particularly if it wasn't true.

'And this is why you're here? To get "my story"?' It suddenly made sense to him; her presence at the hospital – she said she'd done her research. He'd been set up.

'It's an interesting case – as a boy you find your mother dead, murdered and now you're a cop. Come on, you must have a theory.'

'Yes, I've got a theory,' he said, looking at her, angry at her approach. He'd been all over what was left of the original file, copied it and kept it with him. He'd traced some of his mother's old friends and spoken to them, taken statements from some and followed up on any leads they gave. Some had been more forthcoming than others. He even had a hypothesis but he wasn't going to give Sophie Twiner any of that. 'My theory, as you put it, is that thirty-five years ago, they did things differently. The investigation into the death of someone who society considered to be a drug taking, non-tax-paying drop-out who associated with a lot of other druggy non-tax paying drop-outs wasn't exactly a priority. Free living hippy types weren't exactly popular back then. A year later came the 'Battle of the Beanfield', the clash between police and more free-loading, establishment-hating hippy types. There was one unidentified suspect from my mother's murder and all that remains is a poorly put together file and exhibit bags that have been lost in the mists of time.'

Sophie continued.

'What about the officers who worked on it, what do they think?'

'Most of the team who worked on it thirty-five years ago are dead, life expectancy after the job thirty years ago wasn't that great. You retired, got your pension and within five to seven years, you were dead. That is, with one exception, the original senior investigating officer ex-Detective Superintendent Roy Filer.'

'And? Go and see him.'

'When I last saw him five years ago, he was in a care home with dementia. He'd picked up the job two months before retirement. He couldn't remember his own name, let alone what happened with the case.'

'Why did you leave it that late to see him?'

'I didn't. I caught up with him years ago before that, in a pub. I did most of the talking. Trouble is, ex-detectives will talk to you for hours about a good case, one where they got a conviction. When the case doesn't go so well, they clam up. Don't want to talk about it.'

'So, did *you* see who it was – any idea who it could have been?'

'No.'

'I suppose in some respects you were lucky, lucky you weren't murdered too.'

It was something he'd wondered about endlessly since. That and what if he'd gone back just that bit earlier he might have stopped it happening, or what if his presence would have put the attacker off altogether. Endless what ifs. *Why had he been left alive? Why?*

'I read somewhere that you were hypnotized – have you tried since?'

'I was seven years old at the time. Some woman thought it would be a good idea to try hypnosis, it was a load of bollocks.'

'So, what was she like, your mother?'

Temple shot her look of disdain. She persisted.

'From what I've read, you were pretty neglected, she lived an itinerant, hippy lifestyle, took drugs, was a drugs mule. You hadn't ever seen the inside of a school when you were found and ...'

Temple interrupted her. The memories he had of his mother and their lifestyle were far from unhappy. He travelled in the passenger seat with her in their Land Rover, reading the maps and wherever they were, there always seemed to be music from the radio which they sang along to. She always seemed to be singing and dancing to music. Always happy. That wasn't how the press had painted it though.

'I might not have known the rudiments of English or maths then, but I knew a few things about life that they weren't teaching in schools.'

'So, what now? I could help you,' she offered.

'I've had enough therapy, thanks.'

'No, I mean with publicity, run a piece on it, see if anyone comes forward. It was on *Crimewatch*, wasn't it, years ago, as one of their first cold cases – did anything come of it?'

'No, nothing.' Temple didn't want to divulge the fact that the case was his reason for joining the job – and staying in it. The need to find out who murdered his mother and why never left him. It kept him awake at nights, gnawed at him like a sickness waiting for a panacea. It would never go away or let him go until he found her killer.

'Can we change the subject? I need to concentrate on the case I'm working on at the moment.'

Sophie eyed him. 'The offer's there,' she said, wanting him to warm to her. 'When you're ready, let me know.'

They continued the journey in silence, Sophie happy thinking that the atmosphere between them had started to thaw.

The sat nav took them straight to the address. A tired-looking 1930s semi-detached house, it was divided into two flats. Not trusting her to not look in the glove compartment and ordering Sophie out of the car with him, Temple pushed the wooden gate, the bottom of which scraped across a red tiled pathway. At the door there were two doorbells, only one with a name on it. He rang it and it was answered by a young woman.

'Can you tell me if Ian Turner still resides in the flat, please?' ventured Temple.

'I live in the ground floor flat. No one lives in the flat above. The landlord is still trying to find a tenant for it,' the woman said.

'Who is the landlord?' asked Temple.

'Mr Khan, he owns a few houses down here. He lives on the other side of town.'

'Does he come to collect the rent?'

'Yes.'

'So you know where Mr Khan lives?'

'Yes,' she replied, not offering his address.

'Can you give me his address, please?' asked Temple.

Reluctantly, the woman disappeared inside and came back with an address written on a piece of paper.

'Did an Ian Turner ever live there?' Temple said.

'There was a man living there once, but I never knew his name. I barely saw him,' she said.

'No mail or anything for him then?'

'No.'

'Could you describe him?'

'No, I couldn't. The flat's been empty for months now and as I say, we didn't even pass the time of day.'

'Did he have a blue transit van?'

'I don't know, mate, sorry.' The woman shut the door, tired of Temple's questioning.

They got back into the car. Temple put the address into the sat nav and drove to its direction. At the destination, he pulled his car up outside and taking Sophie with him, walked up the drive of a red brick detached house. He rang the bell. Mr Khan opened the door.

'I'm Detective Inspector Temple, Mr Khan. I apologize for the lateness of calling but I wonder if you could help me with my inquiries.' Temple held out his warrant card for inspection.

Khan took it and after examining it, beckoned Temple inside, but kept him in the hallway.

'You have a property in Crofton Road, a house that's two flats. The bottom flat is occupied by a lady, the flat above she tells me is empty. I believe it was once occupied by Ian Turner, a tenant of yours?' he said.

'I can't remember every one of my tenants, Mr Temple, they are just names to me. I have forty-eight houses and flats on my books. My sons help me to collect the rents,' Khan replied.

'I suspect Ian Turner to been involved in the death of a woman that I am investigating. I'd like to go and see the flat if at all possible. I was wondering if you would have a key and could take me there,' said Temple.

Khan looked back at him. 'It is rather late as you say. Are you sure this can't be done in the morning?'

'My inquiry is rather urgent and I really wouldn't ask if it wasn't. Perhaps if I could just have the key and drop it back to you afterwards, would that help?' said Temple.

'Well, I suppose I could give you a key. Wait there.' Khan went off into the house and returned, holding two Yale door keys on a fob with the street name and house number on it. He gave them to Temple.

'It will save me coming out with you. One is for the front door, the other for the inside door.'

Temple drove off with Sophie back to Crofton Road. Once there, Temple got out of the car, with Sophie following.

Temple opened the door and went inside up the stairs. He opened the second door and went inside. The flat was empty. Temple put his hand out and found a light switch but there was no light bulb in the fitting. Sophie followed Temple inside and walked around the room which was lit only from an outside street lamp. Temple looked around; there was a small kitchen and bedroom off the main room, with a small bathroom back out on the landing. In the main room, a worn, creased carpet lay on the floor. Temple noticed the plug sockets with a yellowed outline imprint of the plugs that it had once held.

'Whoever lived here must have been one hell of a smoker,' said Sophie, her face not hiding her disgust at the smell. 'It really stinks in here.'

Temple continued to look around, going from room to room, looking for any signs of life that may have been left behind. He opened the cupboards in the kitchen, looked under the sink, not sure what he hoped to find. His eyes suddenly caught sight of something in the corner.

'Have you got a pin?'

'What? What for?'

'There's a fag butt here. I need to pick it up.' A waste bin had at some time been attached to the inside door of the cupboard. It had obviously got there during the process of emptying an ashtray into the bin.

'I've got a safety pin, you could bend it and use that?' she said, retrieving it from her handbag.

'Give it here,' Temple demanded. 'I need something to put it in. Do me a favour, go downstairs and see if they've got a freezer bag or something. It has to be new, unused.'

Sophie gave Temple the safety pin and left for the flat below. Temple crouched down in front of the cupboard and reached in, impaling the cigarette butt on the pin. He held it in front of his face. If this was Turner's, he had something to take back with him to test for DNA. He heard Sophie come back up the stairs.

'Ta daa!' she said, excitedly. Brandishing a roll of freezer bags, she unfurled one, tore it across the perforation and opened it. 'Here you are, Sherlock.' She went back down the stairs, pleased to have been of some use.

Temple put the butt in the bag and tied the corners together. It had made the trip worthwhile. After a final look around, Temple shut the door. Meeting Sophie at the bottom of the stairs, they left the flat and got back in the car. Temple put the exhibit on the back seat before driving back to Mr Khan's to drop off the keys. Driving back to Marlborough, Sophie sensed Temple's mood had lightened enough for her to attempt conversation.

'Are you married? You're not wearing a ring,' she said.

'Technically,' he replied.

'I don't mind, if you don't. You can come back to mine if you like,' she said. 'You could tell me about the case.'

Temple glanced across at her.

'I rent a place at Upavon,' she said.

'I'll drop you off at Marlborough Station, where I found you,' said Temple. 'I'll have to go back in the office to see my colleague and get the exhibit processed. I need to see if I can get any DNA from it.'

Undeterred by his refusal, for the rest of the journey, Temple bore the unsubtle onslaught of Sophie's attempts to warm their relationship. By the time they arrived back at Marlborough, she knew she still had some work to do but the challenge merely served to make her more determined to make a conquest of him.

'Call me.' Sophie put a piece of paper with her mobile number into Temple's jacket pocket before getting out of his car. He intrigued her and she wanted to get his story.

He went into the station and up to the office where he found Kelly, her eyes glued to her computer screen. He gave her a run-down of his trip to Croydon and told her to get the exhibit over to forensics in the morning. Pleased with the outcome of his visit, Temple suddenly felt an overwhelming urge to go back to Wedwellow House.

Although it was late and dark, Temple went downstairs into a redundant cell area to where the exhibits for the case were held. Searching through, he found a sealed bag with the keys to Greta's Porsche which had been seized when Marcus Hussain had been arrested. He examined them through the plastic; they contained a door key. He took them back upstairs to Kelly and asked her to witness him breaking the seal to the bag to get the keys. They both went off to Ramsbury.

Once inside Wedwellow House, they went straight upstairs to Greta's bedroom. Kelly shivered involuntarily.

'Feels a bit spooky,' she said.

Temple found the light switch on the wall and switched on a central chandelier, which showered the room in bright light.

'That's better. I don't know what I'm hoping to see but just coming back in here makes me feel as though there's something here for me to find. Something I'm missing,' said Temple. The last time he was there, he was distracted by Sloper and the room was busy with the pathologist and Jackie Newly. He needed to take another look around, take his time.

Temple walked slowly around the room. He opened the wardrobe; on the top shelf in rows were all the expensive handbags that Maxwell had mentioned. On the racks were the designer shoes, pairs and pairs of them. Kelly was in awe at the collection.

He studied Greta's photographs again. He went into the ensuite bathroom. He picked through the various bottles that stood on a shelf; shampoo, perfume, aftershave. He went back into the bedroom. There was something in there, something he'd overlooked, he felt. He couldn't explain the feeling. Whatever it was, it eluded him. Maybe it was all starting to get to him, he thought. Maybe this was what happened to you when you were sleep deprived. Maybe I'm going mad, he thought. Maybe Harker was right. They left.

CHAPTER 36

In the morning, Kelly sent the cigarette butt off to forensics and then went off to Newbury to see Caroline Black. She met her at her home, a Victorian terraced house near the town centre. It was light and airy, with a fashionably modern open plan kitchen/sitting area looking out onto a courtyard garden area. In contrast to how Kelly had last seen her, in her BA uniform, Caroline was casually dressed in a t-shirt and sweatpants.

'I just wanted to see if you could help us clear up some points that have come out of our inquiries,' explained Kelly.

'Of course, anything I can do to help you.'

'Things have moved on since I made our appointment. Are you aware that James Ashton-Jones died yesterday?' asked Kelly, carefully.

'Yes, yes, Brett Forrester rang me last night. It's just terrible, it's one thing after another. The poor lad, whatever possessed him to take an overdose, do you know?' said Caroline.

'I interviewed a friend of his who told us that James and Greta were having a sexual relationship …'

Caroline stared back. 'No! No way, no way! How can you be sure the friend isn't lying?'

'I'm afraid we have other evidence ...'

'I don't believe it, you've got it wrong.' Caroline shook her head. 'She wouldn't do *that*.'

'Did you know that Greta was pregnant?'

'No, no I didn't ...' Her voice trailed off. 'But she wanted to tell me something, she said she wanted to tell me something and perhaps that was it. Christ!'

'You didn't mention that before when we spoke.'

'No, I remembered it afterwards. The last time we spoke, she said when she had more time, she needed my advice, wanted to tell me something,' said Caroline.

'Did she give any indication of her relationship with James?'

'Well, no, but now you tell me that, when I think back, perhaps there were telltale signs. They were very tactile with each other, loving, which I just took ...' Her voice trailed off again. She hit the side of her head with the palm of her hand. 'I'm so stupid! Now you say it, she was dreamy eyed around him. Oh God, she loved him! I thought there was someone else, just didn't realize it was James. That's why he took an overdose. Christ! What was she thinking of? Maxwell's *son*.'

'Did you know Olivia Ashton-Jones?'

'No, only of her, as Maxwell's wife, who had died. There were people at work who still talked about her death, so I knew she drowned in Riyadh. It was before my time with the organization.'

'Did you hear any rumours about Olivia and Jonathan Silvester?'

'No, but it wouldn't surprise me, given his behaviour with Greta,' replied Caroline.

'It appears that James was in fact Jonathan's son and not Maxwell's. Do you think Greta would have known this?'

'Christ! No, well, if she did, she didn't tell me. How did you guys find this out?' Caroline sat down as the revelations about Greta left her shocked.

'From DNA testing. The scientists drew familial DNA between the samples given by James and Jonathan. The child that Greta was having was James's. The reason I'm telling you all this is to try and discover who knew what. You see, we are interested in Jonathan's involvement with Olivia and you told us about his involvement with Greta and the nature of their relationship. Your account is slightly different to what Jonathan says, but the fact that both women are dead, having both had affairs with him, means we are seeing parallels in each case. Jonathan Silvester doesn't deny his relationship with Greta but says that it ended some time ago.'

'No, that's a lie. He's lying. She definitely saw him in the last few months because I asked her to come over to me one night and she said she couldn't that evening because she had to deal with Jonathan. That's how she put it, that she had to 'deal' with him. As I said before, it would make me angry that she allowed herself to be used like that by him but she said that he would tell Maxwell about them if she didn't go along with it. She knew I didn't like what she did so she stopped telling me. I wanted to shake her, get her to see sense and stop it.'

'Are you absolutely sure he would at least have seen her in the last few months?'

'That's what she told me. It wasn't over.'

CHAPTER 37

Temple drove his car into Melksham Crematorium for Chris Rees's funeral. The car park was full and cars were abandoned on the deep grass verges that followed a snaking one-way system around the site. A popular man in the force, detectives had taken a break from the Swindon abduction and murder to pay their respects to a man whose absence was keenly felt in that inquiry. Others came from around the county. Temple had to double park in order to be in time to stand with a hundred or so other officers outside the building, as inside it was full to capacity. Large speakers had been erected in anticipation of the turnout due to Rees's popularity and allowed those outside to hear the assistant chief constable eulogizing Rees's police career.

The irony of this was not lost on his colleagues; a few weeks before, still angry from the exchange, Rees had regaled the CID office of the nose-to-nose shouting match he'd had with the same ACC after his last case went west at Crown Court. Having told Rees only weeks earlier that he was a fucking liability and he was considering discipline action against him, those who had heard of the exchange wondered now how ACC Buller had the brass neck to stand and look at the coffin, much less give the eulogy. Temple heard their muffled whispers accuse him of contributing to Rees's heart attack. In death, Rees was described as 'a fine, outstanding officer ...'

After paying respects to Rees's grieving widow, Temple went onto The Wheatsheaf at Seend, Chris's local, where a traditional wake had been organized. The pub would be packed, but all he had to do was avoid Harker. Temple slipped inside. The previously sombre mood of the crematorium had now manifested itself as respectful relief. There was an optimistic buzz of steady conversation. Temple spotted DC Paul Wright getting served at the bar. Temple had joined the job with Wright and they had remained close friends.

'Hello, mate, how are you? You look rough,' said Paul Wright, pleased to see his friend and referring to Temple's heavy lidded eyes and pallor. 'Still, you look better than poor old Reesy. That poor bastard's already spinning in his grave from having old Billy Bullshit trotting out that load of bollocks about him. Funny how you have to be dead before the bastards say anything decent about you. He wasn't calling Reesy an officer of outstanding ability the last time he spoke to him. Senior officers make me puke. What have you been doing to look that rough?'

'Harker gave me the murder over at Ramsbury. Skeleton staff, long hours, you know what it's like. It's been a bit tiring,' said Temple, managing a half smile and starting to feel less tense than he had in a while. It was good to see Wright.

'I was going to ring you; I've got some news.' Wright was taking hold of a plastic basket of chips.

'What's that then?'

'Op Acre.'

Temple's attention was assured. Wright dropped his voice and Temple leaned in.

'A man came into Melksham station the other day. Said his mother had sent him down. He handed in a black bin bag full of stuff that he said had been in the loft. He said his father had died and his mother had sold the house and was moving into a care home. During the course of clearing the loft, they had come across a box. The man who'd died was none other than ex-Detective Superintendent Roy Filer, original SIO on Op Acre …'

'Filer's dead?' Temple interrupted. 'I only mentioned him yesterday.'

'… So they look in the bin bag and there are a couple of exhibits from old jobs going way back. Amongst these is a bag with blue material in it. On the label it says, *Exhibit 13 – Blue t-shirt worn by murder victim's son*. That's you, mate.'

Temple's heart quickened. 'I thought it had been lost. Are you sure?'

'So sure that they're talking about preparing it for DNA testing. There must have been a rat in the loft but even so, there's enough left to clearly see that it's a boy's t-shirt. Anyway, that's on the QT, but I'm keeping tabs on what they do next. It's Harker's call apparently.'

Temple had long given up hope that exhibit had survived. So many exhibits in the case had been lost during the course of thirty years and multiple office moves. How on earth had it ended up in Filer's loft? He must have taken it with him when he retired. Had he hidden it? No, he'd probably seen what happened to exhibits and preserved it. Waiting for advances in technology? Filer could never have envisaged DNA testing back in the early eighties. Neither had Filer mentioned keeping the exhibit when he had met him briefly. Temple was stunned. Could this at last mean that some further progress could be made? His mind went back to the caravan and a large hand grabbing hold of his t-shirt, pulling him forward before pushing him hard in the chest.

'Have a chip, mate,' said Paul, thrusting a plate full of chips towards Temple.

Temple took a couple. The sensation of warm food in his mouth made him suddenly realize that he hadn't had anything hot to eat for a week or more. The comforting feeling the food gave him saw him push more into his mouth as he took a pint of Coke from Wright's hand. He started to feel more human.

'So, who have you been working with?' asked Wright, as he watched his plate empty.

'Simon Sloper,' Temple replied, relaxing in his company.

'That's a fat, lazy, useless bastard if ever I saw one. So, you're having to dodge the Glaswegian handshake on a more regular basis at the moment,' said Wright, referring to Harker. 'How's the job going?'

Taking a couple of gulps of his Coke, Temple gave him an outline of the case and the progress so far. However, all the time in his mind was this new revelation about the t-shirt.

'Got your work cut out, then, especially with Harker on your case. Let me know if I can help but it sounds as if you've got it pretty much covered. You're using all the toys, the only thing you haven't got is surveillance, but then you've got no target. Unlike, of course, the job at Swindon. They don't know whether they're on their arse or their elbow. They're driving the Met boys up the wall. It's a right cluster fuck, the surveillance team have lost the target so many times it's a joke.'

Temple saw Harker out of the corner of his eye. He handed Paul Wright his glass.

'I've got to go, mate, Harker's over there and I need to avoid him right now.'

'We'll have a beer soon, yeah, when you're done,' said Wright. 'I'll keep in touch on Op Acre.'

'Look forward to it.'

Still thinking about the discovery of the t-shirt, Temple called in at Marlborough Station for the keys to Wedwellow House. Another thing Paul Wright had said had got him thinking. He wanted to go back to the house again on his own. Once there, he drove across the driveway and stepped out of his car. He surveyed the outside of the house before putting the key in the heavy oak door.

Inside, he looked downstairs, slowly walking from room to room without knowing what it was he was looking for. Temple had felt something the last time he was there, something indiscernible. He went upstairs to Greta's bedroom. His eyes scanned around. He looked at the charcoal drawing of Greta that hung on the wall and stood at the foot of the bed. He remembered how he'd first seen her, lying with her wrists tied. He stood still and continued to look around.

The silence and his concentration were disturbed by the noise of his phone ringing, making him jump.

'Hello, boss, just thought I'd ring you with a bit of information.' DC Craig Toff spoke in a quiet, conspiratorial tone.

'Nice timing, Toff, the phone going off nearly gave me a heart attack. What have you got then?'

He'd almost forgotten about the recording device fitted inside Jonathan Silvester's house.

'Sorry, boss, but I thought it was worth passing on. The subjects were both talking about the son, James, and his funeral arrangements,' said Toff.

'Yes, and?' Temple began to pace about the room.

'Then things got a bit heated. Jonathan Silvester told Maxwell Ashton-Jones that he was the boy's father. Said he'd known since he was born. He said that Olivia had told him James was his son and they'd hidden the fact from Maxwell. He went on about how he'd been more of a father to James than Maxwell and said – and I've written it down verbatim – "Someone had to help him that night, and as usual, you weren't there. I was the one he turned to, the one he rang, crying down the phone, 'Uncle Jonathan, you've got to help me, Greta's dead.'"'

Temple hung on Toff's every word.

'Then he said – and I've written it down – "I rang you in Sydney because I wanted us to protect him. I told you, he didn't just find her dead, he must have killed her, he *killed* Greta. He told me he was *fucking* her, Maxwell. I saw her lying there, dead. He said he hadn't hurt her, hadn't touched her but he must have. She was dead. I was trying to protect him. I had to. I knew he was my son. It's a fucking mess, Maxwell."'

Temple's mind raced as he listened to Toff continue.

'Maxwell said he didn't believe him, didn't believe that James was not his son. He asked Silvester why he was saying this, after all they'd been through in the last few days. Maxwell said, "We all lied, we lied to protect James and you're lying now." He said that they should have watched James more carefully, especially after Brett phoned and told them that Greta was pregnant. Then Jonathan Silvester said, "That's why he was so ill. He'd killed a child as well."'

'What then?'

'They argued about James. Jonathan said that Maxwell had known he was having an affair with Olivia so what did he expect. Said that Olivia hassled him to marry her but he didn't want to. They started to shout about Riyadh.'

'Yes, Riyadh. It's where Olivia died.'

'Maxwell said that you had asked him about Olivia, boss. He said that since James was dead and couldn't speak, how did he know that he, Jonathan, hadn't killed Greta. Maxwell said he'd said nothing to you about Jonathan and Olivia but felt like changing his mind now. Jonathan said that that would be really unwise and for him to remember the comfortable position Olivia's death had left him in, thanks to him.'

'Anything else on that, Toff?' asked Temple.

'No, boss. Maxwell then said he was going to see some bloke, Anthony Delee or something …'

'Anthony de la Hay, could it have been?'

'Yes, that was it, he said he was going to move out, ask de la Hay if he could move in with him. Hey, that's the crime commissioner, isn't it?'

'Yes, they're mates. Anymore?'

'No, no more, a door slammed and that was it.'

'Listen to the tape again, Toff, and make sure you've got it all written down accurately. Then get a copy of your notes over to Kelly Farmer at Marlborough.'

Temple felt deflated. The comments put James right at the scene at the time and Jonathan was convinced he'd killed her. Jonathan was obviously the first to give Maxwell the news about Greta's death and they both lied to protect James. Maxwell had also lied to him about his knowledge of an affair between Olivia and Jonathan. He had obviously wanted to cover up the same pattern of behaviour of using Jonathan to distract both his wives. He knew he had been right to put in the technical equipment but he was still reluctant to think that Harker and Sloper were right about James. From the sound of the exchange, Jonathan had gone to James's rescue that evening. But there was something more about Olivia and Riyadh; the exchange that Toff relayed had stopped just short of a confession by Jonathan. He'd have to go and get a statement from Jonathan but not yet; James was dead, unable to defend himself and Jonathan could make up what he liked. As Jonathan was unlikely to go anywhere before James's funeral, for now, he'd just let the technical equipment do its job.

Temple looked at the photographs of Greta on the chest of drawers. Irritated at the thought of Sloper and Harker being right, he walked over to the glass doors leading to the balcony and looked out to the pool and fields beyond. He walked back to the foot of the bed.

His neck stiffened and he rolled his head from side to side in an attempt to free it. The case was getting the better of him. Perhaps it had been James after all, he thought. Perhaps that would account for the lack of violence, as from Felix Harmond-Fford's account, he was in love with her. He was a big lad, perhaps it had been a mistake. But would a seventeen-year-old kid have his hands around the throat of the woman of his dreams, reasoned Temple. Would he want to tie her up?

His fingers manipulated the familiar feeling of tension in his neck as he tilted his head backwards, closing his eyes. Opening them, he looked up. The glass chandelier hung from the centre of the ceiling and was now above his head.

Staring up, avoiding the glaring light, he looked at the hanging crystals. As his fingers continued to work on his neck, he noticed that those in the middle were missing. He looked back at the bed and back at the chandelier. Again, he recalled his conversation with Paul Wright about not needing any surveillance and the photographs of Greta and Hussain. It was a perfect vantage point.

CHAPTER 38

TEMPLE'S EYES DARTED around the room. He knew that Maxwell had effectively placed Greta under surveillance with the private investigator but the photographs Maxwell had were nothing like those taken of her with Hussain at Savernake. Taken with a long lens, the ones found at Hussain's house were pornographic in detail. Temple looked at the chandelier again.

Temple slowly left the room and stood out on the landing and dialled his mobile. With it pressed to his ear, he stopped suddenly before he spoke and went outside and sat in his car.

'Is that Technical Support? DI Temple here. What are your commitments like? I need you to come over to Wedwellow House, at Ramsbury.'

Temple instructed them to meet him at the house, outside the gates. They were with him within the hour.

Dan Crayling, the force expert in covert equipment, led the team of two men and a woman. Crayling sat in Temple's car and left his colleagues in a white van.

'Dan, inside the main bedroom, I think I've found where a covert camera may have been hidden, in a chandelier. Do you happen to have one that you could put in there so that I can just test the theory? I might be wrong and if I am, you're going to think I'm an idiot, but I just need to see if it's possible,' Temple explained.

'We'll have a go for you, boss,' said Crayling, brightly. 'There's all sorts of commercial covert cameras on the market now. They come in all disguises, some look like smoke alarms, some look like LED alarm clocks. They can be monitored remotely and can record the content – sound and vision.'

'If I'm right, this would be pointing directly at the bed,' said Temple.

Crayling and Temple continued to work out what they could do. Crayling went back to his colleagues who waited in the white van marked *Swindon Satellite Dish Installation and Repairs* in black letters. Back in the van, they all spoke at length before Crayling went back to Temple's car.

'We've come up with a plan,' said Crayling. 'We think we've got something that would do the job. We'll set it up and mess about with it, record from it and let you know how we get on. It'll take a couple of hours or so.'

Crayling went back to the van and he and his team got to work.

Temple drove off towards Jane's house. With the prospect of having to wait for Crayling to contact him, Temple relished the thought of a hot shower. He had to wash the day off himself. He arrived to an empty house for which he was grateful and went off to the bathroom. Faced with state-of-the-art shower jets, still dressed, Temple negotiated the controls, which resulted in him drenching the arm of his suit, before a hot, powerful stream of water blasted out. Shutting the large cubicle door, Temple bent down to untie his shoes. Before he could get his second shoe off, his mobile rang.

'Temple.' His words met with silence. 'Hello? Hello?'

'It's me,' sobbed a voice.

'Who is it? Leigh?' Temple couldn't hear above the noise of the shower, so he moved out onto the upstairs landing.

'It's Tara.'

'Tara, are you all right?' There was silence to his question. 'Tara, are you all right, where are you?' he asked.

Tara sobbed down the phone. She couldn't speak through her crying and Temple knew he would have to wait until she could calm down before he could get any sense out of her.

'It's all right, it's all right,' Temple coaxed. 'Just tell me where you are and I'll come and meet you.'

Between sobs Tara managed to speak.

'I was so scared,' she cried. 'I can't do this anymore.'

'Where are you? Tell me where you are,' he said.

'They took me to Finch's garage. They put me in the inspection pit …' She continued to sob.

'Tara, just tell me where you are, for fuck's sake.'

'They had dogs. Pit Bulls and Alsatians …' Her voice trailed off.

'Tara, are you all right, what happened? *Where are you*?' Temple knew he had to get to her. He left the house and got into his car.

'They said they were going to put them in the pit with me and rip me to pieces …' she continued to sob.

'Who was it, Tara, who were *they*?' Temple asked.

'The Fortunes,' she whispered.

'What did they want?'

'They said they thought Finch was your source of information, but I didn't tell them anything,' she sobbed.

'Tell me where you are and I'll come and see you,' said Temple, relieved that what Tara had been threatened with obviously hadn't taken place as he was talking to her.

'They put me in the back of a van and drove me over to Devizes. They threw me out outside The Bell,' she sobbed. 'They dragged me out by my hair and left me on the pavement. I was so scared I threw up. I'm outside now.'

Temple wondered if they were telling him they knew where Leigh and Daisy were. Of all the places they could have dumped Tara, they left her there.

'Listen to me, Tara. Listen to me,' Temple shouted, his voice breaking through the noise of her continual sobs. 'I want you to walk down the street and go to The Black Dog, can you hear what I'm saying?'

'Go to The Black Dog?'

'Yes, go there now, I'll meet you there.' Temple ended the call and called Leigh's mobile. There was no answer. Temple rang the reception desk at The Bell Hotel.

'Can you put me through to Mrs Temple, please, Mrs Leigh Temple.'

'Mrs Temple went out, sir, about an hour ago, with her daughter,' said the receptionist.

'How do you know?' asked Temple.

'I saw them, sir,' said the receptionist, 'I was here when they checked in and I saw them leave.'

It was dark as Temple drove into Devizes. Repeated calls to Leigh went unanswered. He drove through the Market Place and parked outside the town hall. He went to go through the door of The Black Dog but out of the corner of his eye, he saw Tara in the small courtyard at the back. It was cold but she was sitting at a table, having a cigarette. With no one else there, he sat at the table, looking across at her. She looked a mess.

'Are you OK?' he asked.

He saw her hand shake as it struggled to hold a cigarette to her lips.

'I can't do this anymore,' she said in a low trembling voice. 'I'm a wreck, just fucking look at me.'

Temple saw her whole body trembled with fear. She was filthy and had grazes on her bony hands and arms. Parts of her clothes and hair were wet. As he sat down next to her, he could smell her, she stank.

'What did they want from you?' he asked.

'Caleb Fortune wanted to know what I knew. I just said I knew nothing. Said nothing. They had dogs, baying dogs, ready to get me in the pit, they were going to set them on me. They were making the dogs go mad.' She held her head in her hands.

'They were just frightening you, Tara, otherwise you wouldn't be here.'

'Well, it fucking worked,' she said, her voice shaking.

'So, where's Finch?'

'I don't know.'

'When did you last see him?'

'When he went to work at the garage this morning,' she said, her fingers trembling as she tried to put a cigarette up to her lips.

'Have you tried to ring him?'

'No, I was expecting him to come home as usual and then, instead, I get a knock at the door and the Fortunes, bloody knuckle heads, are there, telling me they're taking me down to the garage. They must have him.'

'Did you tell them anything, anything at all?' asked Temple. He was thinking about the gun.

'You're fucking joking, aren't you?' said Tara, scornfully, as her puckered lips sucked hard on the tip of her cigarette. 'I knew if I told them anything at all, I was fucked.' Her tear-stained face was now hard; her hands continued to shake as she lit another cigarette with the one she was already holding.

'Why would they think Finch was giving me information, Tara?' Temple pressed, looking at her.

'They said he was your informant, *yours*! Is it true?' she asked.

''Course he's not,' Temple lied, protecting Finch. 'But if they think he is, I need to know where he is now. Do you know anything, Tara?'

'No, they didn't say anything.'

Tears started to roll down her face as she stared impassively, looking past him. She shook uncontrollably.

'What else, Tara?' he asked.

Looking into the middle distance, after a short silence, she spoke, making no effort to stop the tears dripping from her face into her lap.

'They all stood around me, in the pit. Five or six of them. They had these dogs. They were all looking down on me. Shouting at me. Then Caleb Fortune unzipped his trousers. I thought …' Her voice trailed off.

Temple looked at her as her head dropped down.

'I was so fucking scared, I wet myself. He called me loads of names … then they pissed on me …'

'Who did, Tara?' asked Temple.

She was barely able to speak. 'Munt and Caleb Fortune,' she said, got up and turned away from him to be sick. She sat back down, opposite him.

'Was that all they did?' asked Temple.

Avoiding eye contact with him, she hung her head. 'Then they told me to get out of the pit. They grabbed me and dragged me out, into the back of a van.'

She continued to shake. Temple knew she was in shock.

'Did Munt or any of the others sexually assault you, Tara? You must tell me,' he said, gently.

She still couldn't look at him but she shook her head. 'I thought they were going to kill me.'

He questioned her further to be satisfied that they hadn't sexually assaulted her.

'Look, get yourself home. Ring me if you need to. I'll see what I can find out about Finch.'

He felt sorry for her, sorry for the situation she was in with Finch. She was bright and he'd had many a conversation with her in the past about leaving Finch and leaving Trowbridge, but she stuck to the low-life like glue.

Temple had given her a lift home one night when she came to the station to give Finch some fresh clothes when he was in custody. She'd said it was the first time a copper had been nice to her. She'd wanted to repay the kindness by giving him snippets of information about Finch's criminal associates which she gained from working in the pub and pillow talk. She had even been happy to be tasked and had been able to help Temple snare Paul King. Temple figured that after tonight, she wouldn't be in any rush to contact him again. Temple gave her money for a taxi back to Trowbridge and left. He rang Leigh's mobile again. There was no answer.

Temple walked down to The Bell Hotel. The lounge bar, with its central stone fireplace, was welcoming and busy.

He went to the reception desk off to the left. He asked the receptionist if Leigh and Daisy were back. She made a call to the room.

'There's no answer, I'm sorry,' came the reply.

Temple went back into the lounge and through to the bar area. Ignoring the bustle in the busy bar, he looked out through the large front windows onto the Market Place. Relief flooded through him as, in the dark, he saw Leigh and Daisy, hand in hand, making their way towards The Bell from across the road. He headed towards the door. He held the door open as they approached and tried to temper his concern for Daisy's sake.

'Where have you been, Leigh?' he asked, his voice full of tension. 'I've been trying to ring you but your phone's been off.'

'Oh yes, sorry, we've been to the pictures, I had to put it on silent,' she said brightly.

'You can't stay here,' he said, quietly, drawing her into him. 'You'll have to come with me.'

She looked back at him. 'We'll be fine here, as you said, we're thinking of it as an adventure. We've had a good day today, haven't we, Dais?' She looked down at Daisy, who was in between them, looking up at them, her eyes going from face to face.

'They know you're here,' he said quietly.

'We're safe here, look at all these people,' whispered Leigh, refusing to go. 'There's safety in numbers. We're as safe here as anywhere.'

'You don't know what you're dealing with. I do,' he said.

'I want to stay here,' she insisted. Turning away from Daisy, she continued. 'I've spoken to Daisy,' she whispered. 'He hit her but she says he didn't touch her in any other way.'

'Do you believe her?' he asked, relieved.

'Yes, I do. She knew what I meant and I picked my words and moment carefully.'

Temple's mobile interrupted their conversation. It was Crayling.

'I've got something for you, boss, at the house. You'll find it interesting,' he said.

'OK, I'm coming over.'

Temple left Leigh at The Bell with instructions to ring him first thing in the morning and drove over to Ramsbury. Crayling met him outside.

'There's a bit of a complication.'

'What is it?' asked Temple, wanting to go inside. Crayling barred his way.

'Well, we did as you asked. We went into the bedroom, saw what you had explained about the chandelier and took one of our devices in. After a bit of fiddling about, yes, it's possible that a device had been put there, given what had been removed from the chandelier. It would have been held in a small cradle.'

'So, what's complicated?' said Temple, impatiently.

'Given what you'd said about there being a covert camera, I started looking around. You know I said that covert cameras could be disguised, well, I think there's a live one still in there. They've got passive infrared sensors as a security system all over the house. There's one in every room downstairs and I was walking around checking these when I noticed that the one in the hallway was flashing amber. The others are red and only flash when it senses motion or when the alarm is on and when there is an intruder in the room,' explained Crayling.

'What are you saying?'

'I'm saying that I think the security camera in the hallway has been converted to a covert camera and I think it's still running. It's a motion sensor camera. It appears to be recording.' Fit and slim built, Crayling relished the opportunity to demonstrate his knowledge. 'No one would even notice, as it looks just the same as all the other remote sensors used around the house for the burglar alarm system, only amber. It's also completely noiseless.'

'Is there one of these in the bedroom?' asked Temple, still taking in what Crayling was saying to him.

'No. As the householder, if you wanted to put the alarm on during the night, you'd trigger it if there was one in the bedroom and you got up in the night. Which would mean if someone wanted to covertly watch someone in there they would need to put up a hidden camera. The chandelier is central in the room and a good disguise. These cameras can be transmitted to a mobile phone or computer for remote monitoring. Anyway, the crux of the matter is, that whoever put it in, the one in the hallway could still be monitoring now.'

'How sure are you that it's a covert camera?'

'Pretty sure. I've seen them before.'

'If it's still live, do you think whoever's monitoring it knows we're onto them? How obvious were you when you were looking at it?'

'Hopefully, I haven't made it obvious. It was the flashing light that drew my eye and to be honest, you have to know what you're looking at, it is subtle or else there wouldn't be any point,' Crayling explained.

'So, could I have a situation whereby the equipment in the bedroom has been removed but this camera has been left behind – say, if someone was in a hurry?' Temple suggested.

'Yes, that's possible – and of course, as we don't know what else was removed, there could have been any number of devices. Here's the keys, do you want us to change the locks on the house, just in case someone feels the need to come back and get what they left behind?'

'No, don't do that,' Temple said, as Crayling had given him an idea.

'There doesn't seem to be any cameras on the outside of the house,' Crayling went on.

'Put one up outside, would you, as discreet as possible, with a recording device. Front and back,' said Temple.

Given what Crayling had told him, he realized the prospect that far more evidence might exist of Greta's activities. He had to find out who was monitoring the cameras. If Crayling was right and a camera in the bedroom had been removed, there was every possibility the camera in the hallway might yet be retrieved. Temple was also left considering the possibility of Greta's murder having been recorded.

CHAPTER 39

GEORGIE MUNT STOPPED the 4x4 along the Hilperton Road. At 2 a.m. in the morning, it was dark and the middle class residents were asleep behind their lightless windows. He got out of the driver's seat and noiselessly opened the low rear door of the flat bed area. He put his hands under the armpits of Zac Finch who was lying on the flat metal floor of the truck and pulled him out. His lifeless legs hit the tarmac as Munt yanked at him. Moving quickly, all the while Munt looked about him, making sure no one was watching. Bearing Finch's weight, Munt dragged him across to the centre of the road. Once he'd dropped his beaten, bloodied and unconscious body down, he had a final look around and went back to his 4x4. He hoped some unsuspecting motorist might miss seeing Finch's body in the dark and finish him off. He drove away.

Temple woke at 4 a.m. Two generous measures of Jane's whisky had had the desired effect on his tired and almost foodless body, dulling his mind just long enough to snatch three hours' sleep. As he lay in the dark, he started to think through the last few days. *They'd found the t-shirt.* He allowed himself to go back in time, thirty years ago. Like thousands of other times, he relived the same moments in the caravan, with his mother dead and the noise of the blue bottles. Then a hand grabbing at his throat taking a handful of his t-shirt. A hand he had tried to hold in his mind a thousand times for any identifying marks. He wouldn't give up. He'd have to see Harker and ensure they examined the t-shirt for DNA, perhaps re-open the case. They had to do it now, surely?

Then his mind shifted back to Greta. He went back over everything, sifting, remembering faces, conversations, intelligence, recalling the facts and trying to make sense of what he was faced with. He needed more evidence. He needed to make some progress on the covert camera missing from the bedroom.

He remembered Maxwell's face when he confessed to having Greta followed. He seemed to genuinely regret having engaged a private detective, even though he'd paid heavily for the evidence it had given him. But perhaps his regret was due to him knowing Turner had set up recording equipment on her, thought Temple. He already knew Turner had withheld from Maxwell the graphic photos of Greta and Marcus Hussain at Savernake; he must have been responsible for setting up the surveillance in the bedroom but had Maxwell instructed him to do that too? What was it that the woman from Dobson and Byrne had said – he only accepted matrimonials. Temple was convinced Turner was his prime suspect – but he was unsure as to how much Maxwell knew. All he had to do now was find Turner.

Temple drove off early to meet with the Hi Tech Crime team at Gable Cross Police Station at Swindon. He needed their particular expertise to advise him on what the possibilities were for the products gained from covert monitoring. If Turner had been recording Greta, he would be doing it for a reason, to do something with it.

Torrential rain from a flash early summer downpour slowed up the traffic along the A345, causing gridlock at the roundabout for the two lines of traffic. He approached Junction 15 on his way to Swindon. Looking through the windscreen across at the line of cars that had stopped at the traffic lights, out of the corner of his eye, Temple saw a black Chrysler 300 queuing to his right. It looked like Roger's car. As he pushed the button, the descent of his door window revealed Roger sitting in the driver's seat, barely two yards away from him. The sight of him and the thought of him inflicting pain on Daisy caused a rush of anger. Temple looked around, put his window up and yanked on his handbrake. He got out of his car, oblivious to the rain and queuing cars and just focusing on what he had to do. He made his way quickly over to the Chrysler 300 while it was still static and pulled the door open, surprising Roger in the process.

'What the hell ...'

Roger turned, startled by the sudden movement of the door being opened. He looked up and saw Temple standing over him. Temple reached through, grabbing Roger by the throat, pushing him over and pinning him down across the front passenger seat. Kneeling on him on the driver's seat, Temple's punches rained down on his head and body, and caught unawares at the swiftness of Temple's actions, Roger was helpless to defend himself. In his rage and frustrated at the restrictions of the confined space, Temple pulled Roger back towards him, holding him by the throat. Standing back on the road by the open door, Temple continued to pull Roger towards him.

As he reached the sitting position, his body was pulled awkwardly to the side, through the open door, towards the road surface. Temple's movements were now unrestricted. He continued to land blows to Roger's head and body, as he laid half out of the car, both of them becoming drenched with rain. Suddenly, Temple was brought out of the moment by the sound of a blasting horn from an HGV immediately behind. The traffic lights had turned green and both Temple's and Roger's cars were now blocking the road. Letting go, he left Roger hanging out of the driver's seat, his face covered in blood, struggling to lever himself upright after the onslaught.

Calmly, Temple walked back to his car. With one hand, he wiped the rain from his face and looked at his bloodied and grazed knuckles as they clenched the wheel. Roger was sure to drive straight to the police station and complain of assault. As he exhaled, he knew he now faced the prospect of waiting for the Professional Standards team to come for him and charge him. Temple knew his career would be over. While feeling strangely at peace with himself about it and feeling totally justified in his action, he knew he shouldn't have done it. He released the handbrake and drove off.

At the station, he let himself in through the back door to the men's toilets where he washed his hands and checked his damp suit for any of Roger's blood. When he was satisfied that he was clean, keeping his hands in his trouser pockets, he went into the office of the Hi Tech Crime team. Knocking on the door of the locked office, he waited. The door was opened by DS Ceri Lambert.

'You've been caught in the rain,' she said, inviting him in.

Hi Tech Crime were responsible for retrieving evidence from computers and other devices which made them experts not only in software and encryption, but familiar with many of the worst depravities of internet sites available to those who populated them and the voyeurs who knew where to look for them. As a result of the sensitive nature of their business, they worked behind locked doors, ensuring only those who needed to be in the office were allowed entry. Temple needed their expertise, he needed to know the extent of what he thought he might be dealing with. Ceri Lambert showed him inside and took him to her desk in the far corner of a large room, stacked with laptops and computers, all waiting to be divested of their hard drives.

'During the course of your internet trawls, have you come across sites with adult sexual content that seems to be covertly filmed?' asked Temple, stepping through the door.

'We mainly see child exploitation sites as you can imagine, but obviously, we come across all manner of linked sites as a result. There are loads of adult sites where people appear to have been covertly recorded. These are particularly evident where they have been drugged, mainly women but some men, where the drug Rohypnol and the like has been administered. You can clearly see these women and men have no control over what's happening to them. Then there are the sites where they go even further,' Ceri Lambert explained.

'What do you mean?'

'Well, some are drugged as I say, and then there are some where the women are obviously being coerced, beaten and raped. The propensity for this stuff to be filmed and sites to accommodate it are vast, we can't keep up with it. In the most extreme cases, serious harm and even death are shown, the so-called 'snuff' sites. In some cases, just like the child exploitation sites, they don't show the faces, so they go unidentified, but they are getting bolder. Such is the confidence of these people that they will never be caught, they film the faces of their victims in the knowledge that because of the sheer volume of stuff on the internet, which of course, weighs against our resources, we'll probably never identify them. Some of this content is years old but once it's out there, it's out there.'

'What about new content?'

'Oh, they're always looking for new stuff,' said Ceri, matter of factly. 'At least, it's advertised as new stuff. The people who look at this stuff are insatiable. They might start off on Level 1 classed content but then their perversion escalates; fuelled by the chat sites where they exchange views and swap thoughts, many quickly escalate to Levels 4 and 5. There is a constant need for them to advertise fresh content. It's big business.'

'I need some help,' said Temple, as he explained the case. 'In light of what you've said, I've got a theory that the private investigator I'm looking at is somehow involved in the murder. I've considered the prospect that, because of the equipment left at the scene, the act of her death, her murder, may have been filmed. As I see it, there's only one reason it would be filmed and that's for online distribution. The thing is, I don't yet have the evidence to prove it.'

'Look, we're up to our necks in computers, as you can see.' Ceri glanced over her shoulder at a stack of computers. 'There's twenty-eight computers over there, they all have to be looked at and I have three staff to do it. The Swindon job takes priority at the moment.'

Temple, desperate to help his case, was suddenly forced to thrust his hands deeper in his pockets to conceal his bruised knuckles, as he countered an involuntarily action to touch Ceri Lambert's arm. Unable to completely control himself, his right hand then reached for his head, running his fingers through his hair, gripping onto the back of his neck in the process. Ceri Lambert looked at his face; as she saw the familiar signs of sleep deprivation and pressure, she relented.

'I'll give you twenty-four hours. I'll tell one of the team to concentrate on adult sites and conduct a search on new content. Send me over a picture of your victim and we'll see what we can do. I have to say though, don't get your hopes up. Just so that I manage your expectations, we are unlikely to find what you're looking for, it's going to be like looking for a needle in a haystack,' she said.

He knew in reality Ceri Lambert couldn't have used a better euphemism, but he closed his mind to the hopelessness of the situation. At least she was going to try to help him. Before Temple left, he rang Kelly who emailed a picture of Greta to the Hi Tech Crime team. On his way out of the station, Sophie Twiner rang him.

'I hope you like the coverage I've given you in today's *Daily Record*. I've kept it fairly restrained and I've asked for an appeal for information,' she said, referring to a piece in that morning's edition of the newspaper.

'Thanks for that.'

'Perhaps we could catch up later, tonight maybe? You can update me on progress?' she asked.

'I'm actually a bit tucked up with all this at the moment, so I can't promise anything. Text me later and I'll see if I'm free,' offered Temple, concentrating on getting back to the incident room.

'OK, I will.' Sophie ended the call, happy that Temple had invited contact from her.

Back at the incident room, Temple informed Kelly of the conversation with DS Lambert. The phone rang and Kelly answered it. It was the Call Centre at Headquarters. They had a call from a member of the public, a Ramsbury resident who had read the piece in the *Wiltshire Daily Record* and had information for the inquiry about a dark blue transit van they had seen in the vicinity. Kelly asked them to be put through and started to take the details down from the caller. As Kelly wrote, Temple looked over her shoulder, reading her notes. As she wrote out a registration number, Temple was immediately on another phone, contacting PNC for them to run a check. It came back registered to a van hire company in Croydon.

'Go out and get a statement from the caller, Kel,' instructed Temple, 'and I'll ring the hire company.'

The hire company confirmed the hirer to be Ian Turner, with an address at the empty flat in Croydon where Temple and Sophie had visited. The van had been returned to them only days ago, the Monday after Greta's death.

'Where is the van now?' asked Temple.

'Oh, it's gone out again already, mate. As soon as we get them in, they're washed, hoovered and out again.'

'How long had he had it?'

'Continuous hire for about three months, he had another one before that,' came the reply.

'Come back in good nick, did it?'

'Yes, bit dirty, but apart from that, everything was in order.'

'Did you find anything, anything at all, when cleaning?' Temple asked in desperation.

'I'm looking on the inventory here. No, mate, nothing, clean as a whistle.'

'And did he hire another vehicle? What did he drive away in when he left the van with you?'

'He walked off. Walked off down the road.'

Temple let out a deep sigh.

'But what I do have is a photocopy of his driving licence,' offered the assistant. 'It's part of the hiring process. We kept it on our files.'

Temple asked for it to be faxed over to Marlborough Station. For the first time, Temple saw the face of his main suspect.

CHAPTER 40

TEMPLE RANG KELLY and met her at Ogbourne St George, where she was taking a statement. He was able to show the witness, a postman, the picture on the driving licence.

'That could be him. I was picking up the last post in the afternoon from the post box and I saw the van, because it was in my way,' he said, helpfully.

'When was this?' Temple asked.

'About a month ago.'

'Where?'

'He'd parked right in front of the post box. There's a deep verge there and he had reversed back into it and was having to give it some welly to get his back wheels out of the verge. Then he lunged forward and the front wheels did the same on the opposite side of the verge. I was just sat there, in my post office van, not able to get on until he sorted himself out. When I saw the article in the *Daily Record* earlier today, I thought I'd ring in, for what it's worth. I've got an eye for numbers as you might imagine in my line of work and the fact they drum it into you that you are part of the community and to report anything suspicious. We all have a list of registration numbers of unfamiliar vehicles we collect during the course of deliveries. Just in case.'

'Well, it's been a real help, thanks very much,' replied Temple.

Temple took the short drive back to Marlborough Station. He went into the office where he was alone.

As he was considering his next move in the investigation, the door of the office opened and in walked two detectives. Temple looked up from his desk, he recognized them from Professional Standards. His immediate thoughts were that Roger had gone straight to the nearest police station and they were about to arrest him. Temple's mind raced; he wondered where they would take him and how long he'd be kept in custody. Should he just admit to what he'd done or deny it? He wondered how many witnesses they had and for the first time, started to feel a little nervous.

'DI Temple, we've come to serve disciplinary forms on you regarding the voluntary referral to the Independent Police Complaints Commission following the death of James Ashton-Jones.'

Temple remained silent and looked back at them. They were poised to record in their notebooks any reaction he made. He took the forms, read them and signed for their receipt. One of the officers gave him back a copy.

'We've also been instructed to inform you that you are to report to Melksham Police Station in the morning, where you have been posted whilst the investigation is carried out into your conduct. You will now be part of the local uniform shift, reporting to Superintendent Brown,' he was instructed, robotically.

Temple nodded in acknowledgement and the two detectives left. Ordered off the case, Temple knew he now had to act quickly. He dialled his mobile.

'Kelly, once you've finished with the postman, I want you to meet me at Wedwellow House in two hours. I'll meet you outside.'

Temple's desk phone rang at the same time.

'Hello?' he answered.

'I'm calling from Social Services, I'm after Detective Inspector Temple—' came the reply.

Before the female caller could finish her sentence, Temple interrupted, annoyed at the intrusion.

'He doesn't work at this station any more, you'll have to try elsewhere.' He put the receiver down abruptly and left for Headquarters.

He knocked on the locked office door and after a short delay it was opened by DS Lambert.

'Twice in one day, we are honoured. I hope you don't think we've made too much progress yet,' she said, opening the door and inviting him inside. Temple negotiated some laptops on the floor and went in.

'Sorry about them, we weren't expecting any more visitors today,' Ceri said.

'I've just managed to get a photo of my suspect and I thought it might help,' explained Temple. 'He's gone to ground. I don't know where he lives or what he drives at the moment, but I've now got his face.' He handed over a page containing Turner's image.

'I'll give it to the guys who are looking on the sites for you. I'll also fax it up to my colleagues at CEOP, you never know, he might already be on their radar. I see he's got a beard,' said Ceri, looking at the image again. 'That'll be off straightaway, they're pretty resourceful, these lowlife, at changing their appearance once they've had an official photograph taken. They don't vote, so you generally can't find them on Quick Address or on voters' lists, so having their name doesn't normally help, either. They'll rent their houses and cars and use multiple aliases when they're doing it.'

'What do you think the chances are that he'll come up on the internet?'

'Honestly? As I said, very slim. But if you're right and your victim's death has been recorded, sadly, there'll be a market for it. It just may take a while for it to surface sufficiently for us to find it. If, of course, we ever do. There's an international market for this stuff and the thing is, this is unlikely to be the first time he's done it.'

As she said that, Temple remembered that Turner had only ever asked for matrimonial cases. Turner had exploited the perfect pretext for spying on vulnerable women, thought Temple, and he wondered how many more victims there were.

Temple left the unit and headed off to Ramsbury to see Maxwell. He pulled up outside the home of Anthony de la Hay. It was a large thatched property, with its neatly sculptured hedges and a well-kept front lawn matching the precision of the sharp straight lines cut in the thatch. Nothing was out of place to catch the Brigadier's eye.

Temple visited on the pretext that he was updating de la Hay on the inquiry and hoped that Maxwell had already moved in, as Toff had reported. He rang the doorbell. An elderly lady opened the door. She invited Temple in and called for de la Hay in a loud and shrill voice that belied her apparent frailty. De la Hay appeared, with Maxwell by his side.

'How did you know I was here, Inspector?' asked Maxwell.

'I didn't, sir. As promised, I came to update the crime commissioner on the progress of my inquiry,' Temple lied, 'but as you're here, I do need to see you. Would it be all right if we speak please, if you feel up to it and it's not too inconvenient?'

De la Hay ushered them both into a snug room and shut the door. He suddenly recalled Temple's warning about Maxwell being a person of interest in the murder enquiry and felt more than a little uneasy at the visit.

'I'm sorry to intrude at this time, but there are a few questions I need to ask you,' said Temple.

Maxwell stood before him, less sure of himself than Temple had ever seen him. The death of James had obviously hit him hard. He had lost the assurance he had previously had and was a much changed man than Temple had previously encountered. He was nervous – deservedly so, thought Temple.

'Ask away, Inspector,' replied Maxwell, in almost a whispered voice.

'The private detective, what exactly was his remit again?'

Maxwell looked back at him.

'Well, as I've already told you, I asked if he would find me evidence of Greta being unfaithful.'

'And you mean you relayed this to Curtis Coleman who found you the operative and relayed that message?'

'Yes, because as I said, I never met him. His evidence was the photographs that I have shown you of Greta and the other men involved. These he left in a safety deposit box that I had. It had been pre-arranged by Curtis Coleman that he would report every two weeks. Curtis Coleman accessed the deposit box and sent me anything that the detective posted. That was how we communicated. That was how he was paid.'

'Why didn't you just deal with him direct?'

'I actually didn't want to meet him. I didn't want him to know me by sight. I told you, I wasn't comfortable with it.'

'Was that the only kind of surveillance you commissioned, for him to follow her?'

'Yes, what else is there?'

'Did he have the keys to your house?'

'No, of course not,' replied Maxwell, incredulously and increasingly uncomfortable at the reminder of what he had done.

'I asked you once before, so I'll ask you again, did he ever show you any other photos than those you have already shown me?'

'No, Inspector, those I have shown you are all that I received.'

'And you don't have any contact details at all for the investigator?'

'No, I'm sorry I don't. As I've already told you, I left it all to Curtis Coleman.'

Temple was still uncertain as to whether Maxwell was being completely truthful. While they spoke, Temple heard de la Hay answer the front door and welcome someone into the hall.

'What brings you to visit de la Hay, Maxwell?' Temple asked, knowing the answer.

'I, I have asked him if I can stay with him. He has kindly offered in the past and now I shall move in, until I can take repossession of my home,' Maxwell replied, nervously.

'Were you not happy with staying with Jonathan Silvester then?'

Maxwell's face changed into a hard mask.

'We had a difference of opinion over James's burial and I thought it was best for us to both cool off,' he lied.

'I see. Thank you for your time.'

As Temple went into the hall, he found de la Hay standing with a woman. She saw Maxwell coming through the doorway behind him and rushed towards him. It was Antonia Peronelli.

Temple left, knowing that it was probably the last time he would have access to Maxwell. PSD would be contacting him shortly regarding the IPCC investigation and he would know that Temple had been moved off the inquiry.

CHAPTER 41

At Wedwellow House, Temple waited until Kelly turned up and went and sat in her car.

'We're going to go inside and into the hallway. We're going to look around the house briefly and return to the hall. I'll say to you that we'll release the house soon, back to Maxwell, in light of the fact that James is dead and he was responsible for Greta's murder.'

Kelly looked at him. 'Are you serious? I thought you'd said he wasn't responsible.'

'Dan Crayling thinks there is a live covert camera in the hall and if he's right, I want to use it to our advantage. If he's right, there are two things. The first, if he's still remotely monitoring the camera, once Turner knows the police are going to release the scene, he may return to retrieve it. It may have his DNA on it. The second, whatever he has been recording I want him to keep, I don't want him spooked so that he destroys what he has or goes on the run. I want him to think that he's not in the picture, that we've decided that James killed Greta and he's more likely to relax if he thinks we're closing things down.'

'So you're setting a trap?' Kelly asked.

'Yes. But it all hinges on whether or not he is still monitoring the camera.'

'And you think this will work, do you?'

'Look, I might be totally wrong about this investigator. Then again, he might have everything I think he has and kept it and distributed it, or he has already destroyed it. I just don't believe a seventeen-year-old boy killed Greta. There is a flaw in my plan, though,' said Temple. 'PSD are investigating me regarding James's death and Maxwell will be aware of this very shortly. I've been posted off the case and they'll tell him this in the next day or so. This is all I can think of to get Turner to return to the house. If he does, I can arrest him and take his DNA and see if it matches the outstanding profile. If he doesn't and he's the murderer, he'll have got away with it, because I can't convince Harker that it wasn't James.'

'The flaw in your plan is worse than that, boss,' said Kelly. 'It actually might not be him, either.'

Temple and Kelly went into the house and re-enacted the scene he had described in the car. They went back outside.

'I need you to do me a favour now. I want you to go to Jonathan Silvester and take a statement from him regarding a telephone call that took place between him and James on the night of the murder. Tell him that our telephone billing inquiries have shown that there was a call between them at 23.58 on Saturday night. Give him some old moody that we know it came from Wedwellow House …'

'But we don't, boss, cell site wouldn't show us that,' said Kelly.

'I know that and you know that, but he doesn't. OK, I'll be straight with you, I've had some technical equipment put in his house and he made a disclosure. Obviously, I don't want him to know how I've come by this information, so I need him to think that we know it came from telephone inquiries which showed it came from the house.'

'Are you going to tell me what he said?' asked Kelly.

'No, I just want you to go in there and do your job. Give me a call when you're done.'

Temple got in his car and drove off to the Porsche garage at Swindon. Marcus Hussain missed seeing Temple's arrival in the showroom; he had taken a quick break and when he came back out, thought he had an interested customer looking over the latest 911 model. Approaching him from behind, Hussain was taken aback when Temple turned round.

'What do you want here?'

'Don't worry, Marcus, I've just come to ask you a question or two. You can calm down. You can pretend to show me over this car while you tell me what I want to know.'

'This is out of order, man,' he said through his teeth.

'Is it? Is it really? Your boss over there, is he? I'll go and speak to him, shall I, tell him what you've been up to? Now, that might be out of order, Marcus, so if that's what you'd prefer I do ...'

'All right, all right. What do you want?' hissed Hussain.

They both continued to circle the car, Temple opening the doors.

'I want to know exactly when Greta booked her car in over the last six months, would you have that recorded?'

'Yes, I suppose so. I'd have to go into the workshop and have a look.'

'Off you go then.'

Temple kept up the pretence of looking at the Porsche until Hussain returned.

'It came in three times during the last six months. The last time, obviously, three months earlier and two months before that. The second time was for the MOT.'

'And the first?'

'Change of tyres at the front and air con service check,' said Hussain. Temple got into the driver's seat of the Porsche and Hussain followed into the passenger side.

'What did you do with her keys when the car was in here for a service?'

'They were hung up over there.' Hussain nodded towards a rack with a number of keys hanging from it.

'Were Greta's house keys on the same key ring?' asked Temple.

'Yes, why?'

'Did she leave them there when the car was in the garage?'

'Yes, she did,' Hussain replied, puzzled.

'How can you be so sure?'

'Because when I delivered the car back to her, after the second time it was booked in, she texted me to tell me to let myself into the house and go and see her in her bedroom.'

'Oh yes?'

'You asked me, man, when you were interviewing me, whether I had been in the bedroom, well, that was when I was there. She was ready for me. All fancy underwear, lying on the bed, bottle of wine chilling. What was I to do? What would you have done, man?'

'Probably the same as you. And was this before or after you received the photographs?' asked Temple.

'After, man. That's why she asked me to the house. So no one could see us.'

'How long was the car in for?'

'A day. It's a day for an MOT.'

Temple left the Porsche garage and drove back to Marlborough Police Station. He went back into the incident room and picked up his mobile charger and his policy book. Clearing his desk and two drawers, he put the contents into a cardboard box and took it with him. Going downstairs to leave the station, he was met by Sophie Twiner in the foyer.

'I'm going to serve a harassment notice on you,' Temple joked.

'My visit today is strictly professional,' she replied. 'What do you know about a man found badly beaten in the early hours of this morning? A guy called Zac Finch?'

Temple feigned disinterest and kept moving. He needed to get in his car and get away. She followed him as he walked.

'Why don't you ring the press office?' he suggested.

'I have. There's no one there and I just got the usual voice message. So I thought I'd come and ask—' she said.

'I've no idea. I can't help you. Call the hospital. Look, I have to go.' He wanted to get to a computer to look at the overnight logs and find out about Finch.

'What's in the box?' she asked.

'I'm on the move,' he replied. His answers to her questions were curt as his mind was on the visit from PSD and the prospect of a further visit from them. His shortness wasn't lost on Sophie.

'Are we still on for a drink some time?' she asked, a little perplexed at his attitude.

'Yes, sure, call me,' he replied, wanting to end the conversation and realizing she wouldn't get out of his way until she heard something positive.

Temple put the box in the boot of his car and drove off. She had, however, given information he didn't know. He'd need to find his new desk.

Pulling into the car park, he looked up at Melksham Police Station. Temple went in through a side door and up to the DI's office, where he put the box onto a desk. He logged onto the force computer. He looked at the Command and Control log and scrolling down, saw the report of Zac Finch being found by the ten to six night crew and taken to Great Western Hospital. They would have contacted Tara by now so it was no use him ringing her to tell her something she already knew.

His mobile rang, it was Kelly.

'Boss, I've just finished with Jonathan Silvester,' she said.

'And?'

'Once I told him that we had the call on record from the mobile company, he said that James had rung him from a friend's house, asking him to go and get him. He said that he refused to go, telling him to stay where he was for the night. When I said the call came from Wedwellow House, he just said that James had said he was at his friend's house.'

'The bloke's a fucking liar,' said Temple. 'James never went back to school, he was with Jonathan. Look, Kel, you might not see me for a day or two, but I'm on the end of the phone. Should anyone ask, you're finishing the file and I've moved to Melksham. Let me know if there's any news on the cigarette butt.'

Temple knew the next forty-eight hours would be crucial. He also knew he had to keep a low profile. If he stayed at his desk, he'd be easy to find in the likelihood of another visit from PSD regarding Roger. He felt he at least ought to make them work to find him if they wanted to arrest him. Thinking about what he had done even now, he couldn't feel sorry for attacking Roger but he knew it would cause him a whole lot of trouble. In any event, he was supposed to be off the inquiry; in fact, as far as Harker was concerned, there was no inquiry. It was closed.

Temple knew he just had to keep out of the way and hope that something worked in his favour. He'd keep on the move and work out of his car at least until he had explored every avenue with the case; his last case. Then they could have him. *Just as they'd found the blue t-shirt, he'd be kicked out.*

Temple unpacked the box and put the things out on the empty desk. It at least looked as though he had complied with PSD. He then called Superintendent Brown confirming his move. It was Saturday and Brown was having the weekend off.

'A report came in this morning,' said Temple. 'Zac Finch took a beating so if it's OK with you, I'll start taking a look at it.'

Having been interrupted whilst shopping in a lingerie boutique with his girlfriend, Brown was only too happy to comply with Temple's suggestion.

CHAPTER 42

It was dusk when Temple made his way up to Great Western Hospital. Having made the inquiry at the reception desk, he found Finch in a small, six-bed ward with only two other patients. He approached the bed and seeing that Finch was sleeping, pulled the privacy curtain around them. Temple sat in a chair that was next to the bed and waited for Finch to open his eyes.

Temple looked at his swollen face; Finch was a mess. His eyes were black, badly bruised and there was a deep cut above his right eye. His nose was broken and there were blue bruises and red scratch marks and grazes all over the rest of his face. A drip fed saline into one arm, while the other was in a temporary plaster. A crisply starched cotton sheet and a thin synthetic coverlet hid the rest of the damage to his body. When a nurse appeared in a gap in the curtain, Temple left momentarily while she woke Finch to take his temperature. When the nurse left, he went back in behind the curtain. Finch, unaware of his presence until now, looked at him, expressionless, through the blue-black slits his eyes had become.

'Hello, Finch,' Temple said, with a false cheerfulness.

‘What the fuck do you want?’ Finch replied. His voice, although deep and groggy, somehow managed to find its way out of his swollen and bruised lips.

‘Just looking in on you. See how you are.’

‘I fucking told you I’d end up like this, didn’t I?’ he struggled to say.

‘That’s why I’m here. Who did it, Finch?’

The question caused a reflex action which made Finch inhale more air than he could manage. He started to cough but his cracked ribs wouldn’t let him achieve the intake of breath he needed for it to be effective. Finch struggled to lean forward to alleviate his pain, which only served to cause him more discomfort.

‘As if you don’t know,’ he spoke as if it was his last breath.

‘Well, I’m guessing it was Munt and his associates. And in the usual tradition, you’ll deny it because you don’t want to grass on anyone and all I can do is give you an Osman warning.’ The formal letter informing someone that they may be in danger was scorned in criminal circles. ‘Don’t come crying to us’ was its basic message and a legal let off from a duty of care to criminals who chose to keep lawless company and then fell foul of their criminal brothers.

‘You can shove it up your arse. Too fucking late for that,’ breathed Finch.

‘I know who did this to you. If you’ll let me, I can lock him up,’ said Temple.

‘Fuck off, Temple. I ain’t some fucking kid.’

‘If you won’t tell me who did it, then tell me why they did it.’

‘They thought I was keeping the gun. Thought I’d taken it off of Paul King,’ Finch mumbled.

‘What gun?’

‘The gun King says he got from your house.’

‘The fantasy gun. There was no gun.’

‘You would say that,’ Finch struggled to say.

‘Did you see it, Finch? Did you?’

'Why would he lie?'

'Don't make me laugh. Did you see a gun, Finch?'

Finch made no reply.

'Well? Did you see a gun? If he'd had a gun he would have shared that knowledge with you and shown you, so did you see it?'

Finch shook his head.

'Look, I told you before, he's trying to set me up. You got caught in the crossfire because you put him up when he came out. He wants his revenge for his sentence. He told me he would kill me and my family and when he got out. He torched my house. He gets recalled to prison and starts directing things from his cell. You know as well as I do that guns are valuable currency. Do you really think that King would let a gun slip through his fingers when he could make a load of cash out of it?'

Temple needed to deflect Finch's attention away from his flat, where the gun was last placed in the holdall by King. It wouldn't take even Finch's limited intelligence to work out who might have moved the gun, placing Tara squarely in the sights of Finch and Munt. Temple, sensing he had Finch's attention, continued.

'How would I have a gun, Finch? I'm a detective, not a firearms officer. He gets put back in prison in his cell because he's torched my house, but still he has to get his revenge on me – only now, he's really pissy because he thought he was staying out. The lazy bastards in custody don't search him properly, so they don't find the mobile phone stashed up his arse, so he's on the phone straightaway to his mates on the outside. What's he do? He has to motivate his mates somehow. So, he tells them there's a gun on the end of it and you and I know they'll work all day and night to get hold of a gun. You work it out.'

Reluctant at first, slowly, Finch was convinced.

They were interrupted, as Tara appeared through the curtain. Seeing Temple, she was a little wary but she had listened to some of the conversation before entering. This advantage meant she was self-possessed enough to face both Temple and Finch; she was also begrudgingly thankful for Temple's intervention. She went round the side of the bed and kissed Finch on the only space she could find on the side of his head that was free of bruising.

'You look better,' she said to Finch, lying.

Temple stood up to leave, mindful of the need to afford some distance between himself, Finch and Tara, particularly when they were in such close company. Playing her part to perfection in the presence of Finch to hide her complicity, and with some conviction, Tara rounded on Temple.

'Look at him, I hope you're going to find out who did this.'

Finch waved his hand in protest.

'Leave it, Tar,' he mumbled.

'I hope you've told him who did this to you,' she said, her voice rising.

'I've taken some details,' said Temple.

'I want to know that you're going to do something about it. Catch the animals that did this. Fucking animals.' Even though Tara was speaking to Temple, she avoided eye contact with him now by concentrating on Finch.

'I'll be off now, Zac,' said Temple, aware that each of them were playing off each other and wanting to end the charade for all their sakes.

Temple left the hospital. He walked out into the dark night and back to his car. He was thinking about Finch. In his jacket pocket, his mobile phone rang.

'Is that Detective Inspector Temple?'

'Speaking,' Temple answered.

'Now you've seen what we can do to Finch, I think it's about time we had a chat.'

'And who are you?' asked Temple.

'Elijah Fortune, boy.'

'And what could we possibly have to talk about?'

'You've got something I want. You've got a gun. If you give me the gun, I'll call Paul King off you.'

'I haven't got a gun. Even if I did, I wouldn't give it to *you*.'

'Perhaps you want a cut, a piece of the action as they say. I'm not beyond a deal.'

'There'll be no deal, Elijah. I'm not for sale.'

There was a short silence.

'Your wife's pretty, isn't she, boy? Perhaps you've given the gun to her, to protect herself, just in case someone attacks her in her room at The Bell Hotel. You can't be too careful. I'll ring you in the morning to see if you've changed your mind. We'll arrange a meet.'

Temple considered getting police cover but knew he had to deal with Munt and the Fortunes on his own. There was no way he would give the gun to them, so all the time they threatened him and his family, he had to keep it.

'There's no gun, Elijah,' repeated Temple.

'Yes, there is, boy. I've seen it with my own eyes,' came the reply. 'Now I want it back.' The call terminated.

CHAPTER 43

LEIGH PUT DAISY in the double bed back at Jane's.

'You've got to sort this,' she hissed at Temple, as they both stood in the bedroom.

'I'm just trying to look after you both,' he said.

'Well, you're not. I've got a perfectly good home of my own and I want to go back to it. Staying in a hotel's one thing, being dragged around other people's houses is another. I don't even know the woman. She didn't know what to say when you turned up with us,' said Leigh, referring to Jane. 'I suppose you're screwing her,' she said, doing her best to keep her voice down so that Daisy couldn't hear their conversation. She was angry at having to rely on the hospitality of a stranger.

'Hey, no, I'm not,' he said. Leigh looked back at him, desperate to believe him. 'She's helping me out by letting me stay here and now she's helping you out. Look, I'll sort it, tomorrow. For now, just stay here.'

'I want to go home tomorrow,' she said, looking at him. 'I want us all to go home tomorrow, I want us all back together,' she said quietly. She had calmed down on Temple's reassurance about Jane.

'So do I,' he replied.

'You'll come back?' asked Leigh.

'You told me to go in the first place,' he reminded her. 'Of course I want to come back.'

He went to move towards her to hold her but at that moment, his mobile rang, which took all his attention. Leigh threw up her arms in exasperation at the interruption. He turned away from her to take the call.

'Is that DI Temple? This is the Control Room. I've been asked to pass on a message to you. You've placed a marker on PNC for an Ian Turner?'

'Yes.'

'An evening crew have stopped a man in a car at Cadley. He gave an alias Ian John Taylor which has come back with the marker on it, real name Ian Turner.'

'Where is he?' asked Temple, his attention focused completely on the caller. There was a pause. 'Where is he?'

'They're going to ring you. I'll give them your mobile number.'

The call ended. Temple looked at his mobile, frustrated at the caller. A minute later, his mobile rang again.

'You've stopped a man called Ian John Taylor,' said Temple, without waiting for any introduction.

'Yes, sir, out at Cadley.'

'What direction was he travelling from?'

'From Swindon.'

'Where is he now?'

'He's driven off. We stopped him for a rear light out and as we couldn't hold him before the PNC check came back, we let him go. There was a delay in PNC getting back to us but as soon as they did, we alerted Control Room to contact you,' a PC explained.

'What was he driving?' asked Temple.

'A hire car, sir, a black Ford Focus, we've got the registration number.'

'Where was it hired from?' Temple asked.

'Hertz at Swindon.'

'And how long ago did you stop him?' Temple was ready to calculate how far he could have gone in the intervening time.

'He drove off about ten to fifteen minutes ago. We've put out observations on the vehicle to locate and stop.'

'What direction did he go in?'

'Back towards Swindon.'

'Right, I need him traced but I don't want him stopped. I want him followed,' Temple instructed. 'If you locate him, you ring me immediately and I'll get the crime car on him. He's required to help with inquiries in a murder investigation. Go and check an address in Ramsbury while you're at it, Wedwellow House, it's a crime scene and he might go back there.'

Temple called up the Control Room and requested a scene guard to be reinstated to Wedwellow House and then asked them to put him into contact with the night duty crime car. An unmarked police vehicle driven by a pursuit trained officer, with a DS as co-passenger had a remit to respond to any serious crime that occurred during the night and direct initial inquiries. Temple knew that in light of the force surveillance unit engaged on Harker's inquiry and disappearing up their own arse in south London, this was all that would be available to him. Having established contact, he was explicit in his instruction.

'As soon as the Focus is located, it's crucial that you don't stop it; I want it to lead us to where he's staying where I think there will be evidence that relates to a murder.'

Pleased to be able to have a worthwhile task rather than waiting for Control Room to direct them to anything they saw fit, the crime car crew were instantly galvanized.

'You must only follow – and for fuck's sake – if you find it, don't lose it. And ring me immediately,' ordered Temple.

Temple drove out towards Ramsbury. He drove past Wedwellow House and sat outside until the scene guard arrived. He then drove around the village until he was content that Turner wasn't there. Temple knew Turner could be anywhere, but he was convinced that he had been on his way to Wedwellow House when he was stopped. For him to have been found so near Ramsbury couldn't have been a coincidence, he thought. Crayling had been right, he'd kept the camera in the hall running and he'd heard the conversation he'd had with Kelly.

He really needed one of the night crews to find him before he disappeared so the crime car could follow him. Temple was parked up alongside a verge. He knew now he just had to wait to see if he surfaced somewhere. After only fifteen minutes, unable just to sit in his car, Temple decided to drive to Swindon, along the route he thought might have been taken by Turner.

Before an hour had passed, there was a call from Control Room saying that a marked patrol car regularly parked at Leigh Delamere Services had the car in its sights. The driver had replaced a rear light. As the driver was kept under watch by uniformed colleagues, they made contact with the crime car, which was circling the streets of Swindon Old Town. By this time, Temple was in the vicinity. He called the crime car crew to pick him up en route to the motorway. As Temple got in the back, the driver flicked on the blue flashing lights ready for a high speed blue light run out to Leigh Delamere.

The patrol car at Leigh Delamere reported that the Focus had left the services heading west, with Temple and the crime car heading towards it on the opposite side of the carriageway. As they got nearer to the vicinity, Temple ordered the car to cruise and turn off the blue lights flashing in the car's grill, fearing that any speeding emergency vehicle would spook Turner. The crime car radioed ahead to traffic cars on the motorway to monitor exits between Junctions 17 and 16, to see if the Focus turned off. At the next junction, the crime car turned around and resumed the high speed pursuit.

Temple knew that this was his final chance of detaining Turner and securing the evidence he needed to back his supposition that he was the murderer. The fact that he had now had most of the Swindon mobile resources in the pursuit of Turner wouldn't go unnoticed by on-duty senior officers for very long and they would soon start to ask their arse-saving questions that wouldn't necessarily be conducive to Temple reaching the best outcome. He knew he had to get an outcome before they started getting involved.

The Focus remained on the motorway long enough for the crime car to gain ground. With the Focus in its sights, it slowed and pulled in behind a line of cars so that it could follow from a safe distance. It drove on past Junction 17. Detective Sergeant Charlie Eaton in the car with Temple asked him if he was sure he didn't want the occupant stopped.

'No, no, just follow. I need him to take us to wherever it is he's going,' Temple instructed.

As the car sped along in the darkness and Temple considered the prospect of arrest, doubts began to spring into his mind; what did he actually have on this bloke? Harker and Sloper considered the prime suspect to be James and he was dead. What if they were right after all? He was a big muscular lad, maybe he did it – maybe he found Greta with someone else that night and lost it. All he had on Turner was a gut feeling that the creepy bastard had had Greta under surveillance for his own ends. But senior officers didn't like gut feelings – a growing number of them would say there was no place for gut feelings in modern policing. What had nagged him was Maxwell not being given the photos of Greta and Marcus Hussain in Savernake Forest. Temple knew that if he had, the job would have been over, Turner's work would have been completed. He'd deliberately prolonged the job because he liked what he saw. The more he thought of him, the stronger was his feeling that this was the right action.

Junction 16 was looming and the Focus remained in the outside lane. The crime car remained in the same lane, four cars behind.

Suddenly, the Focus swerved across the carriageway, causing other motorists to break hard. It sped down the slip road of the motorway. The crime car struggled to make the same manoeuvre. The brakes were slammed on due to a tight line of cars barring its way due to Turner's quick action.

'The bloke's a lunatic,' said the police driver.

'He either had a quick change of mind or he's surveillance aware and knows or thinks he's being followed. Just don't lose him. Get down that slip road,' Temple ordered.

The blue flashing lights in the grill of the crime car were deployed to force its way across the carriageway through the line of traffic. They went down the slip road and back into Swindon.

'He could have gone off down the B4005,' said Eaton, seeing there was no sign of the Focus immediately ahead.

'Get on the radio for patrol cars to look out for it. I've got someone at Ramsbury, if that's where he's headed. Let's just stick with Swindon, just see if he's here somewhere.' They continued on, driving down the dual carriageway.

Temple realized that the darkness of the night actually enhanced Swindon. As he looked out of the car window under street light, the soullessness that was starkly evident by day was just about hidden from view. The place was totally devoid of any form of beauty, its main claim to fame was Swindon railway works, which had been turned into one of a few museums and what the modern town was founded upon.

'There it is,' said Eaton, looking into the distance. The crime car slowed down and the surveillance operation began again, with Eaton directing the uniform traffic driver in surveillance techniques to minimize their presence in Turner's rear view mirror.

They continued to follow the Focus as it went through the numerous sets of traffic lights that blighted the streets until they were back in Old Town.

'He's going towards the lock-ups,' said Eaton. 'We can't follow him down there, we'll be seen. I'll have to get out. Pull over here.'

'No, I'll go,' said Temple.

The crime car pulled up a distance away as the Focus did exactly as Eaton suggested and turned into a cul-de-sac full of lock-up garages. Temple made his way quickly down the street. As he walked, he took off his jacket and tie and undid the buttons at the neck of his shirt. He pulled out his shirt from his trousers and, holding his jacket in his hand, he walked toward the cul-de-sac. He slowly walked into it and saw the Focus parked up in the distance. He couldn't see anyone in it. There were ten lock-ups on either side of the road. In the dark, Temple could see the ones closest to him were closed. He'd have to venture further down the unlit area to see the rest.

He walked on, tentatively, trying to minimize the crunch his shoes made on the concrete beneath his feet. As he moved forward, he could hear a car engine and was suddenly blinded by the full-on beam of headlights headed straight towards him. He couldn't see anything but white light and didn't know which way to jump to get out of the way but knew he had to make a quick decision. He jumped to his left. The vehicle sped past him, leaving him to get up off the road. It turned the corner back onto the main road and drove off. The crime car screeched at the top of the cul-de-sac and Eaton saw Temple getting to his feet.

'You all right, boss?' he shouted.

Temple ran towards him, 'Yes, let's get after him,' and he got back into the back of the car. 'What's he driving?' asked Temple.

'A BMW 5 series.'

'Did you get the number?'

'No, only partial, our main concern was that we'd have to pick you up off the road covered in tyre tracks.'

The car sped after the BMW. As a roundabout loomed with four possible exits, they had no chance of guessing the way it had gone. Temple instructed the partial index number be relayed over the airway for a stop if seen. With no other indication of where the BMW had gone, Temple asked to be dropped back to his car.

'Good effort, guys, thanks.'

'We'll keep cruising for you, boss, sorry we lost him,' said Eaton, feeling Temple's disappointment.

Temple drove back towards Jane's. With the adrenalin rush of the crime car pursuit already starting to dissipate, he had a sense that he'd just lost his best chance of making any meaningful progress. Without Turner, all he had against Harker's wish for him to write up the case against James Ashton-Jones was gut instinct and he knew that wasn't enough. When he arrived outside the house, despite the time and although he felt tired, he knew he wouldn't be able to sleep so he resolved just to sit in his car, rather than go inside and wake anyone.

He looked at his watch. It was 3.45 in the morning. He checked his phone. There were a couple of missed calls, both from Kelly. Temple considered the meeting he would inevitably have with Harker later that day, as he came to read and sign his policy book and see that the investigation was being written up for CPS.

No doubt Harker would hear about the crime car pursuit and ask him to explain that too, when he'd already given him instructions to close the inquiry. He should have known that he was always going to come off worse working closely with Harker. The past should have taught him that.

The business with Roger would play right into his hands; Harker would have a field day. Any day now and Temple expected to see PSD again. He looked at his hands; they had healed quite well, another day and there would be hardly any marks left. He still couldn't feel sorry for what he did. Given the circumstances, he reasoned, no jury would convict him, surely? He wondered how much Leigh would want him back though, once she knew he didn't have a job. He decided he wouldn't say anything to her until he was served papers.

In the meantime, he had to sort out Munt and the Fortunes because she was intent on moving back home. All he knew was, he had to do something about the situation. There was no way he was going to give a gun to Elijah Fortune, but all the time he had it, he knew he was vulnerable. He suddenly had an idea, a way to get Elijah Fortune off his back, but he'd have to give up the gun. He started his car and as he did so, his phone rang.

'Boss, it's Charlie Eaton. I've arrested your man.'

CHAPTER 44

'WHERE ARE YOU?'

'Wroughton,'

'Are you sure it's him?'

'It's him, boss. We picked him up again, an hour or so after you left us. We kept looking for him. He must have been driving around thinking we were following him when we weren't and when he thought he'd shaken us off, we picked him up and he went home. He took us to a terraced house on the main drag in Wroughton. We sat up and watched him go inside. I was going to ring you then, but after about ten minutes, he came out again. On foot this time. He walked straight past us. I swear he knew we were there. I let him walk on up the road, up the hill, watching him in the wing mirror and then I got out and followed him. He was almost out of sight but I figured there was nowhere really he could go, except into a copse. By the time I saw him, he was lassoing a tree with a rope and putting a noose around his neck. It was already made, so it was premeditated. That's when I ran to him and arrested him.'

'Why didn't you ring me when you located him again?' Temple hit the dashboard with his hand in frustration and anger. 'Where are you now, *exactly*?'

From his tone, this was not the reaction Eaton was expecting, something akin to a verbal high five he thought would have been more appropriate.

'He's literally under my boot, boss,' said Eaton. 'We had a bit of a tussle. We're still in the copse. I'm just about to call up the crime car to come and give me a hand.'

'I'm on my way. Try and stay there until I arrive. Move only if you really have to.'

Temple pushed his car to the extremes of its engine and the winding road to Wroughton. Temple's main concern was what Turner had done in the house for the ten minutes he was in there before he came out. Temple berated himself for leaving; he should have stuck with it, he could have controlled it. By the sounds of it, a few minutes later and Turner would have been swinging from a tree.

Temple arrived on the outskirts of Wroughton. He reduced his speed into the approach, going downhill, into Church Hill, in the hope of seeing the crime car. As he approached a line of terraced houses on the left, he saw it parked up, last in a line along the roadside. He'd passed a copse on his approach. Eaton must be in there, thought Temple. He parked up behind the crime car and got out. In the half light, he strode up Church Hill and into a shallow copse by the church. A little way in, he saw Eaton with Turner stood next to him. He saw a rope on the ground. At last, Temple was able to look at him.

His hands handcuffed behind his back, Turner met Temple's gaze and the two stood looking at each other momentarily. Temple was met with a dead eyed stare from two small eyes that were detached from soul and spirit. Temple looked him over. He was non-descript – with no outstanding features, he had a clump of badly cut straight dark hair and a grey pallor. He'd shaved off the beard he'd had in his driver's licence photo. Average height, clean shaven, blandly dressed, Temple figured his appearance was deliberately designed. Typical of surveillance squads, under his guise as a private investigator, he ensured he wouldn't stand out from the crowd and he wouldn't be remembered.

Temple continued to look him over. Dishevelled from rolling around on the ground with Eaton, Turner's lightweight grey Mac was muddied. Temple noted the greasy stains on the front, near the lapels, remnants of hours spent in cars, eating, while he watched, stalked. Likewise, the front of his cotton trousers. His shirt was also muddied at the front, half tucked in and missing a few buttons from the tussle with Eaton. Temple knew he had to be responsible for Greta's death – he just didn't know how.

'What's he said?'

'Nothing. I haven't asked him anything. Just told him he was under arrest on suspicion of the murder of Greta Ashton-Jones,' answered Eaton.

'What did he say to that?'

'Nothing.'

Temple faced Turner. 'You are going to be taken back to the police station. Is there anything you want to say or tell me before you go?' asked Temple, his breath showing in the early morning air.

'You ain't going to lock me up with nonces, mate,' Turner replied.

It was an innocuous enough comment but to Temple, it was all he needed. Relief flooded through him. This was it, the confirmation he needed. He was sure he had his man.

Temple searched him. In the inside pocket of his coat was his wallet. Temple looked inside and saw it contained bank and credit cards. He replaced it and took a mobile phone and keys from his pocket, then he and Eaton walked him back to the crime car, telling the driver to call for another car to take Turner to custody. Eaton walked down Church Hill with Temple to Turner's address. Arriving at the small terraced cottage, they let themselves in with the keys.

The house was devoid of anything to declare it a home; it was merely a building, from which Turner came and went. The house felt cold in the way that houses did when their owners went away for any length of time; cold from a lack of any human warmth within its walls. They went through a narrow hallway, which had a front room running from it. The place was unfurnished. To the rear was a small dining area which led onto a kitchen. Through the kitchen was a bathroom. Temple gave it all a cursory look around; the place was stale. He noticed the dead flies that peppered the black mouldy window sill. Empty take-away cartons from curries and Chinese meals had been left on the kitchen worktops. Turner had obviously just existed here.

'He probably rents,' said Eaton.

'Find me a computer, a laptop, anything.'

They went from room to room until, upstairs, Temple found what he was looking for. In a small back bedroom, there were two laptops, one lying on the floor and the other on a small table with a chair in front of it. He knew he couldn't touch either and he also knew that because of the early hour, he couldn't contact the Hi Tech Crime Unit who would have to take care of it for him. For ten minutes Turner had been in the house before he went out and was finally arrested. Temple was mindful that he could have done a lot of damage to the hard drives in that time. He rang Control Room for them to put a call in to DS Ceri Lambert to contact him.

They continued to look around. The largest front bedroom had a sleeping bag on the floor and a rucksack in the corner. A pair of thin curtains hung by a couple of rings at the window. A search of the rucksack revealed a compact handheld video camera, memory cards and an extra battery pack. A third bedroom was empty.

'Tip that rucksack out,' Temple instructed, 'Look in every pocket. Look for an address, we need an address. I want to know where he lives because he doesn't live here.'

Eaton hunched down and started to open every zip. There was nothing. Temple instructed him to search Turner's car outside which again produced nothing. Temple's mobile rang, it was Ceri Lambert.

'Ceri, I've made an arrest in the case and I'm at an address in Wroughton. I've got two laptops here and a video camera that will need to come over to your team, how are you fixed for getting someone out here to pick them up?' asked Temple.

'I can send someone out to you at eight. They'll bring them back here,' she replied.

'How long before you can look at them?' he asked.

She thought out loud. 'Well, that's the difficulty. We're still dealing with the Swindon job, a load of Facebook stuff needs looking at.' Knowing that Temple didn't want to hear that, she relented. 'I'll tell you what, we'll get onto it straightaway. Nothing has come of our other inquiries for you so far, there's so much out there. Is it just the two?' she asked.

'Yes, trouble is, he was in the house for ten minutes prior to going out and attempting suicide. He may have wiped files and such like,' Temple explained.

'Don't worry. We have software that will trace deleted files. Leave it to us.'

Reassured, Temple and Eaton finished the cursory search of the premises which revealed nothing more than Turner's eating and hygiene habits. Until he had some hard evidence, Temple knew he had to keep things low key. He couldn't request a search team straight away in case it alerted Harker to what he was doing. But he also had to deal with the Fortunes and Eaton's call to him earlier had interrupted that.

'Take the crime car and go back to the garages where he took us last night,' said Temple. 'Give it a thorough search and when you've finished, come back here and let the Hi Tech guys in to pick up the laptops. Ring me on my mobile if you find anything, I've just got to go and do something else.' Eaton nodded.

Temple looked at his watch; he calculated the time they took Turner away and the time it would take the Swindon custody unit to process him, get him medically assessed and provide him with a solicitor. Temple reckoned there were two hours before he'd be needed at custody. If he was going to get the Fortunes off his back, he'd have to go now. He drove off to Trowbridge, to the flats where Tara and Finch lived.

Parking around the corner from Lambrok Road, he walked to a nearby telephone kiosk. He called 101 and, speaking in his best Birmingham accent, reported that he'd found a gun dumped in a waste bin at the rear of the flats. He then walked quickly to the flats. He'd wiped the gun over with a moist screen wipe he had in the car and, satisfied that he hadn't been seen, he opened the lid of the bin and rested the gun on top of a cardboard box. Walking quickly, he returned to his car and he drove to the end of Lambrok Road. Within ten minutes, Temple watched as a marked police car drove past him.

A uniformed officer and a PCSO casually got out and went to the rear of the flats. After a while, the PCSO returned to the police car and went into the boot and returned to his colleague at the rear of the flats carrying an exhibit bag and blue latex gloves. Returning to the car with the bag, they drove off. Temple went back to check the bin. The gun was gone. Temple then rang Sophie Twiner, waking her.

'If you want a scoop, go to Trowbridge nick and ask them about the discovery of a firearm today, at the rear of some flats in Lambrok Road. You might have to make a fuss but it should give you the front page tomorrow. Remember, this conversation never took place.'

At Swindon, Temple went into the custody unit. Turner was by this time in his cell waiting for his solicitor to arrive. Temple spoke to the custody sergeant.

'Did he say anything when you read out the reason for his detention?'

'Nope, nothing. No reaction at all. We've got him on twenty-four hour watch, given the circumstances of his arrest. DNA's been taken.'

'Fast track it. I also need to seize his wallet. I want to get his bank and credit cards up to the Financial Investigators to see if they can trace his address for me.' The custody sergeant retrieved Turner's wallet and Temple delivered it to their first floor office and returned to the custody suite.

As Temple waited to speak to Turner's solicitor, Kelly rang him.

'Boss, I tried to ring you last night but you must have been in a really low signal area, it wouldn't let me leave a voice message. They found some DNA from the cigarette butt at the flat in Croydon. It didn't match the outstanding profile.'

Temple held his head in his hands. He just had to hope that the cigarette butt hadn't been Turner's. The solicitor approached him and indicated his client was ready for interview. A few minutes later, Temple, in company of a trained interviewer, sat in an interview room across from Turner. After introductions and the usual legal procedures, Temple began his questioning. Turner sat impassive, listening to the questions and responding to each with 'no comment'. Thirty minutes of questioning went by with the same response. Temple knew he was going to be in it for the long haul.

'Can you explain the nature of your work for Maxwell Ashton-Jones?' asked Temple.

'No comment.'

'Can you tell me why you didn't pass onto him photographs that were taken of his wife in Savernake Forest with Marcus Hussain?'

'No comment.'

'Can you tell me about texting Marcus Hussain asking for money for the photographs that you took of him and Greta Ashton-Jones?'

'No comment.' It turned into a mantra.

Turner's demeanour did not change throughout. Temple knew that this first round of questioning would continue like this and it was a case of going through the motions. During a break, Temple rang Ceri Lambert.

'Anything on the laptops yet, Ceri? He's going "no comment" here and I could really do with something,' he said wearily.

'The guys are still going through the preliminaries,' she said. 'I'll call you as soon as we have something for you to view. You're missing a hard drive for one of the laptops. He must have removed it and dumped it somewhere. You might want to tell your search guys.'

CHAPTER 45

Back at Wroughton, Charlie Eaton had been joined by Kelly. His search of the garage had produced no more than a receipt for petrol from an Esso garage in Staines, so he and Kelly were going over the house again, room by room, looking for the missing hard drive. Temple also told them to look further afield in the copse. In the Hi Tech Crime Unit, they were ensuring that the other hard drive was copied and all passwords were undergoing a software check.

As Temple felt the pressure mounting, Harker had got to hear of his presence at Swindon and the prisoner in the custody suite. Going down to the cells, he found Temple talking to the custody sergeant. He ordered him to one of the empty interview rooms.

'What's going on here, Temple?'

'I've traced the private investigator that Maxwell Ashton-Jones had engaged to watch his wife. I've seized his laptops. I suspect he has been filming the victim covertly and possibly uploading this onto the dark web or at least, I think he has it on his computers,' explained Temple.

'What's he saying in interview?' Harker looked back at him, grim faced.

'No comment.'

'DNA?'

'Taken and fast tracked.'

'Well, you know what he'll say, don't you, when it comes to his defence?' Harker's deep voice started to rise in volume. 'He'll just say that they had consensual sex. She had form. She's dead, he's the only witness. I hope you can back up this arrest, Temple, as you say. I thought we were happy with the young lad as the perpetrator?'

'*I* wasn't,' Temple rounded on Harker, who continued, his voice quieter.

'I thought I told you to wrap this up. I'm told that you had most of the mobile resources tied up on this last night.' Harker was strangely calm, as if he knew that Temple was on the edge of a precipice that was about to give way of its own accord. 'When you need an extension for interview, make sure you come to me to review. In fact, just in case you forget, I'll tell the custody sergeant to contact me. You've got eight more hours, Temple.' Temple watched Harker leave the room.

Temple instructed another pair of interviewers to take Turner in for interview for the next couple of hours. He had to get out of the station, go and see Ceri Lambert and make sure they were doing all they could to interrogate the seized computer. He knocked on the locked door of the Hi Tech Crime Unit – she answered and let him in.

'Nice and timely,' she said with a smile. 'They've just got through his passwords and have started to locate some files.' She indicated to where the laptop was sat on a desk.

Temple went inside and sat next to a woman who was intently looking at files on the screen. The office had the air of a library, as she spoke quietly so as not to disturb her other colleagues in the room, all working on computers. Temple looked around the room. There were computers and laptops everywhere.

'What you can see here are tracks of where the owner has gone onto various websites on the dark net. We are able to see exactly where they have been,' she explained, pointing at the screen.

'What does it show so far?' asked Temple.

'Well, let's have a look.' She scanned a list of sites. 'Some of these are very familiar,' she said, 'and some are not.' She opened up the links available and was able to see the content of the actual website. 'It's mostly adult porn, extreme stuff, which will take me a while to go through. There might be other stuff,' she said. 'It also looks as though he's a contributor to these sites, sending content. He's got a pseudonym by the looks of it, Mr PI.' She deftly clicked her way through a myriad of files before Temple had time to blink.

'What I'm particularly looking for is things that may be stored on there that he has filmed himself.'

'OK, let's have a look on the hard drive.'

After some searching, a folder of interest was located.

'I can't open this at the moment as he's password protected it. I'll just run some software on it so that I can open it.'

Temple sat and waited for another operator.

'Right. Here we go.' The operator opened the folder on the screen. 'There appears to be ten sub folders for us to look in.' She started to click on each folder. 'These files are a mixture of photographs and movies, so let's take a look. You did well to get these laptops to us before he destroyed them.'

As she moved the cursor onto the folders, they opened up, revealing a series of files. The first showed a series of photographs of an unknown man and a woman having sex. In another file, a short film of a different woman, naked. Each file contained a different person. The operator continued to click through each file until Temple suddenly saw the familiar photographs of Greta and Marcus Hussain in Savernake Forest.

As they clicked on other files, the quality of the camera revealed with great clarity the surroundings of Greta's bedroom on the screen. The bed was in the centre of the picture and Greta came into view from off camera. Temple watched, his eyes wide, as James then appeared. Temple then saw the recording of them as they cavorted naked on the bed, oblivious to the camera recording them, the sound indicating that they were perfectly at ease with each other.

'Click on another,' he said. He felt strangely calm.

Another file was opened and then another. They went through all of them, each showing Greta either with James, Jonathan Silvester or Marcus Hussain.

'Can we keep looking, I'm hoping there's another, I'm looking for something in particular,' said Temple. Another search of the hard drive and another folder was found. The operator clicked on it and opened it. The file was dated last Sunday.

This time, Temple watched as a camera recorded Greta walking around her bedroom. She had a robe on and was sitting at her dressing table. From her ensuite came Jonathan Silvester fully clothed. He watched as Jonathan told her he was going to tie her to the bed; she told him she didn't want to do it. He roughly pulled at her robe and grabbed her hair, pulling her head back, making her cry out. She asked again for him not to make her do it. As Greta lay on the bed naked, Jonathan began tying her hands to the bed posts. Temple moved closer to the monitor, unable to believe what he was seeing. From the date of the file, this was it. This was the murder. *It was Jonathan Silvester.*

'Stop it, can you please stop the film?' he asked.

Temple's mind was reeling – how could he have been so wrong? *Jonathan did it.* There he was, on the screen, tying her hands to the bed. He had Turner in custody and it was Jonathan – Jonathan had killed her. What was it that he had ignored? How could his instincts have let him down so badly, he thought? His mind seemed to want to battle with itself, as the confusion with what he was seeing made no sense with his reasoning and actions. Temple felt sick.

'Fuck it, *fuck it*,' he said under his breath. He held his head in his hands momentarily, unable to believe he had got it so wrong, as his mind raced through events, trying to find the one thing he missed. The one thing that would have put the right man in custody. Suddenly remembering that he wasn't alone, he sat up. A sickening tense angst overtook him. He didn't want to see any more, see the proof of how he'd got it so wrong. *He had the wrong man.* He could barely mumble for the operator to continue to play the film. They continued to stare at the screen in front of them.

He then watched as Jonathan secured her ankles. He saw Greta protest that her hands were tied too tight. He watched as Jonathan then blindfolded her.

'Stop! Stop the film,' he instructed. He needed to think.

The operator hit the pause button.

'This isn't how we found her,' said Temple, incredulously, speaking his thoughts out loud. 'Her legs were not tied, nor was she blindfolded when we found her dead.'

They continued with the film and watched. He saw Jonathan leave the bedroom, saying he would be back. They sat and watched as Greta lay impassively, waiting for Jonathan's return. After ten minutes, Temple asked for it to be fast-forwarded. Still Greta was alone but her slight movements on the bed kept the motion sensor camera recording. They fast-forwarded again, a timer in the corner of the software showed that nearly two hours passed before suddenly, there was another person in the room. They stopped and re-wound.

'Who's that?'

The light in the room came from the open door of the en suite. The film showed a man entering the room and approaching the bed. With his back to the camera, his face was unidentified. Temple willed him to turn round as he continued to watch.

On screen, it was obvious from the sound recording that Greta thought Jonathan had come back. She had no idea that there was a stranger in the room. The man was carrying something and placed it on the bedside cabinet. Temple spoke his thoughts out loud.

'What's he just put there?'

'Probably another camera,' said the operative, 'some of them want a close up head shot.'

As the man turned, he looked up, directly into the camera.

'That's him. That's him,' said Temple, quietly. 'That's Turner.' Relief flooded through him.

As they continued to watch, Ceri Lambert joined them. Turner circled the bed, silently looking at Greta. He took off his coat, dropping it to the floor, unzipped his trousers and got onto the bed, positioning himself between her legs. His body then obscured Greta's as his hips moved in a frantic motion. They continued to watch, helpless voyeurs compelled to witness a terrible finale. Turner grunted obscenities and still blindfolded, Greta screamed out. Her body jerked against his weight. It was then that his hands moved up towards her head. His actions were obscured.

'He's stopping her breathing now.' Temple's voice was barely perceptible.

Turner's movements slowed before he momentarily slumped on the body. A minute and twenty seconds had passed since he walked in the room. When he got off the bed, Greta lay dead, with her head back on the pillow, hair splayed from the brief struggle. As if startled, Turner suddenly looked up, grabbed his coat and the bedside camera and left the room.

Temple sat in stunned silence, looking at the screen, watching Greta's lifeless body on the bed. Less than three minutes later, the image showed another person entering the room. It was James. Temple watched as the boy made his terrible discovery, lifting the blindfold and shaking Greta as she lay on the bed. He was clearly unable to believe she was dead. Distressed and crying, James left the room. Temple was transfixed. It was almost a re-run of a familiar scene he often played back in his mind. He knew exactly how James Ashton-Jones felt at that moment.

'He's still there,' said Temple. 'Turner is still there, still in the house somewhere.'

The same slight movement in picture and forty minutes later, James returned to the room with Jonathan Silvester. Temple watched as Jonathan, visibly shaken by the sight of Greta on the bed, told James to go into the bathroom. Temple saw the lad could barely walk. They heard him being sick. The toilet flushing. With gloved hands, Jonathan proceeded to untie Greta's legs, placing them together. His hands shaking, he took the blindfold off her eyes and along with the leg ties, placed them in a drawer. He then ushered James out of the bathroom. Ten minutes after, Turner returned to the room, looked around and left.

Temple sat back in his chair, not quite believing what he'd just witnessed.

'Are you all right?' Temple quietly asked Ceri and the operator.

'Yes, yes, we're fine,' replied Ceri matter-of-factly, putting her hand reassuringly on her female colleague's shoulder, as she handed Temple a cup of tea. 'That OK?' she asked him.

Temple was grateful. Taking a drink from the cup, he tried to assess his feelings for what he had just seen. All he could register was relief at having Turner in custody.

'It's not often that you see murder taking place. Normally, we just turn up afterwards,' said Temple.

'She was an adult.' Ceri nodded towards the blank screen. 'We often see that sort of scenario with young kids. They don't show them actually dying but you wonder how they could ever get out of those rooms alive. And even if they do, they're as good as dead from a psychological point of view.'

'How do you do this every day?' Temple asked. Her matter-of-fact approach to what they had just witnessed wasn't lost on him; she'd been there too long and seen too much.

'Someone's got to. For the same reasons as you do it. To catch the bastards.'

'Can you copy that for me?' requested Temple, subdued at what he had just seen.

'Of course. It's been done before,' said the operative. 'There are markers here to show that it's been copied, so as well as being uploaded to the dark web this has already been sent copied and probably sent somewhere, perhaps through the post. Unfortunately, there's a market for this stuff. ' In no time at all, they handed him a DVD as an exhibit.

Temple's suspicions had been confirmed. More analysis of the computer showed that the movie and the others had, at some point, all been uploaded onto the dark net using software to hide Turner's identity. They undertook to trace the websites and search the content. Taking the DVD exhibit, Temple left the office for Swindon Police Station.

CHAPTER 46

Temple pressed his fingers into his neck to relieve the tension; as he walked across the Headquarters car park, images of what he had just seen kept emerging into his head. He didn't know how Ceri Lambert and her team could be shut up in that room, looking at so-called human beings doing evil things to each other every day. Just as he was about to drive off, his mobile rang.

'Hello, boy, we've got some business to do, haven't we?' Temple recognized the distinctive voice of Elijah Fortune.

'We'll have to do this another time,' said Temple, suddenly tired and in no mood for Fortune.

'I'll meet you in twenty minutes. Park in the lay-by on the Beckhampton Road and walk out to meet me on the gallops.' The call ended.

Temple knew he would have to drive past there to get to Swindon. Aware that Fortune still thought he had the gun in his possession, Temple knew he had to convince him otherwise and get him off his back. If he was lucky and Sophie Twiner had done a good job, the *Wiltshire Daily Record* would help do this tomorrow.

Temple drove down the A4 to the wide green expanse of Beckhampton gallops. He approached the lay-by and pulled in next to a tourist information board for the Avebury stone circle, a mile away. Parking head on to a Ford Ranger, he saw a man sitting in the driver's seat. Looking out across to the gallops, in the distance, he saw a line of racing horses walking slowly in the direction of Morgan's Hill. In the middle distance, he saw a man standing, hands thrust in a leather coat, looking in his direction, waiting. Temple got out of the car. He walked across the grassy field towards him.

As he got nearer, Temple recognized him. Elijah Fortune was in his late fifties, a jean-clad, balding, heavy, squat man, with a look of a permanent taste of piss in his mouth. His thick neck was covered in tattoos and draped in chunky gold chains. His hands were thrust so deep into the pockets of a long, tan coloured leather coat that his large knuckles could be seen through the leather. He rocked backwards and forwards on his heels as Temple approached.

Temple stopped and faced him. Fortune wanted to close the gap between them and took a step closer.

'We've been watching you,' Fortune spoke in a quiet, menacing tone. 'Know who you are, where you live.'

'How did you get my mobile number?'

'We read the papers. Take an interest in what the local lawmen are up to, log names, log faces. Get intelligence on what you lot are looking at. You're dealing with a murder so we got your number by saying we wanted to give information. Easy as shit.' Fortune spat on the ground.

'How did you know I was at the hospital the other night?'

'One of ours was coming out as you was going in.'

'I was investigating a GBH. Know anything about it?'

'I think we both know about Mr Finch.'

Temple remained silent, looking back at him.

'Right, where's the gun?' asked Fortune, staring hard into Temple's eyes.

'I don't have a gun. I've never had a gun.' Temple took care to hold his gaze.

'Paul King says he took a gun from your house. He showed it to me. Then, when he got nicked, it disappeared. He thinks either Finch got it back for you, or the arresting officers gave it back to you.'

'Paul King is taking the piss. He may well have shown you a gun, but he didn't get it from my house.'

'And why would he lie to me?'

'To get you interested in taking up his vendetta with me. Look, I put King away and he threatened to kill me and my family. He comes out and my house catches fire. I say it's him, he gets nicked on suspicion and they find a letter of mine that was in my house in his belongings. He took the letter to trace my wife, it had her name on it. That's what put him there. Without the letter, he could have denied it and I couldn't have proved it. If he hadn't taken the letter, he'd still be out. This is between me and him, not you and me.'

'Nice story. I saw the gun. He had it when he left me – then – no gun. What is it – you've got it and you want money for it? I'll give you money. I told you, we can cut a deal.'

'And I told you, I don't do deals and I'm not for sale. Now, I'm not telling you that you didn't see it, or that he didn't have it. But I am telling you that the gun didn't come from me or my house and I don't have it. Be honest, would you have been interested in coming after me otherwise?'

Fortune looked at him. Temple was still thinking about Greta and what he had just seen. His distraction made him appear indifferent.

'I'm being straight with you, Elijah. If King had a gun, he didn't get it from me. Now he's back inside, I just want my family left alone. What's between me and King is to resolve when he gets out.'

'So where do you think this gun is then?'

'Perhaps he hid it, Elijah, ready to come and get me when he gets out again. I don't know, do I? We both know how valuable guns are. You say you saw it, how come you didn't keep it?'

Fortune bridled at Temple questioning him.

'Don't start questioning me, boy. That's not what you're here for. I haven't got no fucking gun. He took it with him. Next thing, there's no gun but your fucking lot have got him. Finch didn't have it and now you say you haven't got it. Well, it's fucking somewhere.' Despite Fortune raising his voice, Temple remained calm and shrugged.

'I can't help you. But I *am* interested in the fact that you say there is a gun, especially since King must know where it is. He might have it tucked away somewhere waiting for when he comes out – waiting for *me*, remember.'

'Fuck off, boy. Now fuck off. This ain't finished. Not 'til I see a gun,' said Fortune, shaking his head. He looked up at the sky. It had started to rain; Fortune hated rain.

'I want my family left alone, Elijah. I haven't got a gun. This is between me and King, no one else. Otherwise I'll have to involve the job.'

'Don't you threaten me. Don't you fucking threaten me.' Fortune's neck moved forward as he spoke, thrusting his face close to Temple's. Temple didn't flinch.

'I want my family left out of this,' Temple repeated. 'Do what you like to me, but leave them alone.'

'I might take you up on that, lawman. I'll speak to Caleb first. Go on, fuck off.'

Temple took his cue and walked back to his car. Fortune followed a little distance behind. Temple sat facing the driver of the Ford Ranger who was waiting for Fortune to get back in the passenger seat. He rang DS Eaton.

'Charlie, I want you to organize some arrests. Go with Kelly and arrest Jonathan Silvester for the attempted rape of Greta Ashton-Jones on the night of her murder, for starters. Send another team out to arrest Maxwell Ashton-Jones. I want him interviewed about the death of his first wife, Olivia. And then Brett Forrester. I want to know what he has to say about having underage sex with his daughter. Take them all to Swindon nick.'

Temple pulled out of the lay-by and drove off to Gable Cross Police Station to get back to Turner and await the other detentions. He didn't know if he'd resolved the situation with the Fortunes until he saw the *Daily Record* in the morning, but if they showed up again, he'd knew he'd have to call it in and get protection.

Once at Gable Cross, he rang Leigh and told her to go home. Temple gathered his interview team into a small office and played them the DVD of Greta's death on a laptop. Turner was in his cell taking a break from interview and they'd scheduled another session in an hour's time. Temple set about arranging a forensic team to attend Turner's address at Wroughton and to visit the lock-up at Old Town. While he was on the phone arranging a search of the copse, Harker appeared in the doorway.

'This place is buzzing with the news that you've got yourself a snuff murder. You'd better let me see,' said Harker quietly.

Temple could see he was visibly calmer than when he had seen him previously; the news was, he had made arrests in Southall on his abduction and recovered the victim.

Temple played him the DVD.

'Seems like you were right,' said Harker.

Temple felt annoyed at Harker's attitude towards him throughout the inquiry and was trying hard to suppress the urge to say 'I told you so.'

'Seems like you were wrong,' said Temple, not able to help himself.

Harker looked across at him. His tired, bulging red rimmed eyes took on almost a demonic look.

'Have you written in the policy book as I told you?' asked Harker.

'No, because the inquiry wasn't closed.'

'Good,' said Harker.

'You thought it was the wrong man,' said Temple, not able to let it go and wanting Harker's acknowledgement of the fact.

Harker shot a glance at him. He was tired from his own inquiry and in no mood for an argument, never mind give Temple any kind of apology.

'Don't write any more decisions, just leave it blank and give it to me. Now, tell me about your inquiry,' he demanded.

Temple looked back at him; he was angry. If he'd listened to Harker and took his order to close the inquiry, implicating James, Turner would still be free and an innocent dead lad would have been labelled a murderer. Temple had stopped that happening but looking at Harker now, he knew the only person who was going to profit from his efforts was Harker. Temple would have confronted him but for the now constant nagging matter of Roger and the inevitable consequences which wormed away at his mind, giving him no peace. Resignedly and stage by stage, Temple went through the investigation.

'Greta was made vulnerable by the men she was surrounded by,' Temple explained at the end of his briefing. 'Both by the psychological effect they had on her and by placing her in danger when they no longer wanted her. Her father abused her, although it's clear she didn't recognize it as such and was a willing participant; when he wanted to pass her onto Maxwell, her feelings of rejection started, which gained momentum when she felt she was being rejected again by her husband. He was content to pass her onto Jonathan Silvester – as he had his first wife – and who is associated with her death. So, looking for security, she began a series of affairs. The exception was perhaps James who loved her, but that was doomed to failure. His hormones would have been racing and he would have had no chance of resisting her – the others hadn't. The strange thing is, it seems he was going back to her that night, he was so close to either seeing her with Jonathan Silvester or Turner. So, along comes Turner, employed by her husband to find some dirt on her for a divorce, to leverage a small divorce payout. Only, no one knows who Turner is; Curtis Coleman farm the work out and lose control over who undertakes the task and in protecting their 'client' from getting his hands dirty, even Maxwell has no direct contact with him.'

Harker sat listening, his face impassive, as Temple continued.

'A loner, Turner preys on Greta, doubtless as he has done on any number of other women he's been employed to follow. The last employers, Dobson & Byrne, have gone bust, shredding their records. There's no record of where he's been. Who knows what will be thrown up now we have his DNA on the database. This won't be the first time he's done this – he dealt only with matrimonial cases because he knows it lets him get really close to a woman, legitimately stalk her and get paid for it into the bargain. I suspect his MO is once he knows they're over the side, he moves in and blackmails them for sex and/or money. In this case, he photographed Greta having sex with Marcus Hussain and blackmailed him as well—'

'But that's just supposition on your part at this stage, Temple—' Harker interjected.

'It's all on his laptop, files of other women, but given his behaviour in this case, yes, I think that's his MO. Turner didn't want to give Maxwell what he'd found regarding Cooper because that was in the first month he employed him as I suspect, he did in the other cases. He saw Greta and what she was about – Cooper, Silvester, Hussain and James and must have thought all his Christmases had come at once. He strung it out. He got the keys to her house from the garage, having been led there by Hussain, and set up cameras which he monitored remotely, transferring what he found onto the internet. I think when he saw Silvester leave her that night, he saw his chance to have her at last. He'd watched everyone else having a piece of the action. He didn't have to do anything; drug her, tie her, all the work had been done for him, all he had to do was help himself. She was left completely vulnerable. But he was a pervert with a predilection for extreme internet porn, a contributor who went by the name of Mr PI, obviously a reference to him being a private investigator. He had an opportunity to carry out a fantasy and he took it. And he nearly got away with it.' Temple shot Harker a look.

'What do we know about this bloke, this Ian Turner?' asked Harker, ignoring his inference.

'No more than I've told you, at this stage. He's been off the radar. His DNA wasn't in the system – perhaps he'd been careful up to now. No one's reported him so far – out of fear or shame, I should imagine – but given his line of work, the fact he has aliases and he moves around, it's going to take some time to build a picture, get some idea of the extent of what he's been doing, if we ever do. Greta may or may not be the first woman he's killed. There's another laptop with a hard drive missing at the moment, so who knows what's on that,' Temple finished.

'We live in a sex fuelled society, Temple. The internet has taken the place of the soft porn mag found on the top shelf at Smiths. Every dirty, filthy, perverted taste is catered for. The difference is, people in the shop could see and give a disapproving eye as the hand reached up for that top shelf. The internet gives access to a world of filth, virtually without anyone knowing who's accessing it. It's creating pervs – you only have to look at what it's doing to kids.' He looked at Temple, still unforgiving. 'Everyone's saying that you did a good job. Maybe. But there's a young boy lying in the mortuary and an IPCC investigation. You're still an arsehole, Temple.'

Maybe I did a good job, thought Temple. He knew that was as close as he was ever going to get to an acknowledgement of good work from Clive Harker. But he knew he was right about James. Temple knew he should have gone himself that day to take the DNA and fingerprints instead of Sloper. He would have taken James to one side. He would have got him to talk to him, to open up, tell him what happened. He would have got him access to professional support. He sensed James had been close to wanting to tell him something when he went to see him initially. He had missed an opportunity, he could have perhaps saved him. He should have done more, Harker was right. He'd failed James. He should still be alive.

'Before you go, Op Acre – I hear you've got an exhibit, a blue t-shirt. My blue t-shirt.'

'Yes,' Harker mumbled. 'I'll be meeting with ACC Buller, tell him what we've got and see whether or not the case will be re-opened. I'll see that the t-shirt is sent to forensics. You'll be updated.' Harker left the room.

Temple's mobile rang. It was Graham Mellor.

'Boss, we've had a result on Turner's bank details. He's got an address in Staines. I street viewed it with Google, it's a grubby looking maisonette so I rang the local station and asked them to go round and gain entry. They're continuing to search the place for us as we speak.'

'They found anything yet?'

'More computer equipment, which they're seizing for us. I'll send a couple of mine up to get it but it's definitely his home. No sign of any other occupants, no female stuff at the house, seems like he lived alone,' said Mellor.

'Great, we need to find out who he is, what he's been up to. Take a video camera up with you, will you, and make another search when you get there.'

Over the internal tannoy system, a call went out for Temple to contact the front foyer. As he went to respond, Leigh called him to tell him she was home and looking forward to him joining them later. It felt good to hear her voice after his conversation with Harker. He needed her comfort, needed to go home, see Daisy, think about the last week, about what to do next.

'I'll be there, don't worry,' he reassured her.

He knew he had to put things right between them and he couldn't fuck it up. He couldn't afford to – he had a feeling his chances were running out with Leigh. She knew he never set out to hurt her but he had. He'd hated the last eight months living apart, it had been a half existence, a shock to his system he hadn't come to terms with. He felt an overwhelming desire to hurry home to them.

'Just one thing,' she said. 'I told Daisy that you were coming home and she's really happy. Thing is, she felt able to tell me that she'd told a lie. She said Roger hadn't hit her after all. She'd made it up to try and get us living together again. Are you still there?'

Temple was silent. He remembered how he'd rained punches down on Roger a few days ago. He remembered how he'd left him. He'd wanted to kill him. He looked at his hands. He forced the words out.

'It's OK. It's fine,' he lied, resting his head in his hand. Leigh filled the silence between them.

'I just want us all back together. Here, where we should be,' she replied.

'Me, too,' he said. Relief should have flooded through him; he'd wanted to hear Leigh say that for months but he couldn't escape what he'd done to Roger and now it seemed, with no justification.

'I've called the solicitor too, called off the divorce. I'll see you later,' she said. 'I love you.'

He wondered if she'd still say that if she knew what he'd done, if she knew he would lose his job – perhaps go to prison. She would know soon. Fuck, he thought, he should have spoken to Daisy himself, he would have got the truth out of her. A sense of gloom enveloped him which stopped him sharing Leigh's happiness with the new situation. All thoughts of a happy reunion dissolved.

He sighed deeply, knowing he had no one to blame but himself. He felt as though he was on a precipice, with Roger deciding his fate. A familiar dead weight of dread embedded itself deep in his guts. Maybe he could sort it, somehow. He suddenly felt as if he just wanted to shut his eyes and sleep but he knew he had to carry on.

Temple went down to the cells to meet the interview teams who were preparing for the hours ahead. With both Turner and Jonathan Silvester in custody and Forrester and Maxwell in transit, they were all in for a long stint of interviews and Temple decided to focus all his remaining energy on them. Coordinating the teams, they went long into the night. He texted Leigh to say he'd see them both tomorrow evening due to the inquiry and at 2 a.m., when the interview teams finished and went home, he sat in an office and continued on.

Early in the morning, he drove into Swindon. He went into a café for a cup of tea and intended to have a fried breakfast but couldn't face it. As he sat down opposite a man reading the morning newspaper, he saw the headline *Police Find Gun at Local Flats*. Sophie Twiner had done her job. Temple waited until the man left, leaving the paper on the table. Amongst quotes 'police said this and police said that', the local MP waded in with his comments. Temple hoped that it would be enough for the Fortunes to realize that he didn't have the gun and give him some peace. He went back to Gable Cross.

CHAPTER 47

ON HIS ARRIVAL, he met with Charlie Eaton, who was coordinating the interviews for a briefing.

'Turner's still going "no comment". We've got the usual extensions to carry on questioning and today we're going to put a DVD in the room and show him the evidence from the laptop. That should concentrate his mind.'

'Let me know what his reaction is. I suspect the brief will ask to suspend the interview. Make sure he's got a twenty-four hour cell guard, I don't want to lose him now.'

'So far as Maxwell Ashton-Jones and Jonathan Silvester are concerned, Maxwell has disclosed that Silvester told him that Olivia Ashton-Jones had hit her head when she was with him in the pool prior to her death. He says that she was in the water at the side of the pool with her arms resting in a hollow that ran just above the water line. He says that Jonathan told him that they had been arguing and Jonathan had gone to pull her towards him at which point, her head jerked backwards, catching the edge of the pool. He said he thought she was just being dramatic when she cried out and turned his back on her and got out of the pool and went inside the hotel. Not long after, she was found floating face down. He said he only disclosed this to him a couple of years afterwards.'

'And Silvester?'

'He denies it, of course,' said Eaton. 'Says they're the ramblings of a jealous man, trying to get back at him for being James's real father.'

'Of course, we've got the technical which is a kind of admission.'

'Yes, so we'll go in with that this afternoon.'

'And Brett Forrester, what does he have to say?' asked Temple.

'Nothing. Fuck all, except "no comment". It's thin, boss. The victim's dead and all we've got to go on is the word of a bitter ex-wife.'

Temple knew what Dianna Forrester suspected was probably true but Eaton was right, they'd never prove it now and the CPS were unlikely to run it on such grounds.

'Keep going,' said Temple.

Eaton went on to update Temple on the search of Turner's address.

'The team are also fetching back stuff from Turner's flat. There's another computer coming back into Hi Tech Crime, but he's spread himself about a bit. Looks like we'll be busy asking other forces if they've got any outstanding jobs where we know he's been in the vicinity.'

'We need to get hold of the experts at the centre, get hold of SCAS, I want to find out why he chose now to leave his DNA behind,' said Temple.

'Already have, boss,' said Eaton. 'I put a call into them myself, having had the same thought. Of course, if he's coerced other victims they wouldn't necessarily have reported it, which is why we have no DNA, but like you, I was intrigued as to why he would have given us the evidence. They said that he probably hadn't intended to, and that he had probably become so excited during the act of strangulation that he just couldn't help himself. When I explained that I'd found him in the process of putting a noose round his neck, they said that he would have known it was only a matter of time before he was caught. They also said they doubted whether he would still be alive when the case came to court. There's precedent for this sort of thing, apparently. They tend to commit suicide on remand.'

What was it he had said again on arrest 'you're not going to lock me up with no nonces.'

'Don't lose him, Charlie.'

Eaton saw that Temple was bone tired.

'Lighten up, boss, you've got a good team on this now.'

Temple left Eaton with instructions for the interview team and reviewed the evidence coming in on Turner. As time went on, he felt as though he'd started to hit a wall. He needed a break from the inquiry, if only for a few hours. He knew he needed to go and see Dianna Forrester to update her on the arrests and tell her that Brett Forrester had been released with no further action. He would do this and then go home, back to Leigh. As he was leaving the station, he walked through the front foyer and was stopped by a man behind the desk.

'Here he is, madam. Here's DI Temple.' He called across to a woman who was seated. 'Sir, this lady's from Social Services, she's been waiting to see you. I was just about to tannoy you, this lady was here yesterday but you probably didn't hear the tannoy.' Temple remembered hearing his name yesterday and ignored it, leaving the building by the rear exit.

The woman approached him.

'Do you keep trying to contact me?' asked Temple, annoyed at the man on the front desk for stopping him. He needed the drive to Salisbury; it was going to give him time to think, think about his next move, think about James. Think about Leigh, Daisy. Roger. Think about his response when he was arrested.

'Yes,' she replied.

'Well, if it's about my daughter, Daisy, I've got some good news on that front—' said Temple. She interrupted him.

'Can we go somewhere to talk?'

Temple looked at his watch. 'I do have to be somewhere, will this take long?'

She looked back at him without saying anything.

'Let's just go in here then.'

He showed her into a small room off the foyer. She stood as she spoke to him.

'I've been trying to track you down, Mr Temple. I'll get to the point. About three years ago, you had a relationship with Marina Delaney.'

'What is this?' asked Temple, not committing himself to answering and not appreciating the stranger asking him personal questions. Marina, he thought, of course he remembered her, but he hadn't seen her in years – probably as much as the woman said, three years ago – and hadn't thought too much about her since, either.

'You knew Miss Delaney?' she asked him to confirm.

'Yes, I knew her.'

'In what capacity?'

'In no capacity, actually,' Temple answered, struggling to see the connection and becoming increasingly uncomfortable with the bluntness of the questioner.

'Miss Delaney was quite adamant that she had a relationship with you, a sexual relationship. She has produced an affidavit to the effect. It's a legal document, drawn up by her solicitor,' the woman explained.

'I'm familiar with what an affidavit is, I'm just not sure why you're telling me this,' said Temple.

'Miss Delaney died recently. She had a terminal illness …'

Temple stared back at her and softened. 'Look, I'm sorry for that but I'm still not sure how I can help you.'

'Well, I think she was rather hoping that …'

Impatient to get on his way, Temple stopped her, failing to see what any of this had to do with him. His relationship with Marina had been fleeting to say the least. A drunken one night stand when out for an evening with Paul Wright that had happened when Leigh had been away, visiting her sister. Not his proudest moment, he acknowledged, but after another meeting and with no harm done, he thought he'd got away with that one. Having just spoken to Leigh, the reminder of this particular peccadillo wasn't welcome. Looking back at her, he wondered who she was, how did she know about him and what did she want?

'You're Social Services, right?' he said, quietly. 'That's what you said. Correct me if I'm wrong, but since when did Social Services get involved in someone's private life?'

'Since there is a young child who now has no mother. Before she died, his mother said that you are his father, Mr Temple. That's how we become involved. We are looking after your son.'

CHAPTER 48

He was dreaming, or he had died and gone to heaven.

She came through the door with her golden hair, long legs and in uniform. From that moment he was lost. It was the golden hair, that exact colour that mesmerised him. Abandoned, like a lamb to the slaughter. He had no chance. No hope. Nothing. Zilch.

In that lovely hair was a white starched hat – smooth – yet with some tightly pressed pleats. Perfect. Snowy white starched apron, tied in a bow at the back (he checked). A starched blue dress, complete with starched white collar. White frilled armlets at the short sleeves of the shirt – an often missed but exquisite detail (she was quality). And then, the watch, the upside down watch (he was already gone by now). Black stockings in those long legs – but he knew what lay beneath – her hair colour told him that – milky white flesh, almost translucent, exactly how he liked it. The hair colour, the nurse's uniform, the flesh – she was like a total eclipse – once in a lifetime.

Drink fuelled lust had told him that if he didn't have her that night, he'd pursue her for the rest of his life. He'd gladly give his soul to the devil for five minutes. Just five minutes. He'd wanted her so badly and she was going to let him have her.

She led him like a bull with a ring through its nose. She liked the look of him. Lovely eyes, not bad looking at all. No wedding ring. He was single? Single! He'd do – for what she had in mind.

His groin leapt at the remembrance of her; he'd tried to have her, there and then, outside, instant gratification. But she took him home, ensnared him. He'd unwrapped her, like a present to himself, taking too much care as he lived his own fantasy. He'd wrapped her white legs around him and feasted on her white body – if this was the prize for sinning, he'd pay the price.

He paid all right.

He woke.

Where was he? His eyes snapped open. He looked to his left and saw Sophie's bleached blonde head lying on a pillow beside him. He closed his eyes and then looked up at the ceiling. His mind was blank. He tried to focus. *Sophie? Shit!*

He couldn't recall how he'd got there.

He'd been in the pub. He remembered that. The King's Arms. Sophie had turned up there. He was finishing his second bottle of wine by then; drinking to make sense of the last eight months, the last two weeks, drinking to think clearly, to work out what to do next.

As he lay there, he continued to try to rewind his mind, pausing at intervals to check his understanding. He felt an odd sense of calm that was deeply unfamiliar and he knew it wasn't right. He never felt like this. Then he remembered - they'd found the blue t-shirt, there was now a way forward, a huge step forward – hope of finding his mother's killer. But he was still out there, somewhere, free. Living whatever life, a good life, a bad life, he hadn't paid for taking a life. And Temple still had to find him. There it was, it returned with full force, the familiar dull sickening heavy weight that felt like a malevolent stone in the bottom of his gut. Only this time, there was more. It wasn't just this, there was something else. He continued to try and remember. Turner was in custody for Greta's murder. He'd left Dianna Forrester and gone back to see Jane, to tell her he was moving back home. She'd seemed pleased for him. Then he went to The King's Arms. That wasn't it, he thought, it was before then. Harker, he'd seen Harker.

Then it all came back to him, as he lay there, in the dark. James – a suicide he could have prevented – could he? Could he really? Perhaps. Leigh. Daisy. Roger. Fucking Roger – with whom now his career rested. That was it, that was what was missing. But no, it wasn't enough. His mind worked away, like a pick, in the darkness until he found it. A social worker. That was it. That was the gut twister. The unexpected life changer. That's why he'd dreamt of her.

She'd showed him a typed statement. Marina.

Just then, his ears picked up the sound of a clock ticking in the room – tick tock. Her biological clock had been ticking. She'd been on a hen night, dressed as a nurse. She'd seen him, weighed him up and chosen him, purely on looks. He could have been a murderer but she didn't care. Nurture over nature, she just wanted one thing and he was the sucker in the room who gave it to her. He'd drank far too much to resist.

She didn't care when she found out he was married, that suited her, she didn't want *him* per se, she didn't want a relationship, just what he could give her. And he gave it to her – a son born nine months later. Only, as a result of her pre-natal checkups, she had been diagnosed with breast cancer, a particularly aggressive form, and had declined treatment until after the birth. Her struggle went on for two years until her death. Now the boy was with social services who were trying to track down his natural father to see if he would take care of him.

He looked across to Sophie sleeping soundly. How had he got *here*? What, if anything, had he said to *her*?

He was in pain. He went to get out of the bed but his head wouldn't let him. It felt as if it was nailed to the pillow. He forced himself up and out of bed, into his clothes. He swayed, couldn't walk straight. Couldn't think straight. In his upright position, the room spun around him. Just as he focused on something, it spun away from his sight again. Spinning. Out. He had to get out.

He staggered outside and along the narrow road. It was pitch black and cold. God, it was cold. He pulled at his jacket to try to cover himself more. Just then a taxi drove slowly by and stopped. Temple got in and directed him to Beckhampton. For the first time in months, he was going home to Leigh. He was going to tell her everything. Well, perhaps not everything.

THE END

DI TEMPLE BOOKS

Book 1: WATCH HER DIE
Book 2: DEAD OF NIGHT

Thank you for reading this book. If you enjoyed it please leave feedback on Amazon, and if there is anything we missed or you have a question about then please get in touch. The author and publishing team appreciate your feedback and time reading this book.

Please join our mailing list for free kindle crime thriller, detective, mystery, and romance books and new releases. http://www.joffebooks.com/contact/

Our email is office@joffebooks.com

http://joffebooks.com

We hate typos but sometimes they slip through.
Please send any errors you find to corrections@joffebooks.com

We'll get them fixed ASAP. We're very grateful to eagle-eyed readers who take the time to contact us.